CARNAL
HOURS

By Max Allan Collins

MAX ALLAN COLLINS

CARNAL HOURS

A NATHAN HELLER NOVEL

A DUTTON BOOK

DUTTON
Published by the Penguin Group
Penguin Books USA Inc., 375 Hudson Street,
New York, New York 10014, U.S.A.
Penguin Books Ltd, 27 Wrights Lane,
London W8 5TZ, England
Penguin Books Australia Ltd, Ringwood,
Victoria, Australia
Penguin Books Canada Ltd, 10 Alcorn Avenue,
Toronto, Ontario, Canada M4V 3B2
Penguin Books (N.Z.) Ltd, 182–190 Wairau Road,
Auckland 10, New Zealand

Penguin Books Ltd, Registered Offices:
Harmondsworth, Middlesex, England

First published by Dutton, an imprint of Dutton Signet,
a division of Penguin Books USA Inc.
Distributed in Canada by McClelland & Stewart Inc.

First Printing, April, 1994
10 9 8 7 6 5 4 3 2 1

Copyright © Max Allan Collins, 1994
All rights reserved.

 REGISTERED TRADEMARK—MARCA REGISTRADA

LIBRARY OF CONGRESS CATALOGING-IN-PUBLICATION DATA
Collins, Max Allan.
    Carnal hours : a Nathan Heller novel / by Max Allan Collins.
      p.   cm.
    ISBN 0-525-93758-7
    1. Heller, Nathan (Fictitious character)—Fiction.   2. Oakes,
Harry, Sir, 1874–1943—Fiction.   3. Private investigators—Caribbean
Area—Fiction.   I. Title.
PS3553.O4753C37   1994
813'.54—dc20   93-30349
                                                     CIP

Printed in the United States of America
Set in Sabon
Designed by Leonard Telesca

To Barb—
with warm memories
of carnal hours in Nassau

Although the historical incidents in this novel are portrayed more or less accurately (as much as the passage of time, and contradictory source material, will allow), fact, speculation and fiction are freely mixed here; historical personages exist side by side with composite characters and wholly fictional ones—all of whom act and speak at the author's whim.

"Life is struggle."
—Axel Wenner-Gren

"*L'homme est un apprentis. La douleur est son maître, et nul le connait, taut qu'il n'a pas souffert.*"
(Man is an apprentice. Pain is his master, and no one understands who has not suffered.)
—Count Alfred de Marigny

"Lay that pistol down, boy, lay that pistol down—pistol-packing mama, lay that pistol down."
—Bahamian calypso folk tune derived from Al Dexter's popular song

One

~~~~~~

The low-flying seaplane made a shimmering mosaic of the tropical waters beneath: blue turning bluer, then graying, even
whitening over coral or sand. Shallow waters seemed emerald one
moment, red as a Chinese robe the next, then—without warning
—midnight blue. Islands, tiny, scraggly, apparently unpopulated
keys—the sort pirates hid out on two or three centuries ago—
dabbed the sea with more color, like a bold impressionist painter:
pink beaches lined with mangroves, or pines, or palmettos. Then,
nearing a larger island called New Providence (a particular pirate
favorite), shallows that were sapphire turned emerald again in a
lagoon surrounded by sand so white it might have been snow.

Beyond the lagoon rose the capital of the Bahamas, Nassau,
sprawling over a modest hillside, white and pink and yellow limestone buildings peeking out among lazy palms, pastel ghosts haunting a world of vivid green under a pure blue sky. Glittering coral
roads coiled through this landscape like sensuously loose jewelry
on the necks and wrists and ankles of pretty native girls. Dazzling
in the morning sun, it was a vista at once exciting and restful—
you couldn't wait to run breakneck to a beach, and fall fast asleep.

A spray of silver brushed the wings, then beaded the windows,
as the seaplane skimmed into the harbor; in other times, a steamer

or two would likely have been anchored there, but during wartime, such pleasure ships were strangers in Nassau. A few wealthy tourist types had taken the thirty-five-buck Pan Am seaplane ride with me from Miami, but no diving boys or dancing girls would be waiting for them. Not during off-season; not during the war. That was okay with me. I was here on business.

A working vacation was the way it had been pitched to me. But I know a contradiction of terms when I hear one.

It didn't start in Nassau, of course. Some would say it began in New England, or maybe Canada; still others might consider the beginning of this tale of murder, greed and romance (is there any other kind?) to have been on the tiny island of Mauritius in the Indian Ocean.

But for me it began, as always, in Chicago.

"Mr. Heller?" he asked, straw fedora in hand. He was of medium height, a square-shouldered, erect man exuding quiet confidence. Even if I wasn't a detective, I could've put together his Southern drawl, his tan, and his tan linen suit, and figured he was from below the Mason-Dixon line. "Nathan Heller?"

"That's right," I said, half-rising in my side booth at Binyon's restaurant. "Mr. Foskett?"

"That's right," he said with an easy white smile in his smooth tan face, sliding into the booth across from me. "But call me Walter, if you would. I hate formality, don't you?"

If he really hated formality, he would have asked me to call him Walt. But I said, "Hate it like the plague, Walter—and call me Nate."

He had unblinking brown eyes and the sort of rubbery mouth that seemed to taste the words he spoke; otherwise, he was blandly, unmemorably handsome in that invisible manner common to so many attorneys. And he was one.

"You mind if I smoke?" he wondered, but he didn't take out his cigarettes first, like most people who ask. He was a Southerner, all right. I knew several in the service and they were so fucking polite I wanted to strangle them.

"Not at all," I said. "I already ordered myself a drink. Can I get you something?"

"A martini would be pleasant." He probably had a good ten years on my thirty-seven. He removed a Chesterfield from a gold case, tamped it down and lighted it with a gold Zippo; his hands looked soft, unused, and his nails were manicured.

I waved one of the waiters over. Binyon's was a male bastion in the Loop; lawyers, brokers and businessmen appreciated its wooden booths, spartan decor, and no-nonsense service. The clatter of busboys fought the loud talk of business and the whir of ceiling fans, while the aroma of unpretentious, well-prepared meat-and-potatoes cuisine mingled with cigarette and cigar smoke. It was as close to heaven as you could get without sex.

It was also close to my suite of offices, which was in a building just around the corner on Van Buren. Despite Binyon's and the nearby Standard Club, the neighborhood was pretty borderline. Street level was a hodgepodge of hockshops and saloons and flophouses and winos in doorways; tenants in our building included a palm reader, a dentist, a probable abortionist and several shysters of the sort Mr. Foskett here wouldn't likely meet in court.

But I'd started out with a one-room suite in trade for moonlighting as the building's night watchman (living in my office) and now, a decade or so later, July of 1943 to be exact, we had most of the third floor, and the A-1 Detective Agency (of which I was self-appointed president) had three operatives and a one-woman secretarial pool.

When the war was over, the male work force would swell, and I could expand further, and move into bigger, better digs. I'd had some financial success and publicity over the years, and occasionally attracted an upper-class client like the Palm Beach attorney sitting across from me in a Binyon's booth.

"I appreciate your willingness to meet for lunch," Foskett said, "particularly at such short notice."

"No inconvenience. I eat lunch here every day, anyway."

"What would you recommend, by the way?"

"House specialty's the finnan haddie. Stay away from the meat dishes—they're good, but the servings are regular kid's portions."

He shook his head. "One of the sad realities of these dark times." He smiled almost wickedly. "Perhaps you'd like a vacation with pay . . . to a tropical isle?"

I guess that was supposed to make me go *ooooh* or *aaaahhh*, but instead I just laughed and said, "I had one of those last year."

His eyebrows raised. "Really?"

"A little tourist trap called Guadalcanal."

Now the eyebrows lowered and tightened. "I wasn't aware you'd served. What branch?"

"Marines."

"I have a brother-in-law in the Marines. Here's to you, sir."

He lifted his martini glass and toasted me; I smiled a little and nodded and sipped my rum and Coke.

"I'm afraid I was too old to lend a hand," Foskett said with what I was supposed to think was regret.

"So was I. But if you get drunk and lie about your age to the recruiting officer, it does wonders. What brings you to Chicago, Mr. Foskett?"

"Walter. *You* do, Nathan."

He said this with quiet melodrama—he was obviously a corporate lawyer, as opposed to the trial variety; but he had a little ham in him, just the same.

"I'm in Chicago just for today, Nathan—flew in yesterday evening, flying out again this afternoon. I'm here to see *you*—on behalf of my principal client."

More melodrama. I'd asked him to call me Nate, but I guess a Walter prefers a Nathan.

"And who would that principal client be?" I asked, just a little testily. The phone call arranging this a week before had been evasive, but when a Palm Beach attorney wants to buy you lunch, why not?

But now I was starting to get a little worried. A Florida attorney just might have a "principal client" of the mob variety, since that sunny state was home-away-from-home for so many of the boys. I had a partly deserved reputation as an ex-cop with mob connections—though with the death earlier this year of my sometime mentor Frank Nitti, those connections were largely severed—and this could be about that.

And I didn't want it to be.

"Sir Harry Oakes," he said with a smug little smile.

He might have said Walt Disney or Joe DiMaggio. The name was a famous one, but out of context, it sounded like nonsense.

"The rich guy?" I said, wincing in confusion.

"The very rich guy," he said, putting a slow Southern two-syllable emphasis on "very."

"The richest man in Canada is what I read," I said.

"Except he lives in the Bahamas, now—in Nassau." Foskett's eyes glazed over with admiration. "Here is a man who could live in a marble palace, big as the Taj Mahal, with a gilded dome sparkling with precious gems. Yet he prefers to live a relatively simple life in a tropical paradise."

I managed not to laugh at that twaddle. "You don't have to tell me why Oakes lives in Nassau—there's no *taxes* in the Bahamas."

Foskett seemed just a little offended. "Well, that too." Then he brightened. "Don't be misled: Mr. Oakes is very generous. I think you'll like working for him."

I shrugged. "I don't mind working for rich people. In fact, I don't mind saying I downright like it. But I do need to know what the job is first."

The waiter came and we both ordered the finnan haddie. A green salad appeared almost instantly.

Instead of answering me directly, Foskett leaned forward chummily and said, "Let me tell you how I came to work for Sir Harry."

I nodded, as if to say, Fine, while I began eating my salad. It was his nickel.

It seemed that once upon a time, in 1932, Oakes had business with the Palm Beach law firm in which Foskett was the juniorest of junior partners. The senior partners kept the bear of a man cooling his heels in the reception area for over an hour; Foskett, walking through, had smiled and apologized to Harry, who was fuming.

"Kid—d'you like working with a rude bunch of goddamn stuffed shirts?" Oakes had asked.

"Not particularly."

"Come with me then," Oakes had said, grabbing Foskett by the arm. "I'll set you up in practice and be your only client."

"Sounds like an interesting fella," I said.

The finnan haddie was here; it was steaming, not particularly aromatic. What the appeal of this bland fare was I couldn't fathom; not that good a detective. I dug in.

He was studying me like a legal brief. "How much do you know about Sir Harry?"

"Just that he's self-made—a gold miner who hit the jackpot. Obviously British."

"No he isn't." Foskett's smile was a trifle condescending. "He was born in Maine. And yet he became a British baronet. . . ."

I looked up from my fish and cast him my own condescending smile. "Walter, you don't need to explain how a mining magnate became a 'Sir'—money talks in England, just like in Chicago. The only difference is the accent."

He frowned. "If you're going to work for Sir Harry . . ."

"We haven't established that yet, Walter."

"If you are, I think you need a little crash course in just who this remarkable man is."

While I ate, he talked. And I admit I was soothed by the Southern inflections of the attorney, even if his admiration for his wealthy client bordered on embarrassing. In any case, the story he told—Sir Harry Oakes' story—really was remarkable.

A loner since his middle-class upbringing in New England, Oakes dropped out of Syracuse medical school, condemning businessmen and professionals for "making money off their fellow men," yet paradoxically possessed by an overwhelming desire to accumulate riches. How could the young idealist accumulate wealth without taking advantage of his fellows? The answer seemed to be in the news of a gold strike in the Klondike.

For fourteen obstinate years, Harry Oakes wandered a penniless prospector, from Death Valley to Australia to the Belgian Congo, with many a stop in between, in search of the instant wealth mining could bring. Along the way he learned the skills of his trade, not to mention a hard-bitten form of self-reliance.

When he finally did find his mother lode—at Kirkwood Lake, Ontario, where Harry was convinced a bonanza awaited beneath its frozen surface—it took eight years of legal, logistical and financial struggles to make it happen; but eventually his Lake Shore Mines made him the richest man in Canada.

Foskett's eyes were tight and gleaming; that flexible mouth savored every Southern-fried word he spoke. "Nathan—we're talking about an individual who could write a check for two hundred million, and *cash* it—in *any* bank, *any*where."

Despite his reputation as a cantankerous loner, Harry was also renowned for paying his debts: a Chinese laundryman who had grubstaked him when everyone else turned their backs was lavishly rewarded by the now wealthy Oakes. On the other hand, a hardware store owner who had refused Oakes credit suddenly found a new competitor opening next door, underselling him item for item, putting him out of business within three months.

More charitably, a teenage shopgirl Oakes had dated in Sydney, Australia, who once lent him money for passage back to America, was rewarded years later with a marriage proposal on a world cruise. He was forty-eight; Eunice was twenty-four. Five children were the happy result.

For business reasons, Harry had become a Canadian citizen in the early twenties; by the late thirties he'd taken Bahamian citizenship, due to the skyrocketing taxes in Canada, and the conspicuous absence of taxes in the Bahamas.

"You must understand," Foskett said, pleading his client's case earnestly, "that Sir Harry was one of Canada's most generous philanthropists, above and beyond the jobs and prosperity his Lake Shore Mines had brought his adopted country. Even before the latest tax hikes, he was already Canada's largest single taxpayer. He felt . . . *plundered*. . . ."

Now a Bahamian, Oakes shifted his charitable giving to London and Nassau, and the title of baronet was conferred upon him by the King in 1939. In the meantime, he became the uncrowned king of the Bahamas, a one-man development boom—adding an airline and airfield to Nassau, purchasing and renovating the British Colonial Hotel, increasing wages, expanding employment through the islands. Giving millions to island charities.

"Much of this charitable work," Foskett said piously, "benefited the colored workers and their children."

"Impressive," I said. I'd finished my lunch. Somehow, despite all his talk, the lawyer had finished his as well. That was almost as impressive as his story. "But what does it have to do with hiring a Chicago private investigator?"

"That's the problem, Nathan." His face twitched in a gesture that pretended he wished he could be more helpful. "I'm not really at liberty to say. You see, it's a personal matter, and Sir Harry wants to present it to you himself. He has asked that I request you meet with him in Nassau."

"I really am *not* fond of tropical climes," I said.

That was no smart-ass remark: Guadalcanal had been less than a year ago. I'd caught malaria there and it still flared up from time to time; only in recent months had the combat nightmares of that sticky, stormy hellhole subsided to where I could get some occasional restful sleep. My condition—what they used to call shell shock—had got me out on a Section Eight.

That's military for crazy as a bedbug.

He was painting a picture in the air with a tanned, manicured hand; he wore a gold ring with an emerald the size of a doorknob in Oz.

"Nassau is a pleasant place, Nathan—an oasis in this war-torn world of ours."

Funny how a Southern accent wrapped around crap like that can be seductive.

"Walter, it's July. A getaway to the tropics is no real inducement. Let's stick to the job itself. I like to know what I'm getting into."

He shrugged. "Your expenses will be fully paid, and your minimum fee will be one thousand dollars, in advance, for one afternoon's meeting with Sir Harry."

That was seductive, too.

"Why me? Why not some Florida dick? Or somebody from the East Coast? Ray Schindler's the society private eye—maybe you ought to call him. I have his New York number. . . ."

"You were recommended by a friend of Sir Harry's."

"Who?"

"Sir Harry didn't share that with me."

"Brother." What if this *was* a mob job? Rich guys had those kind of connections all the time. I sighed. "When does he want to see me?"

"Day after tomorrow, if it's convenient. You'd fly to Miami in the morning. The following morning, you'd be in the Bahamas. It's beautiful there, Nathan, truly it is."

What sounded beautiful was that G-note guarantee.

And my agency could sure as hell use a handsome yearly retainer from a major corporation like Oakes' Lake Shore Mines of Canada. Maybe I could even open up a Canadian branch of the A-1. . . .

"You'll do it, then?"

I frowned at him and shook my finger in his face. "Mr. Foskett, Sir Harry Oakes may be the richest man in the world, but somebody's got to teach him that money can't buy you everything."

His face fell.

Then I grinned and patted his tan cheek like a baby. "But, Walt—that somebody isn't going to be me. I can use a thousand bucks."

T w o

~~~~~~

I barely had a foot on the spongy wooden surface of the landing wharf before I slipped out of my suitcoat; I'd worn lightweight clothing, including a seersucker suit and short-sleeved white shirt, but they couldn't stand up to one minute of muggy Nassau. It was probably only about eighty degrees—child's play for a Chicagoan who could stand up under the coldest and hottest weather the planet had to offer—but that didn't stop my shirt from going immediately sopping.

A houseboat-like affair at the tip of the dock next to the bobbing seaplane was where we waited momentarily for our baggage —mine was a single canvas duffel—and at the end of the short pier in a one-story modern shed was a Pan Am passenger station where a polite, casual Negro in a white shirt as dry as mine wasn't and the crown-crested blue cap of a royal immigration officer asked me a perfunctory question or two and waved me on.

No passports were needed here, I'd been told; and no currency exchange was necessary—though a British colony, New Providence would be glad to take my American money.

Back out in the humid air, I drank in the languid, off-season, wartime ambience of a wharf that no doubt often bustled, but not now. The handful of American tourists who'd made the Miami flight with me—with European travel a memory, the rich had to go *somewhere* in the summer, even if it was the tropics—were shanghaied by a barefoot black troubadour bearing a weather-beaten banjo. In tattered shirt and trousers and a wide straw hat and just as wide a smile, he accompanied himself, plinking, plunking on the banjo, beating out rhythm with his knuckles on the instrument's face as he sang in a jaunty baritone, "Wish I had a needle, so fast I can sew, I sew my baby to my side and down the road we go . . ."

The tourists stood with their bags in hands, with expressions ranging from delight to annoyance, and when the troubadour tipped his hat and then turned it upside down, they pitched some coins in. I wasn't part of his audience, but wandered over and flipped in a dime myself.

"Thank you, mon," he said.

"Always this sticky in July?"

"Always, mon. Even de trees sweat."

And he was off to find new pigeons.

Warehouses and other stone structures—this one labeled Government Ice House, that one labeled Sponge Exchange, another Vendue House, whatever that was—fronted the water's edge. People were on the move, only not too fast. Most of the faces here were dark, with women in sarong-like garments but longer than Dorothy Lamour's, and many of the men were bare-chested, ripplingly muscled, perspiration-oiled; both genders often carried baskets and other objects on their heads (despite frequent elaborate straw hats), perfectly balanced, making a way of life out of a childhood expression: *Look, Ma, no hands.*

As I strolled away from the wharf, duffel bag in hand (not on my head), I glanced back at the harbor, its choppy blueness irresistible to the eye. A strip of land at the immediate horizon (inelegantly named Hog Island, I later learned) defined the harbor; a lighthouse on the tip of the island made a white silhouette against the sky.

A few small sleek white yachts were searching in vain for the fabled Bahamian breezes, while two native schooners were gliding in, as if engaged in a lazy race. Unlike the rich man's pleasure craft, these had a rough-hewn look, were sorely in need of paint and bore sails of patchwork rags. I thought they were fishing ships, but on closer look I could spot bins laden with brainlike objects that my brain finally discerned as sponges. So they *were* fishing ships, in a way, though I didn't relish a fillet of one of their catches.

Another vessel, laden with baskets of fresh vegetables and fruit, drifted by with a colored contingent of young and old, from a granny sitting in a rocking chair to a giggling teenage girl whose nut-brown bare-chested beau was singing her a calypso chantey amidst goats, chickens, sheep and a cow, together on a sloop perhaps twenty-five feet long.

Anchored along the wharf, looking rather lonely, was a ferry-style sight-seeing craft near a sign that said, GLASS BOTTOM BOAT —SEA GARDENS FERRY—PARADISE BEACH. Perhaps fifteen passengers—including some attractive young women, who looked to be either British or American, with some off-duty RAF and Army boys mixed in—sat around the glass well of the boat, looking impatient, while the portly white white-haired "captain," dressed in blazer and cap like a roadshow Captain Andy from *Show Boat*, paced the dock, casting about for more riders.

"You, there, lad!" he called to me.

I waved negatively at him and was about to turn to my left when a voice—a musical, female voice—came from my right.

"That poor man . . . such slim pickin's these days."

I turned quickly toward the voice, with high hopes for who it belonged to.

I wasn't disappointed.

"You know," she continued liltingly, transforming certain t's into soft d's, "there is usually a fleet of those ferries here, even this time of year. And those boats, they keep busy, too."

She was a beautiful milk-chocolate girl in a floppy wide-brimmed straw hat with a red and blue and yellow floral band; her linen dress was robin's-egg blue and buttoned down the front and made no effort to hide or for that matter enhance a slender, high-breasted figure that could speak for itself. She had the full sensual lips of some dark ancestor, and the small well-formed nose of some lighter one, and large, lovely, elaborately lashed mahogany eyes that were all her own. She was probably about twenty-five years old.

A woman this beautiful can take your breath away. Mine, anyway. I opened my mouth to speak but nothing came out.

"But you really *should* see the sea garden while you're stayin' in Nassau, Mr. Heller," she said, as if our conversation was bouncing right along. "That's what the glass *bottom* is for. . . ."

"Excuse me," I said, swallowing. "You have me at a disadvantage. . . ."

She laughed and her laugh was even more musical than her voice, which seemed to put weight on words and syllables in a sweetly random, intrinsically Caribbean fashion.

"I'm sorry, Mr. Heller. Your photo, it was sent ahead to us."

She extended a slender hand; pink-and-red-and-white-beaded wooden jewelry dangled from her wrist, making more music. "Marjorie Bristol."

I shook her hand, and her grip was strong, but the flesh was smooth and soft.

My tongue was thick as one of the sponges on those ragtag schooners. "Uh, I take it you must represent Mr. Oakes, Miss Bristol."

"I do," she said, repeating the dazzling smile, "but he prefer Sir Harry—an interestin' combination of the grandiose and commonplace, don't you think?"

"I was just thinking that," I said.

"Let me take your bag," she said.

"Not on your life, lady!"

She looked at me, startled.

I smiled. "Sorry. That came out rude. It's hot, it's sticky, and I'm in a foreign land. Please lead the way—but I'll carry my own bag."

She smiled again, but in a no-nonsense manner. "Certainly."

She walked just ahead of me and her high, rounded rump moved impertinently under the blue linen dress, as if the globes of her backside were constantly trying to balance themselves and failing, nobly.

"I'm in charge of Sir Harry's household staff," she said. "I hope you don't mind bein' greeted by a female."

"Hardly." I was following along with my coat slung over my shoulder, shirt clinging as if I'd been swimming in it, lugging my bag. Her rear end might be impertinent, I reflected, but Marjorie Bristol herself seemed as polite and businesslike as she was charming.

"We have a surrey waitin' in Rawson Square," she said, tossing me a friendly glance.

Beyond the wharf, native women sold straw headgear and baskets, their own flamboyant woven hats their best advertising tool; others peddled sponges, shells and coconut candies. Miss Bristol walked me past a peaceful palm- and hibiscus-flung postage-stamp park where black little boys rode ancient cannons and black little girls sat primly on green benches before a band shell, possibly while their mothers sold straw goods nearby. A Negro policeman, hands behind him, chin high, stood motionless on a corner of Bay Street, in his white gold-spiked sun helmet, freshly laundered white jacket, red-striped dark blue trousers and black reflective boots. He might have been a statue.

"That's Queen Victoria," Miss Bristol said to me—I was in step with her now—and she was referring to a real statue, pointing to a sun-bleached constipated-looking little lady of marble with crown and scepter sitting on her throne atop a squat pillar with a bright bed of flowers at her feet.

I frowned a little, shook my head. "Funny place to bury her."

Miss Bristol looked at me in sharp confusion, but it only lasted for an instant and was replaced by as quick a smile. "Aren't you a nasty one," she said, and it wasn't a question.

"I am," I said cheerfully, "and it's better you find out now."

Behind the seated stone Queen was a cluster of pink colonial public buildings, a three-sided quadrangle surrounding the stern little monarch.

"That's the Parliament Square," she explained.

But we weren't headed there. We had paused alongside the park, where a lineup of high-roofed horse-drawn carriages awaited passengers who probably weren't coming today; the native drivers slumped in their seats, asleep under their tugged-down straw-hat brims, fanned by their horses who were lazily tail-swatting the air and flies.

One of the drivers was awake, however, a thin, very dark gent in loose white apparel with a brilliant red sash around his waist. He had a grooved, friendly face, close-cropped salt-and-pepper hair and was somewhere between forty and sixty. And his carriage seemed larger and fancier—with both a front seat and back, leather-covered, and red satin side curtains—than the other horse-drawn hacks around him.

"Ah, Miss Bristol. Your guest is here."

He stepped off his perch and found a place at the back of, and under, the carriage to stow my canvas bag.

"Thank you," I said.

He smiled, revealing a gold eyetooth. "My name is Samuel, sir. I work for Sir Harry. If you need anyt'ing, ask."

"Thanks, Samuel," I said, and held out my hand and he seemed pleased to shake it. Then I drew back the carriage's red curtain and helped Miss Bristol into the backseat. It was the closest I'd gotten to her so far, and it damn near made me giddy.

I settled in beside her, put my suitcoat in my lap. "If you don't mind my saying, you smell fresher than all the flowers in Nassau. Particularly since, the way this weather's hit me, I sure don't."

She laughed a little, but took the compliment well. "My sin," she said.

"Pardon?"

When she turned to me, the wide straw hat brim brushed my forehead. "It's a perfume: *My Sin*. That's one of the blessing of living here . . . bargain price on imported scent."

Taking a right onto the left side of the road, British-style, the carriage clip-clopped onto Bay Street, which ran parallel to the oceanfront and appeared to be the town's chief thoroughfare and shopping district. Along the tree-lined street, curio shops peddled more straw hats, shells (conch and turtle), and pickaninny dolls, out of old stone buildings with tiny storm-shuttered windows and overhanging tiled verandas that shaded shoppers. The frequent supporting pillars made me think of horse-hitching posts, which perhaps was how they were still used, from time to time. This Old West touch was offset by the modern, official-looking gilt lettering of registered companies whose offices lurked above the stores—accountants, lawyers, merchants, insurance and real-estate agents, import-export companies . . .

Miss Bristol seemed amused as I took this all in. "Everyone want an office on Bay Street, Mr. Heller. This is where the money in Nassau is."

"Does Sir Harry have an office here?"

"No. I said money, not wealth."

Pharmacy windows advertised the famous perfumes Miss Bristol had referred to; and our surrey rolled past dry-goods stores; liquor stores; saloons; the Prince George Hotel; the Savoy cinema; a produce market that bustled halfheartedly.

"Almost deserted today," Miss Bristol said, the music of her voice mingling with that of the carriage's ever jangling bell. "Many of the Bay Street Pirates are in the U.S. on vacation right now. . . ."

"Bay Street Pirates?"

"That's what the merchants and the other money men on this

street, they always been called. Or the Bay Street Boys, or Bay Street Barons."

For being "almost deserted," there sure was plenty of traffic on the wide white thoroughfare—an odd amalgam of surreys, American and British autos, bicycles, and the occasional horse-drawn cart piled with bales of sponges.

"Funny," I said.

"Funny?"

"I heard of Bay Street back in Chicago." Her talk of money and the Bay Street Pirates had made it dawn on me, finally.

Beneath the vast brim of the straw hat, huge brown eyes narrowed; lashes fluttered like hummingbirds. "Really, Mr. Heller? Why would you hear of our Bay Street back where you come from?"

"They used to call it 'Booze Avenue,' didn't they?"

She laughed silently. "Why yes, they did. I didn't know you were up on our local history, Mr. Heller."

"I'm not. But I do recall that with Nassau so close to the U.S., and with liquor legal down here, rum-running was big business. Not a little of that liquor ended up in Chicago hands."

"Many fortune was made," she said mysteriously.

"But not Sir Harry's."

"Not Sir Harry's. No need for rum money when you have all that gold."

Still, I had another twinge: those fortunes that were made in Nassau, in Prohibition days, meant local links to the mob that were likely still intact. It was enough to make you wonder who was sitting behind the gilt-lettered windows over those curio shops. When they weren't on vacation in the U.S., that is.

"That's where you'll be stayin' tonight," Miss Bristol said, pointing at a mammoth, sprawling, half-colonial, half-Moorish pink wedding cake of a building that seemed to signal the end of Bay Street. "Sir Harry own that."

"No kidding."

Her smile turned mischievous. "A few years ago Sir Harry went into the hotel dinin' room and the maître d' didn't recognize him . . . Sir Harry's apparel is . . . unpretentious, you know? Even unconventional."

"Really," I said, still savoring the odd, almost French-sounding accent she'd put on that unlikely last word.

"Really. So Sir Harry, he's wearin' the shorts and sandal,

lookin' kind of sloppy, you know, and he was refused a seat. And the next day, Sir Harry, he buy the hotel for a million dollar and he go back in and ask for a seat and the same thing happen. Only this time, he fire the maître d'."

"Well. I'll be sure to keep my opinions about Sir Harry's attire to myself."

She laughed again. "Sometime it is best to be discreet."

Pleasant as she was pretty, this Marjorie Bristol. But where did she get that vocabulary? I knew where she got the Caribbean accent—I'm a detective, after all.

But we had gone on past the hotel.

"We're not stopping for me to check in?" I asked.

"No. Sir Harry wants you brought straight to him. He's expectin' you at Westbourne."

"Westbourne?"

We were moving past a public beach, little-used at the moment, the surrey clop-clipping onto an open road, heading away from town.

"Westbourne," she said. "Sir Harry's beach house."

I kidded her with a wry smile. "That name's a little . . . *grandiose* for a cottage, isn't it?"

She turned and grinned at me, her straw-hat brim grazing my forehead again. "It sure ain't commonplace. . . ."

Three

~~~~~~

Following the edge of the sea, past a sprawling, well-preserved stone hillside fortress that guarded the western entrance to the harbor, beyond a budding wealthy residential development, rounding a curve Marjorie Bristol called Brown's Point, Samuel and his surrey ambled past a lush green golf course which provided a vast lawn for the estate next door.

The house itself wasn't visible from the road. Rather, it was announced by a black wrought-iron fence with white stone pillars and a black wrought-iron gate whose metal work, in rococo cursive, spelled out *Westbourne*.

The double gate was shut, but not locked, and Samuel stepped off the surrey, swung open half the gate and returned to shake the reins and get us moving again. He did not get back out to shut the gate behind him before we rolled up and around the crescent-shaped drive across an immaculately landscaped lawn dressed with vivid colorful clusters of gardens, like flowers in a pretty girl's hair. The ever-present palms leaned lazily, as if gesturing toward the large, low house itself.

New Providence was a long narrow island—twenty-one miles by seven—and the house on the Oakes estate mimicked that shape, as well as paralleled it, wide to the west and east, narrow to the

south and north. The elongated front of the haciendalike house—
or was it the back?—dwarfed its two stories, making the structure
look lower-slung than it was; Sir Harry's fabled home reminded
me, frankly, of a motor hotel.

Westbourne was a surprisingly ungainly, shrubbery-surrounded,
white-shuttered gray stucco affair with a reddish tile roof and lots
of latticework on which bougainvillea climbed; a balcony ran the
length of the building, providing a roof for the first-story walkway
below, which ceased to the right of the entry porch where the doors
of several garages stood half-open, revealing pricey vehicles within.
At either end of the structure, open wooden stairways with latticework balustrades gave access to the balcony and many of the
second-floor rooms.

Somebody with money lived here, obviously—this little beach
cottage had to run somewhere between fifteen and twenty rooms
—but not necessarily somebody with taste. Marjorie Bristol had
been wrong: grandiose as its name might be, sprawling and well-
tended as its grounds were, Westbourne had a distinctly commonplace air.

Samuel gave me a smile and I tipped my hat to him as he led
his horse and surrey back toward the gate.

"He seems like a sweet guy," I said. I had slipped my coat back
on and was lugging the duffel.

"None sweeter," Miss Bristol said.

As she walked me toward the wide front porch, she pointed off
to the right. "Tennis court over there," she said. "Swimmin' pool,
too."

The tennis courts peeked through the palms, but you couldn't
see the pool from here.

"Why do you need a swimming pool when the ocean's in your
front yard?"

"*I* don't," she said, with a little shrug.

The main entry was unlocked and she went right on in, and I
followed. The interior was lush dark wood and plaster walls with
paintings and prints that ran to a nautical theme; the ceiling was
higher than I would have guessed from outside. An open staircase
curved to bedrooms above. To my left I glimpsed a formal dining
room, with rich-looking Victorian furnishings and a vast oriental
carpet, large enough for an Arabian village to fly away on. Everywhere I looked was a vase with fresh-cut white flowers.

Miss Bristol noticed me noticing that and said, "Lady Eunice, she loves her lilies. Even when she's away, like now, I keep her vases brimmin'."

Our footsteps echoed on a parquet floor where my face looked back up at me when I glanced down. I wondered if this high polish was Miss Bristol's work, or if she was strictly administrative.

I was led past the open doorway of a gleaming white modern kitchen, out onto a wide whitewashed porch where rattan furniture, potted palms and more cut lilies looked out on the slope of a landscaped backyard that fell to a white beach and blue sea.

Miss Bristol paused on the porch to bestow one of her frequent, but no less prized, smiles upon me. "Time you meet Sir Harry," she said. "Leave your bag up here on the porch. . . ."

Down wide steps off one side of the porch she took me, and I heard a chugging, whirring, that was not the tide rolling in.

"That's Sir Harry now," she said, and she wasn't smiling but her mahogany eyes had a twinkle. "He's playin' with his favorite toy, you know?"

I didn't know, but I soon did. A palm tree that was between me and the ocean suddenly toppled like a twig.

I hadn't noticed the heavy chain around the base of the tree, which had been literally uprooted by a weathered red tractor, its wheels casually churning across the golf-course-like grass, pulling along the palm and its roots and random clinging clods of dirt, like a horse dragging its fallen rider.

Only the tractor's rider, or rather driver, had not fallen; he grabbed the gearshift knob, threw the tractor into a thrumming neutral and hopped off like a frog. Clad in slouch hat, red-and-black lumberjack shirt, khaki jodhpurs and knee boots, he was a small but powerful-looking man with a powerful-looking paunch, which he scratched as he walked toward me.

"Goddamn trees!" he said, working an already harsh, grating voice above the mechanical rumble of the tractor. "What the hell is the use of having an ocean in your backyard if you can't *see* the fucking thing?"

My first thought was whether his salty language had offended Miss Bristol, but when I went to glance at her she was gone. Then I caught sight of her, already halfway up the lawn, heading toward the house.

He whipped off his hat and wiped his brow with the back of a work-gloved hand, leaving the flesh smudged. "You're Heller?"

His hair was brown and wavy and only touched with snow, a younger head of hair than his deeply lined, old man's face.

"That's right."

"I'm Oakes. I'll shut Bessie off and take a little break and we'll have a little talk."

He did, and we soon were walking along the beach.

Sir Harry Oakes had dark, wide-set glaring eyes and a jutting, belligerent jaw that made him seem permanently pissed-off; his nose was a bulbous blob of putty that threatened to touch thin, tight lips.

But he was actually kind of pleasant to me, in an eccentric, assholish sort of way.

Right now his thin lips were doing their tight rendition of a smile. "People think I *hate* trees, 'cause I'm always bulldozing 'em the hell down." He stopped and thumped my chest with a thick finger; he had taken the work gloves off. "I've got a *bigger* 'dozer I use, when I *really* want to tear up the bastards."

"No kidding."

We began walking again; the surf was gently rolling in, and we were walking past a scenic postcard come to life, but some nasty little winged sons of bitches kept trying to make lunch out of me.

"Sandflies," Sir Harry said, slapping one to death on his cheek. It was a stinging slap, as if he were repaying some self-insult. "They're harmless if you kill 'em."

That was a truism if I ever heard one.

But he was back to trees.

"I'm going to plant some palms this afternoon," he said, waving dismissively. "But I like my trees where *I* want 'em. I don't want 'em in my fucking way. I don't want 'em blocking my goddamn view. Right?"

"Right," I said.

"So what do you think of my island?"

He was at least one-third right: Miss Bristol had mentioned that Oakes owned a third of New Providence Island.

"Very lovely," I said, aiming for a sandfly and slapping myself in the face.

He stopped to point at the ocean, as if it were another of his possessions. "This is Cable Beach—where the phone line comes in and connects us with civilization. Sometimes I think that's one hell of a mistake."

"You have a point."

Sir Harry took his hat off to wave the flies away. He smiled again in his stingy way. "What do you think of my little Miss Bristol?"

"A very efficient, attractive young lady."

"She is at that. And a nice little darkie ass on her, too, wouldn't you say?"

I swallowed. Much as I might mentally admire Miss Bristol's posterior, it didn't strike me as a subject for discussion.

"Don't get me wrong, lad."

We'd stopped again, and he had placed a fatherly hand on one of my shoulders; his mean, tiny eyes narrowed into slits and his breath was hot, like a small blast furnace. My trained detective's observation as to this morning's breakfast would be a cheese and onion omelet.

"I have never laid a hand on that sweet child," he said somberly, "and I never will. She's smart and she's loyal and she does her job and then some. That is *one* thing you must always remember, son."

"What is?"

"Never diddle the hired help!"

"I'll try to keep that in mind."

I'd kept my voice flat, but his prospector's eyes searched my face for any irony to be mined. I was glad he wasn't using a pick.

"You're a Jewish fella, aren't you?"

"I don't practice the faith, but that's my heritage, on my father's side. You have a problem with that, Sir Harry?"

His laugh was explosive. "Hell no! But there *are* some narrow-minded bigots on this island. Whenever you have this many niggers and so few white folks crammed together in one little place, bigotry is always going to rear its ugly head."

Coming from a head that ugly, that struck me as a sound observation.

"The thing is, Nate . . . can I call you Nate?"

"Sure."

"Well, and you call me Harry. Fuck this 'sir' shit. We're going to be great friends."

"Great."

We were walking again. Sandflies nipped me while the surf rolled inexorably in—and out.

"The thing is, Nate, there are places you may need to go on this island that are . . . exclusive."

"No Jews allowed, you mean."

"That's right. To me a man's a man, and the only religion I acknowledge is gold . . . but Jesus! Don't tell my wife I said so. Eunice believes in all that heavenly hereafter horseshit."

"Harry, how can I do a job for you in Nassau if this island's restricted?"

"Because I *own* fucking Nassau, Nate. I've got a card for you up at the house; it identifies you as my guest. There isn't a club or restaurant or hotel in town it won't get you in."

"Well . . . that should do it."

"Besides—you don't look Jewish."

"Gee, thanks, Harry."

"You look like a goddamn mick, with that reddish hair." He slipped an arm around my shoulder as our feet padded along the white sand. "You're a good man, Nate. Now, let me tell you about this no-good bastard son-in-law of mine."

Son-in-law? Was that what this about? Some family squabble?

"You're not married, are you, Nate?"

"No."

"So you don't have any kids—not that you *know* of, anyway." He laughed harshly. "Well, if you ever do have, let me guarantee you something: they will break your fucking heart."

I didn't say anything. He took his arm out from around me; he didn't even want a surrogate offspring at that moment. The flinty eyes seemed suddenly moist.

"You give them everything . . . what do they give you back? A broken fucking heart. . . ."

It seemed Nancy, his "goddamned favorite," had—less than a year ago—shown her appreciation for her father's boundless generosity by marrying a "goddamn gigolo fortune-hunting Frenchman."

"Do you know how old she was when he started . . ." He could barely say it, but then it burst out of him. ". . . *fucking* her? Seventeen. *Seventeen!* And him, the slimy bastard, *twice* her age. . . ."

I said nothing; slapped a sandfly, successfully this time, on my suitcoat sleeve. It burst and left a tiny bloody splotch.

"He claims to be a 'count,' this de Marigny." As he spoke, I had no idea how that name was spelled: he pronounced it dee mah-reeny. "Goddamn playboy yachtsman . . . married two other times, lived off his damn wives."

He stopped; sat in the sand. Stared out at several brown pelicans who were swooping in toward the sea, looking for lunch. It was late morning, now, and lunch didn't sound like a bad idea to me, either. I sat next to him.

"We were always close, Nancy and me . . . she liked my stories about prospecting days . . . said she wanted to write my biography when she grew up." He laughed, almost wistfully; odd coming from such an old roughneck. "She always did like the boys. Maybe we shouldn't have let her go to those frolics at so young an age."

"Frolics?"

"That's Brit for dances. She was going to school in London, then—Torrington Park. She had special tutors for art and dance . . . anything she wanted. On her fourteenth birthday, I gave her a year off from schooling, and took her and her mama on a tour of South America. Then I gave her something *very* special. . . ."

He seemed to want me to ask, so I did.

"What was that, Harry?"

He looked at me and smiled wider than those thin lips should have been able to; I thought his parchment skin might crack.

"I took her to Death Valley, Nate."

What teenage girl could dream of more?

He stared at the sand, drew lines in it with a finger. "We retraced my wanderings, when I was searching for gold and damn near died of the effort. It was my way of teaching her . . . showing her . . . just what it had *taken* to have all this. And I think . . . I thought . . . some mutual respect had come of it."

The pelicans cawed, seeming to mock him.

"But then she threw me over for that fucking frog."

He sounded more like a spurned suitor than a father, but I kept that thought to myself.

His face had settled back into a bitter mask. "I sent her to California on a vacation, to get her away from that slimy son of a bitch. But he flew there and *met* her . . . she was barely two days legal, two little days eighteen, when he married her in New York City."

"That's a rough one, Harry."

He gazed hollowly at the ocean. "I tried to make the best of it. Offered 'em money. Offered him land. Offered him a job. He turned me down! Got on his high horse! Like the money didn't matter . . . like he wasn't in it for me to die and Nancy to inherit millions. . . ."

He grabbed at a handful of sand, like he wanted to strangle it, but it only slipped through his thick fingers.

"Now, the son of a bitch has even tried to come between *Sydney* and me!"

"Sydney?"

"My son! He's an impressionable boy, and this Frenchie is smooth . . . so fucking *charming* . . ." The word was drenched in sarcasm. ". . . with his yachting and stories of Europe and his phony *title* . . ."

Sir Harry ought to know all about phony titles.

He was shaking a fist at the sea. "He's turned Sydney *against* me! Fuck him. *Fuck him.*"

Sir Harry's weather-beaten face was suffused with red.

"Then, this most recent outrage . . . he pressured Nancy into writing a vicious letter to her mother, cutting herself off from us 'until or unless' we welcome her beloved husband into the family fold. . . ."

I risked touching his plaid sleeve. "Harry—there isn't much to be done about unfortunate sons-in-law."

His nostrils flared. "*This* one there is!" His eyes narrowed and his thin mouth curled in a sneer as he leaned near me, conspiratorially. "My daughter is spending the summer with her mother in Bar Harbor, studying dance or some damn fool thing. And do you know what that fucking alley-cat frog is doing every night, while his wife is away?"

"No."

He reared his head back and bellowed, "Chasing pussy!"

As I removed one shoe and poured sand out of it, I wondered if all baronets of the British Empire were so eloquent.

He clutched my arm; his grip was a vise. "I want you to get the goods on the smooth-talking bastard!"

"The goods?"

He spoke through a tight smile, vicious little teeth clenched. "I want you to give me a stack of pornographic photos, starring that phony count, that I can spread out in front of my daughter and make her faint *dead* away."

Oakes cackled at his own brilliant plan, while I silently nominated him Father of the Year.

"Mr. Oakes . . . Sir Harry . . . I don't normally do this kind of work. . . ."

He scowled at me—although with his mug, it wasn't that easy

to tell. "Don't go all high-minded on me, Heller. I checked up on you. I *know* your reputation." He thumped my chest with a thick finger again. "Why in hell do you think I called you in?"

I pushed the air with two open palms. "That's not it—my agency thrives on divorce work. I just don't do it myself." I thumped my own chest. "I'm the president of my agency, Mr. Oakes. . . ."

He snorted a laugh. "Well, hell, man—Sir Harry Oakes doesn't want some low-level assistant—I want the top man! Would you send Henry fucking Ford your office boy?"

"Of course not, Sir Harry. . . ."

He put a hand on my shoulder. "Just Harry, Nate."

"Fine. But why didn't you just use somebody local? Why go all the way to Chicago for—"

"There are only two private investigators in Nassau, Nate—both well known by 'Count' Alfred de Marigny. You, on the other hand, ought to be able to blend in with the tourists and military personnel and American airfield engineers . . . the soldiers and sailors lots of times don't wear their uniforms off duty, you know."

"Well . . ."

He stood, planted his feet in the sand like a statue. "What will it take to get you to do the job, Heller?"

I got up, brushing the sand off my ass. "Frankly, I assumed this would be corporate work, or I'd have sent one of my operatives. . . ."

"How much, sir?"

I shrugged; pulled a figure out of the air. A high one. "Three hundred a day and expenses."

Sir Harry shrugged back, and gestured toward his house. "How does a ten-thousand-dollar, nonrefundable retainer sound? Payable right now?"

"Fine," I said quickly, astounded. "It sounds just fine. . . ."

"I'll make you out a check," he said. "I don't think you'll have any trouble cashing it. . . ."

Four

~~~~~~

Marjorie Bristol was waiting on the porch, looking crisp and cheery in her blue linen dress, hands folded before her as if she were holding an invisible bouquet. The wide-brimmed straw hat was gone and revealed dark kinky hair cut boyishly short on a beautifully shaped head.

"I heat up a little lunch for Mr. Heller," she said.

"Good girl," Sir Harry said, slapping his thigh with his hat. "Has Harold stopped by yet?"

"Yes, Sir Harry. He's waitin' in the billiard room."

Sir Harry turned to me and offered me his hand; we hadn't shaken before but his powerful, callused grip came as no surprise. His weather-beaten, deeply lined face cracked in what was, technically at least, a smile.

"I'll leave you to the charming head of my household staff," he said, and bowed a little—he was a baronet, after all. He was heading inside when he called back to me: "Stop and see me before you go . . . I'll make out that check!"

Then he was gone.

"Miss Bristol," I said, "lunch really isn't necessary . . ."

"I already heat it up. Nothin' fancy—just yesterday's turtle soup and some conk fritters."

She directed me to sit on a rattan chair, and put a black-topped, rattan-legged tray table before me; she disappeared, briefly, and returned with a tray bearing a bowl of steaming, aromatic soup on a plate with small, round, irregular fritters. There was also a cloth napkin, gleaming silverware and a tall glass of iced tea garnished with mint leaves.

I tasted the soup and it was very good. I told her so. "You don't do the cooking here, do you, Miss Bristol?"

The sky had turned overcast; the sea looked as moody as it did endless.

"No. The cook, she's out buyin' things for a little party Sir Harry's havin' tonight."

I sipped my iced tea. "No lunch for your boss?"

"Sir Harry and his friend Mr. Christie are goin' to have a bite at the country club."

I noticed I hadn't been asked along. "Why don't you join me, Miss Bristol?"

"That wouldn't be right. You enjoy yourself, Mr. Heller . . . I'll be in the kitchen when you're done. . . ."

"No you won't! Pull up a chair and sit down. Keep me company."

"Well . . ." She thought it over. I knew the hired help—partic- ularly the colored hired help—wasn't supposed to eat with the guests—particularly the white guests (as if there were any other kind at Westbourne). But I wasn't asking her to eat with me . . . just sit and keep me company. . . .

She did.

"A storm is comin'," she said.

"Really? It doesn't look *that* overcast."

"Smell the air. It's comin'."

To me the air was just sea-salty fresh; and I was just glad to finally have something resembling a breeze blowing in.

"How many people are on the household staff, Miss Bristol?"

"Five—three inside, two out. You met Samuel. He's a handyman and night watchman. All-round good fella. And there's another watchman. Also a maid who does the household things. Cook, I al- ready mention. And me, I look after Sir Harry and Lady Eunice."

"How?"

She shrugged. "Help 'em keep their schedules. Put out their clothes in the morning, their night things out at night. Many things."

"Almost a secretary."

She smiled; she liked that. "Almost. I'm always tryin' to be versatile."

"Miss Bristol—if you don't mind my asking . . . where did you go to school?"

She seemed surprised—and pleased—that I'd asked; she hugged a knee as she sat. "Right here in Nassau. I graduate from Government High School."

"Good for you. Any college?"

She almost winced. "No. There's no college here. . . . I have a brother, he is *very* smart, you know. We hope he'll go to college someday—in the United States, they have colleges for Negroes."

"Yes they do. I would've sworn you'd been to one."

She lowered her eyes; this was the first she'd seemed at all shy. "I just like to read, Mr. Heller. I like books, you know." Then she raised those deep brown eyes and her lashes fluttered and she said, "I think ignorance is the most evil thing. Don't you?"

The sky seemed more overcast; maybe she was right—maybe a storm *was* coming.

"Well, Miss Bristol . . . I'm afraid evil's a bigger thing than even ignorance. But ignorance probably has hurt more people than greed or jealousy or even war. I'm kind of in the anti-ignorance business myself."

Her eyes narrowed. "You're not a teacher, are you?"

"No. I'm a detective."

That surprised her. "Really? Police?"

"No, I guess I'm what people insist on calling a private eye."

She lit up. "Like Humphrey Bogart?"

I laughed. "Not quite. Look, I've said more than I should. We're getting into Sir Harry's business now, I'm afraid. I'm sorry, Miss Bristol . . ."

She nodded, as if to say, "You're quite right." I was stupid to mention my profession to her; as far as she'd known, I was just some business associate of her employer's.

We sat in awkward silence for a minute or so, and I ate, and looked out at the vast sea. Somewhere, across it, Mussolini's government was toppling, and Cologne was trying to recover from a visit by a thousand Allied bombers. Back home Charlie Chaplin had attracted near as much attention just by marrying teenage Oona O'Neill in the middle of his latest paternity suit.

But it all seemed abstract, it all seemed to be happening in some other world, when you sat in the Bahamas and studied the sea—a sea that men were dying on right now, most likely, even as I finished my turtle soup.

"Delicious lunch," I said, touching the napkin to my lips. "The fritters were good, too."

"Just heated up. Cook fried 'em last night. They're better fresh."

"What's 'conk'?"

"You spell it c-o-n-c-h. The meat from a pretty pink shell the tourists buy."

"Oh—sure. Well, any way you spell it, the fritters are tasty."

She grinned. "You'll be eatin' a lot of conch while you're here, Mr. Heller."

She wouldn't let me help her with the dishes, but I walked her into the kitchen and said, almost whispered, "Please don't mention that I'm a detective . . . to anyone."

"Mr. Heller," she said warmly, "you're a nice man. I wouldn't do *anything* you didn't want me to."

Our eyes locked, and there was a moment between us—a man/woman moment, that transcended culture and time and taboo—but it was just a moment, and we both looked away, embarrassed.

"I best take you to Sir Harry, now."

She did.

Oakes was in a medium-size room with a fireplace, oriental rug and tall windows that looked out on the ocean; a billiards table took up much of the floor space. On the walls here and there, stuffed big-game fish and mounted wild-game heads were mute observers.

Looking like a sight gag in his plaid shirt, jodhpurs and riding boots—I was reminded of Harpo dressed as a jockey in *A Day at the Races*—Sir Harry was standing bowlegged, leaning on a bending cue as he spoke to a rather disheveled-looking little man sucking desperately on a cigarette.

Both were frowning; perhaps we'd interrupted an argument.

But Sir Harry smiled tightly, seeing us, and said, "Ah! My guest. Have a decent lunch?"

"Swell," I said. "Turtle soup and conch fritters."

He laughed shortly. "We'll make a Bahamian out of you by nightfall, Heller. Marjorie, fetch me my checkbook."

"Yes, Sir Harry."

Miss Bristol left, and Sir Harry gestured to his diminutive but muscular-looking friend, who was so tanned I wondered if he might be mulatto.

"Meet the *real* baron of Nassau, Mr. Heller—Harold G. Christie. Best damn pard an old prospector ever had."

So much for interrupting an argument.

Christie was fiftyish, nearly bald, with an egg-shaped head and shaggy, sandy eyebrows over piercing money-green eyes. He was homely as a toad: face seamed, nose bulbous, chin weak; his lightweight white suit looked slept-in, his dark tie hastily knotted.

This was the *real* baron of Nassau?

"This is Nathan Heller," Oakes told his friend. "He's a detective from Chicago I hired for some personal business."

Christie's eyes widened momentarily as he flashed Oakes a wary look. "A detective? Why, Harry?"

Sir Harry sniggered; put a hand on his friend's shoulder. "It's personal, Harold. You have a personal life. I have a personal life."

Christie frowned up at Oakes, then turned to me and smiled in a surprisingly engaging way; the toad could become a prince when he switched on the charm.

"Welcome to Nassau, Mr. Heller," he said. His voice was mellow. "Though why you'd come to the Isles of June in *July* is a mystery even to a Bahamas booster like me."

"If you want that mystery solved, Harold," Sir Harry said, "you'll have to hire your own goddamn detective."

What was going on here? Was Oakes goading his pal?

But Christie only kept smiling, albeit in the strained way of the underling whose boss has just made a joke at his expense. He crushed his cigarette out in an ashtray on the edge of the billiards table and immediately lighted up another.

"Nate, if you're not careful, Harold here will have you in a villa on the oceanfront before supper."

"You're in the real-estate business, Mr. Christie?"

Christie smiled, blew out smoke and was about to answer when Oakes interrupted. "Saying Harold is in the real-estate business is akin to saying Hitler's in the land-grab business."

That comparison made Christie wince, but Sir Harry bellowed on.

"Few years back, Harold buttonholed me in London, talked me into coming to New Providence, and then managed to sell me half the goddamn place." Oakes snorted a laugh. "Do you know why

Mr. Christie here is the most influential man in these islands? And I'm counting our little friend the Duke of Windsor, too, mind you. Harold understands that the basic asset of these islands is *land* . . . not for mining or crops, mind you: but for selling to rich goddamn fools like me. Ah! Here's Marjorie. . . ."

She was bringing his checkbook; he put down the pool cue and went with her to a small table by a lamp with a silk shade.

Christie said, very softly, "You'll have to forgive Harry. Talkativeness is among his worst vices."

"And tact is not among his chief virtues."

"Hardly," Christie said, and chuckled, and sucked in smoke.

"Nate!" Oakes called, waving at me. "I'll see you out. . . ."

"Pleasure meeting you, sir," I told Christie.

"Likewise," he said pleasantly, and nodded.

Oakes slipped an arm around my shoulder as we walked, handing me a ten-thousand-dollar check that glistened with wet ink. Miss Bristol had gone on ahead to open the door; our conversation remained private.

"That's thirty-four days, approximately," he said, "at your three-hundred-dollar-a-day rate . . . counting today, which was a flat thousand."

"Did you want me to start today?"

"Hell, yes! You'll find de Marigny at the Yacht Club. He's racing there this afternoon. This card will get you in anywhere."

It was a small white card that simply said, "*The bearer is my personal guest,*" signed "*Sir Harry Oakes, Bart.*"

"I'll need de Marigny's photo. . . ."

Sir Harry waved that off. "Just ask somebody to point him out. He's a tall horsy-looking frog, skinny as a plank. He's grown a goddamn devil beard, too. You can't miss the son of a bitch. Look for his yacht." Harry's thin upper lip curled in disgust. "It's called the *Concubine.*"

"It would be," I said.

Miss Bristol had the door open for us. We walked out under the balcony's overhang, toward the garage, the young woman following at a respectful distance. There was a breeze now, Bahamas balmy, but the humidity remained oppressive.

"You're to check in with me every day, by phone. Miss Bristol will give you the number."

I glanced back at her and she smiled. God, I loved her smile.

He was squeezing my shoulder, getting my attention back. "I've a car for you . . . it's rented in your name. Nassau and New Providence road maps in the glove box with a list of pertinent addresses—de Marigny's house, his business interests."

I nodded. These rich guys were efficient.

He swung open the garage door. "But for Christ's sake, remember to stay on the wrong goddamn side of the road!"

"You mean on the left."

"Right," Sir Harry said.

The car was a dark-blue 1939 four-door Buick, big as a tank, which is what it handled like; not the best vehicle for a shadow job, and it *was* unnerving, heading back down Bay Street into town, staying on the left-hand side of the road. The occasional bicycle gave me a start, and the tropical scenery, burning with color, remained a distraction.

I was saved by the sudden appearance of the sprawling pink terra-cotta monstrosity that was the British Colonial Hotel, which even had a parking lot where I could leave the Buick and get back on my own two feet for a while.

The room that awaited me at the British Colonial wasn't a suite, but it was plenty big, and seemed bigger, thanks to the light pink walls and white woodwork. It had a double bed, a chest of drawers, lots of closet space, a writing desk and a good-size bathroom. I could live here awhile.

There was also a wrought-iron balcony and an ocean view to go with it, but the white beach was near empty under the graying sky.

I unpacked, and figured I ought to get to work, but I had a couple of things to do, first. For starters, I'd only brought this one, currently sweat-soaked, suit. The guy at the front desk pointed me toward a little tailor shop near the hotel. I stopped in and from a cheerfully weary, berry-brown tailor named Lunn bought two white linen suits off the rack. He would have preferred to make them to order (promising them within two days!) but reluctantly sold me a couple in my size, sighing, "Can't argue with you, sir! You're a forty-two reg—nothing special!"

Story of my life.

Next stop was the Royal Bank of Canada, which seemed a fitting place to cash Sir Harry's check; I had them wire most of it to my account at Continental Bank back home.

Off Rawson Square, I bought a Panama hat with a light brown

band from a heavyset, gregarious straw lady whose cart was piled high with hats and bags and mats; she asked "fifty cent," I argued her down to a quarter, then gave her a buck for the fun of it.

She gave me a little extra value by pointing me to a camera shop where, since every good bedroom dick needs one, I picked up a flash job, a fifteen-buck Argus with universal focus. Also some 35mm black-and-white film and bulbs.

"Don't you want *color* film, sir?" the cute little Caucasian clerk asked; she had a corsagelike flower in her brunette hair. "You can catch all the beautiful colors of the island. . . ."

"I'm going more for mood," I said.

By the time I got back to the hotel it was nearly two p.m. and I had an armful of clothes—including two short-sleeve white shirts, four obnoxiously colorful sport shirts, some sandal-like leather shoes and three ties with painted tropical scenes—all of which would keep me in comfort and looking properly touristy.

Wearing one of my new white linen suits over a flowery sport shirt, hiding under my Panama and behind a pair of round-lensed sunglasses, I tooled my Buick down the left, remember, *left*-hand side of Bay Street. Most of the cars I encountered were, like the Buick, of American extraction; but now and then a Humber Snipe or Hillman would roll by in the "wrong" lane and befuddle me further, with their drivers sitting on the right. Bell-jangling surreys, donkey carts, wheelbarrows and your occasional straw-hatted native leading a goat kept traffic less than brisk; then at the east end of Bay Street, after the shopping district petered out, near the modern Fort Montagu Hotel and the old fortress the hotel was named for, was the Nassau Yacht Club.

The rambling pale yellow stucco clubhouse, while typical of Nassau's nineteenth-century, plantation-owner-style architecture, was clearly a recent structure; its landscaped grounds, with their not-yet-tall-enough-to-be-sheltering palms, had the unspoiled, sterile look of the new.

I ambled into the clubhouse. Nobody stopped me to see if I was a member or a Jew or anything. I was almost disappointed. The bar had framed photos of famous yachts and yachtsmen, as well as a few customers and a white-jacketed bartender (in the flesh—not photos). A wall that was mostly windows looked out on the eastern harbor. I stepped outside, where I was on the edge of terraced grounds that ran down to a surprisingly modest marina where small yachts were docked.

A handful of other yachts, three to be exact, were clustered out on the water, presumably racing. Not having ever been to a yacht race, I couldn't be sure. Perhaps one of them was de Marigny's *Concubine*.

None of them seemed to be going very fast; there was a breeze of sorts, but it wasn't cooperative. The sky was gun-metal gray now, the ocean a rippling sea of molten lead. The white boats and their white sails seemed trapped in the wrong seascape.

Back in the bar, I took a stool and asked for a rum and Coke.

The bartender was a blond young man of perhaps twenty-four. "Are you a member, sir?"

Finally! I showed him Sir Harry's card, and he smiled, raised his eyebrows and said, "Allow the Nassau Yacht Club to buy you a drink, sir. Could I recommend our special rum punch?"

"Yes to both."

He served it up in a round red glass with fruit in it; I tossed the fruit aside and sipped the punch—it was bitter with lime, sweet with brown sugar.

"What do you think?" the kid asked.

"Delicious and deadly."

He shrugged. "That's Nassau to a tee."

I turned on the stool and looked idly out the windows. "Racing today?"

"Our little weekly regatta. Not much of a turnout . . . lousy weather. They'll be lucky not to get caught out in it."

"Is that fella de Martini racing?"

"De Marigny you mean? Yeah. Sure."

"I hear he's quite a character. Real ladies' man."

The kid shrugged, rubbed the bar with his rag. "I don't know about that. But he's a hell of a yachtsman."

"Really?"

"Really. He's won all sorts of cups, including the Bacardi—and he's only been at it four or five years. He ought to be in in a few minutes. Would you like to meet him?"

"No thanks," I said.

Instead I nursed my rum punch and waited for de Marigny's race to end.

Mine was just about to begin.

Five

When de Marigny entered the clubhouse, he was chatting with two young male club members (possibly his crew), but there was no mistaking him: he was six three, easily, with dark, slicked-back hair and a well-trimmed Vandyke beard; slender, muscular, he wore a polo shirt with the arms of a pale yellow sweater tied around his neck like a clinging lover. I hate that.

On the other hand, despite Sir Harry's unflattering description, I'd assumed the Count would be handsome—most gigolos are— but de Marigny had big ears, a prominent nose and fleshy lips. If you were casting *Legend of Sleepy Hollow*, it would be a close call as to whether to give de Marigny the role of Ichabod Crane or his horse.

He did carry himself well, with confidence, affable if arrogant, and his two friends seemed hypnotized by his discourse. I couldn't make out his words, but he had a thick Charles Boyer French accent, which I suppose some women might find charming. Not being a woman, I couldn't be sure.

He seemed headed for the bar, so I tossed a quarter tip on the counter, slipped away before the bartender could introduce me, and went out to wait in the Buick.

Apparently de Marigny had a drink or two, because it was fifteen minutes later before he emerged from the clubhouse, still in his yachting togs but minus his sycophants, and strolled to a black Lincoln Continental. I wondered if Sir Harry's daughter Nancy had bought it for him.

Beyond Fort Montagu, aping the curve of the island, East Bay Street became the eastern road, along which were fabulous ocean-side mansions on land Harold Christie had most likely sold rich foreigners, and/or rumrunners. But de Marigny took a right, away from this affluence and into the boondocks, and I followed.

The same bushes and trees that so carefully adorned the grounds of wealthy estates grew wild here, pines and palms and bushes with red berries crowding each other alongside the narrow dirt road, like spectators eager for a look.

It was tricky not getting made, but the Lincoln kicked up plenty of dust, so I could keep my distance and still keep track of where the Count had headed.

Then the dust cloud abated, and I knew I'd lost him: he'd turned off somewhere.

Looking frantically right and left, I didn't feel panicked for long: there the Lincoln was, stopped in the crushed-rock driveway of a run-down-looking white farmhouse. It might have been an American farmhouse but for its louvered shutters, and limestone construction that dated back a century or two.

I drove on past, perhaps a quarter of a mile, and found a place alongside the road where I could pull off. Then I left my suitcoat behind but brought along my camera, and walked alongside the road, where the brush was taller than I was, and edged up near the farm.

Back home there would probably have been a fence to climb or at least step over; here all I had to do was push gently, quietly, sneakily through the tropical brush, like a Jap sniper looking for a target. I didn't have a rifle, of course, just my lethal little Argus, ready to snap an incriminating photo or two. . . .

But de Marigny's afternoon rendezvous was not with the wife of some wealthy crony of Christie's, or some dusky native gal; rather, with half a dozen colored workers in well-worn straw hats and loose, sweat-soaked clothing. De Marigny's sweater was no longer tied around his neck—it was gone, in fact—and his polo shirt was sweat-stained and sooty, clinging to a lanky but impressive musculature.

In the yard, alongside the farmhouse, two workers were adding more driftwood to a roaring fire beneath an old, cut-down oil drum that bubbled like a witch's caldron. De Marigny's men were on their haunches, dunking apparently freshly killed chickens—the absence of heads and bloody necks were the tip-off to this trained detective—into what I figured was scalding water.

And de Marigny was getting right in there with them, squatting down and dipping the chicken corpses by their feet into the boiling water. In fact, he seemed to be showing them how it was done, plucking the feathers from the softened flesh of the dunked birds. The ground nearby had a snowfall of feathers and down.

The flames were high, and the smoke was thick—even from my vantage point in the brush, my eyes were stinging.

De Marigny worked hard, maintaining a lighthearted attitude throughout, treating the Negroes like equals. One of them, a handsome, sharp-eyed youth of perhaps twenty-two, his clothes untattered, was clearly second in command. I heard de Marigny call him Curtis.

This went on for about an hour; I was squatting just like they were, only in the bushes, hoping New Providence didn't have nasty lizards or poisonous snakes to give me a surprise. But there was only the humidity to make my life miserable, the faint whisper of a breeze ruffling the leaves. At least there were no bugs, like those damn sandflies on the beach. . . .

Finally de Marigny disappeared inside and came back with his hair combed, the soot smudges washed off and his sweater over one arm. He collected Curtis, spoke for a moment to another of the workers, putting him in charge, and he and Curtis got in the Lincoln, both in the front seat but with the young Negro driving.

I quickly hightailed it back to my Buick, did a dandy little U-turn considering the space I had, and followed the Lincoln's dust trail.

Glancing at Sir Harry's list of de Marigny businesses—which included a beauty parlor, a grocery store and an apartment house —I didn't see anything that sounded like a chicken farm. There was something vague, called De Marigny and Company, which had a Bay Street address.

If de Marigny was such a shiftless son of a bitch, as Oakes had painted him, how'd he assemble such an impressive array of business holdings? Of course, maybe it was his wife's dough that got him set up in them all.

On the other hand, he'd been working his ass off plucking chickens, for Christ's sake, shoulder to shoulder with his black workers. I had been in Nassau only since this morning, but I already could tell that was rare behavior.

The dust led back to the eastern road, where I caught sight of the Lincoln, turning west. My watch said half-past four, so de Marigny ought to be going home, and if my reading of the Nassau Street map was close to correct, that was the way we were headed.

It was. The Lincoln turned off on Victoria Avenue, and that jibed with the address I had on the Count. The sea at our backs, we were going up the hill now, moving along a quaint side street flung with palms where little pastel houses built on the incline had stone garden walls with bougainvillea and creepers trying to climb over them, even as flowering trees on the other side peeked over.

Soon the black touring car pulled into a driveway and drew around to the side of the house to the closed doors of a double garage. Curtis got out and so did de Marigny, not waiting for his driver to come around and open his door for him. What a guy.

De Marigny's house reminded me of places I'd seen in Louisiana: a good-size, two-story, vine-crawling pink affair with green shutters and a screened-in veranda above and porch below, and exterior stairs along the driveway side of the house. Unlike many of the neighbors', with their limestone walls, de Marigny's garden, to the left of the house, was defined by high, manicured bushes.

I drove on by, found a place to turn around a couple blocks up the hill, and came back to park on the opposite side of the street, about half a block from the house. The street was so narrow you had to park on the lip of sidewalk.

De Marigny's Lincoln rolled out less than half an hour later. I assumed he was in the car, and took leisurely pursuit. As I passed his house, I could spy, through the open windows, servants scurrying. One of them was Curtis.

We were back on Bay Street soon, and I was able to put several cars between the Lincoln and the Buick and still keep de Marigny in my sights. It was dusk now, and we both had our lights on. In the thick of the shopping district—it was after five, but shops were still open—he found a parking place. I glided by, found one myself, and was getting out of the Buick when I saw him—in a brown sport jacket, lighter brown pants, cream-color shirt with no tie, and tan-and-white shoes, no socks. Very spiffy. He strolled toward the Prince George Hotel, pausing to light a cigarette beneath the flutter of Allied flags that adorned the entry.

I noticed that the upstairs office over the storefront next door said *H.G. Christie, Ltd., Real Estate, Since 1922.* Small world. Anyway, small town. . . .

De Marigny didn't go inside the hotel, but walked under an archway between it and the adjacent building, to the Coconut Bar and its beach-umbrellaed tables scattered on the terrace to wharf's edge, where small boats, sails furled, swayed uneasily in the restless sea. The ceiling of this bar was a broodingly overcast sky.

Few of the tables were taken, but the Count was immediately waved over by a plump, dark-haired guy of about thirty-five in a handsome pale green suit with wide lapels and a dark green striped tie.

"Freddie! I want you to meet the most gorgeous girls in Nassau!"

"Impossible," de Marigny said, massaging each syllable in his Boyer way, "I know them all . . . oh! I see I was mistaken."

He was: the women sitting with the glad-handing American were lovely young women in their twenties, a brunette with a sexy overbite and a lanky blonde with a nice wide smile. They wore summery dresses and sat with their legs attractively crossed, sipping tropical drinks out of fruit-bedecked coconut shells.

The American was making introductions as the Count joined them, but their voices were lowered to a normal range now and I couldn't make anything out. I risked a table within earshot, ordered myself a Coke with lime and watched the lead-gray sea ripple while I eavesdropped.

"Freddie," de Marigny said, putting the accent on the second syllable and revealing that his plump American friend shared first names with him, "I must insist you bring these charming girls along tonight. My guest list is shockingly scant."

"I've got bad news," the other Freddie said, mock sad. "They're married."

"So am I." De Marigny shrugged. His smile was as wide as it was casual. "Bring your husbands along! Some of my best friends are husbands."

"I'm afraid," the brunette said, "both our husbands are away on missions."

"RAF pilots," the American Freddie said.

De Marigny shrugged again. "My wife's in Maine studying dance. Maybe we old married people, separated from our loved ones, should console one another."

The American Freddie said, "He's got a Bahamian cook who'll knock your socks off, ladies."

I was willing to bet they'd be eating chicken.

The brunette and blonde looked at each other and smiled; damn near giggled. They nodded first to each other, then to de Marigny.

"Splendid," the Count said.

Now we're getting somewhere, I thought.

The quartet chatted—flirted, I thought, though the American was the most obvious—and soon I decided to fade away. I finished my Coke and went back to the Buick to wait for de Marigny to head back to Victoria Street for his party.

Which, before long, he did.

Nassau at night—at least on this overcast night—seemed otherworldly. Giant silk cotton trees cast weird shadows on limestone houses. Garden walls seemed like fortress battlements, and light slanted eerily through the slatted jalousie shutters, closed in anticipation of the storm that had promised itself all afternoon.

I followed the red eyes of the Lincoln's taillights and when de Marigny pulled up onto the lawn beside the driveway, I went on by; again I did a U-turn and found a place on the opposite side of the street.

Before long guests began to arrive, notably a puffy-faced, slickly handsome character with a Clark Gable mustache who pulled his two-tone brown Chevy into the driveway and emerged with a sexy little blonde on his arm. She had Veronica Lake peekaboo bangs and a blue dress with white polka dots and a Betty Grable shape and if she was of legal age, I was Henry Aldrich.

I counted eleven guests, a mixed group as to gender but resolutely white and well-off in appearance—not counting the RAF wives (who'd arrived with the pudgy American) and the jailbait cutie, who were plenty white, but not affluent. Their ticket of admission was their own pulchritude.

My window was down and even half a block away I could hear the laughter and chatter coming from the garden patio, so I got out of the car and joined the party. Sort of. The sidewalk was empty and the nearest streetlight was across the way, so nobody noticed me angle around the side of the well-tended bushes to do some professional peeping.

They were having their dinner party outdoors; a long picnic-type table was set, and several male Negro servants in white coats were in attendance, though nothing but wine had been served.

Three hurricane-shaded candles and two six-candled candelabras were as yet unlit on the attractively set table. Everybody was having a gay old time, but I didn't figure it would last long. The wind was coming up, and mosquitoes were nipping.

This morning, Marjorie Bristol could smell the rain in the air; right now, any idiot could smell it. I could smell it.

De Marigny had a kitchen match going. Sitting next to him was the blond RAF wife, as he half-stood leaning forward to try to light a candle, lifting a hurricane shade to do so. The wind whipped the flame away from the candle and across the back of the Count's hand.

"*Merde!*" he said.

"What does that mean?" the jailbait blonde asked wide-eyed.

"Shit, my dear," her suave puffy-faced escort rejoined.

Everyone laughed. Except me. I slapped a skeeter.

De Marigny singed himself a couple more times, but managed to get all the hurricane lamps lit, and even had the candelabras going, their flames leaning like deckhands on the *Titanic*.

"*Voilà,*" he said, admiring his work, and I was thinking that he didn't seem to know much more French than I did, when the rains came.

The guests laughed, some of the ladies squealing in a manner that I'm sure they thought was delightfully feminine.

"Inside, everyone!" de Marigny called, as his black servants quickly removed the table settings.

The guests, pelted with raindrops, were scattering, fleeing for shelter.

In my spot in the bushes, I was drenched already.

"*Merde,*" I said to myself, and headed back to the Buick.

And there I sat for a very long time. Machine-gun rain battering the car, drumming on the roof, palm trees swaying, fronds rustling, scratching like sandpaper rubbing together, wind whistling disgustedly through its teeth, carrying sickly sweet floral scents. With my windows up, I was hot in the car, windows fogging up. Heat and rain. Yet I was chilled. . . .

When the rains came, we covered the shell hole with camouflage tenting; when the tenting had collected water, we drank from its edge, guzzling it greedily, draining some of it into our empty canteens. The rain seemed to rouse even the wounded among us, and we huddled together, wondering when the Japs would come again, with their machine guns, bayonets, mortar shells. . . .

A crack of thunder snapped me awake, though I at first thought a mortar shell *had* hit. I was in a cold sweat, only there was nothing cold about it. I craved a cigarette.

Not a good sign: the only time in my life I ever smoked was those months I was in the Corps, on the Island—Guadalcanal. The nicotine craving came only rarely, since I got back—like the malaria flare-ups, one of which seemed to have hold of me now.

I cracked the window to unfog the windshield. The rain hammered down. I checked my wristwatch: almost midnight. How long had I slept? Had I missed anything? Maybe I ought to take my camera and go wading across the streaming street and crawl through the soaked shrubbery and see if some sort of Caribbean white-folks-only orgy was in progress.

But about that time the party began to break up; couples found their way to their cars—with the exception of the puffy Clark Gable and his underage Betty Grable. Oh, the happy couple exited, all right, snuggled under an umbrella; but they quickly took the side staircase up to what was apparently an apartment over the garage.

Lightning flared as the American Freddie left in the company of one of the male guests, an older, distinguished-looking man. That meant the Count was alone with the two RAF wives.

Maybe de Marigny was going to live up to his reputation.

Maybe I ought to reach for my camera. . . .

But then de Marigny, his jacket collar up, made a run for his Lincoln on the lawn. He got it running, backed it closer to the steps which led from the side of the porch. Then one of the servants—Curtis, I think—escorted the blond RAF wife, under an umbrella, to the waiting car.

I smiled. Looked like I was in business.

Except that then Curtis went back and returned with the *brunette* under his umbrella, as well. She joined de Marigny and their blond mutual friend in the front seat.

Cozy. I thought of some of the other French words I knew: *ménage à trois*.

I trailed the Lincoln down to Bay Street, the Buick's windshield wipers working furiously. His car swayed in the wind; so did mine. Neither vehicle was exactly a featherweight, either. The rain was unremitting. The street was half flooded, completely flooded around blocked drains; the shops were shuttered and shining with rain, turned silver-blue now and then by lightning. A pharmacy's neon stood out in the night like a modern apparition.

We went past my hotel—alive with occasional lights, a bed waiting there for me—and headed west. This was the way Samuel had taken Miss Bristol and me, earlier today, a century ago. A little ways beyond Westbourne, which was barely visible as I went by, lights ablaze on the upper floor, the Lincoln pulled in past a post with a hanging wooden sign that said HUBBARD'S COTTAGES.

It seemed to be a small development of rental properties. I went on by, but I could glimpse the Lincoln, stopped, and the two young women making a mad dash for the front door of a cottage. De Marigny was sitting with the motor running. . . .

When I had found a place to turn around and coasted by the cottage again, the Lincoln was gone.

I could only sigh. Tonight would definitely not be the night to get the goods on the Count. De Marigny, like a proper host, had merely driven his two female guests home. There were red taillights way up ahead of me—probably his—but I didn't bother trying to catch up.

It was after one a.m. and this long, long day—and night—was over; even at a thousand bucks, I'd earned my pay.

Six

~~~~~~

Thunder shook the sky like barrages of artillery and made my night a fitful hell of delirious combat dreams. I awoke half a dozen times, prowling the hotel room, looking out at the roiling sea and the turbulent sky, wishing I had a smoke. Below, palms bent impossibly, black silhouettes that became blue in the lightning. The goddamn storm kept turning itself up and down, like some ungodly radio tuned to station HADES, a squall followed by gentler wind and pattering rain and then *another* squall, with pealing thunder. . . .

I was finally dreaming about something else, something peaceful, something sweet, swaying in a hammock while a native girl wearing nothing but a grass skirt held a coconut out for me to drink from. She looked like Marjorie Bristol, but darker, and when I'd finished sipping the coconut milk, she soothed my brow with a hand soft as a pillow and, *boom boom boom boom*, an artillery barrage rocked me awake.

Sitting up in bed, breathing hard, sweat-soaked, I heard the sound again and realized it was just somebody at the door. Somebody insistent and knocking in an obnoxious manner, yes: but not artillery fire.

I threw off the sheet and went to answer it, pulling my pants on over the underwear I'd slept in. If this was the maid wanting to make up my room, I was prepared to be indignant—at least, until I glanced at my watch and realized how late I'd slept in: it was after ten o'clock.

Cracking the door, I said, "Yes, what is it?" before seeing who was out there.

It was a black face in a white helmet with a gold spike.

"Nathan Heller?" a Caribbean voice asked.

I opened the door wider. There were two of them, two black Nassau cops in their sun helmets, white jackets, red-striped trousers and polished boots. They might have stepped out of a light operetta.

"I'm Heller," I said. "You fellas want to step in? I just woke up."

They marched in, shoulders straight. Why did *I* feel silly?

"You're to accompany us to Westbourne, sir," one of them said, standing at attention.

"Westbourne? Why?"

"There has been a difficulty involving your employer."

"My employer?"

"Sir Harry Oakes."

"What sort of difficulty?"

"That's all we're at liberty to say, sir. Will you come?" The lilting Bahamian accent, added to the formality of what he was saying, gave the officer's words a stilted poetry.

"Well, sure. Give me five minutes to brush my teeth and get dressed?"

The spokesman nodded.

"I can meet you in the lobby," I suggested.

"We'll wait outside the door, sir."

"Up to you." I shrugged, but it was obvious something serious was afoot.

My police escorts rode in front and I had the backseat to myself as we traveled a West Bay Street slick with rain, sandy with mud. Gutters were clogged with palm leaves. The sky was overcast, making midmorning more like dusk, and the winds were humid and high, blowing an occasional branch across the police car's path.

I leaned forward. "Come on, fellas—what's this all about?"

They didn't seem to hear me.

I repeated my question and the one who hadn't spoken yet still didn't, just glanced at me and shook his head no. They might be native Bahamians, but these two had as much stiff-upper-lip reserve as any British bobbie.

The Westbourne gate was closed, but a white-helmeted black copper was there to open it for us. The crescent-shaped driveway was choked with cars, most of them black with POLICE in gold letters on the doors—like the one I was in.

"Come with us, Mr. Heller," the spokesman said, opening the car door for me politely, and I followed him up the steps onto the porch and inside, where I was greeted by an acrid, scorched smell that seemed to permeate the place. Had there been a fire?

Glancing about, I noticed the carpeting and wood on the stairway to the second floor were scorched; the banisters, too. But intermittently, as if a flaming man had casually walked up or down these stairs, marking his path. . . .

"Mr. Heller?" This was a crisp, male, no-nonsense voice I'd not heard before. British.

I turned away from studying the stairs to see a military-looking figure approach, white, dimple-jawed, jug-eared, fiftyish, wearing a khaki uniform cut by the black leather strap of a gun belt, and a pith helmet with a royal insignia where a badge should be.

He looked like a very efficient, and expensive, safari guide.

"I'm Colonel Erskine Lindop, Superintendent of Police," he said, extending a hand which I took, and shook.

"What crime has been committed here, that would bring brass like you around, Colonel?"

His hound-dog face twitched a smile, and he responded with a question. "I understand you're a private investigator—from Chicago?"

"That's right."

He cocked his head back so he could look down at me, even though I had a couple inches on him. "Might I ask you to detail your business meeting with Sir Harry Oakes yesterday afternoon?"

"Not without my client's permission."

Lifting his eyebrows in a facial shrug, Lindop strode toward the stairs, saying, "Best come with me, then, Mr. Heller."

He paused to curl a finger as if summoning a child.

And I followed him, like a good little boy.

"How did these stairs get scorched?" I asked.

"That's one of the things I'm here to try to determine."

There was mud and some sand on the steps, as well. I said, "If this is a crime scene, we're walking right over somebody's footprints, you know."

He just kept climbing; our footsteps were echoing. "Unfortunately, these stairs were already well traversed by the time I got here." He smiled back at me politely. "But your conscientiousness is appreciated."

Was that sarcasm? With British "blokes," I can never tell.

At the top of the stairs, there was a closed door to the right, a window straight ahead, and a short hallway to the left. The lower walls were scorched here and there. Smoke tainted the air, even more pungent than below. Lindop glanced back, nodding at me to follow him into a room down the hall. Right before you entered, fairly low on the white-painted plaster walls, were more sooty smudges. The inside of the open door had its lower white surface burn-blotched as well, and the carpet just inside the door was baked black, a welcome mat to hell.

Once inside, a six-foot, six-paneled cream-color dressing screen with an elaborate, hand-painted oriental design blocked us from seeing the rest of the large room. The Chinese screen had a large scorched area on the lower right, like a dragon's shadow; a wardrobe next to the screen, at left, was similarly scorched. So was the plush carpeting, but oddly—circular blobs of black, some large, some small, as if black paint had been slopped there.

In here, the smell of smoke was stronger; but another odor overpowered it: the sickly-sweet smell of cooked human flesh.

It made me double over, and I fell into the soft armchair where wind was rustling lacy curtains nearby; a writing table next to me had a phone and a phone book on it—both had reddish smears.

I leaned toward the open window and gulped fresh air; muggy though it was, it helped.

"Are you all right, Mr. Heller?"

Lindop looked genuinely concerned.

I stood. Thank God I hadn't eaten any breakfast.

"Sorry," I said. "It's just that I know what that smell is. I recognize it from overseas."

Charred grinning Jap corpses by a wrecked tank on the Matanikau, a foul sweet wind blowing through the kunai grass. . . .

"Where did you serve?"

I told him.

"I see," he said.

"Colonel, I'm an ex–Chicago cop—I'm not squeamish about much of anything. But . . . being back in the tropics is proving a real stroll down memory lane."

He nodded toward the doorway. "We can leave."

"No." I swallowed thickly. "Show me what's beyond the Chinese screen. . . ."

Colonel Lindop nodded curtly and stepped around it, following the scorched path, leading me to my final audience with Sir Harry Oakes, who was not at all his usual lively self this morning.

He was on the twin bed nearer the dressing screen, which apparently had been positioned to protect the sleeper from the open window's Bahamas breeze, though it had not protected him otherwise.

His squat, heavyset body lay face up, one arm dangling over the bedside, his skin blackened from flame, interrupted by occasional raw red wounds, head and neck caked with dried blood. He was naked, but shreds of blue-striped pajamas indicated his nightwear had been burned off him. His eyes and groin seemed to have taken extra heat; those areas were blistered and charred.

Over the bed was an umbrellalike wooden framework that had held mosquito netting, most of which was burned away. Strangely, this side of the nearby dressing screen was unblemished by smoke or fire. The most bizarre touch in this ghastly tableau was the feathers from a pillow which had been scattered over the blackened corpse, where they clung to the burned blistery flesh.

"Jesus," I said. It was almost a prayer.

"His friend Harold Christie found him, this morning," Lindop said. "About seven."

"Poor old bastard." I shook my head and said it again. I tried to breathe only through my mouth, so the smell wouldn't get to me.

Then I said, "Cantankerous old rich guy like him couldn't have been short on enemies."

"Apparently not."

It was one messy murder scene. Red palm prints, like a child's finger-painting, stood out on the wall by the window across from the other, un-slept-in twin bed; somebody with wet hands had looked out. I didn't imagine they'd been wet with catsup. More red prints were visible on the wall kitty-corner from the bed.

All of these prints looked damp—the humidity had kept them from drying.

Blood glistened on both knobs of the open, connecting door between this and another, smaller bedroom, opposite the unoccupied bed. I peeked in—that bedroom, which looked unused, was about sixteen feet across. Sir Harry's was twice that, and the other way ran the full width of the house, looking out on porches on both the south and north sides.

"Well," I said, "there's not exactly a shortage of clues. The trail of fire . . . bloody fingerprints . . ."

He pointed. "That fan by the foot of his bed seems to be what blew the feathers all over him."

"What do you *make* of the feathers, Colonel? Some sort of voodoo ritual?"

"Obeah," the Colonel said.

"Pardon?"

"That's what the practice of native magic is called here: obeah."

"And the feathers could mean that—or anyway, somebody wanted it to *seem* to mean that . . ."

"Indeed." Lindop's features tightened in thought; hands locked behind him. "After all, Sir Harry was quite popular with the native population, here."

There was a spray gun on the floor near the door to the adjacent bedroom. "Bug spray?"

Lindop nodded. "Insecticide. Highly flammable. . . ."

"Was he doused with that?" I laughed glumly. "Quick, Sir Harry, the Flit."

I was looking out the ajar door to the northside porch—which gave access to an outside stairwell—when Lindop commented, "That door was unlocked."

"So was the front door yesterday, when I showed up. Security here was pretty damn loose. Have you talked to the night watchmen?"

"I wasn't aware there were any."

"There are two. One's named Samuel. Sir Harry's household head, Marjorie Bristol, can fill you in."

He nodded again, eyes on the corpse. "She's downstairs. Taking it hard, I'm afraid. Haven't been able to properly question her."

I went over to have a better look at Sir Harry. I was well past the nausea; cop instincts had long since kicked in. I leaned close. Something behind Sir Harry's left ear explained a lot.

"I didn't figure he was burned to death," I said. "Not with all this blood around."

Lindop said nothing.

Four small wounds, fingertip-size, roundish but slightly triangular, were punched in the man's head, closely grouped; if you were to connect the dots, you'd have a square.

"Bullet wounds?" I asked. I wasn't sure: there were no powder burns.

"That's the doctor's initial opinion. And Christie called it in that way, too. I would tend to agree."

"The body was moved," I said. "At the very least, turned over." I indicated lines of dried blood running from the ear wounds across the bridge of Sir Harry's nose. "Gravity only works one way, you know."

Lindop grunted noncommittally.

A nightstand between the beds had a lamp whose celluloid shade was unblistered by heat, thermos jug, drinking glass, set of false teeth and a pair of reading glasses—undisturbed, as if nothing out of the ordinary had occurred in this bedchamber the night before.

"It's wet under his hips," I said, pointing. "Bladder released on death, probably. Has your photographer been here yet? There's a newspaper Sir Harry's lying on you might want to note."

"We have no departmental photographer. I sent for two RAF photographers, who are developing their photos now, and a draftsman, who drew a floor plan."

"Jolly good." I moved away from the bed, gestured around us. "But you'd better seal off this crime scene before you compromise all this evidence."

Lindop moved his mouth as if tasting something—something unpleasant. "Mr. Heller—much as I might appreciate your insights . . . I did not ask you to Westbourne as a police consultant."

"What, then? A suspect? I hardly knew the guy!"

He cocked his head back again. "You were one of the last persons to see Sir Harry alive. I wish to know the nature of your business with him."

I glanced over at my employer; he was staring at the ceiling with his eyes burned out. He seemed to have no objection.

"His business with me was to have me shadow his son-in-law, which I did yesterday afternoon and evening."

That perked up the Colonel; he took a step forward. "For what reason?"

I shrugged. "Suspected marital infidelity on the part of the Count. Sir Harry wasn't fond of him, you know."

"Damnit, man—give me the details!"

I gave him the details. From picking up the Count's tail at the Yacht Club, to driving the RAF wives home after the party.

"Hubbard's Cottages," Lindop said, narrowing his eyes. "That's near here. . . ."

"Almost next door."

"Then de Marigny drove right past Westbourne!"

"So did I. Around one, one-thirty."

Now his eyes widened. "You didn't follow him back home to his house on Victoria Street?"

"No. I figured he wasn't getting laid, so my night was over."

Lindop heaved a disgusted sigh. "Perhaps it would have been better for all concerned if you'd kept Count de Marigny in your sights a while longer."

I shrugged again. "Yeah, and I should've bought U.S. Steel at a nickel a share."

A voice from the entry area called, "Sir!"

A black face was peeking around the Chinese screen.

"The Governor is on the phone for you, sir."

We went back down—except for Harry—with Lindop requesting I stay on for a few more minutes. I said sure, and stood idly near the foot of the stairs with several of the Bahamian bobbies; I glanced around, hoping to catch sight of Marjorie Bristol.

Instead, I saw a dazed-looking Harold Christie, in the hallway nearby, pacing bleakly, like a father in a maternity waiting room expecting twins from Mars.

"Mr. Christie," I said, approaching him. "I'm sorry about your loss."

Christie, who was dressed in the same rumpled manner as the day before, seemed not to recognize me at first, but maybe he was just distracted. "Uh . . . thank you, Mr. Heller."

"I understand you found Sir Harry. Have you been here all that time?"

He frowned in confusion. "What do you mean?"

"Since you stopped by this morning, around seven, wasn't it?"

Now his confusion was gone, and his expression seemed almost one of embarrassment. "I was *here*, last night."

"What?"

He flipped a dismissive hand. "I frequently stay over with Sir Harry. He had a small dinner party that went on fairly late, and we had an appointment first thing this morning regarding his sheep."

"Sheep?"

Irritation began to edge around his eyes and mouth. "Sir Harry bought some fifteen hundred sheep from Cuba. For food production purposes? The meat shortage, you understand. He's been letting them graze on the country club greens."

That sounded like Sir Harry, all right.

"Now, Mr. Heller, if you'll excuse . . ."

"You weren't in the bedroom next door, were you? That looked unslept-in to me."

He sighed. "You're right. I was in the room just beyond that."

"Well, still, that's only sixteen feet. Did you hear anything? See anything?"

Christie shook his head no. "I'm a sound sleeper, Mr. Heller, and that storm last night must have drowned out any commotion . . ."

"You didn't smell smoke? You didn't hear a struggle?"

"No, Mr. Heller," Christie said, insistently, openly irritated now. "Now, if you'll excuse me, I have a phone call to make."

"Phone call?"

Very irritated. "Yes. I'd just been trying to compose myself when you seized upon the moment for conversation. You see, no one as yet has called Lady Oakes."

Behind him, the front door flew open and Alfred de Marigny stormed in.

Dark hair falling over his forehead like a comma, his eyes wide and almost wild, the bearded Count said, "What's going on here? Who's in charge?"

None of the black cops answered, so I told him.

"Colonel Lindop," I said. I wasn't tailing him anymore. No need to keep a low profile. . . .

"Harold," de Marigny blurted at Christie, "what the hell is this dirty business? John Anderson stopped me outside his bank and said Sir Harry's been killed!"

Christie nodded numbly, then pointed to the living room and said, "I have a long-distance call to make."

Then he walked into the living room, with de Marigny—casually dressed, blue shirt, tan slacks, no socks—tagging along.

I moved to the doorway, to eavesdrop on Christie's side of the phone conversation with Lady Oakes, but couldn't hear much. There was too much chatter in the hallway—not from the cops, but from a group of well-to-do-looking whites who were gathered down near the kitchen. Probably a mix of government officials and Oakes business associates.

Far too many people on hand for a crime scene. This was as bad as the fucking Lindbergh case, everybody and his damn dog tramping through the place.

I watched the silent movie of Christie speaking on the phone to Lady Oakes, de Marigny standing nearby, somewhat impatiently. Finally the Count tapped Christie on the shoulder, like a dancer cutting in.

De Marigny took the receiver.

Christie watched with obvious distaste as de Marigny spoke to his mother-in-law; he spoke louder than Christie, but his thick accent kept me from catching much of it. Obviously he was paying his condolences and asking what he could do to help.

And at least three times he asked her (and this I could hear— he was insistent) to have his wife, Nancy, get in touch with him as soon as possible.

De Marigny hung up the phone and looked at Christie, who turned his back on the Count and headed toward the hallway, and me.

"Why wasn't I called, Harold? Why did I have to hear about this on the street?"

Christie mumbled something, brushing past me. De Marigny was on his heels.

"Count de Marigny," Lindop said.

The Colonel was positioned in front of them like a traffic cop, as if to make them stop.

They stopped.

"I regret to inform you that Sir Harry Oakes is dead. Foul play is indicated."

"When exactly was the body found?" de Marigny asked.

"At seven this morning."

He scowled. "My God, man! It's almost eleven o'clock—this is my father-in-law who's been murdered! Why wasn't I contacted?"

"No slight was intended. We've been busy. A crime has been committed."

De Marigny's wide lips pressed together sullenly. Then he said, "I demand to view the body!"

"No," Lindop said, softly but flatly. "I would suggest you go home, Count. And make yourself available, should we have any questions."

"What sort of questions?"

"I can't say any more."

"Why in hell not?"

"I'm afraid my hands are tied." A pained expression crossed Lindop's hound-dog countenance. "The Governor is calling in two police detectives from Miami, who should be here shortly to lead the investigation."

What was *that* all about? Why call Miami cops in on a murder in a British colony? That "Governor" Lindop was referring to was none other than the Duke of Windsor, England's ex-King himself. That was the phone call that had interrupted us upstairs. . . .

As I was thinking this through, two splendid-looking Bahamian officers came down the curving stairway with a stretcher bearing the bedsheet-covered body of Sir Harry Oakes. Other officers held open the door while they carted him out to a waiting ambulance.

De Marigny watched this, frowning, nose twitching like a rabbit's, and followed them out, as if to press once more for the right to view the body.

I stood on the porch and watched the Count pull his gleaming Lincoln across the rain-soaked lawn to avoid the parked cars blocking the drive. He even passed the ambulance, on his way out the gate.

"You may go," Lindop said, tapping my shoulder. "Those officers over there will drive you. Where will you be?"

"At the British Colonial."

"Fine. We'll contact you there, later today, for a more formal statement."

Then he shut the door.

What the hell. It seemed like a good time to leave Westbourne, anyway. After all, Sir Harry wasn't home.

Seven

By noon the overcast sky had transformed itself into something pure and blue, with a bright but not blazing sun, a reprieve that sent sunbathers scurrying in surprise to the white beach of the British Colonial. During the early morning hours, minions of the hotel had obviously cleared the branches and debris from the sand; the beach was pristine again, shimmering in the sun. The emerald sea rippled peacefully. It was as if the storm had never happened.

Davy Jones' Locker, the hotel café overlooking the beach, was stone-walled, low-ceilinged, slate-floored. A black bartender in a colorful shirt mixed drinks before a mural of Davy himself, fast asleep while nubile mermaids and a school of quizzical comic fish gave him the once-over.

I got myself a hamburger with rare, sweetly marinated meat, a side of conch fritters and an orange rum punch the smiling barman called a Bahama Mama. Then out on the patio, I found a round wooden table under a beach umbrella and ate my lunch and watched the pretty girls on the beach. Occasionally one would even venture into the water.

"You must be in heaven, Heller," a high-pitched, sultry voice said.

I recognized it at once—she had a faint, very sexy, unmistakable lisp—but turned just the same, to confirm this happy news.

Her smile was playful. "Nassau's brimming over with pretty girls . . . all these lonely RAF wives. You must be going to town."

"Helen! What the hell are you doing in Nassau?"

She swept off her sunglasses so we could have a better look at each other. A petite, shapely woman of forty who looked easily a decade younger, she owed some of it to great genes, and some of it to a great face lift.

She wore a wide-brimmed straw hat, tied with an orange scarf under her chin, and a white robe over an orange-and-white floral bathing suit. Her skin was almost white; strands of her dark blond hair, pinned up under the hat, tickled a graceful neck. She wasn't wearing makeup, but her features didn't need any: pert nose, full lips, apple cheeks, long-lashed eyes that were a green-blue shade even the Bahamas could envy.

"I'm just hanging around, after finishing a gig," she said. "How about you?"

"Same. Sit! Have you had lunch?"

"No. Go get me some. Conch salad."

"I'll do that."

I did. I was pleased to see Helen Beck, who was better known to the general public by her stage name: Sally Rand. We went way back, to the Chicago World's Fair, where I worked pickpocket security, and where she made a name for herself (not to mention kept the fair afloat financially) doing a graceful nude ballet behind huge fluffy ostrich feathers. Or, at times, an equally oversize bouncing bubble. Sally—or Helen, as she preferred me to call her—was versatile.

I brought her the salad and a Bahama Mama. She ate the salad heartily—raw chopped conch marinated in lime juice and spices with some chopped crunchy vegetables tossed in for good measure—but merely sipped at her rum punch.

"How's Turk?" I asked.

She grimaced; now she took a belt of the punch.

Turk was her husband, a rodeo rider she'd met when she put together a revue called *Sally Rand's Nude Ranch*; they'd been married since '41, but it had been a rocky ride. Last time I'd seen her, about four months ago in Chicago, they'd been separated.

"I gave him another chance, and he blew it big-time. Son of a bitch *hit* me, Heller!"

"We can't have that."

"Well, I can't. I filed on the fucker." Her expression was as hard as her language. "Sure, I feel sorry for him . . . I mean, he goes overseas to serve his country, can't take it, cracks up, gets sent home on a Section Eight . . . I'd like to stand by him, but the guy's nuts!"

"Sure."

She looked at me and her expression melted; she leaned over and touched my hand. "I'm sorry, Heller . . . I forgot you went through the same damn thing."

"No problem, Helen."

She pulled back and her expression was troubled now. "He's drinking too much. I had to throw him out. Why didn't we get married, Heller? You and me?"

"I ask myself that, from time to time."

"How often?"

I shrugged. "I just did."

That made her smile; that wide smile of hers was a honey.

We chatted for a good hour. Not that we had much catching up to do; a few months ago in Chicago, we'd done our reminiscing about our summer together, back in '34. Some of that reminiscing had been between the sheets, but Helen and I weren't lovers, anymore. Not really.

But we'd always be friends.

"I'm surprised to find you working Nassau in the off-season, Helen," I said. "The wartime nightlife here is a little limited right now, or so I understand. . . ."

She shrugged; she'd finished her lunch and was smoking a cigarette. "It was a Red Cross fund-raising drive benefit. You know how patriotic I am."

And she was. She was an FDR fan, as well as a self-styled intellectual who leaned a bit left, and had attracted non-nude attention when she spoke out for the republican forces in the Spanish Civil War; she'd also got publicity out of lecturing at colleges. In between getting arrested for public indecency, of course.

"Sounds like you're getting respectable in . . ."

"If you say 'old age,' Heller, I'll conk you with a conch shell."

". . . these troubled times."

Her smile turned crinkly. "I am respectable. Saturday night, at the Prince George. The Duke and Duchess of Windsor were ringside."

"Pretty posh audience at that."

She lifted her chin, blew out smoke elegantly. "Not only am I respectable, but my perfectly round balloons . . ."

"You've always had perfectly round balloons."

"Shut up, Heller. The perfectly round balloons I *dance* behind, which are manufactured to my personal specifications by a company that I own, are now being used by the U.S. government for target practice."

That made me laugh, and she laughed along.

"Well, then," I said, "it was *patriotic* of the Duke to watch you strut your stuff. Didn't Wallis mind?"

I referred, of course, to Wallis Simpson, the American divorcée David Windsor, aka King Edward VIII, current Governor of the Bahamas, had abandoned his throne to marry—"the woman he loved!"

"Wallis smiled and giggled throughout. Frankly, the Duke was the one who seemed ill at ease. Embarrassed."

"These ex-kings have no sense of humor."

"I'll say. I hear he's issued an official ban on reporting that the Windsors actually saw my act. Of course, that ban doesn't extend to my press agent back home."

"Of course." I clicked in my cheek. "The poor royal dears . . . banished to a tropical Elba like this."

She lifted an arching, plucked eyebrow. "Well, there always have been rumors the Duke is a Nazi sympathizer. Churchill *had* to get him out of Europe so Hitler couldn't grab him, and set Edward up as a puppet king!"

"What would I do, without a burlesque queen to explain world politics to me."

She slapped my arm, but she was smiling. "You're such a louse."

"That's what you like about me."

"True. But I have to say, I really do *admire* Wallis . . ."

"Admire her? Everybody says she's a shrew who pushes poor ol' Dave around."

"That's ridiculous! You're just threatened by strong women, Heller!"

"Sorry," I said sheepishly.

She smirked. "In fact, both the Duke and Duchess have chalked up a lot of good works to their credit, in the short time they've

been here. The local Negro population has benefited particularly . . ."

"Here we go."

"Be good. Did you know the Duke started a CCC-type farm,
for the native men? And the Duchess works in the local Red Cross
clinic, side by side with black women . . . something the local
whites certainly wouldn't lower themselves to do."

"Really gets her hands dirty, huh?"

"Yes she does. Personally, I think they're a lovely couple. . . ."

"You, and every starry-eyed bobby-soxer in America. This bittersweet romance, these tragic lovers!" I laughed. "I can't believe
you're seduced by this royal horseshit, a left-wing fan-dancing fa-
natic like you."

"Heller, you're getting cynical in your . . ."

"Watch it."

". . . these troubled times."

"Thanks. Actually, I've always been cynical."

"You just think you are. That's why I should have married you:
you're the biggest, most romantic lug I ever met."

"Fooled you."

"You said you were doing a job here. Who for?"

"Sir Harry Oakes."

The green-blue eyes lighted up; lashes fluttered. "No kidding!
He's a real character! You should have seen him at the benefit
. . . eating peas with a knife, swearing like a sailor. But I didn't
get a chance to talk to him. What's he like?"

"Dead," I said.

Helen's eyes were still saucers when somebody tapped my shoulder and I turned to see another pair of those dignified black bobbies.

"You must return to Westbourne, sir," said the one who'd
tapped on my shoulder.

And in their company, I did.

I was ushered into the billiards room, where the lights were off
but for a small lamp on a fancy wooden card table along one wall.
The effect was moody, like the lighting in an old Warner Brothers
gangster movie. Looming above the card table was a huge stuffed
fish—a swordfish or a marlin or something, I'm a city boy myself
—swimming in the darkness.

Two men in baggy suits and fedoras were shrouded in these shadows. One was a tall, ruggedly handsome character in his forties, who looked like what a police detective was supposed to. The other, a fiftyish, chunky, hook-nosed guy in wire-frame glasses, was what police detectives did look like.

If the melodrama of this underlit room and these imposing figures was supposed to intimidate me, I could only stifle a laugh. Once upon a time, I was the youngest plainclothes officer in the history of the Chicago PD, thanks to a little honest graft, and could give these bozos lessons in scare tactics and the third degree.

In fact, all I could think of, when I looked at this pair, was Abbott and Costello.

"Is something funny?" the tall one asked.

"Not really," I lied, and stopped smirking.

"You're Heller?" the shorter pudgy one drawled.

"Yeah. And who would you be?"

"This is Captain Edward Melchen," the tall one said, gesturing to his partner.

"And this is Captain James Barker," the short one said, with a similar gesture.

Maybe I should wait for the applause to die down.

"You're Miami PD," I said.

"That's right," Barker said. Unlike his partner's, his Southern accent was barely noticeable. "Sit down." He gestured to the little lamp-lit table and the chair beside it.

I stayed put. "Why don't you boys turn on the lights, take off your hats, and stay awhile?"

"I don't like this guy," Melchen said.

"I don't like him either," Barker said.

"Who's on first?" I said.

"What's that supposed to mean?" Barker snapped.

"Nothing. What are a couple Miami dicks doing working a murder in Nassau?"

"If it's any of your business," Barker said, "we were invited by the Duke of Windsor. We're acquainted."

Now I did laugh. "You're acquainted with the Duke of Windsor?"

Melchen stepped forward; his bulldog face was tight. If I'd been twelve years old, I'd have been really scared. "We've handled security for him when he's passed through Miami, from time to time. So, do we have your goddamn permission to be here?"

I shrugged. "Sure. Thanks for asking."

Barker barked. "Sit down!"

I sat at the little table. Barker started to turn the lamp toward my face and I batted it away. "I'm from Chicago, boys. Spare me the musical comedy."

Barker said, "You're an ex-cop."

"Mmm hmm."

Melchen was looking at me thoughtfully, which seemed to be an effort. "Most private dicks are."

That was a shrewd observation.

Barker spoke, and he'd drained the intimidation from his voice. "Mr. Heller, why don't you tell us what your business with Sir Harry Oakes was."

"Sure," I said, and did.

Every now and then they would look at each other, and one of them would say, "De Marigny," and the other would nod. Neither bothered taking any notes.

When I'd wrapped up my account, Barker said, "The estimated time of death is between one-thirty a.m. and three-thirty a.m. You've just placed Count de Marigny on the murdered man's door-step in that time frame. Perfectly."

Melchen was smiling tightly and nodding.

"Fellas," I said, "the Count's a good suspect—don't get me wrong. But the behavior I observed the day of the murder wasn't consistent with somebody planning a crime."

"Maybe it was spur of the moment," Melchen said.

"Yeah," said Barker. "He saw the lights on here at Westbourne, driving by, pulled in and had it out with the old man."

"What," I said, "and just happened to have a blowtorch in his pocket? I saw the crime scene, gentlemen. Sloppy as it is, murders don't come much more premeditated."

They both looked at me blankly, the way a dog might.

"Of course," I said, "he may have been killed elsewhere and moved here."

"What makes you say that?" Barker asked.

"The direction of the dried blood on his face. He was on his belly when he was shot."

That made both of them smirk; Barker looked up smugly at Melchen, who was rocking on his heels like a fat top.

"Did I make a joke?" I asked.

Barker laughed soundlessly. "He wasn't shot at all."

"He was killed with a blunt instrument," Melchen said.

"According to who?"

"According," Baker said pointedly, "to Dr. Quackenbush."

"Didn't Groucho Marx play him?"

"Someday, boy," Melchen said, in his molasses-mouth manner, shaking a finger, "you're going to pay for that smart-ass mouth."

"Deliver the bill anytime, fat man."

Barker held Melchen back with an arm.

I don't know why I was needling them, except to see if my initial reading of them as a couple of thick-headed strong-arm types was right. It was—although Barker was clearly the brains. So to speak.

"Hey," I said. "I'm out of line. We're all here for the same reason: to help find Sir Harry's killer. Right?"

"Right," Barker said. But Melchen was still fuming.

"Let me ask you—you fellas *have* seen the body, haven't you?"

They looked at each other dumbly. In both senses of the word.

"It was moved before we got here," Barker said, vaguely defensive. "It's at Bahamas General for a postmortem, then it's being flown to Maine later tonight."

"Maine," I said. "What, for the funeral?"

Barker nodded.

"Well, have a look at those head wounds yourself. I think the old boy was shot."

Footsteps interrupted us, and I turned to see Colonel Lindop silhouetted in the doorway.

"Gentlemen," he said stiffly, addressing the Miami dicks, "the Governor is here. He would like a word with you."

They scurried out of there. I followed, taking my time; Lindop was standing just outside the billiards room as I exited. I looked at him and raised my eyebrows and he shook his head in quiet disgust.

Down the hall, near the front door, by the scorched stairway, the former King of England—sad-eyed, almost slight, dressed in white, like a dapper ice-cream man—was conferring with the Miami cops. A hush had fallen across a hallway crowded with police and various hangers-on; everyone stood around watching breathlessly, respectfully.

I supposed I should have felt impressed. But it wasn't like he was Capone or anything.

What was most impressive, to me at least, was the way the Duke was treating these Miami roughnecks like old friends, shaking their hands, even placing a gentle hand on Melchen's shoulder at one point.

Despite the now-hushed hallway, I couldn't make out anything of their low-pitched conversation. The Duke looked toward the stairs, gestured, and he and the American cops went upstairs, to check out the crime scene. Next to me, Superintendent Lindop— who had not been asked along—watched them go, his face etched with the hollow hurt of a spurned suitor.

"Mr. Heller?" a musical voice said.

Down near the kitchen, there she was: Marjorie Bristol. She wore the same light blue dress as before, or an identical one; perhaps it was a maid's uniform. I went to her.

In the kitchen, white cops in khaki and businessman types milled, while a heavyset colored woman in a bandanna kept busy at a counter, preparing small sandwiches.

"It's a tragedy, Mr. Heller," Miss Bristol said. The whites of her lovely dark eyes were filigreed red. "Sir Harry, he was a fine man."

"I'm sorry, Miss Bristol. Were you here when it happened?"

"No. I left around ten, after I set Sir Harry's nightclothes out on his bed. . . ." She cupped her mouth; just the thought of his bed was jarring. "Then I . . . tuck in the mosquito nettin', and spray the room for bugs."

"Do you live here? Are there servants' quarters . . . ?"

"I live alone in a cottage . . ." She pointed. ". . . 'tween the country club and here. Close enough that when Mr. Christie cry out, this mornin', I could hear. And I came runnin' . . . but there was no helpin' Sir Harry."

"You didn't see anything last night . . ."

"No. The storm was high. So much noise from the sea. I didn't hear or see a thing. Are you goin' to stay and find out who did this?"

"Well . . . no. Why did you think I would?"

Her reddened eyes widened. "You're a detective. You worked for Sir Harry."

"I'd like to help, Miss Bristol, but the people in charge of the investigation wouldn't want my help, even if I were to offer it."

"Well, you should try!"

"No . . . I'm sorry."

"You're goin' back to America, then?"

"Yes. As soon as they let me. But I won't soon forget meeting you, Miss Bristol."

She was pouting, a little; she wasn't happy that I wasn't going to stay and crack the murder case. I had disappointed her—which is something I do sooner or later with most every woman in my life, but usually not this early on.

"Why should you remember *me?*" she asked.

I put a finger under her chin, raised it so she'd look at me. "Because I want to."

The hallway, which had gotten noisy again, fell into another hush, which meant the Duke was returning from the murder room. Edward was coming down the stairs, with the detectives trailing him like schoolboys hanging on their master's every precious word; at the bottom he paused, to shake hands with them again, and then turned to go. Several aides-de-camp fell in place behind him, replacing Barker and Melchen.

But just as he reached the door, de Marigny—making his second impressive entrance at Westbourne today—swept in, accompanied by a white, khakied cop.

The moment that followed is one I'll remember to my dying day. Why? Because it was so goddamned odd. . . .

The Duke froze, like a man confronted with a ghost, and de Marigny stopped in his tracks, too, and looked at the Duke curiously, the way you might pause to view a car wreck as you drove by.

Then the Duke's expression turned hard and frankly contemptuous, and he moved swiftly on, and outside, his retinue following.

De Marigny, his wide lips hanging open, lending this man of obvious intelligence a remarkably stupid expression, gazed numbly toward where the Duke had exited. Then he sneered, and seemed both irritated and confused.

Was there something personal between these two?

The two Miami cops moved in on the casually dressed Count like he was Dillinger and they were the FBI; of course, nobody did any shooting.

But Melchen did place his hand on de Marigny's arm and announce, "I'm Captain Melchen of the Miami Police Department—here at the Governor's request. Would you mind answerin' a few questions?"

"Certainly not," de Marigny said suavely, withdrawing his arm from Melchen's grasp.

They trooped him past me on their way to the billiards room, where they could subject him to dim lighting and dimmer questioning. Just before they went in, Barker motioned to me.

He seemed conciliatory. "You mind stepping inside with us?"

Melchen was already in the billiards room, showing de Marigny to the card table.

"I guess I don't mind. What for?"

"I want you to see if what the Count says tallies with what you observed yesterday. Okay?"

"Okay."

I positioned myself in the darkness, with a mounted moose head or some other damn thing with antlers looking over my shoulder.

At first they treated him almost politely. They played standard good cop/bad cop, with the pudgy Melchen, surprisingly, taking the ingratiating, friendly role. They questioned him about his movements last night, and his every answer—and despite his thick French accent, his English was impeccable—fit the facts as I knew them.

Barker came over to me. He whispered, "How's all that tally?"

"Perfectly."

"He's a cunning son of a bitch."

"Most gigolos are."

Barker went back to the table and withdrew a magnifying glass from his pocket and set it down with a clunk. Great—now we were playing Sherlock Holmes.

"You don't object if we have a look at your hands, do you?" Barker asked, casually snide.

"My hands? No. Go ahead."

Barker took each of the Count's hands, one at a time, and examined them carefully under the magnifying glass, like a palm reader with bad eyesight.

Then, without asking, he shifted to de Marigny's face—specifically, his beard. Melchen turned the table lamp up so it would bathe their subject with light. Conducting a scientific examination in the dark was challenging, you know.

Barker turned and glanced at me, his face smug and tight. Then he looked at de Marigny and said, "The hairs on your hands and beard are singed."

Even now, the house had a scorched smell. The significance of Barker's discovery needed no explanation.

"Can you account for that?" Barker asked.

De Marigny shrugged. For once his confidence seemed shaken.

Then he pointed a finger at them and said, "Remember—I told you I was plucking chickens yesterday over a boiling drum."

The cops said nothing.

"Also," the Count said, "I smoke cigarettes and cigars . . . the dampness in Nassau requires frequent relighting. Oh! And I had the barber singe my beard, recently!"

The cops looked at each other skeptically.

"He also burned himself lighting a hurricane lamp," I said. "Entertaining in his garden last night."

Barker frowned at me. Melchen just looked confused.

"Yes, that's right!" de Marigny said. And then he said to me, "How did *you* know that?"

I didn't answer. He didn't know who the hell I was, and I saw no reason to tell him.

"We're going to clip hairs from your head, beard and arms," Barker said to his suspect. "Any objection?"

"No," de Marigny shrugged. "Shall I take off my shirt?"

"Yes," Barker said. "But speaking of shirts . . . we want to see the clothes you were wearing last night."

"I have no idea *what* clothes I was wearing last night."

"Come on!" Melchen sneered.

"Really! I have an interchangeable wardrobe of white- and cream-colored silk and linen shirts. I think I remember what sport jacket I wore . . . and the slacks . . . but not the shirt. What the hell, gentlemen—go to my house, inspect my laundry if you like!"

"We'll just take you up on that," Melchen said nastily.

Barker rose and came over to me. He gave me a foul look. "That's all, Heller."

"You're welcome," I said, and went out.

I tried to find Marjorie Bristol, to say goodbye, but she didn't seem to be around. So I looked up Lindop, who was in the hallway, amidst an ever-increasing, milling crowd; what a way to run an investigation.

"Can I go, Colonel? Watching those Keystone Kops play in the dark gives me a migraine."

He smiled faintly. "You'll need to give the Attorney General a deposition before you leave Nassau."

"I figured as much, but I meant, right now. . . ."

He touched the brim of his pith helmet, in a tipping-of-the-hat gesture. "As far as I'm concerned, Mr. Heller, you're free to go. But frankly, I don't seem to be in charge."

He had a point; but I found the Bahamian bobbies who'd brought me here and told them they were supposed to take me back to the hotel.

And they did.

Hell—maybe *I* was in charge. . . .

Eight

Palms rustled gently in the sultry night breeze. The sky was a clear dark blue, aglitter with stars, like handfuls of diamonds carelessly scattered on a taut satin sheet; the sliver of silver moon hung like a sideways, Cheshire-cat smile. Ice clinked in fruit-bedecked cocktail glasses while the wind whispered warm tropical kisses. It might have been an idyllic evening in the Bahamas, only I was in Coral Gables, Florida, seated at a table for two in the outdoor dance patio of the Miami Biltmore, where Ina Mae Hutton and her "all-girl" Melodears were playing a bouncy instrumental version of "Pistol Packin' Mama."

Up under the red-and-white stage canopy, Ina Mae, a pretty blonde in a slinky red gown, was swinging a mean baton. She and her musicians were indeed "all-girl," though many of the formerly all-male bands these days had women sprinkled throughout, particularly in the string sections.

I wondered if Miss Hutton, and tonight's headline act, might be a little hep for this somewhat over-the-hill crowd. The audience on this perfect Florida Saturday night was mostly middle-aged and older, although a few sailors on leave with their girls were mixed in, so some wild, throw-her-over-the-shoulder jitterbugging was going on here and there, challenging even the pulchritudinous Melodears for public attention.

Maybe it was the man shortage, or maybe it was just money, but there were a number of older men with younger women here this starlit night, and one such couple—seated ringside—particularly caught my eye. The redhead was petite and pretty and twentyish, slimly attractive in a green gown; twice her age, her well-dressed sugar daddy had close-set eyes, a lined face, a weak chin and a tan from God. He was also small, almost as small as she was.

A fairly ordinary businessman type, he wouldn't have caught my eye, despite the dame, if it hadn't been for the burly bookends seated on either side of them: bodyguards. Was this nondescript little businessman connected? Probably. This was Florida, after all. No shortage of oranges, bathing beauties or mobsters.

Once the Al Dexter tune had abated, and the applause, Ina Mae spoke over a timpani roll, introducing the featured performer of the evening.

"Ladies and gentlemen, the little lady who made so many fans with her own famous fans, first at the Chicago World's Fair, and more recently, the San Francisco Golden Gate Exposition on Treasure Island . . . direct from her command performance before the Duke and Duchess of Windsor in Nassau . . . *Miss Sally Rand!*"

To the big-band strains of "Clair de Lune," she slipped from behind the stage out onto the dance floor, fluttering the enormous pink ostrich plumes, her steps mincing, her smile sweet, blond curls shimmering to bare shoulders, a pink flower in her hair. Applause greeted her, and she acknowledged it with a shy smile, as she began her graceful dance. She moved like the ballerina she was, granting fleeting glimpses of white flesh (no body stocking for Helen, not even at forty) to tommy-gun bursts of enthusiastic clapping. Her pirouettes, as she stood poised on the toes of her high-heeled pumps, saw her caressing the feather fans, like a lover; she seemed lost in a trance, as if unaware anyone was watching.

Of course, they were—many of the men with that agape expression that gets them kicked under the table. Although Sally Rand was, as she'd said, respectable now; a show-business legend, an American institution, her sweet, naughty, only slightly erotic performance pleasing even the ladies.

I'd seen her many times—this, as well her equally famed bubble dance; she alternated them, doing several shows an evening, although wartime curfew and liquor-sale restrictions had the show closing at midnight, after the required playing of "The Star-Spangled Banner." I never tired of watching her, though, and she never seemed to tire of being watched—she had that uncanny star ability to make each audience feel she was performing something unique and just for them, something no one else had ever seen.

The performance lasted a mere eight minutes, but when she lifted her fans high in her famed *Winged Victory* pose, breasts high and bare, lifting a leg coyly to keep one small secret—one she had, happily, shared with me many a time—the Biltmore crowd, over-the-hill or not, went wild.

She covered herself with her fans and took several bows, giving the delighted audience the sort of warm, intimate smile that would make them remember this evening. Then she fluttered coyly out, making herself the center of a sandwich of the two plumes as she did. Intentionally comical, it got a nice laugh that eased any lingering sexual tension.

I sipped my rum and Coke and waited for Helen; this had been her last show of the evening. Tomorrow, or maybe Monday, I would head back for Chicago. What the hell, I could afford to lay back and loaf a little: I'd just hauled eleven thousand bucks ashore, for my little Nassau sojourn.

Actually, I really only worked one day, but several more had got eaten up by questioning and such. I had given my deposition to the Attorney General himself, in one of those pink colonial buildings off Rawson Square.

Attorney General Eric Hallinan was a long-faced, long-nosed, dour Britisher with a tiny mustache and eyes that mingled boredom and distaste, even as he thanked me for my cooperation.

"You'll be asked to return for the trial, of course," he told me, "at the expense of the Bahamian government."

"What trial?"

"Alfred de Marigny's," Hallinan said, quietly smiling, as if savoring the words.

It seemed the Count had been arrested, on the say-so of the two Miami dicks. Their investigation had lasted less than two days—I wondered if they had anything on him, besides a few singed hairs and me placing him near the scene of the crime.

Helen had done me the courtesy of sticking around through all this, and even talked me into doing some Bahamas-style sight-see-ing, including taking a glass-bottomed boat ride to view those Bo-tanical Gardens Miss Bristol had recommended. Watching a bunch of exotic-looking fish swim around amidst exotic-looking coral may not have been my cup of chowder, but it beat hell out of staring at the walls of my room at the British Colonial.

I repaid Helen by agreeing to keep her company for a few days at the Miami Biltmore, during her engagement that opened mid-week. I'd have had a better time if the horses and dogs had been running, but we played a little golf, sat on the sand so I could take a tan home with me (Helen hid her precious white skin under a beach umbrella), and, well, reminisced.

When Helen returned from backstage, she came around through the hotel; wearing a floral sarong-style dress, she was a knockout, but few people recognized her, out of the spotlight, as anything but another of Florida's many beautiful women: her makeup was toned down and the long, platinum-blond tresses were gone, a wig left behind in her dressing room, her own darker blond locks tucked up in a braided bun.

As she skirted the edge of ringside, heading for our little table, high heels clicking, she was recognized by one customer: that little businessman with the redhead and the bodyguards. Helen stopped and chatted with him for some time; she didn't sit, but he rose, politely, and they seemed to know each other.

It was all very cordial, and when he gestured for her to join him, causing the redhead's eyes to tighten, Helen gave the little man a wide, gracious smile and declined.

I pulled the chair out for her and she sat. "Who's your friend?" I asked.

"Are you kidding?" she grinned. She withdrew a pack of Camels from her clutch purse. "I figured you guys must go way back."

So he *was* a mobster.

"He isn't from Chicago," I said. "So he isn't Outfit. East Coast?"

"East Coast," she said, nodding, amused. She blew out smoke. "That's Meyer Lansky, Heller."

"No kidding." I let out a soft laugh. "So that little monkey-faced shrimp is the New York syndicate's financial wizard. . . ."

I glanced over at him, trying not to be obvious, and I'll be damned if he wasn't looking over toward me. Or us. I hoped it was Helen he was gazing at, but somehow I didn't think so, because his two brawny bodyguards were leaning over in conference with him, and were also glancing my way.

I hoped Lansky didn't read lips.

Whatever, I didn't watch them watching me. I told Helen how much I'd enjoyed her show, to which she said, Oh, you've seen it a million times, and I said, It never gets old for me, and it went on like that for a while.

"Sure didn't take you long to add the Duke and Duchess to your intro," I said.

"When did you ever know me to miss a beat, Heller?"

A waiter approached and I was about to order another rum and Coke when he said, "The gentleman would like to see you."

Somehow I knew what gentleman he meant.

I glanced over at Lansky and he smiled a wide, tight, not unpleasant smile and nodded.

My stomach sank.

"Looks like I've been summoned," I said.

Helen blew a smoke ring through kissy lips. "Try to behave yourself."

"I may have a smart mouth," I said, "but I know when to play dumb."

I wandered over, and on my way, a gorgeous brunette who looked like Merle Oberon but prettier gazed at me intensely. She had luscious lips painted blood-red and large, widely spaced brown eyes that bored through you. Her chin was raised patricianly; her hair—which had auburn highlights—was up. She wore a black pants suit with a white shirt underneath, top two or three buttons undone, the mannishness of the outfit offset by the pink swell of her bosom.

She smiled warmly. Sitting alone at a table for two. . . .

I nodded as I went past, returned the smile. My God, I was popular tonight!

As I approached, Lansky rose. "Mr. Heller?"

He was impeccably dressed: that tailored brown suit had set him back three C's easy, and that white silk shirt hadn't come in a Cracker Jack box, either. His tie was green and brown and wide and tasteful. There was none of the flashy jewelry so many mobsters affected.

"Mr. Lansky?" I said.

His smile seemed genuine; he was one of those homely men

whose smile transformed him. Like Harold Christie, he could turn on the charm.

"I hope you don't mind my imposing," he said. His voice was surprisingly rich and resonant for so small a man. "But I know you by reputation, and wanted to pay my respects."

Meyer Lansky, paying his respects to me? At least it wasn't over a coffin.

"You're . . . very kind."

"Please join us," he said, and gestured to an empty chair.

I sat across from him.

"This is Miss Schwartz. Teddie. She's my manicurist."

"A pleasure," I said.

Miss Schwartz nodded to me and smiled politely. Nice-looking girl—not a moll by any means. And Lansky did have nice nails. . . .

He didn't bother introducing the two bodyguards; they were just fixtures, like potted palms. Only these potted palms had eyes, and were keeping them trained on yours truly. They wore identical dark suits that hadn't cost three hundred per (but then neither had mine), with bulges under their left shoulders that I didn't figure were tumors.

One of them, big in both the tall and wide sense, wore a bad toupee and a hairline mustache that was out of date ten years ago; his eyes were small and wide-set and stupid, and his nose was flattened. A former pug.

The other one, not as tall but even wider, had a round face, curly brown hair, sweet-potato nose, slitted eyes and a white, lightning-bolt scar on the left cheek. Probably not a dueling scar—unless maybe it was a duel with broken beer bottles.

They were looking at me with open suspicion and near-contempt. Okay, so I wasn't popular with *everybody* tonight.

"Lovely night," Lansky said. "The Biltmore's a first-rate hotel."

Actually, it was a rambling haciendalike affair, looming behind us; the big attraction was sports—the lawn was a putting green.

"Last time I stayed here," I said, "was back in '33."

His smile was wide. "Really? What was the occasion?"

"I was one of Mayor Cermak's bodyguards."

He grunted sympathetically. "That didn't work out too well."

What he was referring to was that Mayor Cermak had been assassinated.

"Well," I said, "I usually leave that off my résumé."

He chuckled. Miss Schwartz was watching the stage, where Ina Mae and her Melodears were getting started again; this time they were doing "I'll Never Smile Again," which had couples clutching desperately out on the dance floor.

"Can I order you a drink?" he asked, gesturing with his own glass.

"No thanks. I shouldn't stay away from Helen long."

"Helen?"

"Sally. Helen's her real name. We go back a ways."

"Ah. That's nice. Long-term relationships . . . they're valuable. How was Nassau?"

The question hit me like the sucker punch it was.

"Pardon?" I managed.

For a guy with such a nice smile, he sure had cold hard dead eyes. "Nassau. I understand you were doing a job there."

"I, uh . . . didn't know it was common knowledge."

"Miss Rand mentioned it. You wouldn't have heard anything about the Sir Harry Oakes killing, would you?"

Another sucker punch that landed!

"Uh . . . why's that, Mr. Lansky?" I asked, mind reeling, trying not to show the blow's effects.

He squinted in thought. "Well, it's just the Duke of Windsor is censoring all information out of the island, and if that fellow Christie hadn't called some newspaper friend of his, and spilled the beans beforehand, nothing would have leaked out."

One of the first people Christie had called, after finding Oakes, was Etienne Dupuch, publisher of the Nassau *Tribune*, both because he was a friend and because he and Sir Harry were supposed to meet him that morning. To look at those sheep grazing on the golf course. . . .

And Dupuch had put some very basic facts about the crime on the wire before the government ban lowered.

"Actually," I said, "I think that gag order was lifted a couple days ago. You probably know as much as I do, from just reading the papers."

His smile was enigmatic; also, creepy as hell. "I doubt that. I understand you were doing a job for Sir Harry himself."

How the hell did he know that? Would Helen have spilled that much? *Why did Meyer Lansky care about Sir Harry Oakes?*

"I was, but it got cut short by the murder."

He was nodding in interest, but his eyes were so damn expressionless. "Well, that's really something. Isn't that something, Teddie?"

Miss Schwartz nodded, paying no attention.

"So—tell us what the papers haven't. How exactly did Sir Harry Oakes die?"

Maybe Lansky was just curious—the press was all over the case, after all. . . .

"It was kind of grisly, Mr. Lansky. I really don't think it makes for suitable conversation over cocktails."

He was nodding again. He didn't press. "Certainly. I understand. I understand. At any rate, I just wanted to say hello. We have mutual friends, you know."

"I'm sure we do."

He reached over and patted my hand; his was cold. Like a dead man's hand. "And I wanted to express my condolences to you over the loss of one of those mutual friends. I know you were close to Frank. And he thought highly of you."

"Thank you," I said.

He meant Frank Nitti. I'd done some favors for Capone's successor, and he for me, and the mistaken notion had grown up that I was in the Outfit's pocket. Sometimes that came in handy; sometimes it damn near got me killed.

And tonight it put me, uneasily, at Meyer Lansky's table for a few minutes.

"This fellow de Marigny," he said, shifting back suddenly to his favorite topic, "do you think he did it?"

"Maybe. There was no love lost between Sir Harry and him, and the Count's wife stands to inherit millions."

He arched an eyebrow. "Sounds like a murder motive to me. I understand the Miami police are handling the case."

"If you want to call it that."

"What do you mean?"

"Nothing," I said. Barker and Melchen were pals of his, for all I knew; better to keep my opinions to myself.

"Well," he said, with a twitch of a smile, "I'll let you get back to the lovely Miss Rand. You know, she hasn't aged a day since the Streets of Paris."

That was where Helen had danced at the Century of Progress.

"I'm afraid that's more than *I* can say," I said. I'd aged a year since sitting down. "Good evening, Miss Schwartz. Thanks for the hospitality, Mr. Lansky."

"I'm sure we'll meet again."

"I hope so," I lied.

The two potted palms looked at me, coldly, and I walked back toward our table as Lansky and Miss Schwartz headed out to dance to "Tangerine."

I risked a look at the beautiful brunette, who stood and said, "Could I have a moment?"

I stopped. My tongue felt thick as those steaks I used to eat before the war. "Certainly."

"I wondered if I might speak to you," she said. Her voice was a rich alto; but she was young. Sophisticated as she looked, she couldn't be much older than nineteen.

"Well . . . sure."

Despite the strength of her eyes, she had a vulnerable look. "I wondered if you might join me."

"I'm afraid I'm with someone. . . ."

"I know. I meant, in my room."

I mean, *popular.*

"I'm sorry," I said, not believing my ears, "but I just can't. I'm *with* someone. . . ."

She pressed a slip of paper into my hand; hers was warm. The tips of her lovely, tapering fingers were painted the same blood red as her lipstick.

"Tomorrow morning, then," she said. "Ten o'clock."

And she picked up her purse and swept away from the table, disappearing into the hotel.

A tall drink of water. Nice shape on her. Someday Elizabeth Taylor was going to grow up and look almost that good. . . .

"Well," Helen said, just a little icily, "*you're* certainly popular tonight."

"Helen," I said, sitting down, "did you mention to Meyer Lansky that I just got in from Nassau?"

She was genuinely surprised. "Why, no. We didn't talk about you at all. I'm sure you're disappointed. . . ."

"No. Worried." I unfolded the slip of paper and had a look.

"Heller . . . what's wrong? You turned white!"

"Jesus Christ," I muttered.

"What?"

"I've got a date tomorrow morning."

She laughed; blew smoke. "Well, I'm not surprised."

"With Nancy Oakes de Marigny," I said.

Nine

~~~~~~

W hen I knocked on the door of the penthouse suite in the Biltmore's central tower, the lush alto of Nancy Oakes de Marigny called, "It's unlocked! Come in."

Apparently the death of her father hadn't made the Countess tighten up her personal security measures.

I stepped inside to discover, in the modern, pastel living room of the suite, Nancy de Marigny—slender and shapely in white tights and ballerina slippers—with her leg in the air, toes pointing right at me.

This was not a new way of waving hello she'd invented: she was doing a ballet workout. She had a hand against an overstuffed peach-color chair on which she'd piled various thick phone books, using it for a support, in place of a rail. Her free arm arced gracefully in the air.

Without makeup, her hair pinned up carelessly, she was still a ravishing girl—and a girl is what she was: nineteen years old, a child, a woman. The body suit consisted of a white, bathing-suit-like portion that covered her torso, with her legs in white leotards. The outfit left her arms bare and little to the imagination.

"Hope you don't mind if I continue my exercises," she said. "If I miss a day, Miss Graham will tan my hide."

"Miss Graham?"

She turned away from me, working the other leg. "Martha Graham. My ballet instructor. That's why I'm summering in Maine."

"I see."

"But now I'm on my way to be where I belong: at my husband's side."

My hat was in my hands. "Mrs. de Marigny, please allow me to offer my condolences on the death of your father."

"That's very kind, Mr. Heller."

God, I felt uneasy. She was pointing her toes at me again, and I didn't know what the hell I was doing here!

"Would you mind if I locked your door?" I asked. "It makes me uncomfortable, thinking some reporters might get wind of you, and start hounding you. . . ."

She was bending at the knees, now. "Go ahead. But I'm registered under an assumed name. No one knows I'm here."

I locked the door, threw the nightlatch. "Speaking of which . . . how did you happen to recognize me? And know where to find me?"

"To answer your first question, the hotel manager pointed you out, at my request."

Despite her continued exercises, she didn't seem to be breathing hard, though small beads of sweat gleamed on her wide forehead like jewels.

"As for your second question . . . Mr. Heller, my father owned the British Colonial Hotel. You left the Miami Biltmore as your immediate forwarding address."

"True. But how did you even know about me? *What* do you know about me?"

"You were hired to get the dirt on Freddie," she said casually. She might have said, "The Astors will be taking tea with us later."

I didn't know what to say. She had turned her pretty backside to me again, arching her leg at the opposite wall.

"My husband's attorney, Mr. Higgs, told me about you," she continued. "You gave a statement placing Freddie near Westbourne about the time of the crime."

"Well, yes. . . ."

"Would you do me a favor?"

"Okay."

"Sit on this chair. I need to do some stretching, and I don't think those phone books are enough support."

I sighed, went over, moved the phone books and sat down. She was looking right at me, her eyes dark and intense and as naive as a four-year-old child's.

"Uncle Walter admitted he hired you," she said.

"Uncle Walter. Foskett? The attorney?"

This close up, I could tell that she actually was breathing a bit heavy; just a faint huff and puffing.

"That's right," she said. "I saw him yesterday, at the funeral."

"But you were *here* yesterday."

"I arrived yesterday evening. The funeral was in the morning."

"I see . . ." But I didn't.

"I wanted to be at my husband's side as soon as possible . . . allowing time to make contact with you, of course. I take a Pan Am flight to Nassau this afternoon."

"You believe in your husband's innocence, then."

"I have no doubt." And she didn't seem to. Her eyes, her expression, were unwavering. Also, unnerving, as she faced me, leaned in to me, while she stretched each long limb behind her, one at a time of course.

"You see, Mr. Heller, while I may not have made a study of it, I *know* human nature—I've lived with Freddie, and he may not be perfect . . . but he is my husband, and he is *no* murderer."

"That's an admirable attitude for a wife to have."

"Thank you. I want you to do a job for me."

"A job? What sort of job?"

"I want you to clear Freddie, of course. Would you like a cup of coffee? Or orange juice? I think even Miss Graham would agree I've done enough of a workout for one day."

She pointed me to an area where picture windows overlooked the Biltmore golf course, and I sat alone at a carved wooden table shaped like a large seashell and sipped coffee she'd provided from a silver service on a stand nearby.

She emerged in a white terry-cloth robe, belted over her workout clothes, and smiled her multimillion-dollar smile and said, "Would you like breakfast? I can have some brought up."

"No. Thank you. I already ate."

She sipped her orange juice. She looked calm, poised, but it was a mask. Her eyes had the same red filigree as Marjorie Bristol's. Yesterday she had reminded me of Merle Oberon; today I was thinking Gene Tierney. . . .

"Your friend Sally Rand really is quite a gifted ballerina," she said.

"Yes she is. A lot of people don't notice that, though."

"Lovely dancer." Her smile seemed confident, but I sensed vulnerability. "Well, Mr. Heller? What do you say? Will you take the case?"

"No."

Her wide eyes widened. "No?"

"No. Mrs. de Marigny, it's impossible. I'm a material witness . . . for the prosecution!"

She smiled wickedly. "So much the better."

I shrugged. "I don't think it's a bad idea, getting a private investigator to work with this attorney . . . Higgs, is it? I can tell you, frankly, that I'm not impressed with what the police down there are doing, either the Nassau boys or the imported Miami variety."

She rolled her eyes. "I know that all too well."

How? I wondered. But I didn't ask.

I just said, "Really, I apologize, I'd like to help, but . . ."

She locked onto me with that unwavering gaze. "Mr. Heller— I checked with the person who recommended you to my father— an old friend of yours: Evalyn Walsh McLean. She speaks warmly of you, and assures me you are *the* man for the job."

Evalyn. There was a name from the past . . . one of the queens of Washington society, the owner of the famed, cursed Hope Diamond, she'd been at my side during much of the ill-fated Lindbergh investigation. We'd parted rather bitterly—oddly enough, after all these years, it felt good to know I'd been forgiven. . . .

"She claims you solved the Lindbergh kidnapping," Nancy de Marigny said.

"Oh yeah. That one worked out just peachy for everybody."

Her smile was wistful, her eyes glazed. "You know, it's funny . . . that's one of the reasons why my father moved to the Bahamas. . . ."

"What is?"

"The Lindbergh kidnapping."

"It *is*?"

She smiled, laughed sadly. "Oh, I know—everyone thinks Daddy moved to Nassau strictly to dodge the Canadian taxes. Well, I'm sure that was part of it. But after the Lindbergh baby was kidnapped, Daddy received several notes, extortion notes, threatening that *I* would be the next 'rich brat snatched,' if he didn't pay. We lived near Niagara Falls at the time . . . sort of in the same part of the country as the Lindberghs—Mother and Father were friends of theirs, you know. Anyway, for something like two years we had armed guards walking our grounds. I know it was probably only a relatively short time, but in my memory it seems that I spent my entire childhood accompanied everywhere I *went* by armed guards."

I didn't know what to say; so I just nodded sympathetically.

"But in *Nassau*, Daddy had been told, even the richest man in the world could go to sleep, and leave his doors unlocked. . . ."

And now, finally, she began to cry.

She found some tissues in her robe pocket and dabbed her eyes; I rose and went to her and touched her shoulder. After a while, she nodded that she was better, and gestured for me to sit down again.

I did.

"Mrs. de Marigny—I really do wish I could help." And in a way I did, but really I didn't: I just wanted to get back to Chicago. Between Nassau and Florida, I'd had my fill of palm trees, and I sure didn't need to travel to the tropics to find knuckleheaded American cops to tangle with.

"Then you decline?" She took one last swipe at her eyes.

"Yes."

"In that case, I'll have to speak to Mr. Foskett."

"Why's that?"

"Well . . . you'll need to refund my father's ten-thousand-dollar retainer."

"What?"

"I think you heard me the first time, Mr. Heller."

"That was a nonrefundable retainer. . . ."

"Do you have that in writing?"

"Well, no. How did you know . . ."

She smiled blandly. "I'm friendly with the head of my father's household staff—a Miss Marjorie Bristol? She's holding the carbon of the check my father made out to you."

I didn't say anything. I may have moaned.

"And," she continued cheerily, "in his personal ledger, where he recorded the payment, he noted that your daily rate was to be three hundred dollars. He also made a notation that you'd been paid in advance, one thousand dollars for one day's work. And I believe that's how long you did, actually, work? Isn't it, Mr. Heller?"

I nodded. "That was three hundred dollars plus expenses, though."

She shrugged facially. "That's fine. And if you put in enough days to exhaust the retainer, I'm willing to continue paying you at the same rate. Which I understand is top money in your field."

I sighed. "That's correct."

"So. When would you like to head back to Nassau?"

She'd beaten me; Nate Heller, tough guy, pummeled by a nineteen-year-old ballerina.

"This afternoon will be fine," I said.

"Wonderful!" She reached in the pocket of her robe. "Here are your tickets . . . your room is waiting at the B.C."

She meant the British Colonial; I took the tickets, numbly.

She sipped her orange juice. Looked out at the golf course, proud of herself.

"Mrs. de Marigny . . ."

"Nancy." She smiled, and it was genuine enough.

"Nancy. And call me Nate, and how did you know the police are botching the investigation? Did the Count's attorney, Higgs, tell you?"

She shook her head no. "I had firsthand experience with those Miami detectives."

I squinted at her. "Barker and Melchen? How's that possible?"

"They flew to Maine yesterday . . . they crashed the funeral, Mr. Heller."

"Nate. They crashed the *funeral*?"

They crashed the funeral, and afterward they followed Nancy and her mother to the latter's bedroom, where Lady Oakes collapsed in grief. They chose this moment to tell Nancy and Lady Oakes, in gruesome detail, their reconstruction of the murder as Freddie de Marigny supposedly committed it.

She was tightly angry as she told me this; her brown eyes brimmed with tears that seemed of indignation more than sorrow.

"The tall, good-looking one with salt-and-pepper hair . . ."

"That's Barker," I said.

She nodded. "Barker. He told Mother, stood at her bedside and *told* her, that Freddie had taken a wooden picket from a fence

outside the house, and used it to batter and gouge Daddy senseless
. . . this Barker even used his hands to demonstrate the motion,
stabbing the air!"

"Christ. How did your mother take this?"

"She's a very strong woman, *very*—but she became hysterical.
Our doctor advised them to stop with their story, but Mother—
through her hysteria—screamed to let them continue."

"How did *you* take it?"

She spoke through her teeth. "It just made me mad. Mad as
hell."

"Good girl. Go on."

Her eyes hardened even as a tear trickled. "Then Barker said
Freddie splashed Daddy, who was still alive, with insecticide from
a flit gun. And then . . . set him on fire—only the fire roused Daddy,
who rose up, writhing in 'horrible agony.' "

Jesus Christ.

"Even if it were true," I said, "Barker is a sadistic moron, putting you and your mother through that hell."

She shook her head vigorously, as if trying to shake that awful
story out of it. "I didn't believe a word. I was just getting more
and more furious. But it was a cold fury."

"That's the best kind. Did those sons of bitches leave you alone
then?"

"No. Barker added a *coup de grâce*: he said that four or
five fingerprints of Freddie's had been found in Daddy's bedroom."

I shook my head. "I have to be honest with you, Nancy—that's
bad. Real bad."

She heaved a huge sigh and nodded.

"Juries just *love* fingerprint evidence," I said.

"But the odd thing is," she said, frowning, thinking back, "the
other detective . . . the fat one? With the Southern accent?"

"Melchen," I said.

"Melchen. He said, 'No kidding? *Fingerprints?*' It was obvious
it was the first he'd heard of it!"

I sat up. "What did Barker say then?"

She shrugged. "He just shushed him, and they hurried out."

My laugh was hollow. "They fly up from Nassau on the plane
together, they're partners in this all the way, and Barker doesn't
even *mention* to Melchen that he found the accused's fingerprints
in the murder room?"

She seemed confused, as well she should be. "What does it mean?"

"Well, the bad news is they're working up a frame." Then I smiled. "The good news is, they're incompetent dopes."

She was still confused. "But . . . why would they frame my husband?"

"Could be plain old-fashioned bad police work. A true detective accumulates evidence until it leads him to a suspect. A lousy detective finds a suspect and accumulates only the evidence that fits that suspect."

"And even *creates* evidence?"

"Sometimes," I said, making two words of it. "Does Freddie have any enemies in Nassau?"

She smirked humorlessly. "Quite a few, I'm afraid. He doesn't play by the rules; he's his own man, Freddie is."

"These clowns, Barker and Melchen, they were brought in by the Duke. What was your father's connection to the Duke?"

"They were friendly. David and Wallis are . . . *were* fairly frequent guests at Westbourne . . . even stayed there, for several weeks, when they first arrived in Nassau, while Government House was being redecorated to Wallis' specifications. My parents attended many social occasions where the Duke and Duchess were present. Daddy and the Duke played a lot of golf together. And, of course, they had certain mutual business interests."

"Such as?"

She winced in thought. "I'm not really sure. I know that Harold Christie and Daddy and the Duke were involved in *some* business deal or other . . . oh, and so was Axel Wenner-Gren. He's a Swedish industrialist."

"Is that the guy who bought Howard Hughes' yacht?"

"The *Southern Cross*, yes."

"Axel Wenner-Gren." I was sitting up again. "Isn't that guy a Nazi? The Duke and Duchess got bad publicity having him chauffeur 'em around in his yacht. The papers were full of it—the American authorities wouldn't let him dock, a couple times."

She was shaking her head and smiling at me like I was a kid who'd just repeated some wild, unbelievable schoolyard story. "Axel a Nazi? It's preposterous. He's a *charming* man, Nate."

"Well, if you say so."

She raised an eyebrow. "I mean, it's true that he's been blacklisted from the Bahamas, and the United States, for the duration."

I snapped my fingers. "That's what I thought! For suspected collaborationist leanings, right?"

"Right," she allowed. "But it's nonsense."

"Where is the charming Axis what's-his-name now?"

"It's Axel and you know it. Cuernavaca—sitting out the war on one of his estates."

I was grinning. "So there's a Nazi in the woodpile . . . that's real interesting. . . ."

"Nate—don't bother going down that road. I *know* Axel isn't a Nazi."

"How could you 'know' that?"

Her gaze was boring holes in me again. "Because Daddy wouldn't have been *friends* with him if he was. Look—Daddy wasn't very political . . . like a lot of wealthy people, he considered himself *above* politics, I suppose. But he *hated* Nazis. He'd sooner do business with the devil! He was active in all the local war efforts, and when Hitler declared war on Britain, Daddy immediately donated five Spitfires to the RAF! And he's given his airfield to . . ."

"Okay, Nancy . . . okay. You made your point. What about a guy named Meyer Lansky? Ever hear of him?"

She shrugged. "No."

I described him to her. "Ever see anybody who looked like that come around to talk to your father?"

"No."

"Any Americans come around who didn't seem like somebody who'd typically do business with your dad? Somebody . . . suspicious. Somebody with bodyguards, maybe."

"A gangster or something? Hardly."

I didn't want to get into it with her, but I wondered what interest, or connection, Meyer Lansky might have to the murder. Last night his questions had been pointed, and knowledgeable; so knowledgeable that I wondered if he might not have been, in an oblique fashion, warning me off the case. . . .

A knock at the door summoned Nancy, and I stayed and sipped my coffee, watching golfers golf, pondering Lansky's possible warning. I heard Nancy's voice, then another voice, but higher-pitched, and that of an older woman; both voices were raised in something approaching anger.

I went to have a look. Probably none of my business, but I'm a snoop by nature and profession. . . .

"Mother," Nancy was saying, "I did not *sneak* away. I left word where you could find me, and under what name, or else you wouldn't have! Correct?"

Lady Eunice Oakes was tall, handsome, dignified, and royally pissed off. She was also just a tad stout, with a firm jaw and thin wide lips, her hair of medium length and graying blond. She was in black, of course, but stylishly so, with a black fur piece, black soupdish hat and dark glasses and black gloves. Even her nylons were in mourning.

"Don't speak to me in that tone of voice," Lady Oakes snapped. "I don't appreciate having to come running after you . . . chartering a plane at all hours . . ."

"You didn't have to come 'running after' me, Mother. I'm of age. I'm a married woman."

"You *would* have to remind me of that."

Lady Oakes rustled in her purse—also black—for a hanky—white. She lowered her face into the hanky as Nancy tapped her on the shoulder.

"Mother," Nancy said, nodding toward me. "We're not alone. . . ."

She put the hanky away and removed her sunglasses; her eyes, though bloodshot, were a clear, sky blue. Once upon a time, she could have given Nancy a run for the money in the looks department.

Studying me, she said, not unpleasantly, "And who are you, young man?"

A funny way to address me, since she probably only had five or six years on me.

I told her, and expressed my sympathies.

"You're the detective my husband hired," she said, and beamed. She strode over to me and offered me her gloved hand. I shook it, not knowing why this welcome was so warm.

"You provided valuable evidence in the case against my husband's murderer," she said, "and I would just like to thank you personally. . . ."

"Mother—Mr. Heller is working for *me*, now. He's going to prove Freddie's innocence."

She let go of my hand as if it were something disgusting. She looked at me the same way.

"I fail to see the humor in that," she said.

"Me either," I said.

"Mr. Heller," Nancy said, "was paid ten thousand dollars to investigate my husband's activities. I'm keeping him on the case. He'll investigate, and prove Freddie's innocence."

Lady Oakes smiled, and it was a sly, smart smile.

"Am I to understand," she said, addressing us both, looking from Nancy to me and back again, "that you intend to have Mr. Heller continue investigating . . . using up the money that your father paid him?"

"Yes," Nancy said, indignantly.

"I think not," Lady Oakes said. She looked at me. "I'll speak to our attorney, Walter Foskett of Palm Beach, and fix your little red wagon, Mr. Heller."

"Wait a minute," I said. "You can't both threaten me with the same lawyer!"

"Mother," Nancy began, and the two were arguing. Not yelling, but heatedly talking over each other's words.

I put two fingers in my mouth and blew a whistle that would have brought Ringling Brothers to a standstill.

The two women looked at me, startled.

"I have a suggestion," I said. I looked at Nancy. "Your mother has a point. My client here, in a very real sense, is your late father."

Lady Oakes smiled smugly and nodded the same way. She folded her arms across a generous matronly bosom.

"Suppose," I said to Lady Oakes, "that I work for your daughter, on the following condition: if I find evidence of her husband's guilt, I won't suppress it. It goes straight to the prosecution—right to the Attorney General."

The widow's smile turned approving; but Nancy was frowning, and said, "But . . ."

"Otherwise," I told the lovely Mrs. de Marigny, "it would be a conflict of interests. I'd be working *against* your father—who is, after all, my client."

Nancy thought about that. "Well, Freddie's innocent. So you're not *going* to turn anything up that would work against him."

"There you go," I said.

"And you'd answer to me," Nancy said. "*I'm* your client now."

"Yes. With that one condition."

"Well . . . it's acceptable to me," Nancy said, uncertainly.

"It's acceptable to me, as well," Lady Oakes said. She looked at her daughter with a softer expression. "We won't be enemies, you and I. I'm championing my husband, and you are championing yours. I *expect* you to stand by him. . . ."

Now Nancy was getting teary-eyed again; she clutched her mother and her mother patted her, somewhat stingily I thought, but patted her.

"All I need," I said, "is for good old Uncle Walter Foskett to write up a letter acknowledging I'm working out my ten-thousand-dollar retainer—and that when it's used up, my meter is still running, at three hundred dollars per day and expenses."

Lady Oakes smiled frostily at me. "That's between you and your client." She turned to her daughter. "I'll see you in Nassau, my dear."

And she was gone.

Ten

The taxi deposited me at the International Seaplane Base on Biscayne Bay, just south of Miami, and I hauled my duffel bag toward what might have been a fashionable yacht club, with its manicured lawn, decorative nautical pennants, and stream of blue-and-white-uniformed flight crews. Along the seawall, sightseers—some of them tourists no doubt, but locals as well—were passing this dazzling sunny afternoon by taking in the spectacle of the awkward-looking yet streamlined black-and-silver flying boats as they streaked through the water, coming and going. The roar of engines and churn of seawater and noise of sightseers were more air show than airport.

According to the bulletin board in the waiting room, my plane was on time. I knew Nancy de Marigny would not be joining me, as she was going out on a later flight; but I glanced around, wondering if Lady Oakes would be one of the thirty passengers taking the *Caribbean Clipper* to Nassau at one o'clock.

She didn't seem to be, which was fine with me. I didn't dislike her—she was a smart, tough lady, if possessed of that superiority that comes of a shopgirl marrying big money—but the notion of being cooped up with her in the clipper cabin for an hour was less than enticing.

Bag checked, ticket punched, I followed a small, stout, wide-shouldered man in Western shirt and chinos down a canopied walk that opened onto sunshine and the landing dock. I followed the hick down the few steps through a hatchway into the plane; turned out I had the seat across the aisle from him, and he smiled at me, an affable character who was probably a farmer or a rancher or something.

He said, "First trip to the Bahamas?"

He had a grating yet ingratiating voice; for a guy clearly in his mid-fifties—as the broad oval of his tanned, weather-beaten face attested—he had a boyish look. Behind gold wire-frames, his eyes narrowed as he smiled, and his longish brown hair, short and gray at the temples, was combed back carelessly.

"Actually," I said, "my second in two weeks."

"Oh. Go there often, do you? On business?"

"It's my second trip, period—but it is business, yes."

"Don't mean to pry," he said, with a smile, and he looked out the porthole next to him.

The four engines started up, one at a time, the hatchway clanged shut, and the plane began to coast down the watery runway. It took the pilot half a mile of plowing down the bay, pontoons cleaving the water, till he got into position for the wind, and then the plane yanked itself forward into the sky. I looked out my porthole window, but it was washed with spray.

The cabin was full, mostly men, business types.

I leaned into the aisle and said to the hick, "Wonder how many of these guys are reporters?"

He grinned. "On their way to cover the Oakes case, you mean? Probably damn near all of 'em. Myself included."

"You're a reporter?"

"In a half-assed sort of way." He extended a hand. "Name's Gardner. Friends call me Erle."

"Nate Heller," I said, and accepted his firm handshake. I rolled his name around in my head for a couple seconds, then said, "Not Erle Stanley Gardner?"

"That's right." He beamed, pleased to have his name recognized. "Ever read my stuff?"

"Sorry," I said. "I never read mystery novels."

"Not your cup of tea?"

"More like busman's holiday."

"Oh?"

We were both having to work our voices up a bit, over the roar of the props.

"I'm president of the A-1 Detective Agency in Chicago," I said.

His eyes slitted in thought. Then he pointed at me. "Nathan Heller! Damn. I should've recognized the name."

"Hardly."

He was shaking his head, smiling one-sidedly. "No, I should've. The Lindbergh case got you a lot of press. You damn near sprung Hauptmann!"

"Close only counts in horseshoes," I said.

"Point well taken—they *did* fry the boy. But you've been in the thick of all sorts of major cases . . . the Dillinger shooting, this movie union scandal that's *still* in the papers. You're the genuine article! I'm the goddamn pretender. I'd like to pick your brain, son."

"Trust me, Mr. Gardner—if you could pick a brain, it wouldn't be mine."

He had a hearty laugh over that one.

"What's a mystery writer doing covering a real-life crime?"

"I'm Hearst's trained seal," he said with a smirk.

"Trained seal?"

"You know—these big-city papers like to have some famous-name 'expert' who isn't a newspaperman do color on a big story like this. They want me to stick around for the trial and tell the public how Perry Mason would've handled it."

"Who?"

For some reason that amused him. "That's a character I write about."

"Oh." It did sound familiar. "I may have seen a movie based on one of your books."

"Did it stink?"

"Yeah."

"Then you probably did. Those Hollywood sons of bitches pay good money to buy a good story and then invent a thousand new ways to turn it lousy."

"I wouldn't think a successful book writer like you would even want to bother with newspaper work."

He snorted a laugh. "I don't. When they approached my agent, he knew I didn't want the job and made an outrageous offer. That goddamn Hearst double-crossed us and accepted it!"

Hearst sending one of America's most popular writers to cover the case meant Sir Harry's murder wasn't just the hot story of the moment: it would stay big news through the trial, at least.

Gardner was a likable, energetic, jovial guy and made pleasant company on the ride. His Western apparel and leathery complexion were explained by the four-hundred-acre ranch he lived on in Southern California. Seemed he did most of his writing in a trailer that he hauled around his own property, as well as on excursions to Arizona and Mexico.

"I'm strictly a free-lance writer," he said. "It's one of the few businesses where you can take your work with you, anywhere you go."

I'd met my share of literary lions in Chicago, some of whom—like Nelson Algren and Willard Motley—were men's men who belied the artsy-fartsy stereotype. But even so, this Gardner was one of a kind: an outdoorsman who viewed writing as a trade, not an art.

He'd be writing a daily column for Hearst on the Oakes case, for the foreseeable future, while working on a novel and radio scripts for an upcoming show about his Mason character. Like his fictional hero, Gardner—despite his unpretentious farmer appearance—was a criminal lawyer himself, though he didn't practice anymore.

"Novels, radio shows, columns—hell, Erle . . . how will you manage all that out of a Nassau hotel room?"

"Well, it'll be dicey at first," he said, "but my girls will be following me down in a few days."

"Girls?"

"Secretaries—three of 'em. Sisters. Cute as buttons and smart as whips. I dictate everything. Haven't used a typewriter in years."

We fell into silence for a while. The stewardess came by with coffee, which we both took. I was chewing on whether or not to reveal to him that I was working the Oakes case. Before I'd decided, he spoke.

"So," he said, "you're working for de Marigny."

"Pardon?"

"Look, son—stands to reason you're not working for the prosecution. They've supposedly got a couple Miami dicks working the case. What else would Nate Heller be doing in Nassau right now but helping de Marigny's lawyer collect evidence?"

I just looked at his wide, farmer face and shook my head and laughed. Who was the detective here?

"Actually," I said, and I kept my voice down as much as possible so none of these other possible reporters could hear, "I'm working for Nancy de Marigny."

"The poor little rich girl! Is she as cute as they say?"

"As a button."

His brow creased with thought, but he kept smiling; he usually was. "So how the hell did a Chicago op get pulled in on an exotic crime like this?"

I gave him a condensed version, which he ate up eagerly.

Now his expression was wistful. "If I made up a yarn like that . . . gold miner becomes the world's richest man . . . murder in a tropical storm . . . voodoo kill . . . cradle-robbing count and beautiful child bride . . . I'd either make a million or get laughed out of the business."

"Don't forget the part where the victim's best friend in the bedroom next door sleeps through the killing."

"Oh, I haven't. I've read every news report I can, and in a case that smells a hundred ways, that part smells the worst. What do you say we team up?"

"Mr. Gardner . . . Erle . . . I don't think that would be appropriate. I don't think my client would want me working hand in hand with the press."

He scowled; even his scowl seemed affable. "I'm not the goddamn press! Look—these other reporters are going to go check in this afternoon and then head to the hotel bar and start guzzling booze out of hollowed-out coconuts. But you and me, we can go right out to Westbourne and have a look. I bet you could get us in."

I thought about it.

"I'll go with you or without you," he said, head to one side.

"You got a car lined up?" I asked. Nancy had promised to have either a rental or family car for me, by tomorrow, with a ration book full of stamps. But for this afternoon and tonight, I had no wheels.

"Hearst'll have one waiting. I'm at the Royal Victoria. Where are you staying?"

"The British Colonial."

"Sir Harry's own hotel." He clapped his hands, once, like a

sultan summoning his harem. "All right, after we're both checked in, I'll swing by, and we'll go see what's up out at Westbourne."

One of Nassau's finest was on the Westbourne gate, late-afternoon sun gleaming off the gold spike of his white helmet.

Gardner was behind the wheel of the black rental Ford and left it running as I stepped out to speak to the bobbie.

"Is Colonel Lindop inside?" I asked.

"No, sir."

"Damn!"

"Something wrong, sir?"

"I was supposed to meet him here."

"Meet him, sir?"

"I'm one of the American detectives working the case. Damn."

"Well, he's not here, sir."

"Hell. Well . . . I guess I'll just have to go on in and wait, then."

He thought about that for a long couple of seconds, then nodded, and swung the gate open. Several more of the spiffy black coppers were standing around inside the front entry. I told them I was meeting Lindop and they seemed to buy it; then I said I needed to have another look at the murder room.

One of them asked me who Gardner was and I said, "My assistant."

That was explanation enough. Even with Sir Harry dead, security around here stunk.

The air, however, no longer stunk; with the murder a little over a week old, the place was aired out, only the faintest bouquet of the aftermath of fire remained. But Gardner, following me up the curving staircase, was taking in the scorched wood and walls with wide eyes.

The Chinese screen was gone, but the bedroom otherwise seemed the same—the scorched circular area as we stepped into the room, the burnt face of the wardrobe, the blood on the phone book by the French phone on the writing table, wind whispering in the open window, ruffling the frilly curtains.

But as we stepped into the portion of the room where the murder bed waited, we saw an incredible tableau; I couldn't have been much more surprised—or outraged—if I'd interrupted Sir Harry's murder itself.

Kneeling on the floor, in their perfect uniforms, wearing their goddamned spiked helmets, were a pair of Bahamian cops who had, between them, a soapy bucket and two sponges.

They were cleaning the blood off the walls.

Specifically, they were removing—*erasing*—the small, now-dried bloody handprints by the windows overlooking the north porch.

"What the hell are you men doing?" I yelled.

Gardner was frozen, too; he seemed horrified. It was like finding a couple kids with gum erasers removing Da Vinci's *Last Supper* off the wall.

They looked at us mildly; we hadn't even startled them.

"We're removin' the bloodstains," one of them said, even as he was doing so.

"Why, in God's name?"

The other one said, "Because dey is not de Marigny's prints . . . too small."

He was right, of course; they looked like the palm prints of a woman or an adolescent.

"So?" I asked, numbly.

The first one spoke again. "So de Miami detectives say dese only confuse de evidence. Why get some innocent guy in trouble? Wash down de walls, dey say."

"Holy Christ," I said. "Stop it!"

But it was too late.

"Who are you?" one said, standing.

The other said, "He's not from Miami. He's dat guy who saw de Marigny. What are you doin' here, mon?"

"Supposed to meet Colonel Lindop," I lied.

"He's not here."

"I know. But he's on his way."

They looked at each other, and the other one got up; their uniforms remained spotless. So, now, were the walls. As they went out, the one carrying the bucket said, "Don't touch anyt'ing."

"Right," I said. "I'd hate for you boys to have to scrub the room down again."

They gave me blank looks that managed to seem nasty, and left.

"We'd better make this quick," I told Gardner. "I don't know how long my story's going to hold."

He looked properly astounded. "What the hell's going on here, Heller? What sort of criminal investigation *is* this?"

"One of these days you'll meet Barker and Melchen and find out."

I began filling him in on what the crime scene had looked like on my previous visit: the Chinese screen, the state of Oakes' burned and feathered body, including such details as the four wounds behind his ear, and the shreds of blue-striped pajamas hanging down from the scorched flesh. . . .

Gardner was on his knees, looking under the bed, like a husband searching for his wife's lover. "The cloth covering the box spring is burned away—have a look."

I got down and did. "You're right—completely gone. . . ."

We stood.

"Meaning," Gardner said, his broad face gleeful, "the fire on that bed was blazing, at one point. Those torn pajamas should have incinerated."

Damn near the entire surface of the bed was burned black, except a small area under where his hips had been, where Oakes' bladder had put out the fire.

"Notice," I said, pointing, "there's no indication anywhere of the outline of Oakes' body. If his body had been on the bed *before* the fire was set, the sheet and mattress beneath his body would have been virtually untouched."

Gardner was right with me, nodding. "The position of the body, and its weight, would have shut the oxygen off from the fire."

"Add that to the pajama shreds that didn't burn, and the trickle of blood that moved uphill, and what do you get?"

"Well," Gardner said archly, "I don't get Sir Harry asleep in bed, getting shot or bludgeoned and his bed set on fire."

I paced by the blackened bed, studying it. "I think maybe he was sitting on the edge of the bed. Talking to somebody—maybe arguing. . . ."

I put my finger behind Gardner's left ear and said, "Then bang, bang, bang, bang . . . he's shot . . . or *maybe* struck . . . anyway, he collapses on the floor."

"And the bed is set on fire, without Harry on it!"

"Sort of." I frowned. "Look at the ceiling. Right over the bed. What do you see?"

"The charred framework of the mosquito-netting canopy."

"And the mosquito netting is burned away, right?"

"Right," he said.

"But what *isn't* burned?"

Gardner looked; his tiny eyes popped. "The goddamn *ceiling*!"

I smiled. "Right. Look at these weird burns on the floor . . . circular . . . here and there . . . and Sir Harry himself was burned like that, too . . . *intermittently.*"

"That means a torch. Something homemade?"

"Possibly. I think a blowtorch. Something that could be aimed. Something you could point and scorch this bed, even get a fire going, yet still not even touch the ceiling, when you burned the netting away."

Now Gardner's eyes were so slitted they were gone. "You've got something, Heller. You've got something. . . ."

"This bed was on fire when Sir Harry was tossed on it. He was already dead, or nearly dead, from those wounds behind his ear. The killer . . ."

"Killers," Gardner interjected. "With all this going on, there had to be at least two."

"You're probably right. The *killers* then took their time playing voodoo, burning Sir Harry's body here and there, particularly the eyes and his private parts, tossing those feathers on him."

He pointed at the fan on the floor by the bed. "What about that? Isn't that how the feathers got blown around?"

"No," I said. "There were feathers sticking to him on the side of him *away* from the fan. Those feathers were sprinkled over him."

Gardner looked puzzled, now. "Did they *mean* to burn the place down?"

"I'm not sure. Maybe they just wanted to leave this phony voodoo calling card. Or maybe one of them burned and feathered Harry while the body was still on the floor, the other one getting the fire on the bed going real good, then they both tossed him on. . . ."

"And took a powder while the fire was still blazing, figuring the whole place would burn down!"

I nodded slowly. "Maybe. But the wind put it out. You know, usually when a man kills for money—as de Marigny is accused of—he does it as quickly and simply as possible and makes his getaway."

"These killers weren't in a hurry," Gardner said. "They took their time, either out of hatred for Sir Harry, or in an effort to suggest a ritual killing. Unless it *was* a ritual killing. . . ."

"Whatever the case," I said, "it's no hit-and-run job."

"Are you gentlemen in need of assistance?" said a voice from the doorway. A familiar voice, actually.

Colonel Lindop entered the room, his face long and dour under the pith helmet, hands behind him.

"You've been telling tales to my men," he said dryly. His smile was thin and not pleased.

"I told them I was meeting you here," I said. "And here we are—back in the old clubhouse."

"Don't underestimate my people," he said. "Colored or not, they're good men. They had the sense to call me."

But not the sense to stop me from waltzing in.

"I'll admit they do a hell of job destroying evidence," I said. "They were scrubbing bloody fingerprints off the wall when we got here."

Lindop blinked at the bare wall, then looked glumly my way.

"Not my doing," he said softly.

"I didn't figure it was."

"But I must admit I didn't expect to see you in Nassau again so soon," he said, too curious to throw me the hell out, right away.

"I'm working for the defense," I said.

The unflappable Lindop seemed flapped. "Really? For Mr. Higgs?"

"Mrs. de Marigny hired me."

His features froze as he tried to fathom this news. Then he looked at Gardner and said, "And who would this gentleman be?"

"This is Erle Stanley Gardner, the famous writer. He's an old friend of mine. Giving me his reading of the crime scene."

"Fascinating, I'm sure," Lindop said, with the slightest smirk. "You wouldn't be covering this for the press, would you?"

"Actually," Gardner said, with a sheepish grin, "I would. Pleased to meet you, Colonel Lindop. . . ."

Lindop ignored the hand the writer offered. He said, "I'll have to ask you to leave. We'll be bringing the press out, en masse, one day soon."

"Swell," Gardner said.

"Before we go," I said, "I'd appreciate it if you'd let me take a few evidence samples, for the defense."

Lindop looked at me, amazed. "Samples? Such as?"

"Pieces of the sheets and blankets and carpet."

"Why?"

"To conduct experiments about rate of burning."

"Oh. Well, I don't know . . ."

"I'm sure," I said, "that the Miami dicks wouldn't want you to allow this."

He smiled faintly. "I see. Well . . . why don't you go ahead, then. Take your samples."

I did. Lindop watched, then saw us out. He was almost friendly.

"Oh, Colonel," I said, outside on the front doorstep, "I wonder if you'd mind pointing out the picket fence, from which the murder weapon was supposedly plucked?"

Lindop smirked again. "I suppose you want to take one of the pickets, too," he said, "for your scientific experiments."

I exchanged shit-eating grins with Erle Stanley Gardner.

"Now that you mention it," I said.

Eleven

B rilliant late-morning sunlight careened off the high stone walls of the fortresslike Nassau Jail. The structure—which was at the end of a street called Prison Lane, fittingly enough—was atop a hill in a run-down colored district near the southern border of the city. A formidable iron gate swung open to allow the deep-blue Bentley into a courtyard overseen by placid black officers in towers and on walkways—unlike their counterparts on the streets of Nassau, these bobbies were armed, with rifles.

Godfrey Higgs, counsel for the defense, was driving. I was his passenger. I had spoken with Higgs on the phone the evening before, and we'd met for breakfast on a dining porch at the B.C., overlooking lush gardens and busy tennis courts.

I was sitting sipping orange juice when he strode through the hotel dining room over to where I sat by a window. Despite his three-piece suit, my first impression was that the tall, broad-shouldered attorney moved, and looked, like an athlete—even if it was in some ersatz sport like cricket or polo or something.

His forehead was high under dark, slicked-back, parted-in-the-middle hair; the eyes in his oval face were alert and hazel, smile broad and ready, nose sharp.

"Mr. Heller?"

"Mr. Higgs?"

His grip was firm. He sat and ordered breakfast from a black waiter; my food was already on the way.

"One of Sir Harry's good deeds, you know," Higgs said.

"What's that?"

"Giving hotel jobs to the colored population. That's one of the reasons Sir Harry was so beloved."

"I understand your client treats *his* Negro employees well, too."

Higgs' smile moved to one side of his face. "Yes . . . but not in the far-sweeping manner of Sir Harry Oakes. I'm afraid, right now, my client is as unpopular with the black population as he is with the social crowd he's gone to such lengths, over the last few years, to alienate."

"Why so much resentment against him? I've only viewed him at a distance, but he seems at least as charming as he is obnoxious."

Higgs laughed brittlely. "Well put. But you'll find soon enough, in your investigations, that outsiders here . . . unless they're tourists spreading money around . . . are viewed with suspicion and disdain."

I drank some coffee. "So that French accent of his, that charms the pants off the ladies, doesn't win him points with the men."

"That's part of it." His tea had arrived and he was stirring it idly, cooling it. "You see, Mr. Heller, the local people in Nassau . . . of either color . . . are unbelievably lazy. If an outsider comes in, and has the success that Fred has had . . . from his yachting victories to this chicken farm of his, which is so prosperous . . . it rankles."

"But Sir Harry wasn't resented that way?"

"Hardly. Oakes didn't do anything but bring money in and spend it . . . which is what white men are supposed to do in the Bahamas. Freddie, on the other hand, arrived with an accent and a title, worked side by side with blacks, seduced the local ladies, and made himself a general pain in the posterior."

"I like him better already. But the notion that an entire population is 'lazy' seems a little silly to me. . . ."

His smile turned wry. "I understand you're from Chicago. I'm told that's a city where every citizen has his hand in another citizen's pocket. Is that generalization at all true, or am I being offensive?"

Now I had to smile. "No—more like an attorney who's made his point."

He sipped the tea. Muscular-looking as he was, he moved with grace. "You see, Mr. Heller, Nassau is an easy-money town . . . it's part of the pirate mentality."

"What do you mean?"

His expression was almost condescending. "Don't be taken in by all these lovely flowers and this luxurious sunshine—New Providence is a barren island . . . the soil is a thin layer over stone, nothing much can be grown here. The major crop of the Bahamas has always been, and probably always will be, piracy of one form or another."

"Loosely speaking, that would include the rum-running of a few years ago, and the tourism of today."

He nodded. "Exactly. And to this day, wealthy pirates like Sir Harry Oakes—no disrespect to the dead intended—seek shelter here from civilization . . . that is, taxes . . . in much the manner Blackbeard, Captain Henry Morgan, Anne Bonney and the rest found these islands a safe, secluded haven."

I smiled over my coffee. "The roots of the Bay Street Pirates."

Higgs chuckled softly. "Yes . . . and many of them are my clients, so I'll ask you to grant me confidentiality on these views. But always keep in mind, Mr. Heller, as you search for the truth in this island of lies . . . many local residents are descended from wreckers."

"Wreckers?"

He looked out the window absently, then back at me. "One hundred years ago, the major industry locally was luring cargo ships onto the rocks and reefs and pillaging them. It was governmentally sanctioned . . . people had 'wrecking licenses,' ships were registered as 'salvage vessels.' Easy money, Mr. Heller—that's Nassau. And that's why Freddie de Marigny goes against the grain."

"In how bad a position does the local resentment against de Marigny put his defense?"

The smile was gone, now. "There are already signs of government collusion against my client."

"Such as?"

He pointed his teaspoon at me. "Keep in mind there's no love lost between Freddie and our Royal Governor. The Duke once asked Freddie to divert some water on land of his on Eleuthera, one of our 'out' islands, away from the black villagers and onto the property of the Duke's rich friend Rosita Forbes. Freddie declined, and the Duke took angry exception, and Count de Marigny, in his tactful way, within the earshot of several, called the Duke 'a pimple on the ass of the British Empire.' "

"How to win friends and influence ex-kings."

He raised an eyebrow. "Then there's Hallinan. . . ."

"The Attorney General?"

Higgs nodded. "Not so long ago a sailboat washed up on Freddie's beach in Eleuthera—in it were seven half-dead refugees from Devil's Island."

"The prison colony?"

"Yes. When France fell, the prison was shut down, and its prisoners declared free men. Under conditions of enormous physical and emotional strain, these seven had found their way to Nassau. Freddie admired their pluck—fed them, bathed, clothed them. Local churches joined his effort. But Harold Christie objected."

"Why?"

"This 'rabble' was an embarrassment to the Bahamas. At Christie's request, our Attorney General provided a solution: he slapped the refugees in jail."

"On what grounds?"

He chuckled again. "None in particular—and that's why Hallinan has *his* grudge against Count de Marigny. Freddie invoked the War Act and promised Hallinan public embarrassment if he didn't release the prisoners."

"So Hallinan did."

"Reluctantly. Now they all have jobs—three were Vietnamese from Saigon, who found work in a local Chinese laundry."

Around us in the dining room and on the enclosed porches were a number of Army officers; the brass were using the B.C. as their billet.

"All this makes de Marigny an ideal murderer," I said, "from the Duke and his Attorney General's point of view."

He pointed a finger at me. "Yes—and remember, the Duke personally invited these American detectives aboard—who, my sources indicate, are ignoring any evidence that doesn't pertain to my client. Washing the walls of bloody fingerprints being a prime example. . . ."

I had mentioned that to him on the phone last night.

"And there are other suspicious occurrences," he continued. "The two watchmen on duty at the Oakes estate the night of the murder have disappeared . . . blending into the local native population, apparently . . . but the police have made no effort to question or even find them."

One of those was Samuel, who'd been surrey chauffeur to Marjorie Bristol and me.

"The prison doctor, Ricky Oberwarth, is a friendly acquaintance of Freddie's. The day of the arrest, he examined Freddie for singed hairs and didn't find any."

I sat forward. "I was there when Barker and Melchen said they saw plenty of singed hairs."

"Did you see them yourself?"

"No."

He raised an eyebrow, set it back down. "Neither did Dr. Oberwarth. Within hours of the examination, Oberwarth was relieved of his duties at the prison. He asked why, but was refused an answer."

"Couldn't he demand one?"

"Not really. Ricky is a refugee from the Nazis . . . Jewish. He was allowed safe haven here only because a doctor was needed at Bahamas General."

"So," I said, "he decided it was the better part of valor not to press the issue."

"Yes. And most interesting of all . . . when Freddie was arrested, he repeatedly asked the police to call his attorney of record—Sir Alfred Adderley, who is considered the leading defense specialist in the island."

"But I read in your local paper that Adderley was hired to *prosecute* de Marigny."

"Precisely." Higgs smiled humorlessly. "Mr. Adderley claims never to have received the Count's messages. Instead, Freddie's stuck with *me*—a corporate attorney who's not been in court more than a dozen times."

"You strike me as good representation, Mr. Higgs. But why did de Marigny come to you?"

He shrugged those broad shoulders. "I'd been his attorney in several minor business matters. We're yachting club friends, as well. I suggested he acquire top legal counsel from either the United States or Great Britain . . . but he insisted on me."

"That's quite a vote of confidence."

"It is. Even better is Freddie's assurance that if at any point in the case I'm less than convinced of his innocence, I may withdraw."

Our breakfast arrived; mine was scrambled eggs and toast, but Higgs had grits with jelly-coconut milk.

"Mr. Heller," Higgs said, spooning his grits, "I'm pleased to have your aid. An investigator of your reputation is going to make my first major criminal case somewhat easier, I think."

"I'll try. If it won't spoil your breakfast, I'll share some of my thoughts on the murder room . . . I was out there again yesterday with a reporter friend of mine."

"Reporter friend?"

"A well-known mystery writer from America—Erle Stanley Gardner."

Higgs beamed. "Perry Mason! I could use some pointers. Nonetheless, let's be selective about what we give Mr. Gardner access to, in our investigations. The case is already receiving incredible attention in the American press—let's use him to put our best face forward."

"Agreed."

He pushed his half-eaten grits to one side, touched his lips with a napkin. "Why don't you fill me in about the murder scene, on our way."

"Our way?"

"Yes—I think it's time you met our mutual client. . . ."

The warden was a polite, mustached Canadian named Miller; in khakis and pith helmet, he led Higgs and me in a three-man safari down the narrow, clammy corridor. Then, at the last of four cells, he turned the key, admitted us, and turned it again and was gone.

The best thing you could say for de Marigny's cell was that it wasn't a dark dungeon; it was a blindingly bright dungeon. Two light bulbs—five-hundred-watt jobs, easy—were at the apogee of a high domed ceiling and made torture out of the illumination that bounced off the whitewashed walls of the eight-by-twelve cubicle. The floor was unevenly set stones and opposite the door was a barred window—too high to see out of, even on tiptoe, but it kept the warm cell from being stuffy.

The furnishings were limited: an army cot against the wall, a stool on which rested a battered enamel basin of water, and in one corner, a big, uncovered galvanized bucket that served as the incarcerated man's toilet, and gave the cell its distinctive aroma.

De Marigny—in yellow silk shirt and tan pants, but without belt—was standing; with his beard, he looked like a tall, sorrowful devil. He was obviously much too big for the fold-up cot he'd been provided, to which he now gestured.

"Please have a seat, gentlemen," he said. In these surroundings his thick, suave accent seemed very much out of place. "I prefer to stand."

"How are they treating you, Fred?" Higgs asked.

"Well enough. Captain Miller is a fair man. Who is this?" He was referring to me, and now he spoke directly to me. "I've seen you. I saw you at Westbourne. You're one of the police!"

"No," Higgs said, patting the air with one hand. "Freddie, this is Nathan Heller, the American detective your wife hired."

Now the Count smiled; his lips were wide and sensual, so there seemed something wicked about it.

"You're the one who placed me at Westbourne's front door," he said.

"Actually, I did you a favor."

"Oh? Perhaps you might explain."

I shrugged. "I backed up your story. Those two RAF dames might've just been covering for you."

He thought about that, and his smile turned almost friendly. "I never thought of it that way. Had *you*, Godfrey?"

Higgs said, "Yes."

"Sit, sit!" de Marigny said, suddenly a fussy host.

We sat on the cot.

"Have you a cigarette, Godfrey? I've run out."

Higgs provided one, and lighted it with a silver, crested lighter. De Marigny sucked in the smoke hungrily, and shook his head, in relief.

"Bring me more. Even if they're American."

"All right, Freddie," the attorney said. "I thought you and Mr. Heller should meet. He's going to be a vital member of our defense team."

"From hiding in my bushes," de Marigny said, his smile smug now, "to beating the bushes for me—searching for clues, searching for the real killer. Quite a turnabout."

"If you don't mind my saying so, Count," I said, "I find it interesting that you're so unperturbed by all this."

He moved the water basin off the stool and sat; he was all legs, a gawky farmer who misplaced his milk cow. He frowned, mildly. "First of all, Mr. Heller—may I call you Nathan?"

"Nate."

"Nate. First of all, please don't call me Count. I've never used the title, and I've constantly requested the local press not to refer to me as such. Only my wives seem compelled to use it."

"What woman doesn't see herself as a countess," I said.

"Very perceptive, Nate. Second, I'm unperturbed because I'm innocent of this crime. It should be easy enough for you good men to prove it."

"Not with the deck stacked against you *and* us." Higgs shook his head. "Hallinan and possibly the Duke himself are obviously pulling strings. . . ."

"Four-flushers," de Marigny said bitterly. He sucked on the cigarette. He laughed at me. "You're squinting."

"It's too goddamn bright in here," I said.

"All this light does serve a purpose—I can keep track of the rats, spiders and cockroaches more easily. Of course, sleeping is difficult, since they stay on all night. I must apologize for the foul fragrance . . . I've never had to sleep with my own excreta before."

"What the hell," I said. "I've never heard the word 'excreta' used in a sentence before."

He studied me a second, and laughed. "Charming sense of humor. Your manners are questionable, but then of course, you're an American."

"Of course. Why did Harry Oakes hate you?"

I'd thrown him a curve, but he hit it like DiMaggio.

"Because he resented my having sex with his daughter," he said.

"Oh," I said. "Before or after you married her?"

His smile was wide and wicked again. "It never came up *before* the marriage."

That was a straight line if I ever heard one, but I kept quiet; trying to improve my manners.

"A few months after we wed," he was explaining, "we were in Mexico City, when Nancy fell ill with typhoid fever—she also was in need of extensive dental surgery. Our blood type is the same, and I was able to supply blood for transfusions. A few months later, on the advice of her doctors, due to her continued ill health, a pregnancy was terminated."

He paused to inhale on the cigarette again; his jauntiness was absent now.

"Apparently Eunice and Harry somehow got the idea that I had raped Nancy in Mexico City—crawled onto her hospital bed between transfusions, perhaps, and 'violated' my wife. Oakes raved and ranted—called me a sex maniac. Nothing Nancy could say would dissuade him. He was a very uncouth man, you know—rudely eccentric."

"I see," I said, thinking all that was pretty fucking bizarre.

"That's only the beginning," de Marigny said, bleakly amused. "Before long, Nancy went to New York for some further dental surgery; at the same time, I was in need of a tonsil operation. So we checked in simultaneously, took adjacent rooms. Sir Harry discovered the arrangement, charged in like a bull, expecting an orgy no doubt, threatening to kick me out of the room. I told him to get the hell out, or I'd bash his head in."

"A poor choice of words, considering," I said.

That hadn't occurred to him; he sighed and continued: "That was when relations between the Oakes family and myself deteriorated into what was at best a chilly truce. Last March Sir Harry charged into my house to remove his teenage son, Sydney, who is quite fond of both his sister and me, and whose affections Harry felt I was stealing." He shrugged. "That was the last time I saw Sir Harry."

"You know those Miami cops say they have fingerprint evidence," I said.

"Nonsense," he said, with a wave that was like a fly swat. "I hadn't been in Westbourne in over two years. If they found any prints, I left them there during my questioning."

Higgs frowned. "This fellow Barker is being represented as a fingerprint expert . . ."

"That guy isn't an expert on anything but rubber hoses," I said.

"You think the Americans are dishonest?" de Marigny asked.

"Probably. Thick as a plank? Certainly. They've got you pegged as the killer—anything they can't make fit that scenario, they're tossing out."

"With Hallinan's help, no doubt," de Marigny said bitterly. For a moment his cocky mask dropped. "Back home in Mauritius we were brought up to take such little people for what they are—professional civil servants. Lacking the ability to make a success of their life, not good enough for the diplomatic service, eking out an existence on some miserable coral reef. Doing their best to convince themselves and everyone around them that they're so *ve-ree* important."

"Forgive my ignorance," I said, "but what's Mauritius?"

De Marigny looked at me with pity. That so ignorant a boob

could walk the planet must have seemed a reverse miracle to him.

"Mauritius is my home—an island in the Indian Ocean, a British possession but French in language, customs, population and tradition."

"Oh," I said. It was hell being a dumb goddamn American.

The prisoner stood again. He asked Higgs for another cigarette, and as Higgs lighted it, de Marigny asked a question I would have thought he'd have asked sooner.

"Have you heard from my wife? Is Nancy in Nassau yet?"

Higgs nodded. "She arrived yesterday, late afternoon. I expect you'll see her today."

"Good. Good. She's standing behind me, you know."

"I know."

"A rare woman—particularly for an American girl. She has a . . . serious quality. Most American girls, they just giggle . . . so easy to please. None of the inborn reserve of the European woman. None of the cultural maturity. That's why one tires of them so easily, of course."

"Of course," I said.

He turned to me, and his smile was as patronizing as it was wide. "You don't like me much, do you, Nate?"

"Fred, I don't have to like you to take your wife's money."

The smile went away and he just stood there, as if he were waiting for the trapdoor to let loose. Which one of these days it might: murder was a capital crime here, and you swung for it.

The sound of the key working in the metal door alerted us our time was up.

"Mr. de Marigny," Captain Miller said, "your wife is here to see you. I thought you might prefer to meet with her in my office."

De Marigny's delight was obvious. "You're very kind, Captain."

We followed the prisoner and the warden to his office, just outside of which waited a wide-eyed Nancy, who beamed at the sight of her husband. She looked lovely in a white suit trimmed in blue, her dark hair held back by a white ribbon.

I'd thought of her as tall till she embraced the six-three de Marigny; he held her tenderly and she held back her tears. Then they stood staring at each other.

"What do you think of my beard?" he said, stroking it devilishly, smiling the same way.

"It makes you look evil," she said.

That knocked his legs out from under him.

"Should I shave it off?"

She turned to me. Higgs and I had stopped a ways down, to give them some room, but she called, "What do you think, Mr. Heller?"

I was leaning against the stone corridor wall. "Absolutely. Get rid of it. The cops are destroying evidence—why shouldn't you?"

"What do you think of our American private eye?" she asked him.

"He's everything I imagined an American private eye might be," he said suavely.

Her eyes sparkled. "I *knew* you'd like him! He needs a car, Freddie . . . what about the Chevrolet?"

"Certainly . . . uh, Nate—come here a moment. . . ."

I went to him.

He whispered, "You'll need petrol. My man Curtis Thompson will see that you get whatever you need, whenever you need it, out at my chicken farm. Nancy will tell you how to get in touch with him."

"Black-market gas, Freddie?"

"Nate—would you expect less from a disreputable character like me?"

De Marigny and Nancy disappeared into Captain Miller's office; the good captain closed the door to give them some privacy.

"Good thing Sir Harry isn't here," I said.

"Why's that?" Higgs asked, confused.

"He'd have to go in there and break that up. . . ."

Twelve

F orty-seven minutes," Gardner said.

He was watching his wristwatch as we stood on the balcony of my room at the British Colonial, while two squares of cloth burned in a large glass hotel ashtray at our feet. It was as if we were performing some arcane ritual. Smoke curled blackly, the acrid fragrance little diminished by the mild morning breeze. The fragments of unburned Westbourne bedding, which we'd doused in lighter fluid, were charred black.

"So it would have taken around that long, at least, for Sir Harry's bed to have been similarly burned," I said.

"Well," Gardner said, eyes wide behind the gold wire-frames, "I'd suggest we douse those other samples in various other flammable materials—kerosene, gasoline—and see if there's any difference in rate of burning."

Lindop had been generous in the scraps of bedding he'd provided us; they had come, as I requested, from the unburned, unslept-in twin bed next to Sir Harry's.

"I may bring an expert in to do that," I said, "or send the rest of the scraps back to Chicago for testing. But for our purposes, this establishes that the killer or killers spent a longer period of time than forty-seven minutes murdering Sir Harry."

"Not necessarily," Gardner said, shaking his head. "The murderers probably left when the fire was still going."

"But the feathers weren't sprinkled on Sir Harry's body until he was *on* the bed, with his pajamas burned off him. And the bedding was already burned to a crisp when Harry was placed there!"

"True," he admitted. He gestured with an open hand. "So we're talking more like fifty minutes to an hour, minimum."

"Exactly. This killer—killers—were in no hurry."

"Agreed," Gardner said, nodding.

He still looked out of place in the Bahamas, in his green-and-brown Western shirt with bolero tie, and his chinos, against the incongruous backdrop of the white beach and vast blue-green sea.

"But I don't think it was gas or kerosene, anyway," I said, picking up the ashtray, moving back inside. "Maybe something with an alcohol base . . ."

"Why, Nate?"

In the bathroom, I ran water over the smoldering embers, which sizzled and smoked. "Ever see a gas fire, Erle? If that bed had been splashed with gasoline, the flames would've been eight or nine feet high."

Gardner snapped his fingers. "And that ceiling would've been scorched as hell!"

I rinsed out the ashtray. "Or the goddamn house would've burned to the ground. Okay. Whose car shall we take? De Marigny's or Hearst's?"

He grinned. "Let the Third Estate take you for a ride."

"I don't know if I like the sound of that," I said, but I let Gardner drive and this time I would man the wristwatch. But first we had to get to our starting point—de Marigny's house on Victoria Street; I played navigator, pointing the way for Gardner.

The Lincoln was in the driveway.

"Looks like Nancy's home," I said.

"Shall we go in and say hello?"

"You wish," I said, knowing how Gardner would relish an interview. "Drive on, Macduff."

As Gardner guided Mr. Hearst's rental Ford back down Victoria Street onto busy Bay Street, I kept track of the time.

"De Marigny left his house, with the RAF wives in tow," I said, "around one o'clock. After he dropped them off at Hubbard's Cottages, he claims he came back home the same route, via Bay Street. He says when he got home, he moved his spare car, the Chevrolet, from the driveway onto the lawn, so he could put the Lincoln away in the garage, which he did. Then he went up the outside stairs to the apartment over the garage, knocked on the door and spoke to his friend Georges de Visdelou, offering to drive Miss Betty Roberts, de Visdelou's sixteen-year-old date, home."

"Sixteen?"

"Yeah—and honey-blond and more curves than Miss America."

Gardner frowned over at me. We were moving slow, caught behind a surrey on Bay Street, its horse clopping, bell jangling. "Who *is* this de Visdelou?"

"Another Mauritian . . . de Marigny's cousin, a matinee-idol-type gigolo with no visible means of support, although his family is supposedly wealthy—a sugar plantation or something. Uses the title 'marquis,' and isn't as shy about taking advantage of it as Freddie is. According to Higgs, the Marquis and the Count and the first Mrs. de Marigny had a notorious *ménage à trois* that ultimately split up the marriage, but not the friendship between the two men."

"How continental," Gardner said; his expression was that of spitting out a seed. A sour-tasting one.

"Anyway, de Marigny went back down the outside stairs to the driveway, went up the porch steps and in the front way and hit the sack."

"Were his servants still there?"

"Yes," I said. "And they back up his story."

"Are they live-in?"

"No—they were just still there, cleaning up after the party. They were gone by two o'clock. At three o'clock Freddie's dog and de Visdelou's cat were chasing each other around, and when the cat jumped on Freddie's bed, it woke him up. Shortly after that he heard de Visdelou taking the Chevy out, finally taking his date home."

"You should always try to get sixteen-year-old honey blondes home before dawn," Gardner said archly.

"Right—or their folks might worry. Anyway, de Visdelou was back in fifteen minutes, parked his car in the driveway, and Freddie told him to come get his goddamn cat."

We picked up speed, the surrey having turned off at Rawson

Square. Gardner was lost in thought. "What's the approximate time of Oakes' death?"

"According to Barker and Melchen, between one-thirty and three-thirty a.m."

We both mulled that over. At one-thirty or one-forty at the latest, Freddie had been seen by his servants on Victoria Street; also, de Visdelou spoke to him at one-thirty or so.

Soon the big black gates inscribed *Westbourne* loomed ahead. No guard on the gate, today; the crime scene was apparently completely scrubbed down—no need to preserve what's been destroyed.

"Thirteen minutes," I said.

"Double that," Gardner said, pulling in and stopping before the gate, "and it's a twenty-six-minute round trip."

"And the weather is perfect. That night, it was coming down in sheets."

"Yes, but there wouldn't have been surreys and sponge wagons to slow him down," Gardner said, while the engine hummed. "Hell, man, you drove it, same damn night, same damn time— how long did it take *you?*"

"I wasn't paying attention," I said, "but I would guess half an hour easy, round trip."

"So Freddie simply didn't have *time* to murder Oakes, set the fire, do the voodoo routine, before he got home."

"Not even close. We're talking, at best, ten unaccounted-for minutes. I don't even think those are there."

Gardner backed out, pulled onto West Bay Street, and we headed into the city. "But he had between two a.m., when the servants left, and three a.m., when his buddy took Shirley Temple home."

I was shaking my head. "De Visdelou and his date were awake, up over the garage, playing house or whatever. Could Freddie really take the chance that de Visdelou would hear him coming and going?"

"Maybe so," Gardner said, looking over with a raised eyebrow, "if he figured de Visdelou was 'coming.' "

I laughed a little. "Yeah, but he also might be *going*—Freddie had no way of knowing when Georges would finally tire of the blonde and take her home."

"I see what you mean, Nate—cousin Georgie would surely notice the Lincoln was gone. Of course, Freddie could've just lied, if de Visdelou brought that up, and said the Lincoln was in the garage."

"True. But it's still risky as hell. How could Freddie chance de Visdelou running into him in the driveway, either coming *or* going?"

Gardner was nodding. "Besides which, the drive to and from Westbourne took half an hour, and the killing took a minimum of fifty minutes."

"A bare minimum. Even at that, it totals eighty minutes—and there just aren't eighty minutes available to Freddie to do the deed."

"What if the time of death is off? What if our boy did it *after* de Visdelou got back from taking his date home?"

I thought that over, then said, "That was around three-fifteen. With the Lincoln in the garage, Freddie would've had to move, or use, the Chevy. The question is, did de Visdelou leave the keys in the Chevy, or somewhere else Freddie could have got access to 'em? Or did he hang on to them?"

"Whatever the case," Gardner said, "I would say a lot hinges on this cousin of de Marigny's. I hope this gigolo makes a good witness."

Gardner had a point. I needed to talk to the Marquis, who after the arrest had moved out of the Victoria Avenue house, where he'd been living over Freddie's garage, to an apartment over a bar on Bay Street, Dirty Dick's, a place where locals and tourists mingled. Access to the Marquis' apartment was by a wooden stairway in the narrow, sewage-smelling alleyway next to the popular Nassau watering hole.

I knocked on the white weathered paint-peeling wooden door; Gardner stood behind me on the small landing. He had promised that anything he heard on this fishing expedition would stay off the record. I believed him.

"Somebody's in there," the writer said. "I can hear 'em talking."

I could, too, faintly. I knocked again, harder—knocked some paint flakes off.

The sound of speech within stopped, but there was still no response.

Finally on my third assault on the door, it opened. The pretty, puffy, pasty-white face of the Marquis de Visdelou stared at me with indignation, and dark, darting eyes. His brow was wide, his chin weak, his hair black and marcelled; he wore a white silk shirt open at the neck and dark slacks. In one soft hand was a large double-shot glass; it appeared to contain whiskey and ice.

His perfect little Clark Gable mustache twitched as he spoke in a French accent not as thick as de Marigny's, but just as distinct. "I don't wish to be disturbed. Please go away."

"I'm sorry, but it's important," I said. "My name is Heller and I'm working for your cousin Freddie, trying to help his attorney clear him."

For some reason this news made him cringe; he blinked nervously, long feminine lashes fluttering. He looked past me, at Gardner. "And who is this?"

"He's assisting me."

"Oh." He pursed his lips. "*Bien.* Anything I can do to help Freddie." He raised his voice; it did not seem to be for our benefit. "Please step in, gentlemen!"

We did, into a living room that was attractively furnished— matching burgundy-mohair-and-walnut sofa and easy chair, another chair with floral tapestry, coffee table, shaded standing lamp, oriental carpet. A Bahama seascape watercolor was framed over a well-stocked portable bar. A breeze and the noise of Bay Street ruffled the curtains of windows behind the sofa.

"Forgive the drab surroundings," he said, gesturing dismissively. "I was forced to rent a furnished apartment, and the establishment downstairs caters to gauche tourist tastes."

"How sad for you," I said.

My sarcasm was lost on him. "Sit anywhere. Can I get you gentlemen something to drink?"

"Sure," I said. "Rum and Coke, if you've got it. Erle?"

"When in Rome," he said.

De Visdelou smiled condescendingly, went to his liquor cart, freshened his own whiskey, and poured us some Bacardi and Coke on the rocks. We had each taken a chair.

He served us, raised his glass and said something in French, and had a sip. So did we, except for the saying something in French part. He sat on the sofa, where he could lounge against the armrest; he seemed blasé, but he wasn't: a small tic played at the corner of one soulful eye.

"I would so very much like to help Freddie," he said.

I glanced at Gardner, then looked hard at the Marquis. "You say that like there's some doubt."

His prissy mouth pursed, and he sipped the drink again. "Mr. Higgs called. We haven't spoken yet—but I intend to ask him not to call me as a witness."

"Why is that?"

"I gave a statement to the police. . . . It, what is the word? Corroborates Freddie's story, to every detail. But in open court, on the witness stand . . . What I would rather do is leave this island, quietly, and not testify at all."

I sat forward. Gardner's eyes glittered behind the wire-frames; I knew he was kicking himself that this was all off the record.

"What's wrong, de Visdelou? Were you *lying* for Freddie? To cover for him?"

He looked away from me. He seemed about to weep!

"What the hell is going on, de Visdelou!"

He swallowed thickly; he looked toward me, but the darting eyes wouldn't land. "I'm afraid there are elements of Freddie's story that will not . . . coincide . . . with what I would have to say."

"Such as?"

He reached forward to the coffee table and popped open the lid of a silver box; he removed a cigarette, inserted it into a holder and lighted himself up with a silver lighter shaped like a horse's head. The horse's ass.

He gestured with the cigarette-in-holder. "My . . . companion for the evening . . . a young lady . . . I took her home much earlier than Freddie indicates."

Gardner and I exchanged sharp glances.

"How much earlier?" I asked.

He shrugged; the breeze was riffling his silk shirt. "Immediately after the party."

"Before or after the Count took those RAF dames home?" I asked, hoping to catch him.

"After . . . right after. We were gone probably at about the same time. But I returned sooner, because . . . my companion . . . lives only a few minutes from the Victoria Street cottage."

"Fifteen minutes round trip," I said.

"That's right."

"So you didn't leave around three a.m. to take her home? And, earlier, Freddie didn't knock on your door to offer to take her home for you?"

He smiled, as if happy to back up at least part of his friend's account. "Oh, he did knock on my door around one-thirty . . . but merely to say good night."

Gardner's face was clenched with confusion, but I thought I knew what was going on.

"You're a nobleman, aren't you, Marquis?"

"I don't think of myself that way," he said, with a tiny smile that said he sure as hell did. He drew on the cigarette-in-holder.

"And you have certain codes of chivalry, that extend back to days of knights and maidens."

My arch tone was getting under his skin; his smile was gone.

"What are you saying?"

"That you're shielding that little blonde. She's sixteen years old, she probably has parents in town, and you don't want to go on the witness stand and let the world know you two were shacked up."

"That's the most outrageous thing I've ever heard!"

I laughed shortly. "I doubt that. I doubt I can even imagine the outrageous things you've heard, said and done in your Noel fucking Coward world."

"I don't appreciate your crudity."

"I don't appreciate your warped sense of honor. You're going to sell out your cousin, your best friend, you're going to put a goddamn rope around his neck, to protect the 'good name' of some little blond bimbo?"

"He's right, Georgie," a voice said.

A sweet, female, confident voice.

She was standing behind us, to our left, in a doorway that had been closed, but now stood open to reveal a glimpse of a bedroom; in her arms, held gently as if a child, was a dark gray cat.

Betty Roberts was a lovely fair-skinned girl with long, flowing blond hair that covered part of her face, Veronica Lake–style; silky-smooth, it brushed the shoulders of a blue-and-white polka-dot blouse that almost burst with her buxom youth. Her skirt was white and stopped just above the knees of million-dollar legs.

"Ah," de Visdelou said. "My little pussy."

I looked at Gardner and he looked at me; had we been sipping our rum and Cokes at the time, we'd have done spit takes.

The Marquis rose and went to Betty and patted the cat. "My little pussycat. . . ."

Gardner and I traded smiles, rolled our eyes, and both rose.

"I'm Betty Roberts," she said, handing de Visdelou his pussy. She strode over to us assuredly—she might have been sixteen, but she had the demeanor of a career woman of twenty-five. She extended her hand and I shook it.

I introduced myself, as well as Gardner (by last name only), who also shook her hand, and I said, "That must be the famous cat that awoke de Marigny around three in the morning."

"It is," she smiled. "Georgie! Let's all sit down and talk frankly."

He came over, holding the cat tenderly, petting it, and sat next to the cheerful girl on the sofa. She was arranging her skirt so that we could appreciate her crossed legs, within reason.

She looked at me with baby-blue eyes that were as direct as her boyfriend's weren't. "You'll have to forgive Georgie. He has some very old-fashioned ideas. Believe me, this silliness wasn't my doing."

"My dear," he said, "the local scandal . . ."

"Don't be a silly ass, Georgie." She smiled at me; her mouth was wide and her lipstick was candy-apple red. "I live with my mother, Mr. Heller, and she doesn't always approve of my actions . . . but that's her problem."

"You have an interesting point of view, Miss Roberts."

She threw her head back and the blond hair shimmered. "I don't care what people think about me. I only care what *I* think about me. I may not be twenty-one, but I'm free and white and completely self-supporting."

"She's a cashier at the Savoy Theater," de Visdelou said timidly.

"I don't want you to worry about what Georgie is going to say on the witness stand," she said. "You tell Mr. Higgs that both Georgie and I are willing and able to testify for Freddie. Every word Freddie said is true, and we can back him up."

"I'm relieved to hear that," I said.

The Marquis looked at her with admiration and lust. "You're a wonderful child, Betty," he said.

Somehow I didn't think the child in this relationship was her.

De Visdelou handed Betty the cat; she petted it and it purred. "Miss Roberts is right," he said, jutting his tiny chin. "As much as I treasure her good name, I can't put my cousin's life at peril."

"Yeah," I said. "I'll tell Higgs. Thanks for the drink."

I stood, and so did Gardner.

"Oh," I said to the Marquis. "One last thing—when you got back from driving Miss Roberts home, what did you do with the car keys?"

"Of the Chevrolet?" he asked. "They were in my pants pocket."

"In your pants pocket, in your apartment?"

"Yes."

"What sort of sleeper are you?"

"What do you mean?"

"Heavy, or light?" I asked.

"Light," the girl said.

He gave her a scolding look, and she smiled and shrugged.

I asked him, "Does Freddie have another set of keys?"

"Not that I know of."

"All right. Thanks."

He frowned; the cigarette holder was in his teeth now, at a raffish FDR angle. "Is that useful information, Mr. Heller?"

"It means Freddie couldn't have moved or used the Chevy without entering your apartment and fishing the keys out of your pants."

"Oh—well, he most certainly didn't do that."

"It would've woken Georgie," Betty affirmed.

"I know," I said. "By the way, this is Erle Stanley Gardner, the famous mystery writer. He's covering the case for the Hearst papers."

De Visdelou's face fell and Betty's lit up. He looked like he was about to whimper, and she looked about to squeal.

"Everything we've said is off the record," I said, "but I'm sure he'd love to arrange an on-the-record interview."

"That's right, kids," he said.

She grabbed de Visdelou's arm; the cat on her lap seemed bored. "Oh, Georgie, *can* we?"

"We'll discuss it," he allowed.

"I'm at the Royal Victoria," Gardner said, scribbling in his note pad, tearing out a page. "There's the number of my room phone."

She grabbed it eagerly, and, leaving the Marquis behind on the couch with his cigarette holder and his pussy, walked us to the door; she took my arm. She smelled good—like Ivory soap.

"Don't be a stranger, Mr. Heller," she said.

I didn't know if that was a come-on, or just sheer friendliness. But either way, I didn't pay much attention to her.

Unlike the Count and his cousin, I pretty much drew the line at dating teenagers.

Thirteen

~~~~~~

Marjorie Bristol stood in the moonlight, as silent and still as a statue—a lovely statue, at that. But if she were a work of art, the artist was God—the breeze blowing the hem of her dress gave her reality away.

I pulled the Chevrolet—de Marigny's spare sedan, a two-tone-brown number—into the graveled parking lot of the country club; there were a few other cars, and the lights of the clubhouse off to the right indicated activity. But at the moment, no one else was around as she stood waiting for me, on the nearby grass, unblinking, despite my approaching headlights.

I had called her earlier today—using one of several numbers the late Sir Harry had provided me—and asked to see her.

She seemed embarrassed, but said all right; the Westbourne gate was locked, she said, but I could park in the adjacent country club lot and walk over—no wall or fence separated the estate from the country club grounds. She would meet me here.

I locked the car and went over to her; a palm tree was a silhouette behind her. The moon was full. Stars glittered in a sky so clear and blue it should have been day. The breeze was balmy and scented of sea; a perfect evening, but for humidity that hung on you like a woolen overcoat.

I'd almost forgotten how pretty she was—uniquely so, with the huge dark eyes, lashes longer than even de Visdelou's; petite nose; wide sensual mouth, full lips painted a redundant red.

The blue maid's uniform was absent; tonight she wore a white short-sleeve blouse, a wide black buckled pirate's belt, tropical-print skirt and sandals. I'd taken to wearing my white linen suits with sport shirts; it was nice being able to work without wearing a tie. We were as casual, and as ill at ease, as a couple on a blind date.

"Hello, Mr. Heller."

"Hello, Miss Bristol. Thanks for seeing me."

She gestured and the wooden bracelets on her wrists clinked. "The house, we're keepin' it closed up right now, while my Lady stays with friends. We could go to my cottage. . . ."

"That would be fine, as long as it doesn't make you . . . uncomfortable or anything."

She smiled gently. "I trust you, Mr. Heller. I can tell you're an honorable man."

That was a new one.

"But you may not consider *me* very honorable." She looked at the ground. "I promised you I wouldn't tell anyone you were a detective."

"And then you went and told Nancy de Marigny."

She nodded. "I thought she deserved to know. They killed her daddy."

"They?"

"I don't know who. But I don't think it was Mr. Fred. He's many things, you know, but a killer ain't one of them."

"You're probably right. Where's your cottage?"

She pointed. "Just the other side of the tennis courts. You're not mad at me?"

"No. But it's starting to sound like it was your idea to have me give Nancy a hand on this."

We were walking now, toward the tennis courts. The sound of the breeze blowing and the rush of the surf made soothing background music. Her jewelry provided the percussion.

"Maybe it was a little my idea," she said, looking away almost shyly. "I just . . . knew somebody had to do somethin', you know, and I knew Sir Harry, he hired you for all that money, and you only worked one day for it. . . ."

"My Caribbean conscience. Are you Catholic, Miss Bristol, or Church of England, perhaps?"

"Neither. Methodist."

"Ah. Well, whatever the case, the Christian thing to do, after getting me into this, is give me a hand."

I thought that might make her smile, but instead her face tensed.

"I would do anything I could to help find the murderers of Sir Harry," she said. "I know he was a rough man, but to me, he was always fair, and kind."

"You keep referring to his killers in the plural. Why did you think there were more than one?"

Her big eyes were as wide as a naive child's. "I saw the room. Do you think one man could do that?"

Of course, I didn't, and it struck me that we were walking much the same path as the murderers likely had; they had probably parked in the country club lot, as well.

Her cottage was a small square white stucco building with typical Nassau shutters and a brown-tile pyramid roof; it fronted the beach, which sloped gently from the sandy grass that was her front lawn; the sand looked ivory in the moonlight, the sea a shimmering blue-gray.

"I have a teapot on the stove," she said. "Would you care for a cup?"

"That'd be nice," I said.

She opened the door for me and I went in. Neat as a pin, the cottage's interior consisted of a single room and bath; the plaster walls were a subdued pink, the wooden floor covered by braided blue-and-white oval throw rug. A kitchenette was at my right, and at left was what seemed to be a sleeping area—dresser with mirror, even a nightstand with Bakelite radio and streamlined little black-and-white clock, but no bed. Hidden against the wall to the left of the door, however, was a walnut-grain metal cabinet—a foldaway. I knew all about those. For a lot of years I slept on a Murphy bed in my office.

Despite a few rattan chairs here and there, there was no couch or sitting area, other than a round table with four captain's chairs in the middle of the room; pink and white and yellow flowers were arranged in a bowl at its center. Homemade plank-and-brick shelving, under the window along the far wall, brimmed with books, mostly the twenty-five-cent pocketbook variety. The bookcase and its contents were the only aspect of the room (other than perhaps the flowers) that seemed hers; otherwise, this was strictly servants' quarters, albeit pleasant enough.

She bid me sit at the round table, and I did, while she got us our tea. A paperbacked book was spread open there, saving her place: *The Good Earth* by Pearl Buck.

"It's about China," she said, as she served me a small cup of tea and put a plate of fritters before me.

"Really?" I said. I picked up one of the fritters. "Conch, again?"

She smiled as she sat and poured herself a cup. "Banana. Bet you've had your fill of conch."

"Not yet. Hey, these are good."

"Thank you. Mr. Heller . . ."

"Don't you think it's time we started using first names?"

She looked into her tea; her smile seemed shy, now. "I would like that, Nathan."

"I'm glad, Marjorie. But you can make it Nate, if you like. That's what my friends call me."

"I think I like the sound of Nathan better. It has more music."

That was a new one, too.

"Marjorie, I know you didn't work that night. . . ."

"The night Sir Harry was killed? I did work till ten. Sir Harry and Mr. Christie, they were playin' Chinese checkers when I left."

"But Samuel was working . . . he was the night watchman."

She nodded. "Him and a boy named Jim."

"The police haven't talked to them, you know."

She nodded again. "I know. Samuel and Jim, they took off."

"I had the impression Samuel had been working for Sir Harry for some time, was a trusted employee. . . ."

"He is. Or he was." She shrugged. "He took off."

I wondered how hard the police were trying to find Samuel. If they *were* trying to find him. But I sure as hell wanted a word with him.

"Marjorie—does Samuel have family or friends you could check with?"

"Yes. Friends in Nassau . . . family's on Eleuthera."

"Could you help me locate him?"

Her sigh was barely audible; she seemed reluctant. "If Samuel doesn't want to be found, he must have a reason. . . ."

"Exactly. I need to talk to him. What he saw the night of the murder may clear this whole thing up."

Now she nodded, her brow knit. "I will try."

"What about the boy named Jim?"

"Him I didn't know too well. He was hired more recent, to guard some building materials. They're putting up a new building at the country club, you know."

"Could you track him down for me, too?"

"I'll do better lookin' for Samuel. You got to remember, Nathan, workers in these islands come and go, gettin' work and pay by the day or even the hour."

"But you will try."

"I will try. I might hear things you wouldn't."

"I should think. That's why I need your help."

Her brow wrinkled. "In fact . . ."

"Yes?"

"There's a rumor I been hearin'. About Lyford Cay."

She pronounced "Cay" in the Bahamian manner: key.

"What's Lyford Cay?" I asked.

"The west tip of New Providence—it sticks out, like an island. But it's not an island, it's more like . . ." She searched for the word, then smiled as she found it in the dictionary of her mind. ". . . a *peninsula*. Very beautiful—*verdant*. But it's bein' developed, you know."

"Developed?"

"For houses for rich folks. Right now it's just palm trees, beaches and plots of land they cleared, but they say, one day, there will be electric lights and phones and plumbin' and fancy houses."

"And whose project is this?" I asked, knowing.

"Why, Mr. Christie's, of course."

"Tell me about the rumor, Marjorie."

"There's a dock there, and a caretaker. Lyford Cay is private property."

"I see."

"But there's no fence or gate yet. You can still drive right in there. Anyway, the caretaker is a local man named Arthur."

"Colored?"

"Yes. The rumor I've been hearin' is that the night of the killin', after midnight sometime, Arthur saw a boat pull up to the dock with some white men in it. A car was waitin' for 'em."

"That's an interesting rumor, all right."

"I know Arthur. He goes to the same church as me—Wesley Church, in Grant's Town. Or anyway, his sister does. I spoke with her, and she says her brother hasn't talked to the police about this."

I leaned forward. "Would he talk to you?"

"I think so. I talked to his sister this afternoon—she's in house-keepin' at the B.C.—and she said I could probably find him at Weary Willie's this evening."

"Weary Willie's?"

"It's a bar, over the hill."

I stood. "Take me there."

"Over the hill" was more than directions: it was what the area was called, south of where Government House stood on its ridge, looking the other way; in the virtual backyard of the Duke and Duchess of Windsor's plantation-house domicile, the thatch-roofed shacks of blacks crawled up the hill like shambling invaders who would never quite make it to the top.

As the land leveled out, the houses became more substantial, but the flickering of candlelight in windows with shutters, but no glass, indicated the lack of electricity on the far side of the hill. There were no streetlights to guide a pilgrim's progress on these dark streets littered with roadside ice stands (closed at the moment), sheltered by trees of avocado and silk cotton; but the moonlight showed off the sorrowful gaiety of the clustered houses of Grant's Town, doused as they were with blue and red and green and pink.

I wasn't scared, but I had the same white man's uneasiness I experienced in Chicago whenever I ventured into Bronzeville on the South Side.

"It's just up here," Marjorie said, pointing, "on the right. See that fenced-off place?"

"Yeah."

I pulled the Chevy up in front of an unpainted wooden structure with a thatch roof; over the saloon-style swinging doors a rustic-looking wooden sign bore the hand-carved words "Weary Willie's." There were no other cars around, but the open windows leaked laughter and babble and the general sound of people drinking.

"It is okay for a white man to go in there?"

"It's fine," she said, with a reassuring smile. "Tourists come here all the time—look closer at the sign."

I looked up. Beneath "Weary Willie's" it said: "A Glimpse of Africa in the Bahamas."

Only there were no tourists inside, just black faces, with the whites of their eyes large and displeased at the sight of me, or maybe the sight of me with Marjorie. Day laborers in sweaty tattered clothing stood at the bar having bottles of that exotic tropical brew known as Schlitz. The round uncovered tables in this kerosene-lamp-lit, wood-and-wicker world were mostly empty, but a native man and a voluptuous, almost heavy native woman were huddled over their drinks at one, in a mating ritual that knew no race. Against the far wall, which had two African-style spears crossed on it, sat an angularly handsome, jet-black young man in a loose white shirt and tan pants and no shoes. He recognized Marjorie and she nodded and we went over to him.

"May we sit, Arthur?" Marjorie asked.

He half-rose, gestured nervously. "Go on."

A fat barman in an apron that may have, at one time, been clean approached and took our orders; Marjorie asked for a Goombay Smash and I had the same. Arthur already had his bottle of Schlitz.

Marjorie sat forward. "This is Mr. Heller, Arthur."

I extended my hand and he looked at it, as if it were some foreign object, then extended his. It was a firm but sweaty handshake. His eyes were both wary and troubled in his carved mask of a face.

"He's trying to help Mr. Fred," she explained to him.

"Mr. Fred is a good mon." He spoke in a hushed, rich baritone. "My cousin, he works for him."

I said, "I'd like to hear about what you saw out at Lyford Cay the night Sir Harry died."

"I work de night shif'," he said. "In fact, I got to be out there by ten tonight. I use to fish de sponge, you know, before de fungus come."

I tried to get him on track. "What did you see that night, Arthur?"

He shook his head. "It was a bad night, mon. Storm, it whip de island. I see one of dem fancy motorboats come in and dock, 'bout one in de mornin'. Two white mon, big ones, got off de boat—somebody else, he stay behind with dat fancy boat. It was rockin', mon. Thought maybe it was gonna sink."

"Did you approach them? Lyford Cay is private property, right?"

"Right—but dey was white. And I didn't know what dey was up to, in dat storm—didn't *want* to know." He shrugged fatalistically. "Like dey say, strange t'ings happon in de carnal hours."

"Carnal hours?" I asked.

Marjorie explained patiently. "In these islands, that's what they call the time between dark and daylight."

Our drinks arrived and I gave the barman a buck and told him to keep the change and made a friend. The Goombay Smash seemed to be pineapple juice and rum, mostly.

"It was rainin' so hard," Arthur said, "one of de mon, he slip and drop his hair."

"His hair?"

"His hat, it fly off, his hair too—get wet in de rain." Arthur laughed. "He chase it like a rabbit."

One of the men was wearing a toupee, then.

"Did you notice anything else distinctive about him?"

"What?"

"Anything special or odd about his appearance. Him, or the other man?"

His eyes narrowed. "That rain, mon, was really comin' down, you know. But dey walk right past my shed, you know. I was peekin' through de window. The fella dat lost his hair, he had a skinny mustache, his nose was all pushed in. The other fella . . . he was fat, with a scar on his face."

The back of my neck was tingling.

"What sort of scar, Arthur?"

He drew a jagged line in the air with one finger. "Like de lightning in the sky, mon—it flash across his cheek."

Jesus Christ—were the men Arthur was describing the two bodyguards at Meyer Lansky's table back at the Miami Biltmore?

"A car was waitin' for dem—dey come back an hour later. Maybe longer. Got back on dat boat and go back out in de storm. Crazy, doin' that—the sea was real ugly."

"What sort of car was it? Did you see the driver?"

"Driver I didn't see. What do you call dat long square car, with de extra seats?"

"A station wagon?" Marjorie asked.

He nodded confidently. "Dat's it. It was a station wagon."

"You didn't happen to catch the license number, did you?" I asked.

"No."

I didn't figure I'd be that lucky.

"Could it have been Mr. Christie's station wagon?" Marjorie asked. Then to me, she said, "Mr. Christie, he has a car like that."

"Maybe," Arthur said. "It was dat kin' of car. But I didn't see de driver. See, I wasn't thinkin' about dat car so much as dat boat dat docked at Lyford Cay. I'm thinkin', maybe dis boat don't have no business here. So I got de registration nomber, and name on de side."

I grinned. "Arthur, you're a good man. You remember that name and number, by any chance? Or maybe have it with you?"

"No. But I write it down."

"Good. That's very good. . . . Did you show it to anybody? Or tell anybody—like Mr. Christie, say—what you saw that night?"

He smeared the moisture on his beer bottle with his thumb, then shook his head. "No—I got to thinkin', if dat *was* Mr. Christie in dat car, he might not like me askin' him about it."

"You told your sister," Marjorie reminded him.

"Oh, well, I tell a few friends. Guess that's how the story got around."

"But nobody you work for," I said.

"No. More I thought about it, less I want to make a fuss. Still . . . knowin' dat Sir Harry, he was killed dat same night. It makes you think."

Yes it did.

I reached in my pants pocket and fished out a fin. I handed it to Arthur, who took it gratefully. "I work with a lawyer named Higgs," I told him. "He's going to want to get your deposition."

Now he frowned. "What's dat?"

"Your statement about what you saw."

"I don't know, mon. . . ."

"Look—there's more dough in it for you. What would you say to a hundred bucks, Arthur?"

Arthur grinned. "I say, hello."

I laughed a little. "All right. But you got to keep quiet about this till you hear from me."

"As a mouse, mon."

"I'd like to see this Lyford Cay . . . get the layout. Why don't I give you a ride to work, right now, and have a look around?"

He waved that off. "No—no thanks, mister. I got my bicycle. Anyway, I got to try and find dat piece of paper I wrote dat nomber and name on."

"Okay, then—how about I meet you at the dock tomorrow night. You go on at ten, right? Is eleven okay? You could have that information ready for me, and I'll have a time set up for you to meet with Higgs at his office, day after tomorrow."

"Okay. Make dat an afternoon time. I sleep mornin's."

"Not a problem. Now, Arthur—keep all this under your hat. . . ."

"I buy a hat and put it dere," he promised, and grinned again, and this time he offered his hand. I shook it and Marjorie and I found our way out. By now we barely rated a glance from the native clientele. The fat bartender I tipped even waved.

Going back up and over the hill, Marjorie asked, "What do you think it means, Nathan?"

"I'm not sure. Maybe nothing. Maybe everything."

"Could those men Arthur saw be the killers?"

"Yes. But I have to give you the same advice I gave Arthur: not a word to anybody."

I left the car in the country club parking lot and walked her to her cottage. Occasionally our arms would brush, and we'd move away, then eventually drift back together. We weren't saying anything much; suddenly, with business out of the way, things had gotten awkward.

Just as I was about to say good night to her on her doorstep, feeling as shy as a teenager at the end of a first date, something scuttled across the sand, and scared the hell out of me.

She laughed. "It's just a sand crab."

I raised a hand to my forehead. "I know. . . ."

Concern tightened her eyes; she touched my face with gentle fingertips, as if inspecting a burn. "You're upset. You look sick . . . what is it. . . ."

"Nothing."

"It's something! Tell me."

"I have to walk a second. I need to breathe. . . ."

She walked with me along the beach, our footsteps slowed by the sand; the rush of the tide, the beauty of the moonlight, calmed me.

"I'm all right, now," I said.

I didn't know how to tell her that the last time land crabs had skittered across my path, I'd been in a shell hole on another tropical island, waiting for the Japs to come and finish the job they'd started on me and the rest of the patrol. . . .

She looped her arm in mine; she was close to me, gazing up at me. Those huge eyes were something a man could get lost in. Right now, I felt like getting lost.

I stopped in my sandy steps and she stopped, too, and I searched her eyes for permission before I took her in my arms and kissed her. Gently, but not too gently.

Oh, those lips; soft and sweet and they told me how she felt without a word.

Still in my arms, she looked past me. "We're to Westbourne."

The rectangular shape of the place where Sir Harry died was outlined against the sky, haloed by moonlight. We stood where Oakes and I had strolled that first day.

"We should turn back," she said.

I agreed, and walked her home, and gave her one, brief, final kiss before she slipped inside, wearing a haunting little smile.

But somehow I think we both knew there was no turning back.

Fourteen

Off Rawson Square, behind the sullen statue of Queen Victoria and the white-pillared, pink-walled, green-shuttered build-ings she guarded, was an open square of administrative buildings that included the post office, fire brigade HQ, and Supreme Court. At the square's center a plot of grass was home to a sprawling, ancient silk-cotton tree, a beautiful, grotesque thing whose trunk extended in buttresslike waves of wood, branches spreading for-ever, a wonderful monstrosity that would have been at home in the forest Disney drew for Snow White. In the shelter of its shade stood the courthouse overflow: lawyers in wigs and robes, police-men, and citizens black and white (litigants and witnesses, no doubt), discussing their cases, rehearsing their statements, escaping the afternoon sun.

Next to the yellow courthouse, over which the Union Jack flapped, vivid against the blue Bahamas sky, stood a pink building with green wooden veranda, white shutters and a blue-glass, Victorian-looking lamp on a post: the police station.

Colonel Lindop's office was up on the second floor, and his white, male, khaki-wearing secretary sent me right in. From behind a tidy desk, the long-faced Police Superintendent acknowledged me with a nod, not rising, gesturing to a chair that waited across from him.

This little office—with its couple of wall maps and several wooden file cabinets—being that of the city's top cop indicated just what a small-time operation this was. Not that it justified the Duke inviting those two Miami clods in to fuck up the case.

"You wanted to see me, Colonel," I said.

A humid breeze drifted in from the open window behind him; a ceiling fan whirred lazily.

He didn't look at me. "Yes. Thank you for coming. Mr. Heller, I've been asked by Attorney General Hallinan to . . . clarify your role in the de Marigny matter."

"Clarify my role . . . what the hell does that mean?"

"It's just," he said with patience he was having to reach for, "that Mr. Hallinan wants you to understand what it is you're to do, here."

I laughed. "Frankly, Colonel, I don't give a goddamn what Hallinan wants me to understand. It isn't up to him to define my role in this case—he's the prosecution. I work for the defense. Remember?"

Now he looked at me; his eyes said nothing. "Mr. Heller, I've been asked to inform you that you are absolutely forbidden to investigate anyone other than Count de Marigny."

I winced, shook my head. "I'm missing this. What are you talking about?"

He sighed; started tapping a pencil on the desk. "It is the prosecution's attitude that, since one man is already charged with this crime, it would be . . . improper to look elsewhere for a culprit, until or unless the person so charged is acquitted."

I felt like I'd been hit with a pie, but not a particularly tasty one. "You're saying I'm not to go out and try to find out who really did kill Sir Harry Oakes."

He shrugged. "That's Mr. Hallinan's view. You sent a request to our office yesterday . . ."

"Right. I figure, what with the war on, you must have official records of every person traveling to and from Nassau, with dates of arrival and departure. I'd like a look at those records."

"That request is denied."

I sat at the edge of the chair; did my best not to shout. "Why in hell not?"

"It doesn't pertain to the investigation."

"In my view it does!"

"Your view, Mr. Heller, counts for little here."

I almost hurled a curse at him, but then I thought better of it: his expression seemed an odd combination of disgust and sympathy.

Instead, I settled back in my chair. "You don't like this any better than I do . . . do you, Colonel?"

He didn't reply; just studied the pencil he was tapping.

"Where *are* Frick and Frack, anyway?"

He knew who I meant. "Captain Melchen is in the field. Captain Barker has flown to New York to consult with a fingerprint expert."

"I thought Barker was supposed to be a fingerprint expert himself."

He shrugged again, with his eyebrows this time.

"Of course you're aware," I said, "what an insult this is to you. Sure, your department's small . . . maybe it was a reasonable idea to bring in somebody to work with you, or even handle the case for you. But hell—why not Scotland Yard? You're a British colony. Or if it's a problem bringing somebody over in wartime, then the FBI. But a couple clowns from Miami? How can you put up with it, Lindop?"

I pushed back my chair and stood, shaking my head.

"Mr. Heller," he said, looking up at me like a sorrowful hound, "there's a limit on what I can do."

"Well, here's something you can do. I think either a blowtorch or a flamethrower of some kind was used in the killing. A flamethrower could be hard to trace . . . it might be a souvenir from the last war. But a blowtorch ought to be rare on an island like this —except in one place: where wartime building's going on. These airfields under construction, for example. If I can't get permission to check into that myself, you *should*."

He was thinking that over. "All right. I'll take it under advisement."

"Thanks."

I was halfway out the door when he called, gently, "Mr. Heller . . . before you go . . . stop in and say hello to Captain Sears."

"Captain Sears?"

"Two doors down the hall. He's superintendent in charge of traffic. I understand he may have seen something . . . interesting . . . the night of the murder."

I grinned. "Are you giving me a tip, Colonel?"

"Well, let me put it this way . . . you may mention my name in this regard to Captain Sears himself—but *no one else.*"

"Got ya," I said. "You're okay, Colonel."

" 'Okay' is something I've always dreamed of being," he said dryly, and gestured toward the door. I was being dismissed.

Sears was in his office—which was almost identical to Lindop's, except for a few additional wall maps, some of which had pins in them and were sectioned off into patrol areas—and saw me at once.

"Close the door," he said, and I did.

A squarely built Britisher with small, slate-gray eyes under bold black strokes of eyebrow, Sears stood behind his desk and offered his hand for me to shake, and I did that, too. He sat, motioning for me to do the same.

His hair was dark, combed smoothly back; his mouth was a determined line. His khaki uniform looked flawless. His forceful, confident manner made you want to take his orders without question.

"You're Nathan Heller," he said, "the detective."

"You're Captain Sears," I said, "who saw something interesting the night of the murder."

I was almost surprised when he smiled; it was a closed-mouth smile, not rupturing the thin line of his mouth, but it was definitely a smile.

"I am," he said, "and indeed I did. What I would like you to do, Mr. Heller, is convey to Mr. Higgs that I am ready and willing to testify for the defense."

"Why are you?"

"Because I saw something that is of the utmost importance to the defense, and it is, after all, my duty to see justice done; and because I am dismayed by the clumsy investigative technique of the Americans in charge . . . no offense to you, sir."

"Hey, those guys make it clear why American cops are called dicks."

Now he laughed, just a little, but it proved he had teeth.

"You have a refreshing lack of pretension, Mr. Heller," he said stiffly.

"Glad you appreciate it. What did you see?"

"Frankly, I would prefer to speak to Mr. Higgs."

"Well, that's fine—but I'm his investigator. We're going to have to talk, you and I, sooner or later, and sooner is right now."

He nodded, eyes bright under the black slashes of eyebrow. "Your point is well taken." He leaned back in his chair. The wind was rustling the silk-cotton tree in the square in the open window behind him. "When I left the station that night, a few minutes before midnight, it was raining lightly . . . a heavy squall had just passed."

He had driven down Bay Street and had just turned onto George Street when he saw a station wagon coming from Marlborough Street onto George.

"Harold Christie was sitting in the front seat."

"You're shitting me!"

"I assure you I'm not. As our car passed, we were right under a bright streetlight—the new type they have on Bay Street now."

"Christie wasn't driving?"

"No. Another person was."

"You didn't recognize the driver?"

"No. For all I saw, could have been colored or white, man or woman. But I did see Christie quite clearly—our cars were going only fifteen miles an hour or so."

"Christie has a station wagon," I said. "In fact, he claims he had it with him that night at Westbourne. Could it have been his?"

"Possibly. But, frankly, Mr. Heller, I couldn't make a positive identification, and I didn't see the license number. There was no reason to note it."

"But you're sure it was Christie?"

He smiled mildly. "I've known Harold since grade school. I've known him nearly all his life and mine." He was quietly forceful, enunciating each word clearly: "It was Harold Christie, all right, shortly after midnight, in downtown Nassau."

"And what direction was he headed?"

Sears shrugged. "He might well have been on his way to Westbourne."

"I'm a little shaky, yet, on my Nassau geography. . . . When he came up from Marlborough Street, could he have been on his way from the wharf?"

He nodded. "He might well have picked up someone at Prince George's Wharf, had any boat been foolish enough to be out in that weather."

But an hour later, according to eyewitness Arthur, a station wagon at Lyford Cay had been picking up two men who had moored there, despite the storm. Could Christie have picked somebody up downtown, possibly at the wharf, first? And then gone to Lyford Cay to gather the two men who sounded so much like Meyer Lansky's Biltmore bodyguards?

As I left, Captain Sears said, "By the way, Mr. Heller—if I were you, I'd watch my back."

"What do you mean by that, exactly?"

He smiled tightly, shook his head as if to say he'd said more than he should already.

I thanked him for his courage and honesty, and headed back to Bay Street. It was time to drop in on Harold Christie, who I had any number of questions for, particularly in light of a long-distance telephone conversation I'd had first thing this morning.

I had caught Eliot Ness having breakfast at his Washington, D.C., home. We went back many years, and I suppose it says something about the honesty of Chicago cops in general that Eliot had, during his war on Al Capone, considered me one of the few cops he trusted. I'd been an information source for him, in those days, and after I went into private practice, he became my ear in the government.

He still was, though his stint with the Justice Department was long since over. More recently his successful tenure as Cleveland's Public Safety Director had led to a post as Chief Administrator of the Federal Security Agency's Division of Social Protection. What that meant was, he was America's top vice cop, for the duration.

"Still fighting VD?" I asked him.

"With a vengeance," he said.

"I hear Capone's fighting the syph, himself."

"In his own way," Eliot said. "Say, I'll be in Chicago next month, checking out the neighborhoods around defense plants. See you then?"

"No. I'm calling you from Nassau."

"Nassau? You mean the Bahamas? Don't tell me you landed the Oakes case!"

"Okay, I won't. But I did."

He laughed. "And they say *I'm* a publicity hound."

"Yeah, well. It may prove more of an embarrassment than a feather in my cap."

"Why's that?"

"The Duke of Windsor called in a couple of Miami cops to handle the case, and they've got my client, de Marigny, fitted for a noose."

"Is that who you're working for? That slimy count I've been reading about?"

"That's him. He's an utter asshole, but I kind of like him."

"Well, maybe you have things in common."

"Thanks, Eliot. That vote of confidence means a lot. Actually, technically, I'm working for the wife."

"I've seen her picture in the papers. Hubba hubba."

"With you fighting vice, Eliot, America's in knowledgeable hands. These Miami cops, I want you to make a few calls for me . . . check out their background."

"Sure. Why not? You're a taxpayer and a war hero."

"I buy bonds, too. Their names are James Barker and Edward Melchen—both captains. Barker passes himself off as a fingerprint expert, but I doubt he knows how many digits are on the average hand."

"Okay. Got it. Their names don't ring any bells, but I'll check around."

"There's another guy—a real-estate magnate who was Sir Harry's best friend, and claims he slept through the killing, with just a room between 'em."

"Sure. Harold Christie. I've read the papers."

"Well, run a check on him, would you?"

"No need," Eliot said matter-of-factly. "I know all about him."

"Well, then, spill! But why in hell should *you* know anything about a Nassau real-estate king?"

"Because he was pals with Capone's boys—their chief contact in Nassau back in rum-running days. Chicago was a big client of the so-called Bay Street Pirates, you know—that's how Christie made his fortune. Early on, he started sinking his booze money into land."

"Eliot . . . could Christie have done business with the East Coast mob, as well?"

"No 'could' about it. He did."

"Any chance he might have done any business with Meyer Lansky?"

"I'd be surprised if he hadn't. Capone had something of a monopoly in Nassau till around '26, when Lansky and Bugsy Siegel moved in. There was almost trouble over it, but Johnny Torrio apparently settled things down; after all, there was enough English and Canadian liquor on the docks of Nassau to satisfy everybody. You know, I seem to recall Christie doing some business in Boston, too, and having some federal problems there. But I'm vague on it. I can check up on that, too, if you like."

"I like. Eliot, this information really helps."

"Then you can do me a favor."

"What's that?"

"Wear a prophylactic. Help keep vice statistics down."

"Hell, Eliot—I'm wearing one right now. Ever since I saw those movies of yours, back at boot camp, I never take it off."

The pebbled glass door at the top of the stairs said, "H. G. Christie, Ltd., Real Estate," but the sounds coming from behind it said much more: it sounded like a rally at the Board of Trade. I went in to find a large outer office that was a packed waiting room, chairs lining the wall filled with every Bahamian type imaginable: prosperous white businessmen in their three-piece suits sat next to shoeless out-island natives; a proper-looking Englishwoman sat uncomfortably beside a native girl in a colorful tropical bandanna and sheath. The only difference seemed to be that the whites, American and English alike, were speaking to each other, the men sometimes rising to approach, loudly, animatedly, one of two female secretaries—a young pretty one at the desk at left, an older handsome one at right—while the Negroes of either sex sat timidly with hands in laps and eyes lowered. The secretaries were dealing frantically with phone calls ("Yes, Sir Frederick, Mr. Christie has the blueprints ready," "Your roof is leaking? I'll inform Mr. Christie," "New York? I'll see if he's free . . .") while male assistants would emerge from one of the two offices either side of the central pebbled-glass door labeled "H. G. Christie, Private," to deal with the more impatient clientele.

None of them were as impatient as yours truly, however, because I didn't bother to check in with either harried secretary. I walked right past them and went into Christie's office.

The bald, homely, rumpled little toad who wielded such power in Nassau frowned at me from behind his desk where he was on the phone, not recognizing me at first; then his face went blank as he did remember me, before an even deeper frown returned.

"Mr. Christie . . . I'm sorry," a voice behind me urgently said. "I'm afraid this gentleman just rushed right—"

"That's all right, Mildred," Christie said, waving her back.

The older of the secretaries glared at me and I smiled pleasantly at her and she closed the door behind me. Christie was saying into the phone, "Sir Frederick, I'll have to call you back. My apologies."

His inner office wasn't large or fancy, plaster walls lined with wooden file cabinets, a few framed, hand-tinted photos of lush, lovely Bahamian properties he no doubt either owned or had sold someone; framed photos of himself with the Duke, Oakes and other Bahamian mucky-mucks; some local excellence-in-business certificates. The mahogany desk was large, however, almost massive, resting on an oriental rug. The ceiling fan's blades whirled shakily, as nervous as the waiting room out there. Bay Street bustled through the open window behind him, horses clip-clopping, bells jangling, horns honking, a voice raised occasionally.

"Mr. Heller," Christie said, raising his, "I understand the urgency of the work you're engaged in. But I'm a busy man, and you'll have to make an appointment."

"I called for one this morning. I was told to call again tomorrow."

"Well, you should have. You still should. There are many people ahead of you. But if you have something we can attend to quickly . . ."

"I just have a few questions I want to run past you. So we can get Sir Harry's murder cleared up."

His face tightened. "I was under the impression it had been cleared up."

"Oh, you mean the arrest of Count de Marigny? I don't think so. I think Freddie's arrest raises more questions than it answers."

"And why is that?"

"Well . . . the motive's a little fuzzy, for instance. Surely you're aware that Sir Harry had already changed his will, so that Nancy won't come into big dough till she's thirty?"

"I hadn't heard that. I don't believe Sir Harry's will has been probated as yet."

"Well, Nancy says she was informed of this by her father, months ago. So why should de Marigny kill Sir Harry now? What's to gain?"

"Mr. Heller, even assuming you're correct, the blood between Fred and Sir Harry was bad, to say the least."

"But you and Freddie are friends yourselves, aren't you? Didn't he invite you to dinner at his place the night of the killing? And you declined so you could dine with Sir Harry?"

"Certainly not!"

"Freddie says he did."

"He's a liar."

"What were you doing driving around downtown Nassau at midnight, that night? I thought you were supposed to be at Westbourne."

He sat up huffily; beneath those shaggy eyebrows, he was blinking as if he had something in his eye—both eyes. "I *was* at Westbourne—*all night*. Anyone who claims to have seen me elsewhere is a damn liar. Who is making this claim?"

I shrugged. "Just something I heard. You know, even an out-of-towner like me hears things. By the way, do you know a man named Lansky? Meyer Lansky?"

He stopped blinking; his eyes were cold and hard, now. But also a little scared.

"No," he said. "That name is unfamiliar to me. Mr. Heller, I'm a very busy man . . ."

"I just have a few more questions."

"No," he said, standing as he buzzed his intercom, "I'm afraid you don't. And I don't have any interest in speaking further to you, at this or any time. Sir Harry Oakes was my dearest friend, and I do not intend to aid the man who murdered him."

"And who would that be?"

"Freddie de Marigny, of course! Mildred—show Mr. Heller out."

Well, I'd rattled him, anyway. The danger, of course, was that I might be rattling Meyer Lansky, too. If the East Coast syndicate was involved, I might not be getting paid enough for this job, even at three hundred bucks per day. Funeral costs weren't something I wanted my heirs to have to list on my posthumous expense account.

Down on Bay Street, I headed toward Dirty Dick's, figuring a rum punch would hit the spot about now. But I'd barely started ambling down the sidewalk when I noticed I'd picked up a tail.

And an incredibly obvious tail, at that.

This guy was white, about thirty, with a leathery tan but otherwise ordinary-looking, wearing a colorful tropical shirt—tourist-style—and pressed tan pants and the well-polished black shoes of a cop. Which is what he was, pretending to be a tourist. They should have invested in sandals and sunglasses, as well.

So this was what Captain Sears meant when he advised me to watch my back. . . .

I walked three blocks down and he stayed with me, half a block behind. If I paused to look in a store window, he did the same. He was as subtle as the mumps. I crossed the street, walked back three blocks, and so did my shadow.

Ducking into a pharmacy, I asked the pretty, freckled redheaded girl behind the counter if they had any chalk.

"Like kids use?"

"Right—it doesn't have to be colored or anything."

"I think we do."

"And you wouldn't happen to have a magnifying glass?"

"Like Sherlock Holmes?"

"Exactly."

She smiled; nice dimples. "I think we have that, too."

I bought both items, while the cop in the bright shirt pondered the varieties of aspirin on a nearby shelf.

Back outside, I found the nearest alleyway and ducked in. I stood before the brick wall that was the side of the pharmacy and studied it; out of the corner of my eye, I watched for the cop to peek around.

He did.

I studied that wall carefully, like I was an art critic and it was a would-be Picasso. Then I began examining portions of the wall with the magnifying glass. Touching the brick here and there . . .

"Hmmmm," I'd say from time to time, rubbing my fingers together, as if examining a suspicious substance.

Finally I drew a large chalk circle on the brick wall, put my chalk and magnifying glass away and stood smiling at my artwork, rubbing my hands in satisfaction.

"Yes!" I said. "Yes."

The shadow stayed behind as I walked back to the B.C., where I called Marjorie from the phone in my room.

"Nathan," she said. "Before we go out doing things tonight, I was thinkin' about makin' some supper for you. . . ."

I heard a click on the phone line.

"Marjorie, that's great. I'll be over in half an hour."

"That's a little early, but I don't mind. . . ."

"Good," I said. "See you."

And I hung up; it probably seemed a little sudden to her, but that click had made me wonder. I was being shadowed—was I being bugged, as well?

I picked up the phone, got an outside line, and dialed a random number.

"Hello, Watkins speaking," a thickly British voice said.

"Don't say another word," I said. "I'm being watched. Meet me at Fort Charlotte in half an hour. Have the evidence with you."

I hung up.

On my way to Marjorie's in the Chevy sedan, I swung around by Bay Street; it wasn't on the way, but I wanted to have a look. I almost started crying with laughter, at the sight of the half-dozen black coppers, in their fancy dress uniforms, and pudgy Captain Melchen, all standing there, baffled, gazing at that circle I'd drawn on the alley wall.

As I passed by Fort Charlotte, on my way to Westbourne, I thought about pulling in so I could watch the cops show up for my nonexistent rendezvous.

But I was more anxious to see Marjorie Bristol.

F i f t e e n

~~~~~~

I drove past Westbourne and doubled back before pulling into the country club parking lot, just to make sure I'd shaken my tail. Apparently I had, but I got out of the Chevy and ducked behind a palm, anyway, and waited to see if anybody else pulled in. Nobody did.

As I watched, however, I had one of those stupid moments that I assume others must occasionally have, of which I have more than my share: I wondered why it had gotten so dark out so early, before remembering I was still wearing my sunglasses. I slipped them into my sport-shirt pocket—I wore no coat with my slacks, and was hatless, wearing sandals with no socks, looking more like a tourist than a detective, I supposed. Maybe *I* should have been doing the shadowing.

Only a few cars were in the graveled lot, and I walked toward the tennis courts and the subtle thunder of the ocean beyond, a cooler, less humid breeze ruffling the trees and the grass and my hair. At dusk, the palms positioned against a gray sky, the beds of colorful flowers muted now, had an otherworldly beauty; I felt alone, but it was a nice feeling, solitary not lonely.

Even in twilight, the beach looked ivory; the gun-metal sea looked peaceful, tide rolling lazily in. I stood staring for a moment, hands in my pockets, thinking about the invasion that was under way somewhere across these vast waters—the Allies were moving across Sicily, and in the paper today the Pope was bitching about us bombing Rome—but I couldn't make it anything but abstract.

Then a land crab scuttled across my path, and I jumped back, and shivered. Closed my eyes. Breathed slowly.

The little bastard had made it real for me again.

Through Marjorie's open windows the smells of cooking drew me toward her cottage like I was Hansel and she was a wickedly delicious witch and as for Gretel, well, to hell with Gretel.

I knocked once and waited, to give my hostess a chance to put lids on the steaming pots I pictured her tending. When the door opened, she looked a little harried, her brow pearled with sweat under a white bandanna; she grinned, though, and motioned me in. She wore a white blouse with an inadequately aproned wide blue-and-white-checked skirt that swirled over petticoats as she moved back to the stove.

"Smells wonderful," I said, and it did, the spicy fragrances a virtual culinary aphrodisiac. I sat at the round table, where two woven sisal place mats waited, along with the usual bowl of cut flowers.

"I hope you like this," she said. "I been workin' on it all afternoon. The main course isn't so hard, but dessert is gonna be real special."

Watching her slim graceful form, as she moved from this pot to that, I could think of something that would make a real special dessert, myself.

That lecherous thought aside—and despite the lingering memory of last night's sweet kiss—I was determined to be a gentleman this evening. Marjorie Bristol was as intelligent as she was lovely, and as vulnerable as she was ladylike; hurdling the racial barrier between us, not to mention the cultural one, was a peril I didn't wish to subject her to.

Or me either, for that matter. Friendship, possibly mild flirtation, was the limit, here.

"You said you weren't sick of conch," she said, serving me a small bowl of chowder, "and I took you at your word."

"Out of this world," I said, savoring a spoonful. The spicy soup was thick and the chunks of conch mingled with diced potatoes, tomatoes and various other vegetables. I didn't even dip into the oyster crackers she provided.

She seemed to spend more time watching me eat than eating herself, and her childlike smile at my enjoyment was infectious. Halfway through the soup, she added an appetizer to the table, crunch-battered, mild-tasting fish fingers.

"Grouper," she said.

They didn't serve this at Billy Ireland's back in Chicago; but they should have.

The main course was a plate of well-spiced rice with onions and tomatoes and big white tender chunks of meat.

"Crab?" I said, and smiled a little.

"Your enemy," she said. "I thought you might like to triumph over him."

I had a bite and said, "He tastes a hell of a lot better than he looks."

She ate a bite herself, then studied me, those huge long-lashed brown eyes turning soulful. "You don't look like a man who's much afraid of anythin'. Why does a little animal give a big man like you such a start?"

I shrugged; sipped my iced tea. "Not while we're eating, Marjorie. I'll tell you later."

She nodded solemnly, looked down at her food; she had a chastised expression, and I didn't want her to.

"Hey—Marjorie. It's no big deal. It's just not polite supper conversation . . . okay?"

She smiled again, a little. "Okay."

I asked her about herself, her family. Both her mother and her father had for many years worked for various wealthy white households in domestic positions.

"My father . . . really isn't my father," she said. "He is my father to me, and I love him, but . . . he married my mother when she was expectin' me. Some rich man was my blood daddy. I don't know who he is, and I never look into it. But that's why I look like this. Mama's kind of light-skinned, too. Papa, too, a little. That's why we live on the other side of the wall."

"Other side of the wall?"

"In Grant's Town, a concrete wall separates us light brown ones from the darker."

"And you folks are higher up the social ladder, I take it?"

She nodded. "We have a nice house. Two stories. No electricity, no indoor plumbin' . . . not as nice as livin' here by Westbourne. But nice enough."

"You mentioned you had a brother you want to put through college. . . ."

"I have two sisters, one older, one younger. Mabel's married and works at the straw market; Millie's a maid at the B.C."

"I'd like to meet them."

She smiled and ate her food. Somehow, despite her openness, I knew that me meeting her kin wasn't high on her list.

I was finished with my main course; my stomach glowed with it. I looked at her as she nibbled at her food, and thought about how she'd leveled with me about who she was; how personal she'd been with me.

"Last year about this time," I told her, "I was on an island called Guadalcanal."

Her head tilted. "I read about that place in the papers. You were a soldier?"

"A Marine. I was on a patrol that got cut off from the rest of our company. We fought back the Japanese for a day and a night, out of a hole in the sandy ground a shell made. Some of us died. Some of us lived. All the ones who lived were . . . wounded. Not necessarily physically. Do you understand?"

She nodded gravely. "It was a place like this, Guadalcanal. A tropical island."

"Yes."

She smiled ever so gently. "And the land crabs were there."

I laughed, tapped my empty plate with a fork. "Skittering around like ugly baseball gloves with legs. Lots of legs."

"Well, you ate you him, now. Your enemy."

I touched her hand. "Thanks to you."

Her hand was warm; so was her smile. "Now, dessert."

She went to the oven and put on a kitchen mitt to pull out a cookie sheet on which were two steaming, oversize custard cups. Soon the cup with its orangeish-white, crusted-brown contents sat before me, its rising, swaying steam beckoning me like an Arab dancing girl.

When I broke the skin with my spoon, a rich orange-white liquid ran through the custard.

"Coconut soufflé," she said, beaming, obviously proud of herself. "Be careful . . . it's hot. . . ."

It was, but god*damn* it was good; I can taste that stuff this minute: sweet with shreds of coconut and hints of banana and orange and rum. . . .

"I make it with Yellow Bird," she said, taking a little taste herself.

"There's a *bird* in this?"

She laughed musically. "No! Yellow Bird is a drink that mixes banana liqueur, orange juice, Triple Sec, and rum. I put the same things in my soufflé."

"Are you *sure* you're not the cook up at Westbourne?"

"I'm sure. She's so much better than me—but not as good as my mama."

After supper, we sat out on her front stoop and watched the tide roll in; both the look and sound were shimmering. We sat close, but didn't touch. The moon in the dark clear blue sky looked unreal, like a poker chip you could reach out and pluck. There were very few stars to wink at us tonight. The horizon was endless, though I knew the countless islands of the Bahamas were scattered out there; that hundreds of beaches, just this lovely, were ivory under the moonlight, just like this one. But somehow this was the only one. Anywhere.

"You know, Nathan . . . there's something that's been botherin' me. . . ."

"Oh? Something I've done or said?"

"No! No. Something about Sir Harry."

She looked into her lap; she must've slipped out of the petticoats when she went into the bathroom after supper, because the blue-and-white dress was spread out before her now, flat, like a tablecloth.

"Sir Harry seemed kinda . . . funny, a month or so before he died."

"Funny? How?"

"He was always takin' precautions. Like he was scared about somethin'."

I laughed a little. "Some precautions: he left every door in the house unlocked and every window open."

"I know, I know. But still . . . he was takin' precautions like I never see him take before."

"Such as?"

She sighed, shaking her head slowly, thinking about it. The beads of her wooden necklace made brittle music. "One night, he would sleep in one room. The next night, another room, next night, another. Always a different room."

"Well . . . that's a little odd, but I don't know that it means he was necessarily taking precautions. . . ."

"Maybe, but he took to always sleepin' with his gun next to his bed—*that's* a precaution, isn't it?"

I sat up a little. "That's a precaution, all right. That's definitely a precaution. What became of that gun?"

She shrugged. "I don't know. I see it on his nightstand, when I put his clothes out, night of the murder. That's the last I saw of it."

"Jesus. This could be important, Marjorie. What sort of gun was it?"

"Oh . . . I don't know much about guns. I don't know anything about guns. . . ."

"Was it a revolver or an automatic?"

"What's the difference?"

I explained, briefly.

"Revolver," she said.

"How big?"

She thought about it, then held her hands apart about six inches. "A .38, maybe. You'll have to tell Colonel Lindop about this."

"I already did."

"Oh. Well. Thanks for telling me about it. The prosecution sure as hell isn't likely to."

"I'm sorry I didn't mention it sooner. . . ."

"That's okay. There's a lot to keep track of in this crazy case." I checked my watch. "It's almost ten. We'll have to leave in forty-five minutes or so, to meet Arthur."

"Okay. You want to take a swim?"

"Well . . . sure. You got any spare trunks in your place?"

She looked at me with what might be irritation. "Do I look like the sort of girl who keeps a man's swimmin' things in her house?"

"No—not at all, I just . . ."

She rose, and undid something, and the dress fell to the sand.

I was looking, dumbfounded, directly at a dark triangle between her legs when the white of her blouse fluttered past me. Then I looked up and her body rose like the perfect statue of a woman, modeled in milk chocolate by some lascivious confectioner. Her breasts were round and high, not large, not small, the sort of over-flowing handfuls that would outsmart gravity for decades; the waist seemed impossibly small, legs muscular and endless, a dancer's legs, spread apart boldly, unashamed; this modest girl had her hands on her hips and was laughing down at me.

"Why is your mouth open like that, Nathan?" She wore nothing but the wooden beaded necklace. "Are you still hungry?"

Then she ran into the surf, laughing, legs kicking, globes of her behind perhaps too large for some tastes, but not mine; I was scrambling out of my clothes and scampering into the surf like a horny land crab.

She splashed at me, giggling like a young girl, and I splashed her back; the moon was playing on the water, washing her with ivory, the water's surface a ripply mosaic of white and blue and black and gray. She dove and splashed me and swam out a ways and I followed her. Treading water, I looked back at the shore. We weren't incredibly far out but we could see the country club and her cottage and Westbourne and palm trees silhouetted against the sky.

"It doesn't look real," she said. "The world looks like a toy world."

"It doesn't seem real to me, either," I said. "But you seem real."

She smiled, arms and legs moving, keeping her afloat. But it was a bittersweet smile. "Oh, Nathan . . . we shouldn't. We're from different worlds."

"There's only one world," I said. "Just different places and different people. Sometimes they make war on each other. Sometimes they think of something better to do. . . ."

That took the bitter out of her smile, leaving the sweet, and she dove back in and swam to shore and sat half in the water, half on the wet sand, looking up at the moon, basking in it, as if sunning herself.

I sat next to her. I was a little out of breath. She was in better shape.

"You have scars," she said, and touched one.

"I been shot a few times."

"The war?"

"Some of it's the war. Some isn't."

"Your life is dangerous, isn't it?"

"Sometimes. Sometimes it's more dangerous than others. . . ."

And I took her in my arms and kissed her, I kissed her hard, and she returned it, our tongues finding each other, my body on hers, the surf crashing over us, her skin wet and hot and cold and willing under me; I slid down, and was about to bury my face between her legs when I said, nastily, "If I can eat my enemy, the least I can do is . . ."

But then I was doing it, kissing her there, licking her, tasting the coarse hair, sucking the inside of the pink sweet bitter fruit and she cried out, as if in pain, but she wasn't, and then the tip of me was in her mouth, and then more than the tip of me, and when I couldn't endure the ecstasy any longer, I pulled her up on me, and rolled back on top of her, put my hands on her breasts, hard soft cold wet warm breasts, tips of them hard and sweet and salty when I suckled them, and then I was inside her, the mouth between her legs suckling me, and she moaned and I moaned and we moaned, and we churned gently together and then not so gently, and when I pulled out of her, whimpering with pleasure, her hand gripped me as I spilled into the sea. . . .

We collapsed together on the wet bed of sand, clutching each other with a mingled urgency and tenderness, staring up at the moon. There were a few wisps of cloud drifting in front of it, now; it didn't look like a poker chip anymore: it looked alive; it seemed to glow, almost burning, the clouds like white smoke. And we basked in its glow as the tide lapped over us.

I'd almost fallen asleep when she tugged my arm, saying, "Nathan! Time to see Arthur."

She ran to her clothes and I watched with a smile.

Then I hauled my sorry ass over to my own clothes and shook the sand off and put them on.

Some gentleman.

On the way to Lyford Cay I filled Marjorie in on my experience this afternoon with the obvious police tail.

"Do you think they were following us last night?" she asked, sounding worried.

"When we drove over to Grant's Town? Naw. I would've noticed."

She glanced behind her, into the blackness. The sheltering palms made a tunnel of the narrow, unlighted road into the Lyford Cay development area. "What about now?"

"No. I gave 'em something to study in that alley. They're probably still standing there, watching that chalk circle, waiting for something to jump out at them."

The wharf at the tip of Lyford Cay wasn't much of one: a finger of wood extending into the sea with a few rowboats tied there, a couple posts with life buoys draped on nails, a kerosene lantern on another post, giving the scene a jaundiced cast. The road stopped and opened into a small graveled area near the mouth of the dock; we got out of the Chevy and walked over to Arthur's shed, which resembled an oversize outhouse—a four-seater, maybe. His bike was propped up against the side.

"No light on," I said.

"Maybe Arthur has rounds he makes," she said. "He's care-taker, you know."

"Right. Let's peek in, anyway."

We did. There was a chair, a table, a water jug, and no Arthur.

"What time is it, Nathan?"

"About five after eleven. We're late, but not much. I'm going to have a look around."

"I'm stayin' right with you. This place doesn't feel good."

"Don't be silly," I said, but she was right. I wished I'd brought my nine-millimeter along, but it was still packed away in my suit-case. Without official permission to carry it here, I hadn't been risking it—nor had I seen any reason to.

At least, not until I felt the skin on the back of my neck start to crawl, about two minutes ago. . . .

We walked out on the spongy dock; walked clear out to the end. I glanced in the moored skiffs, thinking Arthur might be tak-ing a nap in one—no room to stretch out in that shed—but Arthur wasn't loafing on the job, at least not in one of the boats. We reached the end of the dock, and turned, simultaneously, and looked back toward land.

I think we both saw him at the same time; we each grabbed the other, and were lucky we didn't tumble into the drink.

But we caught our balance, if not our breath.

Because we could see Arthur clearly, in the moonlight, in the kerosene glow: spread-eagled on his back, half in the water, half on the sand. Sort of like Marjorie and I had been, not so long ago.

Only we'd been alive.

We had to drive back to Marjorie's cottage, to use the phone, and I tried to talk her into staying behind, but she insisted on coming along on the return trip.

We beat the police there, but stayed in the car, waiting, until the siren announced their arrival, loudly, pointlessly, the black police car throwing gravel as it ground to a stop. Arthur was dead, and unlikely to get either alive or, for that matter, any deader. What exactly was the rush?

Another two cars arrived shortly, but in the lead car were Lindop, Captains Melchen and Barker, and a uniformed driver.

I went over to Lindop, who wore a black-and-khaki cap in place of his daytime pith helmet; I filled him in, going out of my way to pay no attention to Barker and Melchen, who were standing around, rocking on their heels, like little kids who had to go wee-wee.

We walked over to where Arthur lay on his back, eyes wide and empty and staring up at the moon.

"I gave him a quick once-over," I said. "I don't see any marks, but his clothes are torn around the shoulders."

"He's a native," Barker said. "His clothes are ratty. So what?"

I acknowledged him for the first time, saying, "I thought you were in New York."

His upper lip curled. "I got back this afternoon. Is that all right with you, Heller?"

"I didn't know I had a say in it. Next time check with me and I'll let you know."

Kneeling over the dead caretaker, standing half in the water, Lindop said, "He's apparently drowned. Perhaps he fell off the dock, in the course of his duties."

"Perhaps his clothes are torn because he was held under the water till his eyes popped out. Colonel, he was meeting me here to give me key defense evidence. I hardly think this is an accidental death."

"What sort of evidence?" Melchen drawled. His eyes were like cuts behind his wire-frames; the sneer on his pudgy face indicated his opinion of any "evidence" I might come up with.

I told them that Arthur was to have given me the registration number, and name, of the suspicious boat he'd seen; that we were to have met here tonight, at eleven o'clock.

"So somebody tied up here the night of the murder," Barker said. "So what? Nassau's a big place. Boats come and go all the time."

"In the middle of the worst fucking storm since Noah? Are you on dope or something?"

Barker's face twisted and he raised a fist. "I don't have to take your shit . . ."

"I don't have to take yours, either, Barker. You guys aren't cops here—you're advisers. So think carefully before you start in with me."

He laughed harshly at that; but his hand dropped and his fist turned into fingers.

"Why don't you drop by headquarters tomorrow, Mr. Heller," Lindop said blandly, "and we'll take an official statement. In the meantime, you're free to go. We'll handle things here."

Marjorie had drifted up behind me. "Nathan . . . excuse me. I wanted to say something."

Barker and Melchen turned and looked at her wolfishly. They looked from her to me and back, and exchanged knowing glances.

Colonel Lindop said, "Please feel free to speak, Miss Bristol. We understand you were with Mr. Heller when he found the body."

"I was. I didn't mean to be eavesdroppin' . . . but I heard you say Arthur drowned. Well, Arthur, he was an experienced sponge fisherman. I don't think it's likely he'd drown in shallow water like this."

"He might have hit his head, Miss Bristol," Lindop said reasonably, "if he fell from the dock."

"Does he have a bump on his head?" she asked.

"We haven't turned it up yet, but the coroner will make an examination. . . ."

"He was probably drunk," Melchen said, and laughed.

"Is there any liquor on his breath?" she asked, standing right up to the squat detective.

Barker sighed dramatically, and said, "Colonel Lindop, we only came along because Heller told you this death related somehow to the Oakes case. It clearly doesn't. Do we have to listen to both his cockeyed theories *and* this native girl's?"

"Heller," Melchen said, dragging it out into two molasses-soaked syllables, looking past her, "why don't you gather your little nigger baby and go on home?"

I brushed past Lindop and looked right in the fat cop's fat face. His smile was curdling by the time I said, "Apologize to the lady."

"For what?"

"Apologize or I'll feed you your fucking spleen."

"You don't scare me . . ."

"Then don't apologize. Please don't."

He took a step back. In the moonlight his face looked flour-white, but I had a hunch it would have looked white, anyway.

"Sorry, miss," he said tightly, softly, without looking at her; without looking at anybody. "I was out of line."

She nodded and walked back toward the car.

"Oops," I said, and shoved Melchen.

His feet went out from under him and he landed, splat, in the water. Right next to Arthur.

"You son of a bitch!"

Barker took me by the shirt and said, "You think you're so goddamn tough. War hero. Silver Star. Am I supposed to be impressed?"

I batted his hand away. "Say, Barker . . . where were you girls this evening?" I looked at Melchen, who was back on his feet, scowling as he brushed the soggy sand off his soggier suit. "You two got an alibi for Arthur's murder?"

Both Barker and Melchen were looking at me with burning fury, their posture about to explode into an attack when Colonel Lindop stepped between us.

"Mr. Heller," he said calmly, "before this gets further out of hand, perhaps you should go. We have a dead body to process."

"Whatever you say, Colonel."

"I'll walk you to your car."

He did. And as we walked, he said softly, "Mr. Heller, there is every likelihood that this death will be deemed accidental."

"But . . ."

He stopped me with a raised hand. "But if you choose to investigate this man's death—on the q.t., as they say—I want you to know that if you turn up any linkage between this and the de Marigny/Oakes case, I will be most interested."

"Colonel—like I said before, you're okay."

"Mr. Heller, *you* won't be 'okay' much longer if you continue to treat my American colleagues with such disrespect."

"I'm just treating 'em the way they deserve."

"I didn't say they didn't deserve it," he said, smiled briefly, and saluted with a fingertip to his cap, turned and went.

I drove Marjorie back to her cottage in silence. I went in and sat with her, on the edge of her bed which she folded out from its little metal cabinet. I didn't stay the night, and we certainly didn't repeat our earlier carnal activities. I just held her in my arms and she shivered, though it wasn't very cold at all.

Finally as I was about to leave, she said, "You know something, Nathan?"

"Yes?"

"Maybe they *were* shadowin' us, last night, after all."

She closed the door and I was out on the beach, alone.

Sixteen

A midst tall exotic trees with whorls of feathery leaves, among colorful tropical gardens exuding a scent not unlike vanilla, stood the big pink stucco building that was the Porcupine Club. I'd been warned not to go inside the clubhouse of this exclusive facility, but instead to walk directly to the white beach beyond, where Nancy de Marigny would be waiting.

This was Hog Island, much of which was owned by the black-listed billionaire Axel Wenner-Gren. I'd taken a launch over to the nearby public beach—a five-minute ride—and now was at the private beach next door, winding through striped beach umbrellas and wooden deck chairs, looking for my client among various rich folks, mostly women of various ages, who were soaking up the midmorning sun under a clear blue sky that they probably thought belonged to them. Or anyway should.

She was at a round metal table under a large green umbrella with a leaf design that made it look like a big cloth plant; she sat back in her deck chair, looking tan and lovely, ankles crossed over red-and-blue-and-yellow-and-green leather open-toed sandals, her face further shaded by a colorfully banded straw hat that tied with a yellow sash under her strong jaw, her eyes hidden behind sunglasses. Her slender body was wrapped in a short terry-cloth robe, under which was a glimpse of lime-green swimsuit. Her fingernails were painted candy-apple red, and so were her toenails.

There was a little-girl-playing-dress-up quality about her that didn't diminish her allure—nor did the bottle of Coca-Cola she was sipping through a straw, which made a kiss of her full red-painted lips.

"Mr. Heller," she said, and smiled, sitting up. "Please sit down."

She gestured to a straight-backed wooden chair at the table; there were two of them, as if another guest were expected.

I sat. "I have a hunch you should keep your voice down, when you're using my name."

She cocked her head. "Why's that?"

"This place is restricted, isn't it? Isn't that why you had me avoid the clubhouse?"

She removed her sunglasses; the big brown eyes were earnest and her expression was almost contrite. "It is. I'm sorry. You must think I'm awful, even belonging to a place like this."

I shrugged. "A lot of people belong to places like this."

She shook her head. "You'd think people would change their attitudes . . . because of this terrible war—the way the Jewish are being mistreated by those horrible people."

"I appreciate the sentiment, but that's not exactly your fault. You know, frankly, Nancy, I never felt very Jewish before this war came along. Back on Maxwell Street, I was a *shabbes goy.*"

Her pretty face crinkled. *"Shabbes goy?"*

"Yeah. My mother was Catholic and died when I was little, and my father was an old union guy who didn't believe in anybody's God. I wasn't raised in either faith. Anyway, on Friday nights, the Jewish families needed some non-Jew to do their chores after sundown."

Her smile was sad. "So to the Jews you're a 'goy.' "

"And to the Irish Catholics, I'm just another heathen."

Now there was embarrassment in her smile, and lipstick on her soda straw. "I feel like the heathen, inviting you here. . . ."

I shrugged again. "Hey, obviously, a private club like this is a good place for you to get away from the reporters and other pests."

"It is. Do I seem simply ghastly, sitting in the sun, sipping a Coke, when my husband is rotting away in a filthy cell?"

"No. You're under a lot of pressure, and I don't blame you for relaxing a little. On the other hand, you're paying me three hundred dollars a day, so I'm inclined to cut you a little slack."

Her smile was so genuine, it underscored the phoniness of the heavy lipstick. "I like you, Nate. And I think Freddie likes you, too."

"It's not important he likes me. What's important is we get him sprung. Which is why I wanted to see you today. . . ."

Two days had passed since Arthur's murder, and in those two days I'd run up against a stone wall. A number of stone walls.

"There are people I need to talk to who are simply unapproachable," I said, then laughed, once. "They're probably all members of the Porcupine Club."

Her brow was knit. "Such as?"

"Well, the Duke of Damn Windsor, for starters. I actually went up to Governor's House and managed to talk to the Duke's majordomo . . ."

"Leslie Heape?"

"That's the one. He said that under no circumstances would the Royal Governor see me or speak to me. The reason he gave was that the Duke was keeping his distance from the case."

Her big eyes got bigger. "Keeping his distance! Why, he's the one who brought in those two Miami detectives!"

"I know. And when I pointed that out to Heape, I got shown the door in a hurry."

She placed her Coke on the table. "Who else is giving you a hard time?"

I dipped into the jacket of my white linen suit for my little black notebook; I thumbed to a specific page. "On the night of his murder, your father dined at Westbourne not only with Harold Christie, but also a Charles Hubbard, as well as a Dulcibel Henneage."

She was nodding. "I don't know Mr. Hubbard very well—he was just an acquaintance, and neighbor, of Daddy's."

"He lives near Westbourne?"

"Oh yes. Those Hubbard's Cottages where those two women Freddie dropped off live? He owns those, and lives there himself, but not in a cottage. I believe he's from London—Daddy said Mr. Hubbard made his money in 'dimestores.' "

I sighed. "Well, he's not responding to messages I left at his Bay Street office, or with his housekeeper. This Mrs. Henneage I've left messages for, also—with her housekeeper, and with one of her kids, apparently. She doesn't respond, either."

She made a *tch-tch* sound. "I see."

"I thought, before I went around banging on doors, showing up uninvited on rich people's doorsteps, I should see if you could pave the way, at all. . . ."

"Mr. Hubbard shouldn't be a problem," she said, frowning. "But I've got a feeling Effie will be another matter entirely. . . ."

"Effie?"

"Mrs. Henneage. That's her nickname—Effie. You see, Nate, Effie is a married woman."

"Well, I gathered that from the 'Mrs.' "

"I mean, she's not a widow or anything."

"I'm not following you, Nancy."

She spoke slowly, patiently, as if to a child; a backward child. "She's married to an officer stationed in England; she has two children here with her, and a nurse, who's probably the one you spoke to on the phone."

"So?"

"So—Effie is widely rumored to be . . . friendly with a certain unmarried man of some local prominence."

"Hubbard, you mean?"

"No! Christie. Harold Christie. Oh! Look who's here! You're late—I was starting to worry!"

My mouth had dropped open like a trapdoor at this latest Harold Christie revelation, but it would've been that way anyway, because the party approaching our table was one of the most stunning examples of womanhood this ex-Marine ever had the privilege of feasting his lecherous eyes upon.

She looked a little like Lana Turner, facially, and had other things in common with that famous sweater girl, including ice-blond hair that cascaded to soft, smooth shoulders; but unlike Miss Turner, this lady was a tall one, taller even than Nancy de Marigny. I would say five ten, easy, and lanky, slim-hipped, almost too bosomy for her frame, but as faults go, that was easily overlooked. So to speak.

Her skin was pale, improbably pale for the tropics, and the effect of her white one-piece bathing suit, white open-toed sandals, was that she looked like a seductive ghost. The only hint of something darker was the shadow of her pubic triangle beneath the suit.

Her eyes were almost exactly the light blue of the Bahamian sky, rather small but seeming larger thanks to the framing of thick brown eyebrows and long, apparently authentic lashes. Her lips had a puffy, bruised look, and were painted blood-red, under a tip-tilting nose; apple-cheeked, but not at all wholesome-looking, she had a white terry robe like Nancy's over one arm and white-framed sunglasses in the opposite hand.

You had to look close to tell, but she was not the twenty-some-year-old she seemed at first glance; gentle crow's-feet, extra smile lines, the way her eyes sat deep in their sockets . . . I put her at thirty-five.

"I simply must get out of this sun," she said. Her voice was thin but not unattractive, a brittle, British wind chime of a voice.

Nancy was beaming, half-standing. "Di! You look fabulous in that new suit. Schiaparelli?"

"Travella." Her smile was surprisingly wide, her teeth the dazzling white Pepsodent promised, but rarely delivered.

And now she had turned that smile on me. "You must be Nancy's charming private eye."

I was standing, straw fedora in hand. "Nathan Heller," I said.

She arched an eyebrow. "You *must* be good at what you do."

"Why's that?"

"To sneak in here with a name like that."

I didn't know whether to laugh politely or slap her.

"You're outrageous, Di," Nancy said, almost giggling. "Don't mind her, Nate. Di's the least prejudiced person I know."

"But then most of your pals belong to the Porcupine Club," I reminded her.

"Touché," Di said. She took a seat, got herself in the shade to protect that Aryan skin of hers. "We're not going to be enemies, are we?"

"You tell me," I said.

"Nate, this is Lady Diane Medcalf."

Lady Diane extended her pale white hand to me and I said, "Do I kiss that or shake it?"

"Handshake will be fine," she replied. Then her smile settled wickedly in one dimple. "We'll save the kiss for later . . . perhaps."

Nancy turned earnestly to me. "Di is my *best* friend. She's a fabulous person, you're just going to love her."

"I already love her swim suit," I said. "Travella, huh? I was going to say Macy's."

To her credit, she chuckled and said, "You *are* bad. I understand you're going to clear Freddie of this ridiculous charge."

"Fred's got the deck stacked against him," I said. "I was just explaining to Nancy how some of Nassau's social lions are ducking my inquiries."

"Really," Lady Diane said, and her brow creased and she seemed honestly troubled. "We can't have that, can we? Why don't I arrange a little soirée out at Shangri La?"

"Pardon?"

Nancy said, "Shangri La is Axel Wenner-Gren's estate . . . it's over there . . . *fabulous* place."

"And Axel won't mind?" I asked dryly. "Being as he's in Mexico and all?"

Lady Diane's laugh was brittle, too, but it had a certain musicality. "I'm *sure* Axel won't mind. Who does a girl have to fuck around here to get a drink?"

"Oh, Di," Nancy said, giggling, a little embarrassed, "you're awful."

"I'll get you a drink," I said. "You can pay up later."

"You are b-a-d, Heller," Lady Diane said. "Gin and tonic, darling."

I went over to the portable bar, where a white guy in a tuxedo was bartending under the hot sun, and bought her a drink and myself a rum and Coke; it only cost me about half what a week's rent did back home at the Morrison Hotel. This rich bitch appealed to me, for some strange masochistic reason. If my heart didn't belong to a dusky native girl, I might have done something about it.

I took my seat again, but Lady Diane was gone.

"She went in for a dip," Nancy said. "To cool off."

"With that mouth of hers," I said, "it's no wonder."

"Isn't she fabulous?"

"Fabulous is the word. Who the hell is she? How do you get to be a 'lady,' anyway?"

"In Di's case, by marrying a lord. She's the widow of one of the Duke of Windsor's closest friends . . . his equerry."

"The Duke always did strike me as a little effeminate."

She made a face; a pretty one. "Nate, an equerry is in charge of horses."

"I know. It was a joke."

She smirked. "You are . . ."

"Please don't tell me I'm bad. Tell me more about Di before she gets back."

Nancy shrugged, raised her patrician chin. "She's only one of the most important women in the Bahamas . . . possibly second only to Wallis Simpson. She's a professional woman, Nate, which is something of a rarity around here. She's been Axel Wenner-Gren's executive secretary for almost a decade."

"Who pulled the strings to get her a job like that? The Duke?"

"Actually, yes. He and Axel are extremely close friends. Now that Axel's been blacklisted, so very unfairly I might add, Di is managing the Wenner-Gren assets for the duration."

"And she's bunking in at Shangri La?"

Nancy arched an eyebrow. "More than that—she's running it, maintaining it, with something of a skeleton crew. It's like nothing you've ever seen. I can't tell you what it means to have her offer to throw a party for our benefit . . . *no one* will decline an invitation from Lady Diane."

She came running up, as if fleeing from the sun, pulling a white rubber cap off her mane of blond hair, which sprang free, glimmeringly, the supple muscles of her long legs grabbing as her feet caught the sand.

For a moment she stood there before me, though she must have known that brown pubic patch was showing right through; so were small erect nipples on the oversize breasts. She picked up the drink I'd brought her, guzzled it greedily, set down the empty glass and grinned at me. There was something savage about that grin; the look in her eyes was gleeful.

Then she threw the robe around herself, tossed back her hair. With the rouge washed away from the pouty lips, she looked even better. Naturally pretty, instead of calculatedly beautiful.

"I'll tell you what, Mr. Nathan Heller," she said, biting off each word, sitting forward brazenly. "You tell Nancy who you want invited—Harold Christie, the Duke and Duchess, Humphrey Bogart, Jesus Christ, Tojo . . . and I guarantee you they'll be there."

"You understand I mean to corner 'em one by one, and grill 'em."

"I simply adore barbecue," she said. "It's so . . . *American.* Got a smoke, honey?"

That last was for Nancy, who pulled a pack of Chesterfields from the pocket of her own terry robe, and gave one to Di, had one herself and offered me one.

"No thanks," I said.

"I thought all you ex-GIs smoked," Di said.

"Who told you I was an ex-GI?"

"I did," Nancy admitted.

"I asked all about you," Di said.

"Why?"

"Because I'm bored." She laughed again, a more full-bodied laugh this time. "This must really be paradise for you, Heller . . . all these young women around without their husbands. You see, an old gal of thirty-six like me has to work a little harder to stay in the game."

I had missed it by only a year. Mrs. Heller's son was a detective.

"I would have said twenty-five," I said.

She liked that; threw her head back regally. "It's an effort. Why do you think I keep this precious skin of mine out of the sun? I keep telling Nancy, if she insists on tanning, she'll be as leathery as an alligator's bum by the time she's thirty."

"Di," Nancy protested, shaking her head, smiling.

"Besides," Di said, gesturing with cigarette in hand, "I burn like a son of a bitch!"

Considering how Nancy's father died, that struck me as in bad taste; but Nancy didn't seem to notice.

"And," I said to Di, "you swear like a sailor."

Her mouth made amused little movements. "A lot of men find that attractive."

"You run into a lot of men around these parts, do you?"

"Not real ones." Then she smiled enigmatically, or thought she did: there was no enigma about it, as far as I was concerned.

"I'm glad to see you two hit it off so famously," Nancy said.

"I almost never give beautiful blondes too bad a time," I said.

"So, Mr. Heller," Lady Diane said, blowing the air a kiss as she made a smoke ring, "what do you say? Shall I throw a wingding for you? Cracked crab and caviar and all the champagne my well-heeled boss can afford in his absence?"

"Why not?" I said. "Just so long as it's all kosher."

Nancy looked shocked, but Di only laughed heartily again.

"Bad," she said, smiling, shaking her head.

When I got back to the British Colonial, I had a message to call Eliot Ness in Washington, D.C. I caught him in his office at the Department of Health.

"Remember I said I thought Christie had some fed trouble in Boston, years ago?"

"Yeah," I said. "Come up with something?"

"Oh yeah. My contact there also recalls an outstanding warrant out on the boy, dating back to the early thirties, for false registry of a ship."

"Hot damn. Eliot, if you can get me copies of the documents, that'll go a long way toward discrediting Christie as a witness for the Crown."

"It's going to take a while, I'm afraid."

"Why?"

"There's no listing for Christie in the federal indexes to indicate any infraction."

"Hell! Somebody pulled his records, you mean?"

"That would be nearly impossible—removing a number from the index would be one thing, destroying the actual record would be something else again. I've got a man going through every number in the indexes, looking for any missing numbers."

I was smiling. "And if you come up with any, you can request the records the missing file numbers refer to. Ness, you're a detective."

"Heller, be patient. Even if I can find these records, there'll be yards of red tape getting certified copies. There are a few hurdles in wartime that we don't normally have."

"Just drive a steel-nosed truck through 'em."

"See what I can do. How much time do I have?"

"The preliminary hearing's coming up in a few days. We're at least a month away from the trial itself."

"Good," he said, sounding relieved.

"I can't tell you how I appreciate this, Eliot . . ."

"Don't thank me yet—there's more. Not about Christie, but I did ask some friends in the FBI, and in law enforcement circles down Miami way, about your friends Barker and Melchen."

"And?"

"The word is they're bent."

"How bent?"

"They climbed through the ranks thanks to corruption and mob ties. Unfortunately, there's never been any charges brought against them, except insubordination."

"In other words, they're not popular with the cleaner cops."

"That's it. But it hasn't stopped their mutual rise to captain."

I laughed humorlessly. "And here they are in the Bahamas, at the Duke of Windsor's behest."

"That's what stymies me, Nate—why? Why in hell would the Duke of Windsor invite two crooked cops from Miami in to run an investigation of such international magnitude?"

"Eliot, if you were any more eloquent, I'd have to kiss you."

"I'm glad this is a phone conversation, then. I'll work on the Christie documents. You keep your head up—those Miami boys play dirty."

"I've been known to throw a punch or two below the belt myself," I reminded him.

I made a quick call to Captain Miller, the warden at Nassau Jail, and asked if he could arrange an impromptu meeting with Freddie. I already knew Miller was sympathetic to de Marigny's cause; the warden had made it clear (between the lines of several conversations we'd had) that he thought this was a railroad job.

So within half an hour I was sitting on the stool in Freddie's cell, while the Count sat on his cot, his long legs akimbo. Clean-shaven now, his chin looked weaker, his nose larger, and he didn't look at all satanic: just pale and skinny and troubled.

"Whether the cops think so or not," I said, "we've got two murders now: Sir Harry and Arthur. But before somebody silenced Arthur, he described two men to me who resemble a pair of goons in the employ of Meyer Lansky."

He sat forward. "The gangster?"

"The gangster. Actually, he's more like an accountant these days, but they say the little guy made his bones by going around breaking legs side by side with Bugsy Siegel. Anyway, there's little doubt Christie was in bed with Lansky back in rum-running days —and I just learned this afternoon that both Melchen and Barker are connected, too."

He winced in confusion. "Connected in what manner?"

"I mean, they're in the mob's pocket. There's a lot of mobsters in Florida, Freddie—trust me on that. My question to you is, why the hell would the syndicate have a reason to murder Harry Oakes?"

De Marigny's eyes were bulging; he seemed bewildered. "I have no idea . . . though it is no news to me that Harold Christie and Meyer Lansky have done business."

"Oh?"

"There've been rumors for months now that Lansky and Christie are making plans to put casinos in, here in Nassau, and to develop some of the other islands into, what do you call it in America? Tourist traps."

"Like Lansky's already done with Havana," I said.

"Precisely."

"But isn't gambling illegal here?"

He shook his head. "No. In fact, it was made legal just a few years ago—however, only for tourists, not residents. Before the war, the Bahamian Club operated openly, with the Royal Governor's blessing."

"What was that? A casino, you mean?"

"Yes. For the rich who winter here. But since America entered the war, assigning such licenses has been suspended."

"But when the war's over, the floodgate will open."

He nodded vigorously. "Certainly. Tourism—and, I would imagine, gambling—should flourish."

I thought about that. Then I said, "Could Sir Harry have been blocking Lansky and Christie, somehow, in their plans to bring casinos to Nassau?"

De Marigny shrugged elaborately. "But why? Is a man who owns the largest hotel in Nassau against tourism?"

"You're right," I admitted. "Just doesn't make sense. . . ."

"Anyway, Harry was powerful on the island, but it only went so far—he bought himself a seat on the legislature, but the real ruling class of Nassau is the Bay Street Pirates."

"And the head buccaneer is Harold Christie."

He shrugged facially and gestured with an open hand. "But of course."

I lifted a forefinger. "Suppose Christie had his own reasons for having Sir Harry killed, and just reached out to his mob associates to help get the job done?"

De Marigny looked doubtful. "Christie and Sir Harry were the best of friends, Mr. Heller."

"*Most* murders are committed by friends or relatives."

That made him nod knowingly. "They did share many business interests. . . . Should some matter of money go awry, who knows what one friend might do to another?"

"But of course," I said.

"By the way," he said cheerfully, "if you need any help, don't forget my man Curtis Thompson. How's your petrol holding out in that Chevrolet?"

"I could use a fill-up."

"Go see Curtis. And he may have some insights into the murder of that native, Arthur."

"I will. Maybe he can help with something else, as well."

"Oh?"

"I'm also trying to track down a native named Samuel—Sir Harry's night watchman. I had Marjorie Bristol checking around for me, but I've asked her to limit her inquiries somewhat. After Arthur's killing, I'm afraid of putting her at risk."

He sighed appreciatively. "She's a lovely woman, Miss Bristol."

"Yes she is."

His smile was a wavery, sardonic line. "And what did you think of Lady Diane?"

"That's one beautiful bitch."

His laugh echoed in the high-ceilinged cell. "New Providence is a horrible little island—but aren't the women wonderful?"

Seventeen

A round dusk, with the weather turned almost cool, I drove east on Bay Street and took the right onto the dirt road that led to de Marigny's chicken farm. The gas gauge needle was on E, so I hoped Curtis Thompson was around to provide me with "petrol," or I'd be hoofing it back to town.

When I pulled into the crushed-rock driveway of the almost ramshackle limestone farmhouse, I knew at once something was wrong: six or eight of de Marigny's native helpers, in their somewhat tattered work clothes and straw hats, were milling around, wide-eyed, looking like a Stepin Fetchit convention.

Nearby was a black police car, parked on the grass near the cut-down oil drum where not so long ago I'd seen the Count and his men scalding the feathers off dead chickens; the fire was unlit today, but something was in the air, even if it wasn't smoke.

I hopped out of the Chevy and approached the milling men.

"What's up, fellas? Where's Curtis?"

They looked at each other, nervously; several were shaking their heads. Fear and anger mingled in their dark faces.

"Where the hell is Curtis? What are the cops doing here?"

One of them, a kid perhaps eighteen with sad, smart eyes, said, "Dose son of a bitches take Curtis out back."

"Where out back?"

Another stepped forward, chin jutting bravely; he pointed. "Dat toolshed back dere. Two white cops from de U.S.A."

Melchen and Barker—law enforcement's favorite vaudeville team.

"Are they alone?" I asked. "Did any Nassau cops come along?"

They shook their heads, no.

"Not even a colored driver?"

They kept shaking their heads in the negative.

Those two bastards coming out here alone wasn't a good sign. On the other hand, it did make my job easier. . . .

"You fellas stay here," I said. "If any other cops show up, come running and tell me."

The toolshed was well in back of the house, near where the yard ended and forest began; a limestone building a shade smaller than a one-car garage, the shed had a thatch roof and a dirt-caked window on each wall. I looked in the nearest window but all I saw was a fat back in a white sweat-soaked shirt. Both no doubt belonged to Melchen.

I looked in another smudgy window and got the picture: Melchen was standing, hands on hips, watching as Barker stood barking at Curtis Thompson, who was sitting in an old wooden chair, his hands tied behind him with wire, his ankles bound the same way, to the rungs.

The shed itself was pretty sparse—some shelves of tools and jars of nails and such; some feed bags; some bales of wire, from which they'd probably got what they bound Curtis with. The floor was hard dirt.

Both cops were in rolled-up shirtsleeves, ties loose, no shoulder holsters in sight—which made me smile. . . .

Barker paused and Curtis—his handsome ebony face streaked with blood, his mouth and his left eye looking puffy—said nothing. Barker slapped him savagely.

I went around to the door. On the ground to one side, neatly folded, were the men's two suitcoats. Brutality and tidiness going hand in hand. Just beyond the weathered door I was facing, Barker stood with his back to me, working Curtis over.

I could hear what Barker was saying, through the cracked, ancient wood.

"De Marigny's going to hang, anyhow, and you'll be smack out of work! Be a good little darkie—cooperate and we'll see you get a *new* job, a *good* job. . . ."

Curtis said nothing.

Melchen's Southern-fried voice kicked in: "All you got to do, boy, is say you drove de Marigny out to Westbourne the night of the murder. You didn't take no part in it—you didn't know what he was up to . . . you just sat in the car and waited for him."

"Curtis," Barker said in a mock civil tone, "maybe you need your memory jogged a little more. . . ."

That was when I kicked the door down.

It tore right off its rusty hinges, splintering, and fell straight onto Barker, flattening him; Barker and the door falling knocked Curtis back and down, and left him tied in his chair, on his back, gaping up at me.

Melchen was glaring at me in shock and outrage as light burst into the gloomy little room and so did I.

"Heller! What the fuck are you—"

"You call this the third degree? We invented the third degree in Chicago. Perhaps you ladies need a demonstration."

"You're under arrest, asshole!" Melchen sputtered, moving toward me with fists raised.

I kicked him in the balls.

He was doubled over screaming when I dragged Barker out from under the door; he was only half-conscious, so I helped him wake up by slapping him around a little.

Then I shoved him over onto the feed sacks; the Duke of Windsor's lanky fingerprint expert sprawled there stupidly, his mouth hanging open and a little bloody drool trickling out.

Fatboy Melchen, whose face was streaked with tears, had recovered somewhat and charged me like a bull; his big hard head ground into the pit of my stomach and the air went out of me like a blown-out tire. But I stayed on my feet and belted him in the side of the head, weakly, winded as I was, though it was enough to distract him.

Gasping but better, I straightened him up and slammed a fist into the center of his fat face; the crunch of his nose was a sweet sound. He tumbled backward, hit some shelving, and jars of nails and nuts and bolts rained on him; he sat down hard, breathing the same way. He looked up at me, wondering if he should get up again.

"Mister!"

It was Curtis, warning me that Barker was getting up off the feed bags; the warning helped, because I turned, but it didn't keep me from getting tackled by the tall, loose-limbed cop. He pushed me onto the fallen door and started throwing punches into my midsection. I grabbed a handful of his greasy hair, yanked his head back and gave him a forearm in the throat.

He let go of me, rolling off; then he was like a bug on its back, as he struggled to breathe, hands on his throat as if trying to strangle himself. I got back on my feet, but so had Melchen, who had found a wrench amongst the tools and was looking at me with a face running with blood from his mashed nose. His eyes looked crazed.

"I'll goin' to kill you, you Yankee son of a bitch!"

The wrench cut the air, and I ducked, and it cut the air again, even more viciously, with an arcing *swoosh*, and I ducked again, and Melchen was smiling through the blood streaming down over his piglike teeth, enjoying himself.

Barker was on his knees, as if praying, and with one hand on his throat and the other gesturing wildly, he wheezed to his partner, "Don't kill him! Don't kill him . . . witnesses . . . too many witnesses. . . ."

Barker caught Melchen's attention with this touching speech, briefly, and that was when I kicked the fat fuck in the balls again.

His howl filled the little room, and he dropped to his knees, clutched himself and bawled like a baby. Which is exactly what I'd have done in his place.

I picked up the wrench and walked over to Barker, who was still on his knees. Curtis, on the floor in his chair, was grinning like a fox in the henhouse.

"No . . . don't . . ." Barker whimpered. He didn't look like such a tough Hollywood-type copper now. His hands assumed a praying position. Seeing him beg like that would've made me laugh, if it hadn't made me sick.

I tossed the wrench over on the feed bags.

"Get up and help your partner to his feet." I righted Curtis and his chair. "You mind if I let 'em go in the farmhouse and wash themselves up?"

Curtis said, "Dat's fine."

"Go on," I told Barker. "Go make yourselves presentable."

Barker helped Melchen up and out of the shack; the tall cop gathered their suitcoats, then with an arm supporting Melchen, hobbled toward the farmhouse, through a laughing gauntlet of black faces. The native workers had gathered in the backyard to watch and listen to the fight, and now they were applauding and cheering at the sight of the two battered white cops.

I undid the wire from Curtis' wrists and ankles. "Sorry about the door."

"Dat's easy fixed, boss. Dey work over dis face of mine much longer, it be too broke to fix."

"Well, let's get you inside and cleaned up, too."

"Wait till dey go, mon."

"Okay."

We stood near the house and waited for Barker and Melchen to come down the back porch stairs from the kitchen. The two had washed the blood and dirt from themselves, but their clothes, beneath their perfect suitcoats, were mussed and torn. Melchen was holding a bloody handkerchief to his broken nose.

The natives were milling, but no longer laughing; the sight of the two burning-with-anger cops returned them to a more servile mode.

Barker stepped close. "You're not going to get away with this, Heller. This is assault."

"What you did to Curtis is assault. What I did is a public service."

"We're officially sanctioned investigators here," Melchen said, petulantly, nasally, bloody hanky still pressed to his face.

"Maybe so," I said. "And if you want to go public with this, swell. I witnessed you attempting to beat and bribe this witness into giving false testimony. If any of this gets out, you'll both be on the next banana boat back to Miami."

Barker said, very quietly, "You don't know who you're dealing with, Heller."

"Sure I do. A couple of crooked cops in Meyer Lansky's pocket."

Barker reacted as if I'd slapped him again.

Then I smiled and put a friendly hand on his shoulder. "Look —we should be pals. After all, we have so much in common: you don't play by the rules and neither do I."

"Don't fuck with us, Heller."

"Fuck with me, girls, and you'll wake up as dead as Arthur. You do remember Arthur, don't you? The native night watchman who drowned accidentally at Lyford Cay?"

Barker and Melchen exchanged worried glances, then glared at me, to preserve what little dignity they had left, and limped off to their police car. They departed in a cloud of gravel dust, and to more native applause and derisive howls.

"You go in and clean yourself up, Curtis. Then I need some gas for the Chevy—the Count said you could help me out."

"Sure t'ing," Curtis said. "You wanna go get de gas cans yourself, and fill 'er up, while I'm inside?"

"All right. Where are they?"

Curtis grinned whitely. "In de toolshed—back of de feed bags."

No smells of cooking beckoned me through the open windows of Marjorie Bristol's cottage. Otherwise, the evening was its usual beautifully Bahamian self: perfect sky, scattered stars, a full moon making the ivory sand and gray-blue ocean seem as unreal and lovely as an artist's vision. All this and a cool, soothing breeze— and the humidity had taken the night off.

I knocked and she greeted me with a smile; but it was a smile I'd never seen from her before: sad and reserved and . . . careful.

Then I noticed: she was wearing the blue maid's uniform I'd first seen her in.

"I'm sorry," she said, showing me in. She gestured to the round table, which lacked even its usual bowl of cut flowers. "I know I told you I'd cook for you tonight, but I'm afraid I . . . got busy."

"Hey, that's fine. You've been too generous with your culinary skills already. Why don't we go out somewhere?"

She sat across the table from me, and smiled again, that same sad smile; she shook her head. "A white man and a colored gal? I don't think so, Nathan."

"I hear there's a Chinese joint on the corner of Market Street where blacks and whites can mix and mingle to their heart's content. What do you say?"

She smiled again, tightly; her eyes hadn't met mine since I got here.

"Marjorie—what's wrong? What's the matter?"

She sat staring at her own folded hands for what seemed an eternity; finally she spoke.

"Lady Eunice asked me to open Westbourne today," she said. "That's why I've been busy."

"Oh," I said.

I should have anticipated this; Nancy had told me that her mother was staying at another of their Nassau residences, Maxwellton, but with de Marigny's preliminary hearing coming up, friends and relatives—witnesses, in many instances—were beginning to arrive on the island. The larger facilities at Westbourne would be needed.

She stood and began to pace, hands folded in front of her, brow creased.

I got up, went to her, stopped her aimless moving, put one hand on her waist, and lifted her chin and made her look at me. Her eyes were moist.

"Lady Oakes doesn't approve of you helping me, does she?" I asked.

She swallowed, and shook her head, no.

She said, softly, weakly, "Somebody told her about my bein' with you when Arthur's body was found. Somebody else told her they saw us drivin' in your car together."

"And, what? She's forbidden you to help me?"

She nodded. "Or her daughter."

I winced in confusion. "But I understood Nancy and her mother were getting along pretty well, considering."

"Lady Eunice, she just doesn't want her family pulled apart any more than it already is."

"And she's convinced Freddie's the man who murdered her husband."

"She's . . . adamant about it. She says hangin' is too good for that philanderin' so-and-so."

I smirked mirthlessly. "Does she want him hanged for killing Sir Harry? Or for running around on her daughter?"

She shook her head vigorously, as if she not only didn't want to talk about it further, she didn't want to think about it, either. She pulled away from me, turned her back; she was slumped, her posture caving in on itself.

"I can't be helpin' you anymore, Nathan."

I came up behind her, put a hand on her shoulder; she flinched, but then she touched my hand briefly with hers.

"Nathan—my family and me, we depend on Lady Eunice for our livin'. I cannot go against my Lady. Do you understand?"

"Well, sure . . . but that's okay. I didn't want you involved anymore, anyway, what with Arthur's murder and all. I talked to Curtis Thompson this afternoon, and he's going to check around for Samuel and that other missing boy."

She laughed once, hollowly, turned and faced me, but stepped back a little, to put some distance between us. "Do you really think either of those boys is still in the islands? They've flown like birds, Nathan. They be long gone."

"You're probably right. Is it a problem meeting here? You know, now that Lady Oakes will be around. Maybe there's some . . . neutral place we can meet. . . ."

She swallowed hard and her eyes were welling with tears. "You don't understand, do you? I can't be seein' you no more. For any reason. Not anymore."

I stepped forward, and she moved back.

"Don't be silly, Marjorie. We mean something to each other. . . ."

She laughed bitterly. "You can't be serious. I'm just a summer romance to you, Nathan Heller. Just a . . . shipboard romance, without the ship."

"Don't say that—"

Her jaw went firm and yet trembled. "Can you ask me back to Chicago, to live with you? Can I ask you to stay here with me in Nassau? Would your family, would your friends, accept a girl like me? Would my family, my friends, want a white boy like you around?"

I shook my head; I felt thunderstruck. "I admit I haven't thought any of that through . . . but Marjorie, what we have is special, very special . . . on the beach . . ."

"The beach was very nice." A tear rolled down her cream-in-the-coffee-brown cheek. "I won't say it wasn't. I won't make a lie of the sweet truth of that. But Nathan . . . I got a brother! I got a brother who wants to make something of himself. He's going to go to college. But he needs my help to do it. And I need Lady Eunice to help him."

Now I swallowed. "So we're quits then?"

She nodded, once.

"I'm just a . . . summer fling to you, Marjorie? Is that it? Something that just . . . happened? During carnal hours?"

"Yes."

She brushed the tear from her cheek with a thumb; then she

brushed the tear from my cheek, and kissed me there, and showed me to the door.

For maybe five minutes, maybe half an hour, I stood on the beach and watched the ocean; looked at the moon. Looked at the moon reflect on the ocean. Watched a land crab scuttle by; and all I did was smile at the goddamn thing.

Then I headed for the Chevy in the country club lot and drove to the B.C., where the man at the front desk told me I had till tomorrow noon to get out.

"The owner of the hotel has requested that you leave," the white clerk said.

"Lady Oakes, you mean."

"Lady Oakes," he said.

Eighteen

For days I'd been hearing that local displeasure with de Marigny, particularly among Nassau's native population, was threatening to erupt in a lynch-mob assault on the jail; but on this hot Tuesday morning in late July, in the square outside the yellow colonial Supreme Court building, the racially mixed, overflow crowd—straw market vendors and Bay Street big shots alike—seemed almost festive. They might well have been waiting outside a theater, not a courtroom.

Inside, the play that was de Marigny's preliminary hearing began with the accused standing at the rail, before a dour, black-robed, powdered-wigged magistrate, who read the charge against the accused: that he had "intentionally and unlawfully" caused the death of Sir Harry Oakes.

Freddie wore a conservative, double-breasted brown suit and stood clean-shaven and somber, his colorful yellow-brown-and-red-patterned tie the only faint thumbing of his nose at authority.

"What is your full name?" the magistrate asked from behind the bench.

"Marie Alfred Fouquereaux de Marigny," Freddie said, and then spelled out each word for the magistrate, who was taking his own notes in longhand. There seemed to be no court stenographer.

"I appear on behalf of the prosecution," a resonant voice intoned.

The man who rose to speak at a table shared by both prosecution and defense was a giant of a bewigged, berobed black man, whose clear diction and cultivated English accent seemed at odds with his African features and ebony skin. This was the Honorable A. F. Adderley, Nassau's foremost trial attorney, who had never lost a murder case, and who had, until now, been de Marigny's attorney of record.

"I appear on behalf of the accused," Godfrey Higgs said, standing, his athletic frame holding its own with the massive prosecutor's. He too was wigged and robed; his smile was confident, eager.

Now two statuesque black officers—to whose already ostentatious uniforms had been added the touch of sheathed bayonets hanging from black leather belts—escorted the prisoner to a wooden box, six feet long, five feet high, inside which was a narrow wooden bench, where Freddie sat, as a door of widely spaced iron bars clanged shut on him. This slightly elevated cage was on the left, as you faced the magistrate behind his bench, with the jury box (empty, for this hearing) directly opposite.

The 150-seat courthouse was packed with mostly white faces, black servants for the wealthy having arrived before sunup to be first in line for their bosses. Nancy was not present, as she would later be called as a witness; I would be her eyes and ears, from the front row.

In addition to the lawyers' table—where Attorney General Hallinan and the two Miami police captains also sat—two other tables had been squeezed in, in front of the gallery, to accommodate the press. Mere war news took a backseat to a juicy case like this. Newshounds from New York, London and Toronto sat with the local Nassau press, and reps from UPI and the Associated Press were on hand, too. Jimmy Kilgallen was there for INS, sitting next to Erle Gardner, with whom I'd chatted briefly before the proceedings started.

"Have you been ducking me, Heller?" the feisty little mystery writer had asked.

"Yes," I said.

He laughed harshly. "Is this fellow Higgs going to cross-examine the prosecution witnesses?"

"I don't really know. Why wouldn't he?"

A smile twitched in his round face, his eyes glittered behind the gold wire-frames. "Well, burden of proof's on the prosecution. Usually, in a preliminary hearing, these limey defenders don't like to tip their hand by asking many questions."

"Personally," I said, "I hope Higgs goes after Christie with a hatchet—or maybe a blowtorch."

That made him laugh again, before we each scurried to our seats as the doors had opened letting in the surge of spectators at nine-thirty.

Now all was quiet, but for the booming voices of the lawyers and magistrate, and the more halting ones of an array of prosecution witnesses, in the slow, steady campaign to place a rope around de Marigny's neck. That, and the buzzing of flies and the occasional flap of a bird that would find its way through the open windows of the stiflingly hot courtroom.

The poised, mannered Adderley spent most of the morning laying routine groundwork. The first witnesses were the RAF draftsman who'd drawn a floor plan for Lindop, and the RAF photographers who'd taken the death photos—large blowups of which were briefly displayed on an easel, like ghoulish works of art, making the gallery gasp.

Dr. Quackenbush, a bland, trim little man in his mid-forties who (as it turned out) did not resemble Groucho Marx in the least, described the crime scene as he'd found it on the morning of July 8, in clinical but grisly detail; described the four wounds grouped behind Sir Harry's head as "punctures," the diameter of a pencil, penetrating the skull.

He neglected to mention that his first instinct had been that these were gunshot wounds.

In discussing the autopsy, the doctor mentioned that "on removing the skullcap, a quantity of blood was seen inside the brain capsule," and that "there appeared to be a slight contusion of the brain, but no hemorrhages."

Which to me meant the bullets, having lost momentum on their journey through the skull, could still have been in Sir Harry's brain—which had not been cut open for examination—which, with the rest of Harry, was currently in a coffin six feet under in Bar Harbor, Maine.

Quackenbush also spoke of "approximately four ounces" of an as yet unidentified "thick, viscid, darkish fluid" in Sir Harry's stomach. Had Sir Harry been poisoned, or maybe drugged?

I jotted a reminder to myself in my pocket notebook to nudge Higgs about it.

Meanwhile, another of Nassau's wartime parade of lovely women was taking the stand: the elusive Dulcibel Henneage, who described herself as "an English evacuee with two children." I would describe her as a pretty blonde in her late twenties, looking shapely despite her conservative suit and hat; if this was Harold Christie's mistress, he was a lucky man.

But her story of playing afternoon tennis with Charles Hubbard, Harold Christie and Sir Harry Oakes, and later having dinner at Westbourne, shed no particular light on the case. She seemed to have been called simply to help establish a chronology.

The local beauty pageant continued with blond Dorothy Clark and brunette Jean Ainslie, the RAF wives Freddie had escorted home in the rain; like Mrs. Henneage, they looked very proper in their new suits and hats and with nervous precision established Freddie's presence in the neighborhood of Westbourne on the murder night.

I had not been subpoenaed by the prosecution; now that I was in Freddie's camp, it began to seem unlikely I'd be asked to back up the girls' story at the trial. More likely, I'd testify for the defense, showing that de Marigny's activities on July 7 didn't seem to be those of a man preparing to end his day with a premeditated murder.

The RAF girls really hadn't done Freddie any damage; after all, everything they said tallied with his own story. More troubling was the testimony of Constable Wendell Parker, who told of de Marigny stopping at the police station to register a new truck purchased for his chicken farm, at seven-thirty a.m. on July 8.

"He appeared excited," the constable said. "His eyes were . . . *bulging.*"

Over in his cage, de Marigny's eyes were bulging now, at the apparent stupidity of this testimony, but I knew a jury could well interpret his dropping by the police station the morning after the murder as anxiety over whether or not Sir Harry's body had been discovered yet.

The next witness was all too familiar: Marjorie Bristol, looking crisp and beautiful in a red-and-white floral dress as she stood (as all the witnesses did, in the British style) in the witness box, without leaning on the rail. She told her story simply and well: of setting out Sir Harry's nightclothes, arranging his mosquito netting; of answering Christie's cries for help, the next morning.

Higgs rose to cross-examine, briefly, breaking Gardner's rule for limey lawyers.

"Miss Bristol," he asked, smiling affably, "I believe you said you 'flitted' the room with the insecticide spray gun?"

"Yes, sir."

"What did you do with it then?"

"I left the spray gun in the room, because Sir Harry, he always told me to leave it there."

"How much insecticide was left in the spray gun, would you say?"

"Well, sir . . . I filled it the night before."

"So you had used it once?"

"That's right. I would say, it felt about half full."

"Thank you. No further questions."

She walked right by me, and we made the briefest eye contact. I smiled, but she looked away, raising her chin.

Two ceiling fans were slicing the stale air; smaller electrical fans sat here and there, whirring futilely. My shirt under my suitcoat was sticking to me like flypaper. But the next two witnesses—native police officers in full regalia, except for the bayonets—took the stand looking cooler than a milk shake.

Both men told painfully similar stories of their various duties at Westbourne the morning and afternoon of the body's discovery. They spoke in a curious mixture of Caribbean and British inflection; neither man seemed nervous, but their stony demeanor underscored the coached nature of their testimony.

"I saw de Marigny upstairs with Captain Melchen at three-thirty p.m.," they both said.

This was on July 9; that morning, the scorched Chinese screen had been moved from Sir Harry's bedchamber out into the hall, where Miami's finest had done some fingerprint work.

"Captain Barker had finished his fingerprint processing by that time," they both said.

Over at the press table, Gardner glanced at me and frowned; I did the same to him. We both knew something was up. So did Freddie: behind the bars of his cage, he was frowning, shaking his head slowly.

Nancy de Marigny shook her head the same way, hearing my

account of the Tweedledum and Tweedledee testimony of the officers. We were meeting over the lunch break in the dining room of the British Colonial, sharing a table with her friend Lady Diane Medcalf.

"What are they up to?" Nancy wondered aloud. She looked as charming as a lovely child in her plain white sports dress and wide-brimmed straw hat tied in place by a white silk scarf.

"No good," Di said needlessly, arching a brow as she lifted a gin and tonic to her bruised red lips. She did not look like a lovely child, in her vivid-blue clingy crepe dress, big silver medallion buttons like a row of medals in a vertical ribbon between her full breasts. She wore white gloves and a white turban, which hid most of her blondness.

Between steaming spoonfuls of conch chowder, I said, "My guess is that the fingerprint evidence we've been hearing about comes from that screen."

"So what if it does?" Nancy asked, almost petulantly.

"So," I said, "they have to establish that Freddie couldn't have touched that screen while he was in the house being questioned."

Di frowned with interest. "What time does Freddie say he was taken upstairs for questioning?"

I got my notebook out and checked it. "More like eleven-thirty that morning."

Nancy sat forward. "Can we trip them up?"

I nodded. "If Freddie's story is backed up by some of these other witnesses who were also at Westbourne being questioned at the time—like those RAF dames, for instance—we can trip 'em up Duke of Windsor style."

"Duke of Windsor style?" Nancy asked, puzzled.

"Royally," I grinned.

Di was still frowning. "Why were those women taken to Westbourne for questioning, instead of the police station?"

I shrugged. "That was the Miami boys' doing. Sometimes it comes in handy when the bad guys are idiots." I looked at Di and smiled. "And that party you're throwing this weekend is going to be very helpful, too—*if* the guest list shows."

"They'll show," she said with a wicked little smile. She curled a gloved finger at a black waiter, summoning another gin and tonic.

"You know," I said, smirking at Nancy, "I feel kind of funny coming back to the B.C., having been so recently banished and all."

"Is the guest room at Higgs' suiting you?" she asked, with earnest concern.

"It's okay. I'm afraid I'm getting on the nerves of his wife and kids."

Under the table, I felt a hand on my leg.

"I have a guest cottage," Lady Diane said, ever so casually, "at Shangri La . . . if you don't mind the inconvenience of having to take a five-minute ride by launch every time you're coming and going."

With her hand on my leg like that, I'd be coming before I was going.

"That's very gracious," I said, "but I'm afraid you'd be the one who'd be inconvenienced. . . ."

She squeezed my thigh; it was more friendly than sexy, but it was sexy enough.

"Nonsense," she said, in her brittle British way. "You'd be welcome company."

"Well . . ."

"I think it's a simply fabulous idea," Nancy said, eyes sparkling. "I spend half my time over there with Di, anyway. So we could have planning sessions and talk strategy."

The hand beneath the table slipped away.

"All right," I said, and looked at Lady Diane, narrowing my eyes and sending a signal. "I'll be glad to come."

"How delightful," Di said, and those Bahama-blue eyes locked onto mine and sent their own signal.

"Besides," I said, "I know all about how no one in Nassau can dare refuse your invitation."

She laughed a little, then stopped cold to pluck her latest gin and tonic from the hands of the waiter, who seemed a little startled to have his cargo snatched so rudely away.

Nancy leaned in. "Who else do you think will testify today, Nate?"

"To keep the chronology at all coherent," I said, "there's only one man Adderley can call. . . ."

Harold Christie clutched the rail around the witness box till his knuckles went as white as his double-breasted linen suit. As he gave his testimony, the little balding lizard of a man swayed from side to side, as if his balance were constantly at risk.

After establishing that Christie had been a real-estate agent in Nassau for about twenty years, Adderley asked him to describe his relationship with the deceased.

"I considered Sir Harry one of my closest personal friends," Christie said, but prosecution witness or not, his tone was defensive.

Nonetheless, his story of the day—and night—of the murder was a dull, rambling recap of his previous statements: tennis at the country club in the afternoon, dinner at Westbourne with a few guests, Chinese checkers until eleven o'clock when Mr. Hubbard and Mrs. Henneage departed, after which he and Sir Harry went up to bed.

He'd chatted with Sir Harry in the latter's bedroom, and Oakes was in bed, in his pajamas, reading a newspaper, when Christie went to his own bedroom, to read for half an hour or so himself.

Under Adderley's respectful, even fawning questioning, Christie gradually calmed down. In a firm, natural voice, he told of waking up twice in the night—once to swat some mosquitoes that had gotten under his netting, another time because of the "strong wind and heavy rain." But he'd heard nothing from Harry's room, nor had he smelled smoke.

The next morning, when Sir Harry wasn't waiting on the porch, where they usually breakfasted, Christie claimed to have called out, "Hi, Harry," as he went into the bedroom, only to find his friend—scorched and sooty—on the still smoldering bed.

"I lifted his head, shook him, poured some water into the glass on the night table, and put the glass to his mouth." He reached in his back pocket and began swabbing the sweat beading on the shiny dome of his head. "I took a pillow from the other twin bed, propped his head up, got a towel, wet it and wiped his face, hoping to revive him."

Behind the iron bars, de Marigny's expression was incredulous; he looked over at me, for the first time, and I shrugged at him. I'd been at the crime scene, and de Marigny—like everyone here—had seen the large blowups of the charred body.

The notion that anyone could have mistaken the corpse of Sir Harry Oakes for a living person seemed like something out of Lewis Carroll.

But something else was gnawing at me, as well: why in the hell would Christie—why in the hell would *anybody*—go to such great lengths to insist he was within eighteen feet of the scene of the crime, *during* the crime?

Before long, the preening Adderley, enjoying the booming British sound of his own voice as it filled the little courtroom, asked Christie, "And are you acquainted, sir, with the accused, de Marigny?"

Christie, shifting yet again in the witness box, one foot to the other, nodded. "I am. I think I've known him since he first came here."

"What was your most recent encounter with the accused?"

"About two weeks ago, he enlisted my services in connection with selling property of his on Eleuthera. He said he had considerable expenses to meet."

"Did Sir Harry Oakes' name come up in your conversation, sir?"

"It did. He stated that he and Sir Harry were not on friendly terms."

"Did he state a reason?"

"No, but I think perhaps there were a number of reasons. I think Sir Harry felt de Marigny had treated his former wife, Ruth Fahnestock de Marigny, unfairly—"

"Objection, my lord," Higgs said, rising, his tone one of weary patience.

"Withdrawn," Adderley said, and smiled condescendingly at Higgs, then turned back to his witness. "Could you limit yourself, sir, not to your own opinions, but those expressed to you by the accused, on that occasion?"

Christie nodded again. "At the time, he told me that Sir Harry had not treated him fairly, since his marriage to Miss Nancy Oakes. That Harry had been unduly severe."

"I see. And this was the last time you spoke to de Marigny, before the murder of Sir Harry Oakes?"

"No. That was the last time I *saw* de Marigny. I spoke to him on the phone, the morning of the seventh."

"The day of the night of the murder?" Adderley asked, with pompous melodrama.

"Yes," he said. "De Marigny called me about helping him obtain a permit for his poultry business."

"Did the accused, at that time, invite you to have dinner at his home on Victoria Avenue on the night of the seventh?"

"No, he did not."

"Could he have asked you . . . casually? Is it possible you may simply not recall an offhand invitation of his?"

"If de Marigny had invited me, I would have remembered it."

De Marigny's face was almost pressed into the iron bars; his frown was pressed just as deeply into his flesh. Christie was directly contradicting de Marigny's statement to the police.

What followed was a description of Christie calling out to Marjorie Bristol from the balcony, telephoning Dr. Quackenbush and Colonel Lindop, and the subsequent arrival of the Nassau, and then Miami, police; there was no mention of communications with the Duke of Windsor, much less of the personal appearance His Royal Highness put in.

Soon it was Higgs' turn, and I was pleased to see he intended to break Gardner's first rule of English law.

"Mr. Christie . . . Were Sir Harry's eyes open, or closed, when you wiped his face?"

Christie was dabbing his own face with the sopping hanky. "I don't recall."

"We've all seen the photos of the deceased. What made you think Sir Harry might still be alive?"

"I thought he still had some hope. His body was warm."

"I should think. It had been set afire, after all."

"Objection!" boomed Adderley.

"Withdrawn," Higgs said, flashing his boyish smile at his colleague. "Mr. Christie, could you explain the blood smeared on your bedroom and bathroom doors?"

"I may have gotten blood on my hands, wiping Sir Harry's face."

"And the blood on your sheets, in your bedroom?"

He swallowed thickly, braced himself against the railing. "As I stated earlier, I awoke in the night and killed a few mosquitoes with a magazine."

"The blood on your sheets, then, came from the little mosquito corpses."

De Marigny was leaning back in the cage, smiling; he seemed more relaxed now, picking his teeth with a wooden match.

"I would presume so, yes," Christie said, fingering his black four-in-hand tie nervously. Another fine mess.

Higgs was smiling again, but there was nothing boyish about it, now. Relentlessly, he took Christie on an excursion of the upstairs in the aftermath of the murder, showing that the little real-estate giant had no grasp of which doors had been open or closed before, or shut by him after, his discovery of his beloved friend's warm body.

"I put it to you," Higgs said, "that Count de Marigny did in fact invite you to dinner at his Victoria Avenue address on the seventh of July."

"No, sir, he did not," Christie almost shouted.

"No further questions, my lord," Higgs said, faintly sarcastic, and returned to his table.

Christie, his suit soggy with sweat, stepped down from the witness box and shambled out of the courtroom, a wreck of a witness. Nothing in his testimony had really incriminated Freddie, or anybody else for that matter—except perhaps H. G. Christie.

I smiled to myself. *If you think that was rough, Harold, wait till the trial, when we hit you with Captain Sears' tale of your midnight ride around Nassau. . . .*

The next witness was Detective Captain Edward Walter Melchen, Chief of the Homicide Bureau of the Miami Police Department—a grand-sounding title for this pudgy, crooked cop. His hook nose was swollen into something resembling a sweet potato, but otherwise no signs of the recent beating he'd taken from me were obvious.

Adderley treated his client with smarmy respect, eliciting an accurate, detailed description of the crime scene, as well as a vivid and ridiculous reconstruction of the crime, delivered in Melchen's thick-tongued Southern drawl.

"The pattern of burned areas indicates Sir Harry momentarily escaped his killer," Melchen told the court, "and staggered into the hall, his pajamas flamin' . . ."

Over at the press table, Gardner was rolling his eyes.

"Then Sir Harry gripped the railin' and tottered against the wall before his killer overtook him, and dragged him back to his room."

Higgs didn't object to this nonsense, possibly because later it might be helpful for Melchen to have gone on the record with such a cockeyed, unsupported theory.

Adderley questioned Melchen in detail about his interrogation of Freddie, during which the cop claimed the accused had shared such thoughts with him as his hatred of "that stupid old fool," meaning Sir Harry; and his similar hatred of the Oakes family attorney, my old friend Foskett, who had supposedly shown a "filthy" letter from Freddie's ex-wife Ruth to Lady Oakes in an effort to further cause a breach in the family.

De Marigny, still chewing his matchstick, seemed almost amused; and it did seem unlikely he'd say any such things to an interrogator.

After describing Freddie as "uncooperative" in making an effort to find the clothes he'd worn the murder night, Melchen established the time of the July 9 interrogation as three-thirty p.m.

Just like the canned testimony of the two colored cops.

Smelling a rat, Higgs, on cross, asked, "Are you certain of the time you led Mr. de Marigny upstairs?"

"I recorded it," Melchen said, matter-of-factly. He looked to the magistrate. "May I refer to my notebook, your honor?"

The magistrate nodded solemnly.

He withdrew a small black notebook from his suitcoat pocket, thumbed its pages. "Yes—it's right here: three-thirty p.m., afternoon of July nine."

Soon the final witness of the day strode to the box—tall, Hollywood-handsome Captain James Barker, Supervisor of the Criminal Laboratories of the Miami PD—looking none the worse for wear from our recent difference of opinion. On his heels were two grandly uniformed colored cops who carried in the scorched cream-color Chinese screen, which they placed to the right of the magistrate's bench.

Even from this angle, I could see that behind the passive mask of his face, Higgs knew that the Chinese screen was an ominous intruder upon these proceedings.

And I knew immediately why it was a silent, dual witness as Adderley led Barker through an endless, and, frankly, impressive recital of the detective's credentials as a fingerprint expert: FBI Academy training, a director of the International Association of Identification, expert fingerprint witness in hundreds of other cases.

Barker was smooth; he had the magistrate entranced as he gave a lecture on the characteristics of fingerprints.

"With the millions of fingerprints that have been examined throughout the world by experts and scientists," he said with casual authority, "there have never been any two found alike—and from the viewpoint of an expert, I feel justified in saying, none even remotely alike."

He referred to the fifty million sets of prints on file with the FBI;

he explained how fingerprints themselves were formed ("When an individual presses his finger against a surface, small deposits of fatty substances or oil remain on the surface"); he explained the function of fingerprint powder, and the use of tape to lift a print.

On the same easel that had earlier displayed the grisly death-scene blowups, a card with a giant enlargement of a single fingerprint was placed by one of the colored constables. It looked like something out of a modern art museum.

Adderley said, "And whose fingerprint is this, Detective Barker?"

"It's the little finger of Alfred de Marigny's right hand—taken from a rolled impression after his arrest. May I step down, sir?"

"By all means."

Using a crayon and a pointer, Barker identified "the thirteen characteristics of de Marigny's fingerprints." The magistrate, the press, the gallery, even de Marigny himself, were caught up by this bravura performance.

When he had marked up the blowup entirely, each of the thirteen points indicated by lines and numbers, he removed the blowup and an almost identical blowup, already so marked, was revealed.

"And what is this, Captain?" Adderley asked.

"This is an enlargement of a latent impression of the little finger of de Marigny's right hand . . . taken from the surface of that Chinese screen."

As murmuring filled the room, with the magistrate too caught up in Barker's spell even to call order, the lanky detective moved to the screen and pointed to the extreme top of an end panel.

"It was lifted from here," he said, volunteering the information, not waiting for Adderley's prompting but seizing instead the correct theatrical moment.

"I marked the place previously," he continued. "You see, on the morning of the ninth, I raised several dozen impressions of various prints from this screen, nearly all illegible. But there was one print raised which after examination proved conclusively to be the latent impression originating on the number five digit of Alfred de Marigny."

De Marigny was no longer chewing his matchstick cockily; it hung limp in his lips as he sat forward, his face flushed.

"At what time did you raise this latent impression?"

"Between eleven a.m. and one p.m."

I glanced over at de Marigny, caught his eye and smiled; he seemed confused momentarily, then his eyes tightened and he smiled back. The matchstick went erect.

We had them. With a little luck—we had them.

Higgs hadn't made the connection that Freddie and I had. When we met in a small room in the courthouse, before Freddie was to be taken back to jail, the attorney confronted his client.

"You told me you hadn't been inside Westbourne for months!" Higgs raged, still wearing his black robe, but with his white wig off.

De Marigny sat in a chair, legs crossed nonchalantly; he was chewing his matchstick again. "I hadn't been. If I did touch that screen, it was in the morning."

Higgs frowned. "What morning?"

"The morning of the ninth," Freddie said. "That's when I was taken upstairs by Melchen for questioning. Around eleven-thirty. I walked right past that screen in the hallway."

"Could you have touched it?"

"Certainly."

"But the testimony of not only Barker and Melchen, but those two Nassau police officers, places that time at three-thirty p.m."

"Yes," I said, "doesn't it?"

Higgs looked at me with narrowed eyes. I was sitting on the edge of a desk. "What's your point, Heller? That all *four* of these police officers are lying?"

"Yes. Back in Chicago we call it a frame, counselor. Actually, a fucking frame."

"Mr. Heller is right, Godfrey," de Marigny said, his prominent lips curled into a self-satisfied smile. "But remember: there were others present when I was taken upstairs—Mrs. Clark and Mrs. Ainslie, to name two. And Colonel Lindop himself! *He* wouldn't lie."

"No he wouldn't," I agreed.

Now Higgs' irritation was gone and the boyish smile was back. "Now isn't *that* interesting."

I held my hand out to Higgs. "Let me see that copy of the fingerprint Adderley provided you."

He dug it out of his briefcase.

I studied the photo. "I thought so."

"What?" Higgs asked.

De Marigny's attention was caught, too; he stood.

"You fellas happen to notice the background of that Chinese screen? It's a wood-grain pattern—whorls, sort of. Now look at this print . . . look at the background. . . ."

Higgs took the photo. "It doesn't resemble a wood-grain pattern at all."

"It's more like a pattern of small circles," de Marigny said.

"What does this mean?" Higgs asked, puzzled.

The presentation I was about to make wasn't as elaborate as Barker's, but it was every bit as impressive.

"It means," I said, "that this print did not come from that screen."

Nineteen

So that's the infamous Axel Wenner-Gren," I said.

Tall, white-haired, hefty, blandly handsome, with a pink complexion, apple cheeks and a small white smile, the blacklisted billionaire stood leaning against an armchair, gazing at me with pale blue eyes that radiated a cold intensity.

"Yes, that's the notorious Nazi sympathizer you've been hearing about," Di affirmed in her wryly British way.

The huge oil painting in its glorious gilt frame hung over the fireplace in a round living room otherwise decorated with primitive artifacts of some kind.

Di saw me looking at the grotesque clay masks, garishly decorated pottery and gold-and-turquoise ceremonial daggers, displayed on walls and on shelves, and said, "Inca."

"Dinka Doo," I said.

That made her laugh; she put a hand on my shoulder, shook her head, making her shoulder-length silver-blond hair shimmer. "No, seriously. My employer's avocation is anthropology. He's made countless expeditions, to the remotest digs in Peru. Simply everything you see here is museum-quality."

She sure didn't look like she belonged in a museum: white silk gown with shoulder pads and silver-sequins collar that plunged to the wide matching silver-sequins waistband. She was ready for this evening's party—a dance to be held here at Shangri La, in my secret honor.

Our absent Swedish host's estate on Hog Island was a sprawling white limestone hacienda affair set against a lush tropical garden, with enough rooms to give the British Colonial a run for its money. The place was filled with antique mahogany furniture and polished silver pieces, trays, bowls, plaques, platters; the dining room I glimpsed must have been sixty feet long with a twenty-foot mahogany table.

Right now a lot of the mansion was closed off, however; as Di had explained, Wenner-Gren's staff of thirty servants had been cut to a meager seven, when he had been forced to relocate to Cuernavaca for the duration.

"That's one of the reasons why we'll have such a grand turnout," Di had told me earlier, as she'd helped me settle in at my guest cottage, which was a single room but larger than my entire suite at the Morrison back home.

"Why's that?"

"Well, I've thrown several parties since Axel's departure, but all of them were at hotels in town. This is the first opportunity Nassau society has had to see Shangri La, post-blacklist. Their curiosity will bring them around."

My curiosity, as we stood in the living room under the oil portrait's cool watchful gaze, was piqued about something else.

"Never mind the Incas," I said. "What's the story on the elephants?"

With the exception of those rooms given to primitive Peruvian artifacts, it seemed everywhere you looked was a statue of an elephant—from tiny as a beetle to big as a horse, these gold, silver, ivory and wooden pachyderms ruled the estate, trunks held high.

"It's the Electrolux symbol, silly," she said. "My boss made his fortune by inventing, and selling, vacuum cleaners, and those elephants signal his triumph."

"Oh."

"A lot of them came from the estate of Florenz Ziegfeld—he collected elephants, too."

"Ah."

"You notice their trunks are erect, every single one of them? Can you guess why?"

"They're glad to see me?"

Her smile settled on one side of her pretty face. "No, you fool. An elephant with its trunk down is a symbol of bad luck."

"So is an elephant with his foot on your head."

She took my arm and sat me down on one of two facing, curved couches that fronted the unlighted fireplace. In the Bahamas I would imagine you wouldn't light it often.

"You're in a smart-alecky mood," she said, almost scolding me; she looped her arm, bare in the white silk gown, in mine. She had been treating me like an old friend—or even, old lover—since I'd gotten here. Complaining would have seemed ungracious.

"It's just that I feel awkward in a monkey suit," I said.

I was wearing a black tuxedo that I'd rented from Lunn, the tailor kitty-corner from the B.C.

"Balls! You look elegant, Heller."

"I'm going to be mistaken for a waiter."

"I don't think so. My waiters are too distinctively attired."

"Oh, yeah—I saw that. Why in hell is the help wearing those Navy uniforms? And frankly, all those blond boys do look like Nazis. Don't you have *any* native help?"

She was shaking her head, but smiling. "You *are* bad. Of course we have native help—the boy who brought you over in the launch, for one. But our house staff wears the same uniforms as on the *Southern Cross*."

"Oh—your boss' yacht."

"Exactly. And those blond boys are five Swedes and a Finn."

"One of my favorite vaudeville acts."

"Bad," she said, laughing. "I don't know why I'm helping you."

"Actually, neither do I—but I'm glad you are."

She fixed her Bahama blues on me, serious now. "Nancy's just about my best friend in the world. I'd do anything to help her get her Freddie back."

"A true romantic."

"I am. Are you, Nate?"

"A true romantic? I don't know."

"What are you, then?"

"A true detective," I smiled.

"Well, you'll get your chance tonight," she said, looking away from me, leaning forward to a coffee table and popping open a gold cigarette box on the top of which an elephant reared—trunk erect.

"Thanks to you, Di. I do appreciate it. Very kind of you."

She shrugged, as she lighted her smoke with an elephant lighter, flame bursting from its trunk. Its erect trunk.

I shook my head. "If your friends figure out why you've invited them here—that is, to be grilled by yours truly—you may drop off the social register with a thud."

"Heller," she said, and despite the blood-red bruised lips her grin was almost mannish, "if you have enough money, you may behave as insufferably as you wish."

"Hell—I've managed that without the money."

She leaned her head back, blew smoke out through her mouth and nose, and chuckled.

I thought about kissing her, but it was too easy. And too soon. She was blond perfection; trouble was, I was still possessed by a darker girl. As impossible as that was, as *over* as that was, I was still full of Marjorie Bristol. . . .

The band in the ballroom—which with its high ceilings, Gobelin tapestries and crystal chandeliers seemed to belong in some other house—wore tuxes like mine while playing jazz-tinged renditions of, mostly, Cole Porter. Classy as hell—you could dance to it or listen to it or ignore it. My kind of music.

The guest list, I understood, ran to around fifty people: twenty couples and five singles who could bring an escort. I didn't recognize most of the people in this room—lots of older men with slightly younger wives, black tie and black jacket or sometimes white jacket, gowns and glittering jewels. The guests had names like Messmore and Goldsmith and Merryman; the Duchess of Leeds here, Sir Fredrick Williams-Taylor there. Winding among them, blond boys in blue naval-style livery carried alternating trays of brimming champagne glasses and mixed drinks. I wasn't out of place. Not any more than Marlene Dietrich in a convent.

Occasionally I spotted someone I recognized. Over at an *hors d'oeuvre* table—where cracked crab, caviar and shrimp mingled with fruit under the supervision of a tropical centerpiece—Harold Christie, in a wrinkled black tux, spoke briefly with an attractive blonde in a green gown before moving nervously on.

The blonde was Dulcibel Henneage—Effie, to her pals, and Christie's reputed married-lady lady friend. They weren't here together; he merely had a furtive moment with her before joining a group of men who were chatting and smoking over in one corner.

What the hell: time to mingle.

"Lovely evening," I said, joining her as she filled a small plate from the table of goodies.

She smiled sweetly; her blond hair was marcelled, and she was definitely too pretty for that iguana Christie. "Yes it is—we're lucky to have such a cool breeze."

"We haven't met, Mrs. Henneage, although I recognize you from your appearance at the preliminary hearing the other day."

She gave me a sharp look, though her smile didn't falter. "You must have got there early, to get a seat."

"I have connections. My name's Nathan Heller."

She put the little plate down to offer her hand for me to take by the fingertips—anyway, I hope that's what I was supposed to do, because I did—and said, "That name sounds familiar. . . ."

Then her smile fell, and her eyes went glazed and damn near frightened.

"You're the detective. . . ."

"That's right. I'm working for Nancy de Marigny, on behalf of her husband, and his attorney, Mr. Higgs."

She backed away, till the table stopped her. "Mr. Heller, I don't mean to be rude, but . . ."

"I've been leaving messages for you for days now. Could I impose on you for a minute or two? I need to ask a few questions."

She was shaking her head, no. "I'd really rather not. . . ."

"Please. If at any time you're uncomfortable, I'll just go. Why don't we go out on the patio and see if we can find a table. . . ."

Reluctantly she allowed me to escort her outside, onto the balconylike patio that overlooked, and led down to, a fountain in the middle of which a cement elephant rose, erect trunk high and spouting water; around this was an open grassy area where couples could stroll along the edges of a tropical flower garden. The night indeed was cool, the sky as clear as a sociopath's conscience. Wrought-iron tables and chairs were scattered at left and right, and there were two more tables of appetizers and a well-stocked bar with one of those blond naval cadets playing bartender—Aryan boys in the glow of Japanese lanterns. Just being here seemed unpatriotic, somehow.

We sat. She didn't look at me, instead studying her little plate of caviar like a head doc's inkblot she was trying to find meaning in.

"I suppose you want to ask me about having dinner at Westbourne, the night Sir Harry was killed. But I'm afraid there's really nothing much to say about that. . . ."

"What I want to know, Mrs. Henneage—and I mean no disrespect—is if it's true that you and Mr. Christie are . . . friendly."

She looked up sharply, and she wasn't smiling this time. "Well . . . of course, we're friends. Acquaintances."

"Please don't pretend to misunderstand my question. I don't mean to embarrass you. I'll be discreet."

She began to rise. "I'm feeling uncomfortable. One of us should go. . . ."

I touched her arm, gently. "Mrs. Henneage, Mr. Christie is going to great lengths to place himself adjacent to the murder room. His story is incredible—nobody in Nassau believes him."

She sat back down, and swallowed. "I don't think Mr. Christie would lie about something like that."

"Rumor has it he's protecting a woman. That woman is you, isn't it, Mrs. Henneage?"

"Please . . . Mr. Heller . . . I'm going to go now—"

I held my hand up in a gentle stop gesture. "If Count de Marigny is acquitted . . . and I have reason to believe he will be . . . then the police will start looking for another suspect. If you care about Mr. Christie, your alibi would prevent him from being the next innocent man to stand trial."

Her eyes were as earnest as they were beautiful. "Do you . . . do you believe Mr. Christie is innocent in this?"

"I don't know. I know he was seen driving at midnight in Nassau, the night of the murder. Was he on his way to see you?"

She frowned, but it was a hurt frown. "Mr. Heller, I'm a married woman. I love my husband. I *miss* my husband. I have children, and I love them, too."

"I appreciate that. But just answer this question: did Harold Christie spend the night of July seventh at your home?"

"No," she said.

But her eyes said something else.

"Now, if you'll excuse me, *please*," she said, starting to rise again.

"No, I'll go. Enjoy your *hors d'oeuvre*—I won't bother you again, tonight."

She smiled tightly and nodded, relief and irritation merging, and I wandered back toward the ballroom.

Damn! She was lying, but her eyes had told the truth. That son of a bitch Christie had spent at least part of the night with the lovely Effie. Which meant he wasn't the murderer, or at least, his hand wasn't on the murder weapon. . . .

As I entered the ballroom, Di was suddenly on my right, touching my arm. "Here's someone you should meet, Nathan."

She was standing chatting with a handsome little woman in white and gold, down to her gold-trimmed white gloves; her gold necklace and earrings collectively probably weighed more than she did.

Wallis Simpson looked more attractive than her photographs—what I had always taken for rather plain features were, when animated, beautiful: luminous violet eyes; high cheekbones, broad brow, firm jaw, but most of all a wide, generous smile, her lipstick startlingly scarlet against flesh too pale for the Bahamas.

"Your Royal Highness, this is Nathan Heller," Di said. "Nathan, the Duchess of Windsor."

"Quite a thrill for a Chicago boy," I said, taking the fingertips she offered, returning her smile, though mine couldn't compare.

"A pleasure for a girl from Virginia to meet up with another American," she said. Her Southern accent had a tinge of British; mannered, perhaps, but not without a certain charm.

"I've heard impressive things about your work with the Red Cross, Duchess. And a canteen for soldiers of both races. . . ."

"Why thank you, Mr. Heller. Who's been telling you these stories about me?"

I smiled. "I don't know if I should say."

The wide smile twisted whimsically. "Come now, Mr. Heller—you're among friends."

"Well, actually, it was Sally Rand."

For just a second the Duchess seemed shocked, her big violet eyes frozen; then she laughed ripplingly. Di was already laughing.

The Duchess arched an eyebrow. "How is it you know Miss Rand?"

"We go back to the Century of Progress together—where she first made fans with her fans. I was arresting pickpockets."

"She did give a charming performance for the Red Cross," the Duchess admitted, "although, frankly, I'm afraid David was a little embarrassed. But I was impressed by the funds she helped raise."

"She should be doing another benefit right now."

"Really? Where?"

"Cleveland. She opens there tonight, according to a postcard I just got from her—and I know her policy is that the first Saturday of every engagement is a Red Cross benefit."

"What a sweet girl," the Duchess said.

A description Helen deserved but rarely got.

"Diane tells me you're a good friend of Evalyn Walsh McLean," the Duchess said.

I nodded, smiled sadly. "I haven't seen her in years—but we were close, once. Close enough that I petted her pooch while he was wearing the Hope Diamond around his neck on a dog collar."

She laughed again. "Ah, poor Evalyn. How did you happen to meet?"

"The Lindbergh case."

The violet eyes narrowed. "Ah . . . she *was* fascinated by that, wasn't she? I hear from a mutual friend that she's similarly fascinated by our local Oakes tragedy."

She turned to Di, took one of her hands in both of hers.

"Lady Medcalf, I must thank you for opening Shangri La's gates once again—giving our hot little island a cool breath of sea air. You know, I keep expecting to turn and see Axel and that wonderful smile of his." She sighed. "Since Harry's death, social functions have been at a standstill. I must say, New York will be a relief."

The band suddenly shifted from its Cole Porter kick and went into a lilting waltz. The Duchess' face, already radiant, lit up.

She said, "You'll have to excuse me—they're playing 'The Windsor Waltz'. . . ."

Then she moved gracefully away, going near the bandstand to join the sandy-haired sad-eyed little man in a double-breasted white jacket and black tie who used to be the King of England.

And they waltzed, with the dance floor to themselves as the other guests looked respectfully on, two tiny celebrities smiling at each other in what might have been great love or just a practiced public pose. Either way, there was something bittersweet about it.

I turned to Di. "You had the perfect opportunity to tell her what I'm doing here."

"You mean, by saying Evalyn McLean recommended you to Nancy?"

"That's right. Don't you think the Duchess will be irritated with you, when she finds out who I really am?"

She smirked and shrugged. "I can get away with murder where

those two are concerned. I've known David longer than Wallis has, remember."

"Well, when this waltz is over, would you introduce me to 'David,' and then spirit Wallis away? I want a word with the Duke."

"You have but to ask."

"Lady Diane, why are you so good to me?"

"No offense, but it's not you, Heller: it's Nancy. I want her to get her husband back. I lost mine a long time ago, and it still hurts."

"Sorry. Where *is* Nancy, anyway?"

"She wasn't invited; neither was Lady Oakes. It's easier for you to do what you have to without those two around reminding the room about what they're all here to forget."

When the waltz was over, and the applause had died down for the Duke and Duchess, who nodded their recognition of the crowd's kindness, Di took me over to them and said, "Your Royal Highness, this is . . ."

"Nathan Heller, isn't it?"

His voice was soft, gentle.

"That's right, Your Royal Highness."

He extended his hand and I took it and the handshake was so brief it seemed almost not to have happened.

He turned his disappointed little boy's gaze on his wife. "This is the detective whom Sir Harry hired to follow de Marigny. He's working for Nancy Oakes, now."

Not Nancy de Marigny: Nancy Oakes.

Wallis winced, ever so slightly, at this news, and when she smiled at me, it was a little chilly.

"Mr. Heller and I met, but he didn't mention that fact."

I tried to smile it off. "Seemed an unpleasant topic of conversation, Duchess. Forgive me if I seem to have misled you."

"Not at all. David, Mr. Heller worked on the Lindbergh case for Evalyn McLean."

"Is that so?" the Duke said pleasantly but skeptically. "Do you know Charles?"

"Once upon a time I did," I said. "I haven't seen Slim in years."

His eyes flickered. I'd just used a nickname only Lindbergh's closest friends were privy to.

"Duchess," Di said, "Rosita Forbes has been dying to say hello, all evening."

"Oh, well, I'd love to chat with Rosita. Lead the way, dear."

And that left me with the Duke, standing to one side of the bandstand, where the musicians were taking a break while a piano player noodled Gershwin. We were standing near a potted palm and a pedestal with a bronze statue of an elephant with the mandatory erect trunk.

"Would you mind if I asked you a question, Your Highness?"

"By all means," he said, and smiled, but his eyes were cold.

"Why did you call Melchen and Barker in to handle the Oakes murder, rather than go to Scotland Yard, or just leave it to your own local police?"

He twitched another smile as he plucked a glass of champagne off the tray of a blond waiter. "Mr. Heller, we had a riot here last year—perhaps you've heard about it."

"Actually, yes," I said, wondering what this had to do with my question. "I understand natives, hired to help build airfields, discovered they were being paid much less than the imported white American laborers doing the same work. Am I close?"

"More or less. Things got out of hand, Bay Street was a shambles, a pity all the way 'round. As it happened, I was in the United States on a diplomatic mission . . . and, frankly, I was, and am, unhappy with the performance of the Nassau police in that matter. If they had been *tougher*, they might have contained the problem."

"I see."

"In addition to which, our police department does not have the proper fingerprint equipment. Captain Barker is an acknowledged expert, you know. And, frankly, the Nassau department is simply altogether too black."

He sipped his champagne.

"With all due respect, sir, Scotland Yard isn't 'too black.' "

"Very true. But this is wartime—with the transport problems we have, Mr. Heller, it might have taken weeks for a London detective to reach Nassau. I knew Captain Melchen to be reliable—he's been my bodyguard in Miami, on several occasions—and I knew he was literally minutes away."

"I see."

He smiled again, tightly. "Now, I simply must circulate. I wish you luck with your inquiries, despite my own antipathy toward the Count de Marigny."

"Your Highness—forgive me. But I've tried to make appointments to see you, and haven't gotten anywhere. Could you chat with me for just a few minutes more?"

The smile was lost in the folds of a face that for all its boyishness seemed prematurely old. "This is hardly the place for such a conversation."

"Who else but you can explain why I've been denied access to official records of those coming and going to Nassau? And why I've been stopped from searching for a blowtorch? And . . ."

"My dear fellow, you are not an official investigator on this case. Your role is to aid the defense of Count de Marigny—a gentleman who I personally find indefensible, but that's of no consequence. *Excuse* me. . . ."

He moved away, and there was no following him. Soon he was at his bride's side again, as they chatted pleasantly with Di and several other guests.

Out on the patio I spotted Christie and Mrs. Henneage, down by the elephant fountain, having a heated little discussion; she seemed worried, he was placating her. I'd rattled them. Good.

She came up the stone stairs first, while I faded into the background; but when Christie emerged onto the patio, I approached him.

"Mr. Christie—beautiful night. Speaks well of these islands of yours."

He frowned. "Yes. It is a lovely night. Excuse me."

I put a hand on his arm. "Let's just step over here and talk for a moment."

"You're hurting my arm."

I guess I was gripping it a little tight. I let go. "Sorry. Say, you remember my mentioning a fellow named Lansky, in your office last week?"

"Not really. Excuse me. . . ."

I grabbed his arm again; just as hard as before. "You're not still denying you know him, are you? I have friends in Washington, D.C., who say otherwise."

He shook free of me, then smiled perhaps the least convincing smile I've ever witnessed. "Perhaps I did run into a man of that name, back in my rum-running days." And now he chuckled just as unconvincingly. "You know, a lot of people around here prefer having lapses of memory where those days are concerned. . . ."

"I hear Lansky's Hotel Nacional in Havana is running into some trouble. Seems his dictator pal Batista is on shaky ground, lately."

"I really wouldn't know."

"Expanding into the Bahamas with gambling would be a nice way for Lansky to hedge that bet. . . ."

He sighed heavily. "Gambling will come into the Bahamas after the war, Mr. Heller. But if you think any of this has anything to do with Sir Harry's death, I'd say you're gravely mistaken."

"You mean, Sir Harry wasn't against gambling here?"

Christie snorted. "He couldn't have cared less about it. Now, good *evening*, sir."

And he moved quickly into the ballroom.

I stood in the breeze, wondering what the hell Lansky could have to do with this, if casino gambling wasn't in the picture. Of course, Christie might be selling me swampland; wouldn't be the first time for a real-estate agent like him.

By shortly after midnight, the guests had all gone home, and I'd found my way to the guest cottage that was my Nassau home, now. The cottage was one big room with bath, not unlike Marjorie Bristol's, but bigger, with a living-room area, a fancy console radio and a fully stocked wet bar. I got out of my tux and sat on the soft cushions of the wicker couch; I was in my shorts with my shoes and gartered socks on, drinking a rum and Coke of my own design, and figured the night was over. I'd already thanked Lady Diane for possibly the hundredth time.

But I'd had a few too many drinks tonight to make much sense of the various conversations I'd had. What the hell had I accomplished? Christie seemed guilty of nothing more than boffing Mrs. Henneage; HRH David Windsor actually had acceptable reasons for bringing in the Miami dicks; and Harold Christie claimed Sir Harry didn't give a shit if gambling came to the Bahamas.

"Heller?"

She was silhouetted in the side doorway.

"I'm not decent," I said.

"I know that," she laughed, and came on in, a bucket of iced champagne in her arms, two glasses in hand.

She was wearing a sheer robe over a sheer nightgown; you could see everything and nothing, the swell of her breasts, their rosy tips, sort of, a dark blond triangle between her legs, maybe. She came over, set down the bucket on the bamboo coffee table before us, and poured herself a glass.

"There was bubbly left. Want some?"

"No thanks." I raised the rum and Coke. "I'm all set."

She clinked her glass against mine, turning my gesture into a toast.

"How did you do tonight, Heller?"

"I'm not sure. Anybody indicate they were unhappy with you for having me as a guest?"

"No one dared. Not even David. I'm a law unto myself, you know."

"So I've noticed."

She smelled good; it was a familiar scent.

"What's that perfume?" I asked.

"My Sin."

Marjorie had worn that, the day we met.

I stood. I walked over to the double glass doors along one side of the cottage and studied the dark shadows of the palms and ferns. Listened to the caw of exotic birds and the roar of the ocean beyond.

Then she was at my side, touching my arm. "You look charming in your shorts, Heller."

"The shoes and garters *are* a nice touch, don't you think?"

She slipped an arm around my waist. "You've got a nice body."

I swallowed. "All the girls think so."

"What's wrong with you?"

"Nothing."

She took me by the chin and reached up and kissed me; it was a hot, sticky kiss, lipstick and booze and cigarette smell, kind of sickening and wonderful at the same time. Those soft, bruised lips of hers played my mouth like a cornet.

When the kiss was over, I said, "It's just too soon, Di."

"Too soon for us?"

"You don't understand. I'm . . . I'm not ready. I'm trying to get over somebody."

"Well, you know, my brother used to play rugby."

"Really."

"And he told me what a good coach always says."

"What's that?"

"Pick yourself up, get back into the game."

She dropped to her knees and her hand slipped inside the front of my shorts and she took me out and held me. Stroked me. Kissed me.

"Oooo," she said. "What a sign of good luck *this* trunk makes. . . ."

"I . . . I'm not sure you should . . ."

"Shut up, Heller." Stroking me. "I just love a man on the rebound."

And then I was in her mouth. And then more of me was in her mouth, and she worked me, and worked me, and worked me some more. . . .

Then I was panting like a winded runner, looking down at her and she was looking up at me smiling whitely, and it wasn't her teeth.

She stood, smoothed her robe out primly, withdrew a handkerchief from a pocket and touched it to her lips, dabbing politely, as if she'd just finished a petit four.

Then she regarded me with amused eyes.

"They say once a woman does that for a man," she said, "she owns him."

I could hear the surf crashing out there. A bird cawing.

"Okay," I said.

Twenty

~~~~~~

U nder a cloudless midafternoon sky, on the patio balcony behind the ballroom at Shangri La, a pleasant-looking if intense
middle-aged man in a tropical sport shirt, tan slacks and sandals
knelt over a hairy coconut about the size of a man's head, holding
high above it, in one tight hand, a white fence picket, its pointed
tip pointed down. Modestly handsome, with dark hair, a high,
scholar's forehead and round, wire-rimmed glasses, the slender figure seemed about to perform some strange native ritual, the picket
poised like a spear about to strike.

And then with sudden, surprising force, it did strike—only the
picket splintered, leaving the coconut intact, its hair barely mussed.

"You see!" Professor Leonard Keeler wore a triumphant little
smile. He pushed his glasses up on his nose. "And I guarantee you
the mastoid bone is stronger than that coconut's shell."

"Could *any* blunt instrument have caused those four wounds
behind Sir Harry's ear?" I asked. "What if a demented old miner
Harry screwed over in the Klondike sneaked in, and took four
swings with a pickax?"

Keeler, shaking his head no, said, "His whole damn skull would
have shattered!"

Coconut in hand, he took a seat next to Erle Stanley Gardner at one of the wrought-iron tables with a view of the elephant fountain and the brilliantly colorful tropical garden that surrounded it. Tropical birds were calling; a humid breeze was whispering.

I had run into Gardner at Blackbeard's pub, where I'd spent the morning chatting with several prosecution witnesses—Mrs. Clark and Mrs. Ainslie, as well as the American Freddie, Freddie Ceretta—who were sympathetic to the defense. All of them confirmed that they had been taken to Westbourne for questioning on the 9th of July, and all of them confirmed de Marigny's assertion that he'd been taken upstairs by Melchen at eleven-thirty a.m., contradicting police testimony placing that time at three-thirty p.m.

This was good, to say the least: all I had to do now was talk to Colonel Lindop, which I intended to do later this afternoon. If Lindop confirmed Freddie's time, we would not only cast doubt on that Chinese-screen fingerprint, but on Barker and Melchen themselves.

Wearing a Western shirt with a string tie, Gardner had sauntered up to me like a pudgy pint-sized gunfighter, surrounded by his three wholesomely pretty secretaries, the fresh-scrubbed trio of sisters to whom he dictated his daily columns as well as radio scripts and chapters in his current novel, in a suite over at the Royal Victoria. They were taking a lunch break, and I was alone in the booth, now.

"Girls, this is the dimestore detective I've been telling you about," he growled good-naturedly. "Still ducking me, eh, Heller? Don't you know every good Sherlock needs a Watson?"

"Which role do you see as yours?"

He had laughed in his gargling-razor-blades way, and I asked them to join me for lunch—I was already having the pub's specialty, the Welsh rarebit.

"Thank you, son," Gardner said, sliding into the booth next to me; the trio of smiling curly-haired girls squeezed in across from us, without a word. They were like mute Andrews Sisters.

After some food and chitchat, Gardner finally said, "Come on, Heller—give an old man a break."

He probably had all of seven years on me.

But he pressed on: "Like the used-car salesman says, you can trust me. . . . Anything you say or do that you don't want me to put in my articles, all you got to do is say so. Just don't exclude me from the fun."

"All right," I said, pushing my plate of mostly eaten food aside.

"How would you like to meet the inventor of the lie detector?"

His pop-eyed grin reminded me of a kid being offered his first peek behind the hootchy-kootchy show curtain.

And now Gardner—minus his "girls"—was spending the afternoon with me at Shangri La, as I got my first in-depth appraisal from Len Keeler on the evidence he'd been going over and the tests he'd been making.

Despite his relative youth, Keeler had indeed invented the polygraph, an improvement on a German device that measured changes in a suspect's blood pressure; Len's device also monitored respiration rate, pulse and the skin's electrical conductivity during questioning.

"Do you know what mastoiditis is?" Keeler asked us.

Gardner and I were seated at the wrought-iron table, on which were a pitcher of limeade with glasses, the splintered picket, the coconut, and various death-scene photos, fanned out like a hand of cards. In Sir Harry's case, a losing hand.

An old friend of mine via Eliot, Keeler—Director of the Chicago Crime Detection Lab at Northwestern University Law School—was more than just the top polygraph man in the country; he was also an authority on scientific crime detection in general. Including fingerprints. . . .

But the subject now was the cluster of four wounds, which the prosecution claimed had been produced by a "blunt instrument."

"To treat mastoiditis, a surgeon has to take a hammer and chisel to break through the thickness of bone," Len told us, "and even then, the thinner bones around the mastoid would tend to shatter with the impact."

"Then what could have produced those holes?"

He pushed his glasses up again. "A small-caliber gun . . . at the very largest, a .38, but *not* a .38 Special; more likely a .32."

"Were there powder burns?" Gardner asked.

"Somebody played tic-tac-toe on the corpse with a blowtorch," I said, "and you're wondering if anybody noticed powder burns?"

"You can't tell from these photos," Keeler said, fanning them out some more. "Even so, smokeless powder doesn't leave burns. As for these triangular entry wounds, bullets fired at close range tend to make larger, irregular holes because of escaping gases."

I tapped a photo of Sir Harry and the four holes in his head. "Then these are gunshot wounds—no question?"

"No question," Keeler said flatly.

Eyes narrowing with thought and Bahamian sunshine, Gardner said, "Might this old shyster offer the defense a piece of free legal advice?"

"Sure," I said. "I'll pass it along to Godfrey Higgs."

"Don't introduce this evidence," Gardner said somberly. "If you do, the prosecution will shrug it off somehow, explain it away."

"What do you suggest?" Keeler asked.

Gardner shrugged. "Let them try to convict your client for bludgeoning the deceased. If they get their guilty verdict, you'll have this new evidence in your pocket, to help get you a new trial."

Keeler was smiling, nodding. "That's a Perry Mason stunt, all right—but I agree with you. I see no advantage in contradicting their ridiculous assertion that four holes in the toughest part of the skull, an inch apart, are *stab* wounds."

"You've had a chance to go over the fingerprint evidence," I said. "What do you think?"

Keeler smirked. "I think as a fingerprint expert, Captain Barker would make a swell traffic cop. Whole sections of the room were never checked for prints—that infamous Chinese screen was carried out into the hall by three cops before it was even dusted! God knows how many grimy paws clutched that thing before Barker got around to it a day later."

"Not to mention those bloody handprints being washed off the wall," I said, "because they seemed too small to be de Marigny's—mustn't have facts muddying up the case, after all."

Keeler was shaking his head. "Unbelievable. Barker did dust some of the bloody fingerprints, you know—*before* they were *dry*, ruining 'em forever." He looked toward Gardner. "And do you gentlemen of the press realize that these Miami geniuses didn't even have any of the blood in the room analyzed, to see if it was Oakes' type?"

Shaking his head in amazement, Gardner muttered, "It's a goddamn botch."

"No," I said. "It's a goddamn frame."

Gardner gave me a doubtful look.

"Consider this," Keeler said, eyes bright. "Barker was called in as a fingerprint expert, but all he brought with him was a small portable kit—and *no* fingerprint camera."

A special camera was required for fingerprint shots, with a lens you held flush with the surface of the dusted print, almost touching.

"No *fingerprint* camera?" Gardner said. "Didn't the local boys have one he could borrow?"

"No," I said. "Of course, he could have got one from the RAF. . . ."

"But he *didn't,*" Keeler said ominously. "He just dusted the prints, lifted 'em and filed 'em away."

"Destroying the sons of bitches," Gardner said, wide-eyed.

Keeler shrugged. "In some cases, lifting 'em with Scotch tape *might* leave enough of the print behind to dust again and take a photograph . . . but Barker was out of Scotch tape, too."

"*What?*" Gardner said.

"He used rubber," I said. "And that does remove the print from its original surface—destroying it in the act of its supposed preservation."

"Anyway, it doesn't matter where Barker says it came from," Keeler said, picking up the photo blowup of the fingerprint. "There's not one chance in ten million this came from that screen—I'd swear to that on a stack of Bibles."

"Just one Bible will do," I said.

"How can you be so certain?" Gardner asked him.

Keeler stood. "See for yourself."

He led us into the ballroom, where on the same parquet floor on which the Duke and Duchess had waltzed last weekend, a cream-color six-panel Chinese screen stood.

"But isn't that . . ." Gardner began. "No, it can't be—it isn't scorched. . . ."

"I found the shop where Lady Oakes purchased the screen," I said, "and bought another. The painted design is different, but otherwise it's identical."

Len had a hand on it even now, studying the enigma of its wood-grain surface; the photo of the print was in his other hand. "I've taken samples from every nook and cranny of this damn thing . . . and every time, I come up with a print with a wood-whorled background."

I nodded. "*Not* that pattern of circles in the background of their blowup of the print supposedly from the screen."

"That pattern's either flattened beads of moisture," Keeler said, patting the Chinese screen as gently as an infant, "or a very different surface than this."

"Their print is a forgery?" Gardner asked.

"No," I said. "It's a substitution."

The writer stood with hands on hips like a rancher surveying his spread. "How so?"

I took the photo of the print from Len. "That's Freddie's right pinkie, all right," I said. "A perfect specimen they lifted elsewhere. I spoke to Freddie yesterday about this. . . ."

In his cell, Freddie had shrugged when I asked him if he'd handled anything during the interrogation.

"Well, I did pour Melchen a glass of water," de Marigny had said. "From a glass pitcher. . . ."

"Did he specifically *ask* you to pour it for him?"

"Yes," de Marigny said, nodding forcefully, then he winced with thought. "Funny. . . . Right after I poured the water, the tall one . . . Barker . . . he was standing watching from a distance. He called over and asked, 'Is everything all right?' And Melchen called back, 'Just dandy.' "

Now, a day later, Keeler was suggesting the circles in the print's background might be flattened moisture drops. . . .

"Do you realize what you're saying?" Gardner asked us, dumbfounded. "That your client's in the middle of a police frame-up, engineered by the Duke of Windsor's handpicked sleuths?"

I shrugged. "It's not news to me. I caught 'em coercing a witness a week or so ago."

Disturbed, Gardner turned to Keeler. "Professor—have you given de Marigny a polygraph test yet?"

Keeler looked at me and smiled humorlessly, shook his head.

"The court has forbidden it," I said. "Even for our purposes, let alone admitting it as evidence. They won't permit us to use it on any other witnesses, either."

Keeler grinned. "How I'd love to get ahold of Christie. . . ."

"What a waste of your talents," Gardner said almost sorrowfully.

I put a hand on the writer's shoulder. "Len's got plenty of other talents, as you've already seen. He did more burn tests on those remaining bedclothes scraps, and confirmed our conclusion that the killer stayed on the scene for around an hour."

"And, I'm afraid, destroyed a valuable piece of furniture in the process," Len said, chagrined. "I don't know why Lady Diane hasn't kicked me out already, let alone give me a room to stay in. Ah! Let me show you my latest discovery. . . ."

He walked over to the table where not long ago cracked crab

and caviar had been arrayed. Now—on its white cloth, which was dotted with strangely familiar scorched circles—there was an insecticide spray gun, and a glass jar of the sort you might put up preserves in, filled with clear liquid, its screw top off. There was also a box of kitchen matches, with a few burnt ones scattered.

"I've found something you've been looking for," Len said smugly.

"What do you mean?" I asked.

"This spray gun is similar to the one found in Sir Harry's room."

"I'd say identical," I said.

"But the flit gun couldn't have figured in the killing," Gardner insisted. "After the prosecution suggested it might've been used to set Sir Harry on fire, Higgs himself established the spray gun was found half full of 'Fly-Ded,' exactly as the maid had left it."

Keeler merely smiled as he lifted the spray gun and screwed loose the can of insecticide below, removing it, setting it on the table; then he hefted the glass jar, as if making a toast.

"Your hunch, Nate," he said, "was that the flammable material spilled on the floor, not to mention Sir Harry, wasn't a petroleum product, as has been assumed . . . but alcohol."

"Right," I said. "A gas fire would've scorched the ceiling to shit."

"And left a stronger odor behind," Gardner added.

"There are a lot of uses for alcohol in the tropics," Keeler said casually, screwing the glass jar onto the bug sprayer, "besides drinking it, or rubbing it on yourself or a friend. It's used for lamp fuel, for instance, cooking on boats, and for cleaning paint brushes . . . you'll probably find a jar or bottle or can of the stuff in any toolshed, like the one by where that construction's going on next door to Westbourne. Take those matches, Nate, and light one, and hold the flame to the end of this spritzer. . . ."

He was pushing the plunger in and I held a burning match to the mist of alcohol and it caught, burning a dull blue.

"Watch this," he said, grinning like a kid.

The harder he pumped the thing, the bigger, the longer, the blue flame; it was like a homemade acetylene torch!

"You can direct this anywhere you like," he said, "as long as you keeping pumping."

When he finally stopped pumping, tiny puddles of the still-burning alcohol fell from the nose of the thing and landed on the table and made circular scorches, the flames burning briefly, then winking out.

"I'll be damned," I said.

"There's your blowtorch," Keeler said, placing the spray gun on the table.

I took a look at it. The tip was a little blackened; I took out a handkerchief and wiped it off, clean. You'd never know it had been spitting fire moments before.

"Just screw the alcohol jar off," Keeler said, "and screw the bug spray can back on, and you have a seemingly unused flit gun."

I hefted the spray gun. "Weren't you lucky that the threads of both were the same?"

"Maybe. But if they don't fit, you can just hold on to the glass jar with one hand and work the plunger with the other. It's a little awkward, but a child could do it."

Gardner was watching with amazement.

"Erle," I said, "not a word of this in your column, now. . . ."

He nodded. Then he lifted a cautionary finger and said, "Keep this one in your pocket, too."

Keeler looked at me and nodded. We'd tell Higgs, but Gardner was right: the more the prosecution got wrong about the details of the murder, the easier Higgs could land an appeal, if he ended up needing one. On the other hand, straightening out those details in this trial wouldn't help de Marigny at all. . . .

"I have to go, gentlemen," I said. "Len, when Di and Nancy get back from Paradise Beach, tell them I should be back around seven-thirty. Erle, you want to take the launch over with me?"

"I wouldn't mind staying and chatting with Professor Keeler awhile, Heller. You mind?"

"Not at all."

Gardner turned to Keeler. "Is that okay with you, Professor?"

"As long as I get to ask some of the questions," he said. "You see, I'm a big Perry Mason fan. Nate, where are you off to, anyway?"

I was already leaving. Over my shoulder, I said, "I need to drop by Colonel Lindop's office before his shift ends at six. Even with the doubt you can cast on their fingerprint evidence, Len, I think we need Lindop's statement about seeing Freddie questioned in the morning, not the afternoon. . . ."

Within the hour I was on the second floor of the police station, where at the door of Lindop's office, I found a native painter in cap and coveralls applying the finishing touches to the name MAJOR HERBERT PEMBERTON on the pebbled glass.

"Excuse me," I said, "isn't this Colonel Lindop's office?"

"Not anymore, mon," he said. "He been transfer."

"What?"

The guy shrugged, and went back to finishing the final N.

I stopped by Captain Sears' office, but he wasn't in, either. I asked the captain's male secretary about Lindop, and his answer was chilling.

"Colonel Lindop has been transferred to Trinidad," the man said, a skinny white guy with a skinny black mustache and insolent eyes.

"Trinidad? When?"

"As of the first of this week."

"Well . . . what in hell for?"

"For now and forever," he said with quiet sarcasm, "as far as I know."

Minutes later I was at the top of George Street, bolting up the long stone stairs, above which Government House sat like a big stale pink-and-white wedding cake; halfway up the stairs was a landing where the statue of Christopher Columbus, one hand on his sword, one hand on his hip, kept swishy watch. At the top of the stairs, across a cement drive, a black sentinel in white standing before the front door's archway asked me my business. I said I had an appointment with the Colonial Secretary, and was allowed to pass.

When I opened the door with its elaborate E and royal crest inset in the heavy glass, I practically fell over a pile of suitcases, bags and trunks.

I heard footsteps echoing in the high-ceilinged foyer with its marbled wallpaper and pastel drapes (the Duchess' touch, no doubt), and the man I'd lied about having an appointment with— Colonial Secretary Leslie Heape—was striding over to me, dragging one leg as he did. A First World War injury, I'd been told.

"How did you get past the sentry, Heller?" Heape demanded loudly, frowning.

"He asked me who Babe Ruth is," I said, "and I knew."

This humor was lost on Heape, a colorless career soldier in his mid-forties whose white uniform was far sharper than its wearer.

"If you still have the deluded notion that you'll be granted an interview with His Royal Highness," Heape said, "you're wasting my time, and yours."

"I'll talk to you, then. What the hell happened to Colonel Lindop?"

"Nothing happened to Colonel Lindop. He's had a request in for a transfer for some time; the Governor put it through."

"But he'll be back for the de Marigny trial, surely."

"I sincerely doubt it—what with wartime transport difficulties, and the extent of Erskine Lindop's new duties as Commissioner of Police in Trinidad."

I sneered. "That's convenient—right before the trial opens, a key defense witness is suddenly transferred off the island onto the moon."

Heape's jaw was as stiff as his leg. "Colonel Lindop was a *prosecution* witness, and my understanding is that he's given a signed deposition detailing his knowledge of the case. His replacement, Major Pemberton, will be available for testimony."

I didn't know Pemberton, whose name I'd just seen wetly on Lindop's door; if he'd been in on the investigation, it could only have been on the fringes.

"Who's leaving?" I asked, jerking a thumb toward the pile of luggage.

He smiled faintly. "Other than yourself? His Royal Highness and Her Grace."

"What? Don't tell me *they've* been transferred to Trinidad!"

"It's their American tour."

Then I remembered the Duchess making a seemingly offhand comment at the dance at Shangri La: *New York will be a relief. . . .*

Feeling a little dazed, I said, "So, then, His Royal Highness won't be around for the de Marigny dog-and-pony show?"

"No," Heape said. "Why should he be?"

And he escorted me to the door.

Twenty-one

Under a nighttime sky that seemed a deeper blue than usual, with few stars and no moon, on an otherwise lonely stretch of beach, around a sparking, crackling bonfire glowing orange and yellow and red, swayed forty or fifty natives, arms and legs pumping as they danced around the blazing driftwood, to the beat of crude congalike drums and plaintive tuneless tunes blown on twisted conch-shell horns. Though the women wore white sarongs and white bandannas, and the men wore colorless tattered shirts and trousers, the reflected shades of flame mingling with the shadows of night made of them a living, colorful design.

From a respectful distance on the sidelines, where the coconut palms began, Lady Diane Medcalf and I watched. Like the native women, she wore white—a man's shirt and ladies' trousers; I was in white too, a linen suit under which the bulge of my nine-millimeter Browning was both uncomfortable and obvious.

This excursion to one of the out islands, Eleuthera—where at night, white men were seldom seen outside the large settlements—represented the first time I'd dug my automatic and shoulder harness out of my suitcase on either of my Bahamas trips. Maybe it meant I was a coward, or a bigot, or maybe a bigoted coward.

But whatever I was, I preferred to be a live one.

After all, some of the black men dancing around that bonfire were cutting the air with machetes about four feet long. They would dance close to the fire and seize driftwood branches from its edge and then hold them in closer, getting them burning good, after which, bearing them as torches, trouser legs rolled up, the men waded into the shallow water.

And then their machetes began to slice the air, and more significantly, slice the sea. It was as if the machete-wielding men were attacking the water itself.

"What the hell are they up to?" I asked, working my voice up and over the pounding native drums. "What the hell sort of voodoo ritual *is* this?"

Di's brittle British laughter found its way over the "music." "It's not voodoo, Heller—not exactly. This is a fish chop."

"Fish chop?"

"Those men aren't trying to cut the water, they're fishing."

And I'll be damned if they weren't: now the men were reaching in the water and coming back with silvery objects that were then tossed up on the sand. Fish, attracted by the driftwood flares held over the water's surface, were swimming up to the men and getting a slash from a machete for their trouble.

"Later the whole gang'll eat their catch," Di said.

But right now men and women alike were gyrating, twirling, leaping, in an abandoned frenzy, even as the slain silvery fish were tossed onto the beach by the flailing fishermen.

An old woman was wailing, "*Come down, Mary! Come down!*"

"They sure know how to have a good time," I said.

"I wish the guests at my affairs would loosen up like that," she said.

"I bet you do."

We had come here by motor yacht, a gleaming white vessel called the *Lady Diane*, a gift to her from the absent but ubiquitous Wenner-Gren. While no *Southern Cross*, it had a large white cabin with a bar and modern white-leather furnishings. The three-hour journey from Hog Island had been painless—cocktails and conversation and cuddling—and her colored "boy" Daniel had tied us up at a ramshackle little dock by a native village near this beach.

We were supposed to meet someone named Edmund, but he—and everyone else, apparently—had gone to the fish chop. We had followed the drums here. . . .

What brought us to this island was a story Di had told me
several days ago, in my bed in the guest cottage at Shangri La.

"Have you given any thought," she asked casually, sitting up
nude to the waist with a silk sheet covering her lap and a gin and
tonic in hand, "to the motive for Harry's murder being those fucking gold coins of his?"

Now I sat up; I was also nude to the waist, but that was con-
siderably lesser a deal. "What fucking gold coins?"

She had made an astounded, but cute, face. "Surely you know
about those! I can understand the police discarding that possibility,
considering they were busy fitting Freddie a frame, but you . . ."

"What the hell are you talking about?"

"His gold coin collection! Everybody on the island, black or
white, knows that Sir Harry Oakes was hoarding a fortune in gold
coins somewhere."

"Not everybody. I never heard a word about it. How about
Nancy? Has she ever seen any of this coin collection?"

She shook her head, blond hair shimmering. "No, but she's
never had any interest in anything related to her father's wealth.
Remember, a girl like Nancy grows up in the schools she's been
sent away to—for most of her life, she only spent summers with
her family."

I gave her a doubting sneer. "A hoard of gold coins—that
sounds like the sort of fairy tale poor people dream up about rich
people."

"I think this may be more than a fairy tale."

Patiently, she explained. She was completely oblivious to the
nudity of her large, round, tiny-nippled breasts, jiggling gently as
she spoke. I wasn't.

It seemed the hoard—sovereigns, napoleons and other gold
coins—was believed to be kept at Westbourne; Di herself had
heard Sir Harry speak of his disdain of paper money, which could
lose value overnight. At the beginning of the war, British citizens
were ordered to turn in any gold, whether coins or bullion, a request Oakes largely ignored.

"Daniel carried some interesting rumors to me," she said, referring to the young man who piloted the launch that carried me, and
other guests at Shangri La, back and forth from Hog Island to
Nassau.

"Such as?"

"Some gold coins are turning up on the out islands. Eleuthera —Abaco."

"Isn't there . . . pirate treasure around here? I mean, wouldn't doubloons and such just naturally turn up from time to time?"

"Yes . . . but these are said to be newer coins than that."

"Would Daniel talk to me about this?"

"Perhaps. But he doesn't trust outsiders. He trusts me, though. Why?"

"I'd like to get ahold of one of those coins. Talk to somebody who has one."

"I don't know, Nate . . . that could be a little dicey."

"See what you can do, Di. But you said 'rumors'—plural."

She sighed, folded her arms, covering her breasts, somewhat; there was a lot to cover. "I kind of hate to get into this . . . it seems disrespectful of Nancy's late father. . . ."

"Force yourself."

She rolled her eyes; smirked. "Okay. Old Harry had something of a . . . reputation."

"A reputation."

"Yes. I never witnessed it myself—he was never anything but a gentleman around me . . . but there are those who swear Sir Harry was a horny old goat."

"What?"

She nodded, smirking again. "There may a large group of suspects you haven't even touched upon yet: cuckolds."

The notion of an army of betrayed husbands converging in Sir Harry's bedchamber with torches seemed more than a little absurd.

"Your two rumors," I said, smirking back at her, "seem somewhat at odds, don't they? Is it voodoo, or some cheating wife's hubby?"

"Maybe both."

"Oh, come on, Di . . ."

She gave me a hard, no-kidding look. "There were rumors that when Eunice was out of town, Harry would go down to the straw market and find some native wench who'd like to make a year's wages in an evening. In which case, the voodoo-like killing begins to make sense."

"You mean, sprinkling feathers on the burning body was ritualistic repayment by some native for Sir Harry's committing adultery with his woman?"

"That is one rumor going around Nassau, yes. If indeed that's true, then that native—poor, deluded, crazed, vengeance-seeking soul or not—might have remembered the stories about gold coins, searched the house, found them, and made off with them."

"There were no signs of ransacking. . . ."

Her wicked little smile settled on one side of her face. "Does that preclude burglary, Detective Heller? And who was there to stop such a leisurely search? If you're correct about Harold Christie, he was sleeping . . . or something . . . with Effie Henneage at the time."

There could have been something to what Di was saying.

So I did some follow-up of my own. A conversation with Daniel—a shy kid barely twenty—confirmed everything she'd told me, but in a halting, mumbling manner that brought nothing new to the table.

De Marigny, in his cell, paced nervously, smoking a Gauloise, deriding the notion that Sir Harry was a ladies' man.

"The idea of that old prude chasing women is almost blasphemous," Freddie said. "In matters of sex, the old boy was positively puritanical. That's the very thing we were always scrapping about! My loose morals, and the notion that I might be 'raping' his daughter, who happened to be my wife."

"A lot of people talk puritan," I said, "and behave heathen."

"True," Freddie admitted. "But Sir Harry? Positively unthinkable."

On the other hand, de Marigny had indeed heard about the gold coin collection, though he'd never seen it.

"Neither has Nancy," he said. "It never occurred to me that this might have been the motive. Hell—I should have said something before. . . ."

"Well, there were no signs of robbery. It was a natural omission."

I could only think of one person who could help me confirm or rebut these rumors. But I didn't dare call in advance. I took a chance. . . .

The beach didn't have the ivory cast I remembered; it was more a washed-out gray under a sickle moon. I knocked at the cottage door and she seemed stunned to see me. The lushly lashed dark eyes were a little hurt.

"Nathan . . . I asked you not to come here."

My straw fedora was in hand. "I know, Marjorie. I apologize.

But you're the only person I can think of who can help me. . . ."

She began to close the door. "I told you before, I can't be helpin' you."

Like the Fuller Brush man, I put my foot in the door. "Please. I'll only stay a little while."

"If Lady Eunice sees you . . ."

"She and her daughter are having dinner this evening, at the British Colonial. A sort of meeting of truce."

She looked doubtful. "How do you know?"

I risked a smile. "I arranged it."

Her smile seemed both wary and weary. She shook her head. "All right, Nathan. Come in. But don't sit down."

I stood in the neat-as-a-pin cottage, taking in the familiar sight of fresh flowers in a bowl at the round table, where a paper-covered book was open, facedown: *Lost Horizon*.

"I need to ask you a couple of things."

She stood with arms folded, chin up, slightly; she wore the blue maid's uniform. "All right."

"Do you know anything about Sir Harry having a gold coin collection?"

She blinked, cocked her head. "Sir Harry had some gold coins, yes."

"A lot of them?"

"Well . . . he had a little strongbox."

"Like a pirate's chest?"

She nodded. "But smaller."

"Did he keep it locked away? In a . . . wall safe or something?"

She shook her head no. "He had a padlock on the chest, but Sir Harry, he kept it right out in the open; it was in his study, sittin' on a bookshelf."

"How do you know there were gold coins in that chest?"

She shrugged, almost casually. "I saw him once, counting them in his study."

"Counting them?"

"Yes . . . he'd been drinkin'. Drinkin' too much. Gold coins, they was scattered all over his desk. He was makin' little stacks of them. Little strongbox open at his feet."

"That's the only time you ever saw any coins."

"Yes."

It was possible other servants had, from time to time, seen that chest of gold, open; or that Harry, in his cups, had opened it to show to friends. So word about his cache of coins could easily have spread. . . .

"Has Lady Oakes said anything about the chest being missing?"

"No. Come to think, I . . . I don't remember seein' it on the bookshelf, though."

"I don't suppose you could ask her. . . ."

"No."

Well—I could have Nancy check on that.

"Marjorie—do you think that Sir Harry could have been the victim of voodoo? Or . . . what is the other term?"

"Obeah," she said.

"Right. Or a victim of that."

She motioned me to the table, where I sat. She went to the stove and got me a cup of tea.

"Obeah is not voodoo," she said. "It's the practice of Bahamian magic."

"That sounds like voodoo to me."

She put the cup before me, then got herself one. "Obeah is part African, part Christian—a mixture."

"That also sounds like voodoo."

"But it's not a religion, Nathan." She sat across from me. "It's a way to cure sickness, or for a farmer to protect his crop from theft or the bad weather, a way to get success in business, or love . . ."

"I could use some of this stuff."

She smiled faintly and looked into her own cup of tea. "It's *not* a religion . . . obeah is somethin' one person, a shaman, sells to another."

"Like somebody who wants somebody else dead, you mean?"

She frowned thoughtfully. "I don't think so. Obeah doesn't kill by hittin' a man in the head and settin' him on fire. Obeah kills from a distance."

"Like with a spell, or potion, you mean."

She nodded gravely. "And what motive would any black man have for killin' Sir Harry? Sir Harry, he was good to us. And only a black man would think to use obeah."

"What if Sir Harry had been fooling around with a black man's woman?"

"Foolin' around?"

"Sexually, I mean."

She looked puzzled. "Sir Harry? He loved my Lady Eunice."

"He never had other women at Westbourne? When your Lady was away, perhaps?"

"Never!"

I sipped my tea. "This is good. How'd you sweeten it?"

"Honey."

I smiled. "I wish you were calling me that."

That embarrassed her. "You should go now."

"All right." I stood. "Thank you, Marjorie. I won't bother you again—you have my word."

She nodded her thanks. "Has Curtis Thompson had any luck findin' Samuel or that other boy?"

"No. You were right, Marjorie. They're long gone."

She shook her head sadly. "Some people, some things, you just can't get back again."

I don't think she knew what she'd said till she said it, then she looked away and her eyes were moist and so were mine, and I just slipped out of there.

Now, a day later, I was standing with another beautiful woman, an unlikely escort considering, at the fringes of a native, voodoo-tinged ceremony or party or some damn thing, called a fish chop. Right now, they had stopped the music, and the musicians were holding their drums close to the flames, I guess tightening the skins that were their drumheads. As the other merrymakers swayed gently, almost sleepily, waiting for the music to start up again, a figure broke away and, trudging slowly across the sand, approached us.

He was perhaps fifty years of age, his hair and eyebrows and mustache snow-white, his skin still smooth, shirt open to the waist, trousers rolled up; he'd been one of the fishermen, but he had, thankfully, left his machete behind.

He stood a few feet away, respectfully. "I am Edmund. Do I have de priv'lege of speakin' to my Lady Diane?"

"You do," she said with a smile. "This is my friend Mr. Heller."

"Mist' Heller," he said, nodding. He had sleepy eyes.

I held my hand out and he seemed a little surprised, but shook it.

"Do you know why we're here?" she asked.

"Yes—Daniel say you're interested in de gold coin."

"That's right," she said.

"Follow me, please," he said.

Even under a moonless sky, the garish painted colors of the village huts—green, blue, purple—were obvious; the windowless, precarious-looking shacks of wood and/or corrugated metal had dried palm-frond roofs and doors made of packing-crate panels or large tin advertising signs—here Typhoo Tea, there Pratts High Test Petrol. It was a tropical Hooverville.

Edmund opened the door for us, a red Coca-Cola sign loose on its leather hinges; it was hot within, filled with the staleness of no ventilation, and I could make out the sweet stench of muggles in the air. What was it they called it here? Ganja.

But Edmund's shack was not filthy—there was a hammock, several wooden crates and cardboard boxes serving as furniture; the dirt floor was as hard as a wooden one.

"Sorry dere's no real place for a lady to sit," he said.

"That's all right," Di said. "What about the coins?"

"Just one coin," he said. "A fella from Abaco give it to me for some work I done on his boat."

"Could we see the coin?" I asked.

He went to one of the packing crates and lifted back a piece of frayed white cloth, rustled around and came back with a gold sovereign.

I had a look at it and so did Di.

"This isn't pirate's treasure, is it?" she said to me.

"Not dated 1907, it isn't," I said.

"Is dat coin worth somethin'?"

"Twenty shillings," Di said, "but I'll give you twenty dollars American for it."

"Sold."

She gave a twenty-dollar bill to Edmund and the coin to me; I slipped it in my pocket.

"This guy from Abaco," I said, "what's his name?"

He shrugged; his eyes were rheumy. Too much ganja. "Dunno, mon. Just a colored fella who need help with his boat."

"Not somebody who comes around here often?"

"No, sir."

Before long, Di and I were back in the cabin of the motor yacht; Daniel was up on the bridge, taking us back to Nassau on a glass-smooth sea. The night beyond our windows was dark. The cabin was dark. But the leather of the sofa we lay on was so white, it seemed to glow.

"Did we find something, do you think?" she asked.

"Buried treasure? I don't know."

"You look . . . confused."

"It's a look I often get. I wake up with this look."

She was lying on top of me; we were both clothed, though I had taken off my coat and my holstered gun. I might have been aboard the *Lady Diane*, but Lady Diane was aboard me.

"I didn't mean to confuse things," she said.

"It's just that this . . . voodoo stuff, and Sir Harry catting around, and stolen gold coins . . . none of this fits in with other things I know."

"Such as?"

Her blond hair was brushing my face. It smelled good.

I didn't really want to get into this with her. "Well . . . all of that involves some things and some people that are a little outside your royal circles."

She stuck her chin out snootily. "Oh? Such as?"

Okay, then. Insistent little know-it-all rich bitch. . . .

"A New York gangster named Meyer Lansky, who's got some kind of connection to the murder. What exactly, I can't figure."

"Oh. Him."

I sat up, pushing her gently off as I narrowed my eyes at her. Now she was sitting beside me, looking at me like a schoolgirl who got caught with cigarettes in her lunchbox.

"You've heard of Meyer Lansky?"

She shrugged. "I've met him. He's friendly with Harold Christie."

"Harold Christie doesn't say so."

"Well, he is. I understand Harold accepted a 'gift' of a cool million from Mr. Lansky, in return for certain services."

I mimicked her: "Such as?"

"Such as convincing the Duke and Sir Harry to go along with Mr. Lansky's plans to build casinos in Nassau and on Grand Bahama Island."

Back to square one!

"Is it possible," I asked, "that Sir Harry would have balked at that prospect?"

"Very possible. I would say probable. Harry didn't much care for tourists—and the casinos, and modern resort hotels that would make stiff competition for his B.C., would've gone up in his very neighborhood. Right on Cable Beach."

"But I understand Sir Harry didn't have the power to block the casinos. . . ."

That made her smile. "Sir Harry and Harold Christie were in

all sorts of financial beds together. The Duke, too. I think to underestimate Harry's power in that regard would have been a serious miscalculation."

Now we really were back to square one: who needed gold-stealing voodoo-killer cuckolds with Harold Christie around? Or had Christie hired some native to perform a ritualistic-style killing? Or had those two Lansky goons, at Christie's behest, tried to leave a misleading obeah-style calling card?

Whatever the case, we were back to a Harold Christie who was so tied to Sir Harry Oakes that the only way to get around him was to remove him.

She was still smiling, but more pleased than amused, now. "Heller—suddenly you don't look so confused."

She began unbuttoning her blouse. She undid her artillery-shells bra and unleashed those impossible breasts, round, firm, tiny coral tips inviting kisses; my mouth accepted the invitation.

"What about Daniel?" I asked, as she loomed over me.

The bridge was closed off, but he was right up a few steps, on the other side of the door.

"Let him get his own girl," she said, stepping out of her slacks, then her panties.

The yacht's motor thrummed as she buried her face in my lap, reclaiming her ownership, and before long, in the near-darkness of the cabin, her flesh a ghostly white, she sat on top of me, grinding, head back, eyes shut, hair swaying, moving hypnotically, as lost in herself as I was, moaning and gasping and shuddering, her slim, top-heavy body undulating like a dancer on drugs, working herself to a fever pitch and animalistic cries that put those natives around the bonfire to shame.

Twenty-two

After hours in Godfrey Higgs' modest Bay Street second-floor office, his secretary long gone, the affable, athletic-looking lawyer sat behind a battle-scarred desk with his feet up, vest unbuttoned and tie loosened, jacket over the chair. His hands were locked behind his head, making wings of his arms and elbows.

He was smiling, but it was a frozen smile, a crack in his oval face; his parted-in-the-middle dark hair, usually slicked back, fell wearily over his forehead.

"Perhaps I'm no judge," he said, "this being my first major criminal case . . . but I can't imagine a better, more diligent, thorough investigator than yourself."

"Thanks," I said. I was reclining on his leather couch against a pebbled-glass-and-wood wall. His offices were not unlike those of A-1's back home. The only light came from the green-shaded banker's lamp on Higgs' desk; that, and some neon glow from busy Bay Street outside the window behind him. It was close to eight o'clock and neither of us had had supper.

"However," he began.

I groaned. "I knew there would be either a 'however' or a 'but' in there somewhere."

"*However*, very little of what you've come up with is usable, or even admissible, in court."

"Well, now, I wouldn't say that," I said, doing a serviceable imitation of Peavy on *The Great Gildersleeve*.

That made Higgs chuckle. "All right—I'll grant you your expert witness is damn near the backbone of our case . . . between what you came up with regarding the time limitations of the crime, and what Professor Keeler will have to say about the fingerprint evidence, we may well be able to clear Freddie."

"Let's not forget Captain Sears," I pointed out. "His placing Christie in downtown Nassau when Christie says he was sleeping at Westbourne diverts suspicion from our client."

"No, you're right. I shouldn't have generalized. It's just so damned frustrating that so much of what you've dug up isn't going to make it into court. . . ."

"Like what?"

He hauled his feet off his desk, brushed his hair back in place, shrugged, just a little. "The crime syndicate connection. Everything you've put together linking Lansky and Christie . . . we simply can't establish relevance."

I sighed. "If that caretaker out at Lyford Cay hadn't 'accidentally drowned,' we could."

"What we need to discredit Christie," Higgs said, "is for your friend's letter to show."

He was referring to the letter Eliot had sent me over two weeks ago, containing the certified copy of the federal records indicating that outstanding warrant against Christie; but it had not yet arrived.

And we now knew it most likely wouldn't: Eliot's letter, like any letter arriving in Nassau, was subject to wartime censorship; it seemed likely the censorship board—populated with Christie cronies—was withholding it. Contacting the censors directly about the letter was against regulations, and there was not time, before the trial, to have Eliot run the red-tape hurdles for a second time.

Higgs asked, "You haven't had any luck establishing that Sir Harry was a rounder, either, have you?"

I shook my head no. "I've asked some questions, but here's where my limitation as an outsider really hurts us. You might be better off putting a local dick on it."

He arched an eyebrow. "Frankly—no offense meant—but I have. He's come up with nothing, either. He runs into the adultery rumor, now and again, but no substantiation. And as for the gold coins . . ." He shrugged again. "Another dead end."

I had checked with Nancy, who asked her mother about the coin collection; Lady Oakes was unconcerned about its being missing, saying that Sir Harry liked to move the little treasure chest from here to there, and it would most likely "turn up" at one of their many residences—they had four homes in the Bahamas, after all, and three more in the United States, another in Canada, and two in Great Britain.

"You could ask Lady Oakes about the coins on the witness stand," I said. "She's going to testify, isn't she?"

He nodded. "I certainly could do that. But she'll only reiterate what she told Nancy—that the collection is *not* missing, merely misplaced; that, at any rate, it isn't very valuable, anyway."

"It might seem pretty darn valuable to a native."

He shrugged elaborately. "Then why didn't that native take anything else from Westbourne? There was cash in Harry's desk; valuable objects everywhere—from a gold nugget paperweight to Lady Oakes' jewelry box."

"It is thin, isn't it?"

"Yes. So the horde of gold, like Meyer Lansky, like Sir Harry's randy reputation, stays out of court. On the other hand, assuming Adderley doesn't spring too many surprises on us, I think we have a formidable case."

"Hell, Godfrey, all you have to do is fillet Barker on the stand."

He arched an eyebrow. "He's a damn good witness, Nate. He's no virgin when it comes to giving expert testimony."

"He's no virgin, period. Godfrey, you can nail him—no fingerprint 'expert' can justify those bullshit methods."

Higgs sighed, smiled in a less weary fashion, lifted his suitcoat from the back of his chair and slipped into it.

"My wife is waiting dinner on me. Care to stop by? The kids have been asking about you."

I dragged myself off the couch. "I won't impose. You guys put up with me enough, when I was staying with you. I'll grab a bite at Dirty Dick's."

"How's life at Shangri La?"

"Swell. I'm a Ronald Colman kind of guy, you know."

"Where's Di?"

"Oh, she had to fly to Mexico City for a few days, to confer with her boss."

He was opening the door to his outer office for me when he narrowed his eyes and said, "If you don't mind my asking . . . when did you start carrying that weapon around?"

"I thought this new suit Lunn made me disguised the fact."

"It does, fairly well. You're on shaky legal ground—would you like me to try to get you a temporary permit?"

We were walking through the outer office now.

"No thanks. I'll just plead ignorance, which is something I'm used to. If we ask permission, they'll only take it away from me."

"You haven't answered my question."

"Why am I heeled, as we say back in the States? I don't know. With Lansky involved, with Barker and Melchen beating the shit out of witnesses, with voodoo and jealous husbands and burned-to-a-crisp millionaires, it just seemed . . ."

He opened the door. "Prudent?"

"Prudent," I said.

We headed down the stairs to the street with Higgs in the lead.

"At least they're not following you around anymore." Higgs grinned. "With those practical jokes you played on them, and wild-goose chases you sent them on, I would imagine our local constabulary—and their Miami advisers—have learned their lesson."

We stepped out onto Bay Street; the balmy Bahamas breeze felt good—not hot, not cold.

"I'm not so sure, Godfrey. The last couple days I've felt like they had a tail on me again."

"Really?"

"Yeah—a couple times I've spotted a guy. Tall. White. He's good—in a car, he turns off on a side street before he gets made; on foot, he disappears into the nearest store or restaurant, and doesn't reemerge . . . but it's the same damn guy every time."

"Could be a reporter, you know. They've been streaming in of late."

"I don't think so. This one's a cop of some kind."

Higgs shook his head. "Well—with the trial coming up in a few days, it'll be over soon. This harassment will end."

Higgs nodded and headed toward where his car was parked, and I turned the other way; Dirty Dick's was just two blocks down. I'd gone half that distance when I noticed him.

Not you again, I thought, catching his reflection in a shop window.

He was across Bay Street, keeping half a block behind me; tailing me from the opposite side of the street was a good touch, but with all but a few of the stores closed, and hardly anybody on the sidewalks, painfully obvious nonetheless.

For a tail, he just wasn't anonymous enough: tall, lean, dapperly touristy in a powder-blue jacket, yellow shirt and tan pants; a long, cruel, handsome face interrupted by a nose that had been broken at least once, with high cheekbones and sunken cheeks; dark hair falling in a comma over his forehead; cigarette dangling from tight, thin lips.

I unbuttoned my jacket and crossed the street; he kept walking as if he hadn't seen me. I was walking toward him now, and when I passed him, I turned on a dime and came immediately up behind him and put the nine-millimeter's nose in the small of his back.

"Let's talk," I said.

"Why don't we?" he said, blandly British.

"The alley should do."

"It should do nicely," he agreed.

I walked him to the alley; an American sailor and a woman who was probably some RAF pilot's wife walked by arm in arm, smiling at each other. My shadow—who I was sticking to like his shadow—marched calmly into the alleyway, where I escorted him into near darkness. I could smell his lime cologne.

"Turn slowly," I said, "and stand with your back to the wall."

But he didn't turn slowly—he whirled, and then his hand was on my wrist, and the fucker flipped me.

When I landed on my ass, hard on the gravel, I was sitting up with both my hands empty. I looked up at him and he was studying me with an expression of sheer boredom. My gun was in his hand, casually.

"Do let me help you up," he said.

"Thanks ever so," I said.

He dropped my gun in his sport-coat pocket and offered me his hand and I buried my head in his stomach and rammed him up against the nearest wall.

"Perhaps I should introduce myself," he said, groaning, as I held him pinned there. I threw a fist toward his midsection and a hand gripped my wrist and stopped me.

"I'm . . . an agent with His Majesty's Royal Naval Intelligence," he said. "So let's dispense with the foreplay, and get right to the intercourse—shall we?"

I backed away, breathing hard. I held out my hand. "Give me back my gun."

His smile was faint and crinkled. He viewed me as a parent might a petulant child, though he was no older than me, I'd wager.

"Certainly, Mr. Heller," he said, and lifted the gun gingerly from his pocket and held it out to me by its barrel.

I put it back under my arm. "That was a nice job of knocking me on my ass."

"Judo," he explained, smoothing out his jacket. "Those bloody Japs do know their stuff."

"You seem to know my name," I said, brushing off the back of my pants. "You got one—or just a number?"

He was withdrawing a cigarette from an oxidized gold case, tamping it down.

"Fleming," he said. He lighted up the cigarette and turned the harsh angles of his face orange. "Ian Fleming."

We took a back booth at Dirty Dick's. A steel band was banging away on the little stage, and a high-yellow native woman in a skimpy two-piece outfit was doing a dance called the limbo, which amounted to an acrobatic feat of shimmying under a progressively lowered pole held by two darker grinning male cohorts. The crowd was grinning, too, and I recognized among the faces many of the reporters here to cover the trial.

"Remarkable dexterity," Fleming said, exhaling smoke.

"She's more flexible than I am. What the hell's this about, anyway?"

"Just a moment—let's let this charming girl take our order."

The almost-pretty dark-haired waitress was white, but she wore a well-filled floral sarong and had a matching flower in her hair. She was probably twenty-five and fairly immune to come-ons by now, but she warmed to Fleming immediately, though he did nothing but bestow her a mild smile.

"Bourbon and branch water, dear," he said.

"Rum and Coke," I said.

She beamed at Fleming, fluttering elaborate fake lashes, and he granted her another little smile.

"As you may have guessed, Mr. Heller, I'm taking an extended layover in Nassau to . . . shall we say, keep tabs on the Oakes case."

"Why would British Naval Intelligence have any interest in a murder case involving civilians? Even rich ones?"

Fleming stamped out his cigarette in a glass ashtray and immediately withdrew another from his gold case and lighted up. "Well, one of the people involved on the periphery is not, after all, strictly speaking, a civilian. He's what you call a VIP—and he's in a . . . delicate position. A vulnerable position."

Now I was getting it.

"The Duke of Windsor, you mean. The ex-King with the Nazi sympathies. He's a living, breathing embarrassment to your country, isn't he?"

Fleming's smile was almost a sneer. "On the contrary—the Duke is beloved, worldwide. My government's concern is that he not be . . . misused. That he, himself, not be embarrassed."

"Yeah, right."

The waitress brought our drinks; she and Fleming exchanged smiles, hers generous, his miserly.

"I'm afraid the Duke is rather easy prey for financial operators. He's known to . . . resent the limitations of his annual allowance, particularly in wartime."

"I may bust out crying."

"The Duke also resents the limitations imposed on exchange control—limitations designed to keep British money available to the British war effort?"

"I'm afraid I don't follow any of this, let alone see how it relates to the Oakes murder."

"Oh but it does." Fleming sipped his drink; smoke curled from the cigarette between the fingers of his other hand. "You see, several years ago, the Duke entered into a partnership with Sir Harry Oakes."

"So?"

"The other partners included Harold Christie, as you might well imagine, and a certain Axel Wenner-Gren." Fleming raised an eyebrow. "Now, the Duke's friendship with Wenner-Gren has, I will admit, been a source of embarrassment for the Crown."

I shrugged. "There are those in Nassau who say Wenner-Gren got a bum rap when he was blacklisted."

He laughed silently. Then he said, "Allow me to tell you a little story about the wealthy Wenner-Gren. In September of '39, Wenner-Gren was sailing the *Southern Cross* from Gothenburg to the Bahamas. Off the northern coast of Scotland, he quite coincidentally happened to see the British liner *Athenia* as it was torpedoed by a German U-boat. He picked up several hundred survivors on his yacht, great humanitarian that he is, and wired President Roosevelt, encouraging him to utilize the 'horror of this disaster' as a basis for peace efforts with Germany. Now, we in Naval Intelligence were just wondering why the *Southern Cross*, with its many radio aerials, and unusually powerful transmitters and receivers, just happened to be in that particular spot in that ocean at that particular moment."

"That is an interesting coincidence."

"Other fantastic coincidences were to follow—the *Southern Cross* was also conveniently on hand when Allied pilots, training in the Bahamas, crashed into the sea. He rescued these pilots—but had he been watching them train? Before he was banished from these waters, Wenner-Gren liked to keep aboard his ship samples —in depth—of the various armaments manufactured by his company, the Bofors Munition Works. He also kept unusually large fuel tanks aboard the *Southern Cross*, which led to the nasty rumor that he'd been refueling U-boats."

I sat forward in the booth. "And this is the same ship that the Duke and Duchess would take little outings to America on?"

"Oh yes. Wenner-Gren would ferry the Duchess to Miami so she could see her dentist. The Windsors' favorite dessert? An immense sherbet replica of the *Southern Cross*."

"Charming."

"Isn't it? Still, there are those of us in Naval Intelligence who are just cynical enough to consider Axel a . . . bad influence on our boy."

The native band was still clanging away at their steel drums, but I barely heard them.

"Well, Wenner-Gren's in Cuernavaca or someplace, isn't he? What harm can he do now, where your Duke is concerned?"

"The harm, Mr. Heller, if indeed there is any, has to do with that business relationship I mentioned—the one the Duke shares with Christie and Wenner-Gren, and the late Sir Harry Oakes. That mutual business venture, you see, is a bank. Specifically, Banco Continental in Mexico City."

I shrugged and sat back. "So what? International finances are what you'd expect of people on that level."

Fleming drew on his cigarette. Blew out smoke, smiled mysteriously. "Mr. Heller, I am being frank with you, but there are limits on just how much I can explain. Let me see if I can put this succinctly for you. During wartime, certain practices are . . . discouraged. Such as sending money illegally from a struggling Empire to invest alongside blacklisted neutrals in a country ripe for sabotage."

"Oh."

"The Duke's involvement with Banco Continental is unfortunate—it's a rather well-kept secret, however, and I doubt the Duke even knows that Naval Intelligence is aware of it. But we are. And now, so are you."

"Why me, for God's sake?"

The waitress was back, bringing another round, exchanging smiles with Fleming.

"You mind if I duck your question? Just for a moment?"

"Do I have a choice?"

He sipped his second bourbon and branch water. "When I was nine, vacationing with my family at St. Ives, Cornwall, I was searching the caves off the beach for amethyst quartz when I stumbled onto a lump of ambergris as big as a child's football."

I wasn't sure what ambergris was, but I knew it was valuable. I should have been irritated, but this aloof son of a bitch was a good storyteller.

"Now, I knew at once I would be *rich*—I would live on milk chocolate, and I wouldn't have to go back to my private school, or indeed do any work at all—I'd found the short cut to success and happiness. But on my way home it began to melt, and soon I was a bit of a mess. My mother asked me what I was carrying, and I told her, 'It's ambergris! It's worth a thousand pounds an ounce, and I'm never going back to school!' "

He paused to sip his drink again. Then resumed.

"But my ambergris, as it turned out, was actually a lump of very rancid butter, which a supply ship had dumped off the coast. My mother was not amused."

"Neither am I. What's the point?"

"The point, Mr. Heller, is merely that sometimes ambergris turns out to be rancid butter." He smiled again, mostly to himself; blew smoke through his nose. "Wenner-Gren is your host right now, so to speak."

"I've never even met the man. Never seen him, outside of an oil painting."

"But you're spending time with the charming Lady Medcalf, are you not?"

"Yeah. She's been helpful, too."

"Has she? I wonder. What do you know about her?"

His perpetual mild amusement was starting to irritate me. I said, "She's the widow of some pal of the Duke's; she's very high up in royal society or whatever the hell you call it."

He smiled and showed his teeth now; it turned his handsome face horsey. "Diane Medcalf is the former June Diane Sims of the Blackfriars settlement in the East End of London. Strictly lower-class."

I blinked; swallowed thickly. "How is it possible she could wind up married to a lord?"

He shrugged one shoulder, gestured mildly with his cigarette-in-hand. "David Windsor gave up the throne for a twice-divorced American said to have done a stint in a Hong Kong brothel." He put out the cigarette and flipped open his gold case to get another. "Hell, man—you've seen 'Lady Diane' . . . a damn sight closer up than I have. She's a smart woman and a beautiful one."

"I still don't see how . . ."

He lighted up his new cigarette and said, almost impatiently, "She was a lowly clerk with the Royal International Horse Show, an annual event held at the Olympia in London—home of the Windsor Cup, till the abdication. At any rate, it's a year-round organizing job, and Miss Sims worked her way up to assistant manager—where she came in contact with the poshest toffs in town."

"All right," I said defensively. "So she wasn't born with a silver spoon."

"I just thought you should know who exactly it was you were . . . seeing."

I laughed. "You don't look like the kind of 'bloke' who checks a girl's pedigree before climbing in the sack with her, yourself."

He nodded agreement. "Women do have their uses . . . for release of male tension. Although Englishwomen have little appeal for me. They so seldom bathe. Or is Lady Diane an exception?"

"What exactly is your objection to Diane? Other than maybe she doesn't take enough baths to suit you?"

He waved that off with the cigarette-in-hand, making smoke trails in the already smoky air. "Oh, I have no particular objection. But you may find it of interest that your lovely friend is . . . how

would your Raymond Chandler put it? Wenner-Gren's bag woman
. . . and the Duke's, for that matter. Making frequent trips to
Mexico City, to Banco Continental, freighting currency and such.
By the way, isn't that where she is now?"

I wanted to smack the smug son of a bitch. "Even if that's true,
why the hell would it have anything to do with Sir Harry's
murder?"

"It doesn't, necessarily. But I find it intriguing that Sir Harry
himself made numerous sojourns south of the border, in the past
year or so, with serious talk floating about of his relocating from
the Bahamas to Mexico."

"I still don't see the connection."

He waved it off, cigarette trail making a lazy S. "Perhaps there
isn't any. Nonetheless, I would very much like to catch Lady Di in
some illegal act. It would be a pleasure to shut down the Duke's
activities without having to . . . embarrass him."

"Or the Crown. So why the hell are you keeping an eye on *me*?"

"I'm not, really. Lady Medcalf is my interest."

I got out of the booth. "Well, you're right about one thing: Di's
my friend. And I have no intention of helping you catch her in *any*
act."

He shrugged with his eyes, exhaled smoke. "I don't remember
asking you to."

Suddenly the native band's steel drums seemed deafening.

"Then why tell me all this?"

"Strictly to keep you informed. You see, I've already gathered
that if anyone might happen to unravel the truth of this case, Mr.
Heller—it's most likely to be you."

I just looked at him. He smiled his faint smile and raised his
glass to me.

"Do stay in touch," he said.

When I glanced back before I went out, he was chatting
smoothly with the waitress, who seemed entranced.

It was enough to make you wonder who was getting fucked
tonight.

Twenty-three

~~~~~~

O yez! Oyez!" the dark-robed little man cried, shortly after capturing the packed courtroom's attention by beating his crown-tipped staff on the hardwood floor. "God save the King!"

And the assemblage was on its feet as a short, rather stout individual in shoulder-length white wig and fur-trimmed scarlet gown took the bench. Sir Oscar Bedford Daly, Chief Justice of the Bahamas, was in his mid-sixties, though he didn't look it: streaks of black eyebrow were the sole harsh element of a face as round and smooth as a child's.

According to Higgs, Daly was fair-minded and incisive, with a reputation for cutting through red tape and red herrings alike to find the heart of the matter. Right now this pleasant-looking jurist was casting a rather benign smile on the crowded courtroom.

And crowded it certainly was: cane chairs, camp stools and wooden folding chairs took every spare inch of floor space at the center and side aisles and back of the room. Again, the wealthy had sent servants hours ahead of time to get in line and hold seats for them. Nonetheless, about half of the faces here were black, belonging to native spectators who had no intention of giving up their seats for anybody.

The morning was hot, if not particularly humid, and the buzzing of flies could be heard over the churning ceiling fans. As the principals settled into place, and English justice took care of its formalities, the only major difference between this and the preliminary hearing was the jury box, all male, all white, merchants mostly. The foreman was a grocer.

Otherwise, all else was much the same—from the two teeming press tables, including Western-garbed Gardner, who sat forward like a hungry bulldog, to the robed, wigged lawyers: boyishly handsome Higgs sitting quietly confident, albeit with the addition of his second-chair counsel, W. E. Callender, a handsome mulatto with an ebullient manner and theatrical flair; charcoal-complected Adderley, a hulking presence surveying the courtroom as if he owned it, sitting next to the dour Attorney General, Hallinan, with his long, expressionless face and tiny twitching mustache.

And Freddie? He was sitting in his mahogany cage, chewing idly on his ever-present wooden match, his suit lightweight and blue, his tie bright as a Bahamas sun. The only indications of the toll all this had taken were his paleness and the fact that somehow the lanky Count had managed to lose weight.

For all his cheerful manner—grinning, winking at acquaintances—he looked damn near skeletal.

Adderley opened the Crown's case with a lengthy and, frankly, powerful address to the court. He arranged the prosecution's sorry jigsaw puzzle of circumstance into a picture of remarkable clarity, stressing Freddie's "desperate financial condition," and his "burning hatred" for Sir Harry.

"The details of this murder," he said in his commanding, more British than British tones, "surpass by far any misdeed previously recorded in the annals of the history of crime in our fair land."

Now his voice boomed.

"Murder is murder, and a life is a life," he said, "but this murder is, as Shakespeare says, 'as black as hell and as dark as night' in its foul conception . . . a deed which could only originate in a depraved, strange and sadistic mind . . . a mind indeed which is *foreign* to the usual mind, with a complete disregard for humanity in so vile a murder which besmirched the name and peace of this tranquil land."

Nice piece of shifty work, I thought, the way he emphasized the word "foreign."

Adderley, hands clutching the front of his black robe, moved with a kind of lumbering grace, stalking the courtroom, intimidating the jury even as he wooed them. Beneath the eloquence and the so-very-proper accent was a latent brutality that gave the melodrama of his words credibility.

"Return a verdict of guilty," he told the mesmerized jurors, "without fear or favor, knowing that you will be doing the thing which will satisfy your God . . . your conscience . . . and the demands of British justice!"

He sat, heavily, craning his neck, jutting his chin.

This stirring if pompous preamble was followed by a dull recital of familiar testimony from the RAF photographers and draftsman, and from Marjorie Bristol, who looked charming in her floral print dress with pearls, but seemed a little nervous.

On the other hand, she did grant me the briefest smile as she walked away from the witness box and up the aisle.

Over the lunch break, I sat in the B.C. dining room with Di and Nancy de Marigny—again, barred from the courtroom until her testimony—a procedure I would repeat over the coming days, reporting what I'd seen and giving my views.

"Adderley was good?" Nancy asked.

"Better than good. Even Erle Stanley Gardner was spellbound. I think it may have thrown Godfrey, a little."

"He may have to lean on that boy Callender," Di said. "I hear before he went into law, he was considering a stage career in London."

Nancy was nodding. "Ernest was actually a newscaster with the BBC for a while. He's got a fabulous personality—never at a loss for words. . . ."

I'd spent enough time with Ernest Callender to know Nancy was right; but neither Higgs nor Callender was a match for Adderley's showmanship.

"Christie should be up next," I said.

Nancy smirked. "I wonder if he'll make a better showing, this time around."

"I wonder, too," Di said, arching an eyebrow. "As good as Harold is with potential land buyers, you'd think he'd be able to sell a better bill of goods from the witness box. . . ."

But Harold Christie's showing, second time around, was if anything worse: he looked as if he hadn't slept for weeks, his voice quavery and weak, requiring frequent requests from the bench for him to speak up as he gripped the rail, shifting in search of balance or comfort that would never come. If his double-breasted white linen suit with pearl buttons and his dark four-in-hand tie made him seem better groomed than usual, his flop sweat and fingering of that tie betrayed him as incredibly ill at ease.

He told his by-now-familiar tale of the murder night; he denied having been invited to de Marigny's; nothing new.

But Adderley, knowing that Captain Sears would be testifying, did his best to deny the defense one of its bombshells.

"What would you say," the prosecutor asked his witness, "if Captain Sears said he saw you out on the night of the murder?"

Christie's knuckles were white at the railing as he summoned righteous indignation. "I would say he was seriously mistaken, and should in future be more careful of his observations."

Adderley's smile was wide and dazzlingly white; he nodded sagely, turned to the jury and played to them as he spoke to the bench: "My lord, that is all!"

This tactic from Adderley may have thrown Higgs somewhat, because at first his cross-examination of this uneasy witness seemed unsure. For example, he wasted five or ten minutes exploring which end of a towel Christie had used to wipe Sir Harry's face, until Christie finally exploded with, "For heaven's sake, Higgs, be reasonable!"

Yet Higgs pressed on, in an apparent attempt to convince the jury that Christie's memory was unreliable. Fishing expeditions about why Christie had parked his station wagon in the country club lot that night, as well as whether or not the decision to stay at Westbourne was a spontaneous one, brought forth nothing. Nor did Higgs' efforts pay off to underscore the absurdity of Christie's claim that the stench of burning wasn't present until he stepped into the murder room itself.

It was frustrating to see a sharp lawyer like Higgs do so little with an already off-balance witness.

Finally Higgs found his own footing.

"Mr. Christie, did you leave Westbourne at any time that night?"

"I did not."

"Do you know Captain Sears, Superintendent of Police?"

"I do."

"You are friendly with him?"

Christie shrugged. "I'm not friendly or unfriendly. I see very little of him."

"Isn't it true you've known each other since boyhood?"

Now he swallowed. "Yes."

"He has no ill will against you, that you know of?"

"No."

"I put it to you that Captain Sears saw you at about midnight in a station wagon in George Street!"

Christie swabbed his endless forehead with a soggy handkerchief. "Captain Sears is mistaken. I did not leave Westbourne after retiring, and any statement to the effect that I was in town that night is a very grave mistake."

Higgs was pacing before the jury, now. "Would you say Captain Sears is a reputable person?"

"I would say so." He swallowed again. "Nevertheless, reputable people can make mistakes."

Higgs allowed the jury—in fact, the entire courtroom—to chew on the possible meanings of Christie's last statement before saying, "I've finished with this witness, my lord."

Over the rest of that day and extending throughout the next morning, Adderley continued to lay the foundation of his case. First came medical evidence from Dr. Quackenbush, much of which was centered on an unresolved discussion of whether or not Oakes was set afire alive or dead, based upon blister evidence. A little time—just a little—was given to the unsuccessful laboratory efforts to identify the "four ounces of thick and viscid" black liquid found in Sir Harry's stomach.

The best moment came when the Chief Justice solemnly asked Dr. Quackenbush, "How long would it take for a normal, healthy person to die?"

And Quackenbush replied, "A normal, healthy person wouldn't die, my lord."

The tension in the courtroom disintegrated into much-needed laughter, over the cries of "Order! Order!" I found it a relief that the bland Quackenbush was finally living up to the Groucho Marx persona his name promised.

The afternoon of the second day found the pretty blond Dorothy Clark repeating the story of Freddie taking her, and the other RAF wife, Jean Ainslie, home in the rain; this innocent tale gave the Crown the element of opportunity it needed.

This testimony was hardly a surprise—and, had they called me, the prosecution could have got one Nathan Heller to back that up as well—but Higgs on cross took the opportunity to punch a major hole in the other side's boat.

After establishing that Mrs. Clark had seen de Marigny burn himself lighting candles, helping explain the notorious singed hairs Barker and Melchen claimed to have found, Higgs asked, "Did you see the accused, Alfred de Marigny, taken upstairs at Westbourne for questioning the morning of July nine?"

"Yes I did."

"I put it to you—was it between eleven a.m. and twelve noon?"

"Yes, I'm certain it was."

The murmur that swept the courtroom was an indication of how damaging this testimony was. One of the prosecution's own witnesses had now established that Freddie could have left his fingerprint on that Chinese screen by touching it on the 9th of July. At the same time, this witness called into doubt the reliability of sworn police testimony.

This moment of victory was followed by hours of attack, as a succession of prosecution witnesses painted a grimly unflattering portrait of Freddie.

Dr. William Sayad of Palm Beach told of the quarrel between Sir Harry and Freddie, in which Freddie had threatened to "bash Sir Harry's head." The smooth Southerner who had gotten me into this—Walter Foskett, the Oakes family attorney—detailed various family squabbles, making Freddie look as bad as possible.

Appearing as the absent Colonel Lindop's surrogate, Major Pemberton—a proper, mustached figure with an air of authority—presented the police version of the investigation leading to de Marigny's arrest—backing up the unavailable Lindop's own deposition, which incidentally mentioned nothing about what time Freddie may or may not have been taken upstairs for questioning by Melchen on the 9th.

Lieutenant Johnny Douglas—a jaunty Scotsman with a hawklike profile, impeccable in his khaki uniform—had been assigned to stay with de Marigny, keeping him under informal guard, prior to the Count's arrest. As he and Freddie were friends, the accused had apparently let his guard down, asking Douglas if a man could be convicted in a British court solely on circumstantial evidence, particularly if the murder weapon was not found.

In his rolling burr, Douglas also claimed Freddie had said of Oakes, "That old bastard should have been killed anyhow."

Higgs handed the cross to his young second chair, Callender, oval-faced, handsome, slightly overweight but light on his feet as he asked Douglas, "You do understand the accused is a Frenchman, and that the French have different laws than the British?"

"I understand so."

The Chief Justice sat forward and posed his own question. "Were you aware the accused came from Mauritius?"

"Yes, my lord."

Callender smiled tightly. "And didn't the accused ask whether the murder weapon had been found?"

"I believe he did."

"Now, under the circumstances, wasn't it a perfectly normal question for him to ask? If a man could be convicted without the weapon?"

"Not an unusual question, no, sir."

"And did you not say to the accused, 'They are making a fuss about Sir Harry because he has dough. If it had been some poor colored bastard in Grant's Town, I would not have to work so hard'?"

"I don't recall saying any such thing."

"Don't you frequently use the expression 'bastard'?"

"I seldom ever use that word."

Callender's smile was gone; he thrust a finger at the dapper little Scotsman. "I put it to you, Lieutenant Douglas, that 'bastard' is a favorite term of yours!"

"I deny it."

"And I further put it to you that *you* were the one who said, 'That old bastard should have been killed anyway.' "

"I deny it. Those are the accused's words."

"That is all, my lord," Callender said.

An effective piece of cross-examination—but Douglas was a solid witness. Freddie looked glum in his cage, his cockiness knocked out of him.

The following day began melodramatically, even for the Oakes case: Lady Oakes, allowed to sit in the witness box, in black silk dress with black veiled hat and black gloves, spoke softly, convincingly, of the strain placed upon their family by her daughter's marriage to Count de Marigny.

She would cool herself with a palm fan, raise a glass of water to her lips with a trembling hand; it was a performance that garnered much sympathy. And, cynical though I may sound, it *was* a performance: this gaunt, teary-eyed, frail widow was not the strong woman I had met in Nancy's room back at the Biltmore in Miami Beach.

Not to mention the iron-willed broad who had got me bounced out of the B.C.

Still, I thought of the parade of witnesses designed to make a devil out of Freddie, Eunice Oakes was the weakest. She just didn't have anything to say: Freddie wrote a "horrible" letter, critical of Sir Harry, to their impressionable son Sydney; Freddie had apparently encouraged Nancy to break from her parents if they would not accept him "into the family circle."

That was about it.

Higgs asked only six gentle questions by way of cross, including: "Lady Oakes, did you ever hear the accused make any threat of bodily injury to your husband?"

"Of course not," she almost snapped.

That was the Lady Oakes I had met at the Biltmore!

"And to your knowledge," Higgs was saying, "the accused's only complaint was that you and Sir Harry had not accepted him into the family?"

"I assume so."

"My lord, I have no further questions."

The rest of that morning and afternoon, too, found the pride of the Miami Homicide Bureau, Captain Edward Melchen, standing in the witness box, fat, florid, fidgety. For several hours, Adderley led Melchen through a rehash of his preliminary hearing testimony, covering the investigation, the arrest of de Marigny, remarks about Sir Harry the accused had allegedly made.

Higgs handed the cross to his eager assistant, and Callender went for the throat almost immediately.

"Captain, what important piece of evidence did your associate James Barker reveal to Lady Oakes and Mrs. de Marigny, at Bar Harbor after Sir Harry's funeral?"

Melchen licked his lips. "Captain Barker informed them that de Marigny's fingerprint had been found on the Chinese screen."

"*A* fingerprint?"

Melchen shrugged. "He might have said 'fingerprints.' "

"Did you and Captain Barker travel together, from Nassau to Bar Harbor?"

Callender's precise British-Bahamian diction somehow made Melchen's Southern drawl seem lazy, even stupid.

"Of course we did."

"Did you discuss the Oakes case?"

"Yes we did."

"Did you discuss the discovery of this most vital piece of evidence?"

Melchen winced; he seemed confused.

"The fingerprint *or* fingerprints, Captain Melchen. Did you discuss them with your partner?"

Melchen tasted his tongue for a while; then said, "Ah . . . it never came up."

"Sir?"

"We did not discuss them."

The courtroom's surprise was evident in the wave of muttering that passed over it, and so was the Chief Justice's, as he looked up from the longhand notes he was taking.

Callender closed in. "You and Captain Barker had been called in on this case, and worked as partners?"

"Yes."

"You had traveled all the way from Nassau together?"

"Yes."

"And the first time you heard of this vital evidence, Captain Melchen, was when Captain Barker informed Lady Oakes and Nancy de Marigny of it?"

"Uh . . . yes."

"Yet Captain Barker claims to have known about this evidence since the ninth of July, the day the accused was arrested. And now you stand here, swearing under oath that you traveled with Captain Barker from Nassau to Bar Harbor, during which time you discussed the case but Barker never once *mentioned* this important fact to you?"

"That, uh, is correct. Yes."

Callender walked over to the jury and smiled and shook his head; behind him on the bench, Chief Justice Daly was asking Melchen, "Do you not now consider it strange, sir, that Captain Barker did not tell you about the fingerprint on your journey to Bar Harbor?"

"Well," Melchen said lamely, with the wide-eyed expression of a child reporting to his teacher that his dog ate his homework, "now that I think of it . . . I do remember Captain Barker goin' with Major Pemberton to the RAF laboratory to process a print they said was of the accused. On the ninth of July?"

The Chief Justice rolled his eyes and threw down his pencil in annoyance.

Callender took advantage of the moment and moved in for the kill.

"Then let us move to July nine, Captain. That is the day you and Captain Barker recommended the arrest of the accused?"

"Yes."

Callender thrust an accusatory finger. "I put it to you, Captain Melchen, that your preliminary testimony, fixing the time of the accused's questioning on July nine as between three and four p.m., was a fabrication designed to prove that the accused was *not* upstairs before the fingerprint was lifted!"

Melchen loosened his sweat-soaked collar; his smile was pained, strained. "That wasn't my intention at all—my . . . my memory was at fault on that point. It was just a mistake."

"Ah, and *what* a mistake!" Callender sneered. "And what a remarkable coincidence that you and two local constables should make the *same* mistake."

Melchen smiled feebly, and shrugged.

"Nothing further, my lord," Callender said disgustedly.

Next up was Barker himself, but the rugged-looking, lanky detective—with his direct blue eyes and dark graying-at-the-temples hair—was (unlike his partner) no easily rattled boob. He presented a professional, almost distinguished demeanor, standing casually, confidently, in the witness box, hands in the pockets of the trousers of his gray, double-breasted suit.

The Attorney General himself took the witness, and both the questions and the answers seemed too pat, too precise to me. Over-rehearsed. But the jury—despite the sorry shambling act presented by his partner, Melchen—seemed to be hanging on Barker's every expert word.

Much of the afternoon was spent establishing Barker's impressive-sounding credentials, and going back over the investigation of the crime and the arrest of the Count. Shortly after Hallinan guided Barker into a discussion of the fingerprint evidence, however, Higgs made a major play, objecting to the admission as evidence of the de Marigny fingerprint.

"This print is not the best evidence," Higgs told the Chief Justice. "The screen with the print on it is."

The Chief Justice nodded, his white wig swaying. "There should be no objection to that. Let's have the screen itself brought in, then."

Higgs smiled. "Ah, but my lord—there is no print on the screen now."

Now the Chief Justice frowned, irritation edging in on his confusion. "What more do you want than the raised print itself, and the photograph of it?"

"The print was not 'raised,' my lord, but rather *lifted* by a piece of rubber. And we only have Captain Barker's word that the print came from that screen at all—this needless destruction of the evidence in its best state has not been satisfactorily explained, and the print should not be admitted into evidence."

The Chief Justice's expression was grave. "Do you mean to imply that the prosecution's print is a forgery?"

"I do, sir."

The stirring in the gallery was broken by the Attorney General rising to protest. Hallinan asserted the reliability and propriety of lifted fingerprints, explaining that Captain Barker, called to Nassau at short notice, had not brought a fingerprint camera, incorrectly assuming one would be available at the scene.

"Could you not have sent a telegram to your office," the Chief Justice asked the witness, "and had your special camera arrive by the next plane?"

"I suppose I could have done that, your honor," Barker admitted. "But I did not."

It looked like Higgs had them, but the Chief Justice ruled that the fingerprint—Exhibit J—would be allowed in as evidence.

"Mr. Higgs, your argument speaks to the weight of the evidence, rather than its admissibility," the Chief Justice said, "and I will so instruct the jurors."

Court was dismissed for the day: it was a tie game at the half.

The following morning, Barker was back in the witness box, and Higgs sat rather placidly while Hallinan finished up with his presentation of the fingerprint evidence; his expert witness was vague about where exactly the de Marigny print had been lifted from the screen, which had been brought into court and stood to the left of the bench.

I wondered if Higgs would sic his pit bull, Callender, on this key witness. But Higgs rose from his chair and tackled Barker himself.

"You're not prepared," Higgs said in an astounded tone, even as he moved aggressively toward the witness box, "to say that the fingerprint came off the area marked in the second panel? You yourself marked it!"

"I'm certain the print came from the top portion of the panel I marked. Not necessarily the specific place marked."

"Captain Barker, step down, would you, and walk to the screen and point out the area marked in blue pencil at the top of the panel."

Barker stepped down and moved smoothly past the Chief Justice and went to the Chinese screen. He studied the top panel, looking closely at the blue line which he'd previously indicated had been made by him.

"Your honor," Barker said numbly, "the blue line on this screen wasn't made by me. There's been an effort to trace a blue line over the black line that I made myself on August first in the presence of the Attorney General."

As the courtroom murmured, the Chief Justice came down from the bench, joined by Higgs and Hallinan, who stood with Barker examining the blue line.

"I see no black pencil line," I heard Higgs say conversationally.

And Hallinan, in a whisper, said to Barker, "Look there, man —those are your initials. . . ."

Court was called back to order, the Chief Justice took the bench again, and Barker, back in the witness box, did something remarkable.

"I—I wish to withdraw what I just said," Barker almost stammered. "On closer examination I located my initials by the blue line."

Higgs, moving restlessly up and down before the jury, was smiling. No great point of evidence had been made, but Barker's confident demeanor was shattered: Higgs had him on the ropes, groggy.

"You consider yourself a fingerprint expert?"

"I certainly do."

"Have you ever, in the many cases in which you've given expert testimony, introduced as evidence a lifted fingerprint without first photographing the actual impression of that print on the object in question?"

"Certainly—many times."

"Name one."

Barker paused. Gestured nervously. "I would need an opportunity to check my records. . . ."

"I see. When you forgot your fingerprint camera, did you make any effort to get one here in Nassau? We understand the RAF has several."

"Actually, no."

"Did you wire Miami and send for one?"

"You know I didn't."

"When you dusted the bloody handprints in Sir Harry's room, didn't you know—fingerprint expert that you are—that they would be obliterated?"

"I knew it was a possibility."

"Were they in fact obliterated?"

"Yes."

"Well, did you at least measure these bloody handprints, to ascertain whether they came from a large hand or small?"

"I suppose I could have."

"I put it to you that there were other prints on that Chinese screen, which were destroyed by the humidity."

"That's true."

"If the accused was there that night, why weren't his fingerprints similarly destroyed?"

"We got lucky, finding that one print."

"Lucky? Is that the appropriate word? Perhaps you should say, 'It was a miracle that we found it.' "

Melchen, seated in the courtroom, stood; his face was green and desperate. He rushed outside, pushing aside spectators seated on folding chairs in the aisle. At the press table, Gardner stood to look out the nearby window and started grinning. Faintly, despite the churn of fan blades overhead and the buzzing flies, the sound of vomiting could be heard.

"Did it ever occur to you, Captain Barker, that the burns on the accused's face and arms could have been caused by sunburn?"

Barker glanced over at de Marigny, who sat smiling, eating this testimony up; his pale face mocked Barker.

"Sure," Barker told Higgs, "but I saw how white he was and ruled that out."

"Really. Were you not aware that the accused is a yachtsman, and constantly in the sun?"

Barker hadn't realized de Marigny's current complexion had to do with spending many weeks indoors of late—in the Nassau Jail.

"I, uh, was struck by the absence of sunburn in a yachtsman."

Higgs hammered Barker like that all day. He put Barker and Melchen's slipshod investigative practices—in particular the botched fingerprint work—under a merciless magnifying glass. He made Barker admit that he hadn't told Melchen about the print until Bar Harbor.

"Captain Barker, I would like you to look at two photographs of fingerprints lifted experimentally by defense expert Leonard Keeler from the area on the screen from which you have testified Exhibit J came."

Barker took the photographs.

"Can you explain why Exhibit J is so perfect a print—without the wood-grain markings in the background exhibited by these other lifted prints?"

"Well . . . perhaps these prints were not lifted from the same precise area as Exhibit J."

"Would you like to experiment yourself, Captain Barker? Would you like to step down and take various sample prints from the Chinese screen, in full view of the court? Perhaps you will be 'lucky' again."

"I, uh . . . don't think that would be appropriate."

"I see. There is, however, a pattern of sorts in the background of Exhibit J, is there not?"

"Yes."

"Is there anything on the background of that screen that resembles these circles?"

"No, sir."

"When you were lifting prints from that screen on the morning of July nine, did Captain Melchen bring the accused upstairs?"

"I understand that he did."

"And didn't you go to the door of the room where Captain Melchen was interviewing the accused, and ask, 'Is everything okay?' "

"I did not."

"Wasn't the accused's latent print obtained from some object in that room, possibly the drinking glass Captain Melchen asked de Marigny to hand him?"

"Definitely not!"

And the accusatory finger was thrust. "But it was after he left that room that you claimed to have discovered the print, was it not?"

"Yes."

Higgs walked away, and his voice filled the courtroom in a manner even the theatrical Adderley could have envied.

"I suggest that you and Captain Melchen deliberately planned to get the accused alone in order to get his fingerprints!"

"We did not!" Barker's composure was a memory now; he was shouting, sweating.

"Your expert testimony has never before been called upon in a case of such great public interest, has it? May I suggest that in your desire for personal gain and notoriety, you have swept aside the truth and substituted fabricated evidence!"

"I emphatically deny that!"

"My lord," Higgs said, his face solemn with disgust, "I am quite finished with this witness."

Barker was slumping in the box, his face long, haggard; he'd taken a worse beating from Higgs than the one I gave him. He walked out of the courtroom cloaked in silence—his own, and that of everyone present, a silence that spoke eloquently of its contempt.

The court was adjourned for lunch, and Gardner caught up with me as the crowd pressed toward the outside.

"The prosecution hasn't rested yet," Gardner said, "but the defense could win this without calling a witness."

"Think so?"

"Cut and dried, son—thanks to that fingerprint evidence you came up with. That was a piece of detective work worthy of Paul Drake."

"Who's Paul Drake?"

Gardner laughed and slapped me on the back. "I *like* you, Heller!"

"You're cute, too, Erle."

Gardner was right. For all intents and purposes, the trial was over: the frame de Marigny had been fitted for was obvious. The defense held the courtroom for several days, but all was anticlimax.

De Marigny himself was a strong, intense witness who told his own story well, gesturing expressively, his French accent reminding the jurors that this man was fighting for his life in a foreign land. With the help of Higgs, Freddie convincingly portrayed himself as not only a solvent, but successful businessman.

The prosecution was singularly unsuccessful in penetrating his shield of self; Hallinan almost pitifully focused on whether or not

Freddie had a right to call himself "Count," only to find out he indeed did, but chose not to, even having instructed the local newspapers never to use the title.

De Marigny's American friend Ceretta, as well as other guests at the party, testified to the events of the murder evening, including Freddie burning himself; these witnesses included teenage Betty Roberts, blond hair brushing the shoulders of her green-and-white-striped dress, her pretty smile and shapely figure making a hit with the press table.

Captain Sears was a predictably strong witness, and even Adderley's best shots couldn't budge him: he had seen Christie at midnight in downtown Nassau that night and that was that.

Len Keeler beat the dead horse that was the fingerprint issue.

Neither side called me as a witness; the defense didn't need me, and the prosecution didn't want me.

Adderley's last stand—and the only really bad moment the defense suffered, presenting its case—was a devious effort to make Freddie's pal the Marquis de Visdelou seem a liar.

The dapperly dressed Georges de Visdelou, so nervous he was shaking, had testified that at three in the morning he had, at Freddie's request, fetched his cat. But Adderley confronted him with the following from his own signed statement: "I did not see de Marigny from eleven p.m. until ten a.m. the next morning."

The Marquis responded to the forceful Adderley, "Perhaps I was confused when I said that . . . I am French, and very emotional. . . ."

Over the lunch break I had helped Higgs and Callender pore over the original de Visdelou statement; it was in longhand, and we passed the pages around over lunch at the Rozelda Hotel.

"Here it is!" I said. "That Adderley is one sneaky son of a bitch. . . ."

In court, Callender went over the statement with de Visdelou, demonstrating that the witness had indeed not seen de Marigny—they had spoken through the door!

"The statement makes this clear?" the Chief Justice asked.

"Yes, my lord," Callender said, and handed the papers to the Chief Justice.

"Mr. Adderley," the Chief Justice said sternly, his round face bunched as tight as a fist, "you gave me, and the jury, reason to believe that Mr. de Visdelou's signed statement contradicted his courtroom testimony."

Adderley rose; he cleared his throat. His usual self-confidence seemed to elude him. "My lord, I was only attempting to show that the witness did not *see* the accused from midnight on. My learned friend's statement does not contradict that—it merely says the witness *talked* to the accused."

The Chief Justice was red with fury. "I don't appreciate such a fine distinction when a man's life is at stake! Mr. Adderley, do not try my patience again."

The final witness of note was Nancy de Marigny.

Looking pale and a little weak, in a white hat and black dress trimmed in white, the dead man's daughter marched bravely to the witness box and supported her husband by way of her testimony. Her calm broke only once: her chin trembled and tears flowed as she told of Barker and Melchen's coming to the New England funeral to deliver their horror story of how her husband supposedly murdered her father. De Marigny, in his cage, dabbed his eyes with a hanky; women in the gallery wept openly.

"Mrs. de Marigny," Higgs asked her, "has your husband ever asked you for money?"

"No. Never."

"Did your husband at any time ever express any hatred toward your father?"

"No. Never."

When Nancy stepped down from the witness box, Higgs announced, "The defense rests, my lord!"

Higgs kept his closing remarks short; Hallinan, unwisely, gave the prosecution's closing. Adderley, even embarrassed, would have done better. The Chief Justice's summation to the jury was a virtual instruction for acquittal, and in particular was critical of Barker and Melchen.

After court recessed, Erle Gardner found me again, clapped me on the back and said, "Stay in touch, son!"

"Where are you going? The jury's still out!"

"Like hell it is. I'm catching a plane back to the States this evening."

Gardner was right. In less than two hours, the verdict came in: not guilty.

Cheers rocked the courtroom. The Chief Justice said to de Marigny, "You are discharged," and Higgs hugged Callender, saying "We've won!" as both their wigs flew off; nearby, de Marigny was embracing his wife, and they were sharing a storybook kiss as Adderley and Hallinan stalked sullenly out.

But the foreman of the jury had been saying something, just after the verdict, making some recommendation that got all but drowned out by the cheers. And now, as de Marigny was carried out into the street on the shoulders of a good-natured multiracial mob, to the tune of "For he's a jolly good fellow," I wondered if what I thought I'd heard could be true.

If so, this wasn't as happy an ending as de Marigny and his fair-weather fan club thought. . . .

Twenty-four

The reception for the de Marignys at Shangri La that evening
—actually, night, because it didn't get under way until after
nine p.m.—was both less formal than Di's previous party and
smaller, but far more festive and intimate. Many of the dozen or
so guests had been in court today, and none had taken time to
change from the clothes they'd worn there. The refreshments were
limited to sandwiches, brandy and coffee, and a few bottles of
champagne, liberated from our absent host's wine cellar. Di's cook
was here, and one helper, but the blond servant boys had the night
off. We were roughing it.

The little group was gathered in the circular living room where
Axel Wenner-Gren's oil-painting visage oversaw his collection of
Inca artifacts. Present were the Marquis de Visdelou and his blond
cupcake Betty Roberts; Freddie Ceretta and the attractive RAF
wives; Godfrey Higgs and his glowing spouse; Professor Leonard
Keeler; Lady Diane, of course, our hostess; Freddie and Nancy; and
myself. Also a handful of other friends of de Marigny's, who I
didn't know.

In addition—making a brief if surprising appearance—was the
man we were toasting, now.

Standing embarrassed, Curtis Thompson—chauffeur's cap in

hand, having driven his boss and Mrs. de Marigny to the Hog Island launch, and then been invited along by the ebullient Freddie—was the man of the moment, if not the hour.

Freddie lifted his champagne glass high, his other arm around his black driver, who was grinning shyly.

"Here's to my best and dearest friend!" he said. "Curtis stood by me despite the best efforts of our Attorney General and his Miami hoodlums!"

"Hear hear," Higgs said, raising his glass.

Everyone joined in (though I imagined Wenner-Gren himself just might not have relished the idea of a colored guest in his living room) and de Marigny shook Curtis' hand. Then he embraced him.

"There's no way I can repay you for the beating you took," de Marigny said, his eyes moist.

"Mist' Heller, he did his part, too," Curtis said.

"I know he did." De Marigny saluted me with his glass, and I smiled and nodded.

"Boss, excuse me now. Kitchen staff, dey may need my help. . . ."

And he was gone.

Was it my imagination, or did Di seem relieved to see him go?

What the hell—she looked lovely tonight, the only one who'd taken time to dress, in a shoulderless pink satin blouse under which the tiny tips of her cantaloupe breasts were apparent, and a short black skirt trimmed in black with matching black gloves.

She latched on to my arm. "You really pulled it off, Heller."

"Freddie's win? I think Higgs and Callender had a little to do with that."

I noticed the mulatto Callender had either not been invited or had chosen not to attend.

Her blood-red bruised lips formed a wicked smile. "Can you stay for a few days? I'm supposed to fly to Mexico City to meet with Axel tomorrow, but I could postpone if—"

"I don't think you should. I think this'll be my last night in Nassau."

Those sky-blue eyes, so elaborately framed by long brown lashes, looked genuinely sorrowful; she touched my face with a gloved hand. Leaned in and whispered, "Then we'll get rid of these people as soon as possible . . . we have things to do tonight. . . ."

My friend Leonard Keeler was in the process of finally finding some use for the polygraph equipment he'd dragged here from Chicago.

Betty Roberts had asked to see the famous machine, and then boldly stated she could "beat it." This led to much light-hearted discussion and, with a little prodding, Keeler dragged the apparatus out of his room (he'd been staying at Shangri La) and proceeded to play parlor games.

One by one the ladies present took Len's test. He would have them pick a card from a deck of fifty-two, and hold it high for everyone in the room to see but himself. Then the subject would replace the card in the deck, and Len would attach the machine's gizmos around their chests (a job I believe he relished), and on their upper arms and middle fingers.

"Now, I'll begin asking you which card you picked," he said, hovering over his precious needles and dials, "and when I guess correctly, tell me I'm wrong. That is—lie to me."

He caught them all.

Len, looking professorial in his wire-frame glasses and off-the-rack brown suit from Marshall Field's, was the life of the party.

De Marigny—who had removed his tie and stood looking very casual, a glass of barely touched champagne in one debonair hand, his other arm around Nancy's waist—called out, "Professor! Let me try that infernal apparatus. You've been wanting to have at me, ever since you arrived in Nassau."

"True enough," Keeler said. He fanned out the deck. "Pick a card. . . ."

"No children's games, Professor. Hook me up, and ask me about the murder of Sir Harry Oakes."

A moment of stunned silence was followed by encouragement from several of the guests. Then Higgs stepped forward and put his hand on his client's arm and said, solemnly, "I advise against this, Fred. You have nothing to prove to anyone."

Professor Keeler, looking sick suddenly, said, "I agree with Godfrey. These conditions are hardly suitable. . . ."

"Suppose something went wrong," said Nancy, who had turned ashen. "We're all friends here, but if word got out that you'd failed such a test . . ."

De Marigny looked at her sharply; his expression was as close to a rebuke as I'd ever seen him give her. "I have nothing to fear.

The jury found me innocent. I'm merely curious to see if this machine agrees."

There was no stopping him. Soon he was strapped up—chest cable, blood-pressure cuff, finger cup—and Keeler was standing behind him, regulating the clunky box that was his mechanical baby. The only sound in the room, besides the voices of the professor and his subject, was the scratching of three needles crawling over the rolling graph paper. The guests gathered around, trying not to crowd, but hypnotized by the thin, wavy-lined pattern the needles made.

"Is your name Alfred de Marigny?"

"Yes."

"Do you live in Nassau?"

"Yes."

"When you took your guests home, after your dinner party on July seventh, did you come straight home yourself?"

"Yes."

"Did you enter Westbourne?"

"No."

"Did you kill Sir Harry Oakes?"

"No."

"Were you in the room when someone else killed Sir Harry Oakes?"

"No."

"Do you know who killed Sir Harry Oakes?"

"No."

"Did you put your hand on the Chinese screen between the time of the murder and the discovery of the body?"

"No."

Throughout, the needles recording Freddie's blood pressure, respiration and pulse rate remained steady, never jumping.

When he finally looked up, Leonard Keeler was grinning like a kid. "What do you know—this is an innocent man."

Unperturbed, Freddie, still hooked up to the machine, glanced back to say, "I'm not sure if that's an accurate statement—you haven't asked me about my *past* life . . . and don't you dare!"

"He isn't lying about *that*, either," Keeler said, still grinning, and the room rang with laughter and cheers.

I'm afraid I wasn't laughing or cheering, although I did smile. But I was preoccupied, thinking about what I thought I'd heard the foreman of that jury say, during the first outburst of celebratory whooping and hollering. I had told Higgs, before any of us took the launch to Shangri La, and he said he'd look into it.

Right now the barrister was at my side, champagne glass in hand, his boyish face broken by a half-smile. "I guess there's no stopping that client of ours."

"Actually," I said, "my real client is Nancy Oakes de Marigny —but there's no stopping her, either."

Higgs chuckled. Then he turned somber. "I talked to Ernest just before we left. He's checking into that matter."

"I told you what I thought I heard."

He shook his head dismissively. "It's preposterous. The jury has no such authority."

"It was just a recommendation, Higgs. Christ, I'm not even sure I heard him right."

"We'll know soon enough."

"Mr. Heller!"

It was Nancy.

I went to her, smiled, raised my champagne glass to her; she smiled at me sweetly, with those lush red lips that any man would kill for, even if de Marigny hadn't.

"You're a fabulous private eye," she said.

"That's what my business card says."

"Oh, you. Listen . . . I know this isn't the appropriate time, but we simply have to talk."

"Well . . . all right."

I walked over to a corner where we found two comfortable if modern-looking chairs beneath a glowering Inca mask.

"I owe you some money," she said.

"Never mind that right now."

"You more than used up the retainer Daddy gave you."

"Not by much. Mostly I have a few expenses, but hell—you put me up at Shangri La. How often does a hired hand get housing like this?"

She touched my arm; her large brown eyes were luminous. They reminded me of Marjorie's. "This isn't over."

"It isn't?"

"You know it isn't. My father's killer is still at large. Until whoever killed Daddy is brought to justice, there will still be people who think Freddie did it."

I shrugged. "He's innocent. The jury thinks so, even Len's lie detector thinks so. And you and I *know* so."

Her eyes were getting wet. "Yes. But that's not enough. The murderer or murderers should be found. Don't you think?"

"That's how I generally prefer it, when I work a murder case."

"And Mr. Heller—Nate—my mother is still convinced Fred is guilty."

"I thought you two had reconciled."

"We're trying. But until she's convinced of Freddie's innocence, it will never be the same between us. Now that Daddy's gone, I need the rest of my family. A lie detector test isn't enough to sway her. Find out who did it."

I sighed. "I've been away from home a long time, Nancy."

Her strong chin was trembling. "You and I both know that so very much of the evidence you uncovered didn't find its way into court. Now the authorities are without a suspect."

I thought about how handcuffed I'd been in my inquiries; I remembered Lindop telling me, reluctantly, that it would be "improper to look elsewhere for a culprit, until or unless the person so charged is acquitted." Well, Freddie was free, wasn't he?

"What do you want me to do?"

She smiled firmly; gripped my forearm. "Stay on awhile. Gather more evidence if you like, but at the very least, present the rest of your evidence to the Nassau police. Tell them how Daddy actually died by gunshot, how the bug sprayer was the blowtorch, how Harold Christie is connected to Meyer Lansky, how Lansky's bodyguards fit the description of the men at Lyford Cay—"

"Whoa! Nancy. You don't have to tell me. I know all that, and more."

"Will you do it?"

I sighed again. "I'll give it a week. Same rate?"

She looked down. "Well . . . I'm afraid that might not be possible. I know it seems absurd for Sir Harry Oakes' daughter to cry poor mouth, but at this point, my funds are limited. . . ."

"Fifty a day and expenses."

Her expression melted into a smile; she kissed me on the lips. It was just a friendly little kiss, but I tell you, she would have been easy to fall for.

Her husband walked over and joined us. We stood and he was smiling, but it looked a little strained.

"Fred! I'm so thrilled. Mr. Heller has agreed to stay on."

His lips smiled, but his forehead frowned. "Stay on?"

"Yes—he's going to keep investigating Daddy's death."

De Marigny looked mystified. "Why?"

"Well . . . because somebody has to!"

"My sweet, you're probably right that the Nassau police won't investigate," he said, one eyebrow arched casually. "My guess is that they view the case closed."

"That's exactly why we have to pursue it!"

He seemed almost drowsy. "Your father's murder has twenty or thirty angles—could have been blackmail, for instance, or bad business dealings. It's the sort of case that could take forever and still never be solved."

"But we have to *try* . . ."

"I owe a debt of thanks to Mr. Heller," he said, almost as if I wasn't there, "but he *is* expensive. I don't know if we can afford him."

"He's lowered his rate," she said, almost pleadingly.

"Well, my dear . . . it's up to you, I suppose."

"Freddie," I said.

"Yes?"

"Don't you care who killed the old boy? Don't you have a theory yourself, after all we've been through?"

"I have no idea who did it," he said blandly. "It might have been Harold Christie or some crazed native or God knows who. All I know is, it wasn't me. Anyway, you must remember, Heller —I wasn't tried for the murder of Sir Harry Oakes."

"Oh?"

He slipped his arm around her shoulder; it was a gesture at once affectionate and condescending. She looked at him with wide, hurt eyes.

"I was tried for marrying Sir Harry's daughter," he said.

He kissed her forehead. "If you'll excuse me, darling . . . I should mingle with our friends. . . ."

We watched him as he made a trio of the Marquis and his teenage cutie and the three were laughing and drinking within seconds.

"Please stay on," Nancy said with quiet, desperate urgency. "I can get the money."

I took one of her hands in two of mine and pressed. "I already said I would."

She hugged me.

Higgs was coming back into the room; I hadn't seen him go. But his face was white and grave.

"Excuse me!" he said, working his voice up above the laughter and chatter. "I have some unfortunate news to share with you. . . ."

A hush settled and we all gathered around the somber lawyer.

"In the excitement, no one . . . with the exception of our keen-eyed and sharp-eared investigator, Mr. Heller . . . heard the foreman of the jury's full statement. I have inquired as to the contents of that statement. It seems that after announcing the not-guilty verdict, the foreman read the jury's recommendation that Alfred de Marigny and Georges de Visdelou be deported from the Bahamas forthwith."

Gasps of horror filled the room, and de Marigny, frowning, coldly indignant, said, "They have no jurisdiction to do so!"

"You're right," Higgs said, "and we can fight this. Unfortunately . . ."

"Unfortunately?" de Marigny asked.

"Ernest Callender did some asking around—and, while we must consider that tension runs high right now, the word is that this recommendation is one that the Governor is likely to act upon."

The Duke of Windsor would have his way after all.

"Apparently," Higgs said hollowly, "they intend to act upon violations of yours regarding the rationing of petrol."

De Visdelou looked like he might weep; de Marigny stared at the floor, a glazed smile on the sensuous lips, while Nancy hugged his arm supportively.

A funereal pall fell across the little party, and people began to drift away, stopping to express both their congratulations and condolences to the de Marignys.

Before she and Freddie left, Nancy said to me, painfully earnest, "*I* may have to leave this island—but you're going to stay! Right?"

"Right," I said.

An hour later, I was sitting on the couch in my cottage, feet on the coffee table, when I heard the key being worked in the lock of my side door; my shapely landlord, wearing high heels, panties and a nasty little smile, was bringing yet another bottle of champagne around.

"Nightcap?" she asked. She had two glasses in one hand.

"Sure." I hadn't really had much.

Di was a little giggly, but not really drunk. She sat in my lap and put her tongue halfway down my throat and nibbled my ear and nuzzled my neck.

"I travel," she said.

"Pardon?"

"I travel. Even get to Chicago, from time to time. I'll come see you. . . ."

"That would be nice. But I understand full well that we're just . . . a summer romance."

"Oh, we're more than that, Heller."

"Good. Marry me, then. Bring your money."

"You are *so* bad. You know I'm not exactly the housewife type. You'll need another kind of girl to have your babies and clean your house and load your revolvers."

"I use an automatic."

"Whatever. But from time to time, now and then, I'll show up on your doorstep, and, married or single, you'll have a wonderful time with me. . . ."

"That would also be nice."

Her giddiness disappeared and she looked on the verge of tears. "How I hate to see you go. . . ."

"I'm not going."

"Not going?"

"I can leave if you want. But I was hoping you'd let me stay on awhile."

She grinned. "I'll cancel my flight. How long can you stay? We both deserve a vacation, after the hell of these last weeks! We'll dine elegantly, we'll lounge on the beach sinfully, and we'll fuck like bloody heathens."

"Actually, I'm still working."

I filled her in on what Nancy had requested I do.

"That's a wonderful idea. But you won't get much cooperation out of Hallinan."

"I doubt I will—but I have a shitload of evidence he doesn't know about."

"Some of your best qualities *are* hidden away," she said, as she undid my zipper.

Outside the glass doors, palms were swaying; a storm was coming, but not now: now it was just warm wind, and a blonde goddess sitting in my lap, with me buried in her, hands on her slim ass, the globes of her breasts brushing my face like fruit wanting to be picked, our moans, our cries, lost in the caw of exotic birds and the music of the impending tropical squall.

Twenty-five

I saw Leonard Keeler and Di off at the seaplane dock late the next morning. Both were taking the noon flight to Miami to make their connections, Len to Chicago, Di to Mexico City. An almost cold wind whipped us; the sky was a dingy overcast gray that nearly blended with the choppy ocean, the Pan Am clipper bobbing on the water like an oversize buoy. That storm, which had been threatening to arrive since late last night, still hadn't shown.

I told Len that we couldn't have won without him and promised to buy him a meal at the Berghoff when I got back.

"When should that be?" he asked.

"A week or so," I said. Even if I kept working this case, I needed to get back for a few weeks, at least, and tend to A-1 business.

He waved and smiled as he entered the houseboat-like shed to check his bag and board the plane, while I stayed behind on the springy wharf, talking to Di, who wore a mannish tan slacks outfit with a military cut and matching turban, trouser legs flapping like flags in the breeze. Her sunglasses were black and her lipstick crimson. She managed to look both glamorous and businesslike.

"I can't believe you were able to get Hallinan to receive you," she said.

"Neither can I. But he seemed almost eager to meet with me."

"Where? At Government House?"

"No—Major Pemberton's office. It's just a preliminary meeting. Still, if I can convince them to cooperate, then Nancy isn't wasting her money on me." I touched her cheek. "You're not sure exactly when you'll be back?"

"No, but it'll be just a few days," she said, shrugging. Then she said, "Oh!" and dug in her purse for something. "Here are the spare keys to the main house—I've given the servants the weekend off, with the exception of Daniel, who'll be at your beck and call when you need the launch, to and from."

"I'll be lonely."

The bruised lips smiled crookedly, but the sunglasses made her face inscrutable. "The birds will keep you company. The kitchen's well stocked—just help yourself, and don't worry about the mess."

"Thank you. For everything. For last night especially. . . ."

She lifted her chin, mock-snooty. "I did it all for Nancy."

"All?"

"Almost all."

She kissed me; a sudden gust made us clutch each other, or otherwise risk being dropped in the drink. It turned the little good-bye kiss into something desperate, even passionate, and when she pulled away she had an oddly off-kilter expression.

"You mussed your lipstick."

"You mean *you* mussed my lipstick. I'll fix it on the plane." Her pretty smudgy mouth smiled, just a little. "Bye, Heller."

And she trudged toward the shed to check her one suitcase, a well-strapped leather affair large enough to make me wonder what was in it. Something for Axel?

It wasn't any of my business. I wasn't about to repay Di's hospitality by sitting in judgment on whatever she was doing for her blacklisted boss.

That afternoon, at the police station, I met with the long-faced Hallinan and the jug-eared Major Pemberton. We sat at a table in a small conference room, with the Attorney General at the head and Pemberton in impeccable khakis across from me. Both wore tiny mustaches and airs of British imperturbability.

"Mr. Heller," Hallinan said with a smile as small as his mustache, "you may be wondering why I granted your request for a hearing so readily."

I leaned back in my hardwood chair. "Frankly, yes. I didn't figure I was very high up on your hit parade."

Hallinan shrugged one shoulder. "You were doing your job, as was I. As was Major Pemberton."

Pemberton nodded.

"With no offense meant to Major Pemberton," I said, "I would have rather Colonel Lindop continued doing *his* job—his testimony would have been useful to us."

"As it turned out," Hallinan said, with the mildest facial twitch of irritation, "the defense didn't require that testimony to win. However, let me say that I don't consider the Crown to have 'lost'—I am satisfied that we presented the case cogently and fairly."

"Do you think Barker and Melchen's techniques were 'fair'?"

His face tightened; Pemberton glanced away.

"I was referring only to *our* practices—and, with the possible exception of Mr. Adderley's ill-conceived strategy where the Marquis de Visdelou was concerned, I believe we were indeed fair. Now, when you call and suggest you can help us find the 'real' murderer, I must say to you, frankly, that so far as I am concerned, this case is completely closed. I believe Major Pemberton agrees."

Again Pemberton nodded.

"We're prepared to call it a day," Hallinan said. "In our view, acquitted or not, the accused was the guilty party."

"Then why did you agree to see me?"

"To give you a fair hearing. You may find this difficult to believe, but I admire the work you did regarding that fingerprint evidence."

"You admire it?"

"I certainly do. Mr. Heller, the Governor may well have been right in his assessment that the Oakes case was too big for the local police to handle . . . with all due respect to Major Pemberton, our facilities *are* limited. But if I may confidentially say, the Duke's request for aid from the Miami city police was . . . unfortunate."

"That's an example of that British understatement I've been hearing so much about, right?"

Hallinan ignored my sarcasm and pressed on. "Weeks ago, I wrote to your federal CID—that is, your FBI—about my grave doubts concerning the fingerprinting procedures Barker and Melchen were following. In the FBI's view, my doubts were well founded. Barker's lifting of that print, his neglect to photograph it *in situ*, was the Achilles' heel of our case. And you found it."

"I did at that."

"Therefore," Hallinan sighed, "I feel you deserve a fair hearing."

"I appreciate that," I said. "I think you know that any statements, and evidence, that failed to point to the accused were ignored."

"I don't know that I entirely agree with that. But you indicated on the telephone that you had evidence the defense itself failed to introduce. . . ."

I shrugged. "It would have been ruled irrelevant. But once you grasp the fact that de Marigny is innocent, these facts became not only relevant, but crucial."

"De Marigny's 'innocence' is a legal judgment; it does not rule out his literal guilt." Hallinan's expression was one of cold distaste. "I consider the Count, and his amoral companion de Visdelou, to be sorry, irredeemable, reprehensible examples of humanity. I am pleased to say that their deportation is a certainty . . . deportation, or prison. We have found four drums of petrol, bearing RAF marks, in their mutual possession."

"De Marigny isn't my favorite guy in the world, either. But that doesn't make him Sir Harry's murderer."

"You would like to continue investigating the case."

"Yes—but first I'd like the opportunity to present you with evidence and theories you haven't been privy to. Would you like me to start right now?"

Hallinan waved a hand, gently dismissive. "No. What I would like is for you to put something in writing . . . nothing formal, not a statement. But a letter to me, which I can share with His Royal Highness on his return."

"I see. Without the Duke's blessing, I'm out of business."

"You are indeed. However, if your evidence is so persuasive that any man of good conscience could not stand in the way of reopening this investigation, I would say your 'business' might well flourish."

I nodded. "Fair enough."

Major Pemberton, who'd been a mute participant till now, spoke up. "You would have my full cooperation, as well."

I grinned. "Glad to see Barker and Melchen didn't sour you fellas on *all* American detectives."

Both of them returned the smile; not exactly warmly, but this reception had been far more positive than I could ever have dreamed.

"I'll take the weekend to work on the letter," I said. "You'll have it Monday."

Hallinan rose and offered his hand, which I took and shook. "Thank you, Mr. Heller. Good day."

That evening I dined with Godfrey Higgs and his wife, who had invited me to see Nassau's fabled Jungle Club at the Fort Montague Hotel. With the ocean on one side, a lake on the other, and a fragrant tropical garden everywhere else, the deliberately rustic structure beckoned us inside its underlit interior, filled with ferns, palms, waitresses in skimpy sarongs, and green tables under thatched umbrellas, at one of which we feasted on plates of food we'd built ourselves from a buffet of (among other things) crab, lobster, fresh fruit, creamed vegetables, and pepper pots of mysterious, delectable contents.

"I'm delighted our Attorney General gave you such a warm reception," Higgs said, between sipping spoonfuls of creamy soup. "If a bit shocked."

"It does tell us one thing."

"Which is?"

"Hallinan wasn't in on the fix to frame Freddie."

"Interesting observation, Nate. Who was?"

"Well, Barker and Melchen, for sure. The question is, whose bidding were they answering? The Duke of Windsor's? Or Meyer Lansky's?"

"The Duke called them in."

"True. Which may mean I'm on a fool's errand writing this letter."

A steel band was beginning to play.

Higgs arched an eyebrow. "At least you'll know where you stand."

"At least I will."

Higgs put down his spoon and gave me an earnest look. "Nate—with Freddie cleared, I'm no longer an official part of this case."

"I realize that."

"Nonetheless, I want you to know you can depend on me and on whatever resources I might provide."

He smiled, and I returned the smile; and we spent the rest of the evening talking about the case not at all. Mostly I sampled the Jungle Club's "famous" (the menu said so) rum-and-lime punch. I sampled quite a bit of it, actually.

Alone at Shangri La in my little guest cottage, I slept soundly and well, despite the impending storm moving the trees and sending ghostly wails of wind through the gardens, keeping those exotic birds unnerved.

The next morning, Saturday, I slept in, and it was ten-thirty before I went over to the main house and fixed myself some scrambled eggs and bacon; rationing and shortages didn't seem to have any effect on Shangri La's pantry and king-size Frigidaire, which could have kept a hotel dining room going. I sat alone at the table in the big, gleaming white modern kitchen and listened to the approaching storm rattle the windows.

I had that letter to write, and I'd even found a typewriter to write it on in an office of Di's; but I was letting the back of my mind chew on it for right now. I was ready for a day off.

Daniel took me over to Nassau, where I thought about calling Marjorie, but didn't. That situation, despite Freddie's acquittal, would most likely remain unchanged: as Nancy had made clear, Lady Oakes still considered her son-in-law the murderer of her husband.

Besides, I was involved with somebody else now, wasn't I? My other summer romance. . . .

So I figured the best thing to do was get my mind off the Oakes case, and toward that goal, I took in a matinee at the Savoy. The movie playing was *Above Suspicion* and the pretty cashier I bought my ticket from was Betty Roberts.

I had a bite at Dirty Dick's, and spoke with a few reporters left over from the trial, who were lingering on expense account till Monday; and when I got back out onto Bay Street, it was dark before it should be, thanks to the black, rolling clouds. A few tiny raindrops kissed my cheek. The wind was cold and a chore to walk against; with one hand I pulled the collar of my now too-light linen suitcoat around my neck and with the other held my straw fedora on.

The sky finally exploded as Daniel was taking me back to Hog Island; out in the small exposed motor launch, sheets of rain pummeling the sea, artillery-fire thunder splitting the sky and jagged white lightning revealing the cracks in it, I hung on to the sides of the rocking boat, shivering with cold and maybe fear, and getting soaked to the bone.

In my cozy cottage, I got out of the sopped clothes and took a hot shower and toweled off and climbed into bed, naked. I pulled the extra blanket up over me, as the cold was finding its way in, and the double glass doors facing the trees, and the windows of the little cottage, were shimmying like Little Sheba. Outside the palms bent and fronds fluttered, and hysterical birds screeched as they sought cover that wasn't there. The machine-gun fire of the rain on the roof, and on the windows and one side of the structure, kept pace with the howl of the hurricane-like wind.

Somehow I got to sleep, but it wasn't sleep, it was a sort of hell, *it was a tropical hellhole where land crabs skittered and Japs with bayonets stalked while my buddies and me hid in a trench, hoping they'd just walk by, but they didn't, they saw us, and they charged and my buddies got shot to shit and skewered by the bayonet blades but I was still alive and firing as torrents of rain fell, only it wasn't rain, it was blood, I was covered in blood. . . .*

I sat up in bed, gasping. A mortar shell exploded, and I hit the deck.

But it wasn't a mortar shell, it was thunder, and I was bare-ass on the floor, feeling foolish, sweating like Christie in the witness box.

I crawled back into bed. The sheets were soaking; my perspiration had done as good a job as if I'd been sleeping out in the storm, which continued unabated, shaking the windows, the dark shapes of palms bending impossibly beyond the double glass doors.

Leaving behind a twisted mass of damp sheets and blankets, I moved to the couch, and lay there on my back, naked, panting, as winded as if I'd run a mile, and stared at the blackness above me. Now and then lightning would strobe the room, and the pebbled plaster ceiling would be there, above me, protecting me, reminding me I wasn't in some tropical jungle, even though I was.

Using breathing exercises they'd taught me back at the psych ward at St. Elizabeth's, I managed to settle myself down; I was almost asleep when I heard a key working the lock at the side door.

For a moment I thought it was Di, back early from her trip.

But then lightning lit up the room, and there they were, stepping inside: two men, standing in their own puddles, their dark suits soaked, big men—one taller than the other, but both wide, massive specimens.

The first one wore a toupee which was plastered to him like a dark, many-fingered hand gripping his head; his glowering, battered, boxer's face, with small, glittering wide-set eyes, flat nose, hairline mustache, was like a parody of those Inca masks.

The shorter one was no less massive and his eyes were slits in a round, slash-scarred face.

Both had big guns in their big fists—automatics, possibly .45s —the kind of gun that makes a small hole going in and on the way out leaves a picture window to your insides.

They were the men I'd seen with Lansky at the Biltmore.

They were, I had no doubt, the men the late Arthur had seen at Lyford Cay on another wind-swept, rain-lashed night.

All of this I gathered in the particle of a second that the lightning gave me before the room settled back into pitch black.

They were moving toward my bed, to their left as they came in; the tangle of sheets and blankets may have looked like a person, in the nonlight—and they hadn't seen me stretched out on the couch, when they entered in that flash of lightning, looking instead toward the bed where even now they were firing their automatics, the thunder of the guns, the orange fiery muzzle flashes, drowning out the storm as they killed the mattress, sheets and blankets, making scorched smoky holes.

My nine-millimeter, goddamnit, was in my suitcase, over by the bed, over near them; I lifted a lamp off an end table and pitched it at them. The heavy base caught the short one in the forehead, and he yelped and tumbled back into his partner, who saw me charging and fired at me, but was too tangled up with his pal to aim and managed only to shatter a window.

Then I was on them, pushing them to the wall, the groggy round-faced short one waking up as I clutched his balls in one hand and squeezed and yanked and as he cried in agony, screeching like a parrot, his partner behind him did an awkward dance, trying to get around him to me, where he could shoot me or club me or anything, but I had snatched the short one's .45 from limp fingers and fired it past the screaming smaller man, aiming for the tall one's face but missing, in the commotion, and succeeding only in shooting off his left ear, which flew off his head and landed in a sodden scarlet lump against the wall, splattering, sticking there like a big squashed bug.

Now they both were hollering, but the one whose nuts I'd squeezed had recovered enough to elbow me in the midsection, and I tumbled back onto the bed, rolled off the other side, onto the floor, but retaining the .45 even as another .45 from a howling one-eared asshole was chewing holes in the wall just over my head behind me.

I leapt up to return fire, but after one round the goddamn thing was empty, and I threw it and caught somebody somewhere, because I heard a scream as I hit the deck again, with more slugs zinging overhead.

The darkness allowed me to crawl on the wood floor toward the couch, which could provide cover till I got to those double glass doors, where I could get the fuck away from these guys. Without a gun, there was only so much damage I could do.

But when the next stroke of lightning lit the room, I found myself exposed, crouched like a dog on the floor, bare ass in the air, with one of them at my right—the tall one, whose little eyes were big as he pointed the .45 with one hand and held on to the bloody place where his left ear used to be with the other—and standing right in front of those glass doors that were my escape route was the shorter one, the slits of his eyes widened into something savage and furious now, his hands held out like claws. He looked like a sumo wrestler in a wet business suit. . . .

I dove into him. He was the unarmed one, after all, and I'm not sure whether we shattered the glass of the doors, or whether the one-eared man behind us did with his barrage of gunfire, but shatter it did as we flew through the disintegrating glass into the rain, and I was nicked by some shards, but the fat human cushion below me was really cut to shit, a bloody punctured unconscious thing, probably dead. I scrambled off him, the rain splattering my bare flesh like hard wet bullets, the cold a shock even under these circumstances, and scurried into the trees.

"You fucker!" the one-eared man screamed, standing over his fallen partner, and he fired the .45 into the darkness where he'd seen me go.

Only I was behind the biggest tree I could find, a tree too big to sway in the still-punishing wind, and when the lightning gave the night a silvery instant of day, I saw my weapon.

Despite the storm, I heard him snap the new clip into the automatic. And I heard his feet crunching on the twigs and leaves and splashing puddles, and when he came lumbering by with his rain-plastered toupee and his red used-to-be ear, I stepped out and hit him in the forehead with the coconut so hard I heard a crack; whether it was his head or the coconut, I couldn't be sure. But I had more sympathy for the latter as I stood there, pelted by rain, palms bending around me, naked as Tarzan before Jane sewed him a loincloth, grinning down crazily at an unconscious man with one ear and a wet off-center toupee.

I took the .45 out of his loose fingers and maybe I wouldn't have done it if he hadn't somehow reached out and grabbed my leg, but I emptied the thing into his face, three bullets that turned his battered pug's puss into a mask more grotesque than even the Incas ever imagined.

I stumbled away from him and fell to my knees, in the muck, gasping. I must have looked like some crazy native making a sacrifice to the gods. Winded, hurting, I hung my head, let the .45 fall to the wet ground, listened to the sky rumble, let the water purify me, or try to.

He didn't say anything.

He was laughing; or maybe he was crying.

But when I looked up, the short one, his face cut and soiled and red-streaked, his suit soaked with as much blood as rain, a big goddamn shard of glass sticking out of one leg like a lightning bolt that got stuck there, was standing over me with the other .45 in one hand.

Somehow I knew it was loaded, now.

"Are you praying, you bastard?" he shouted over the rain. "You should be."

He raised the .45 and I was looking into the black eye of its barrel about to dive to one side when the gunshot stopped me.

But it stopped him worse.

The shot hadn't been from a .45—from a much smaller weapon, I would say—and the short wide lightning-scarred thug staggered before me like a tree about to fall. In his forehead, not quite exactly between his eyes, was a quarter-size black hole; a comma of red welled out and was washed away by the rain and now I dove to one side as he fell, heavily, throwing water from the sodden ground every which way.

Behind him, in the jagged doorway we'd made through the glass doors, was a tall, slender figure. From where I knelt I couldn't make out his features, but he wore a black turtleneck shirt and black pants, like a commando.

Then the lightning showed me the harshly handsome angles of his face.

"For God's sake, man," Fleming said, "come in out of the rain."

He came to me, skirting the corpse he'd made, helped me up,

and took me around to the side door, to avoid the broken glass. Once we were inside—though the storm was coming in after us, through the broken doors and a bullet-shattered window—he wrapped me in a blanket and said, "Would you excuse me?"

I didn't say anything. I wasn't quite ready to say anything.

He went into the bathroom and closed the door and I heard the sound of violent retching.

When he came back, touching his lips with a tissue, he seemed chagrined. "Sorry."

"Didn't you ever kill anybody before?"

"Actually," he said, sitting next to me, "no."

I told him he'd picked a good place to start.

"I had a report that those two arrived by clipper this afternoon," Fleming said. "I've been looking for them. I thought they might be coming to call on you, so I dropped by. Hope you don't mind."

"Next time," I said numbly, "do try to ring first."

He withdrew his beat-up gold cigarette case and lighted himself up.

"Give me one of those," I said.

He did.

We sat and smoked quietly and as we did, the storm began to abate. I asked him if he'd seen the boat they'd used; I figured there might be a third man, piloting the craft. Fleming said no. Was Daniel still in his shack near the dock? Yes. Within fifteen minutes, the rain was pattering, not pelting, and the wind was a whisper, not a howl.

"The worst is over," he said.

"Is it?" I asked. "Tell me, Naval Intelligence—what suddenly turned me into a loose end those assholes had to tie up?"

Fleming was lighting a new smoke. "Why don't you ask Meyer Lansky and Harold Christie?"

"What do you mean?"

He smiled as he waved his match out. "They're in a suite at the British Colonial, right now—talking business. I can give you the room number, if you like. . . ."

I was dressed and out of there within fifteen minutes—and I had my own weapon now, the nine-millimeter Browning. With an extra clip.

"Is the main house open?" Fleming asked. "I need to use the phone."

I gave him the keys. "You're not coming?"

"No. I'll just stay behind and . . . tidy up. Happy hunting, Mr. Heller."

Somehow I knew what Fleming meant by "tidying up": those two bodies would soon be gone, as if they'd never been here.

But that wasn't my concern.

I had tidying up of my own to do.

Twenty-six

The world was a pale ghostly green as I padded across the tar roof, feet splashing big pools into little ones. After the storm, the wind had turned lazy and gentle and cool. Getting up here had been no problem—stairs led to the flat roof of the central tower of the British Colonial Hotel—but now things would get tricky.

Meyer Lansky had the sixth-floor suite, the penthouse, in the six-story tower that was the axis of the hotel structure. Right now I was directly above that suite, leaning up against a terra-cotta facade which extended up another half-story and faced the ocean; on the other side was a massive plaque of Columbus, which jutted up higher than the rest of the facade, and atop it like a huge coachman's lamp was an electric lantern that must have been a good five hundred watts. This was the source of the pale green mock moonlight.

By standing on tiptoe, I could peer over the wall of the facade to the balcony a story below. Meyer Lansky's balcony. About a fifteen-foot drop, if I wanted to climb over at the point just before the abrupt jut of the Columbus plaque. If I didn't break a leg or two, trying that drop, and instead missed the balcony altogether, five stories below the cement patio of Davy Jones' Locker café was patiently waiting.

For a Saturday night, things were quiet—despite my already active evening, it was not yet eleven p.m., but the storm had hit early enough to keep people home or in their hotel rooms. Below, a few couples stood looking out at the restless sea and wind-brushed palms, doing their best not to step or stand in puddles, dodging the occasional fallen branch.

About six feet down was a decorative overhang above the balcony; it was probably just under a foot wide. I reached in my pocket for one of half a dozen cigarettes I'd bummed off the British agent. Lighted one up with a match from the British Colonial matchbook I'd picked up when I was checking the lobby for Lansky muscle. I hadn't seen anybody who seemed to qualify, but when I went up to the sixth floor, there was a pockmarked burly sentry in the hall by the door to the suite; he wore a two-tone blue suit and sat in a folding chair too small for him, reading *Ring* magazine. I had walked on by him and taken these stairs to the roof.

Now I leaned against the back of the facade, sucking in the smoke, a strong, bitter blend, my white linen suit washed green by the lantern, the nine-millimeter snug under my arm in the shoulder holster, jacket unbuttoned. I could go find some rope . . . with all the boats around that wouldn't be hard . . . I could tie it around the base of that big electric coachman's lamp and . . .

Fuck it.

I tossed the cigarette and it sizzled in a puddle and I climbed over the facade and dropped myself down the stucco face of the building until my hands were hooked over and gripping the edges above, wrists bent, while below my feet stretched and danced in the air, searching for that overhang.

I didn't dare risk just dropping there—not enough width to maintain my balance. Over to my left was the lower part of the Columbus plaque; it was recessed and ornate, with a lot of rococo design work.

I let go with my left hand and every muscle in my body pulled as my right hand held on and my left scrambled over the plaque's surface, like a blind man searching for a light switch, until finally my fingers clutched some sculptured rococo work that served as a handle for me to grab on to.

I let go with my right hand, and my body swung toward where my left hand held on, but suddenly my feet were touching the overhang—and not just my toes; my feet, turned sideways, had footing, at least as long as I had hold of whatever I had hold of in that damn ornate plaque.

Then my right hand searched for something else to grip among the design work, found another rococo handle, and my feet were securely under me and I had my full balance, and I dropped to the floor of the balcony below.

The water puddled there made me slip and I fell back, hard, against the wrought iron of the balcony itself, shaking it, but I didn't lose my balance, and it didn't give way, and I had my gun out from under my arm and in my hand when the French doors opened and a heavyset bodyguard in a straw fedora and tropical shirt—he looked a little like Wallace Beery—peeked out, his hands empty, to see if a branch had fallen or something.

I was on my feet with my gun in his belly before the stupid surprised expression was off his face. In fact, it was still there when I plucked his long-barreled .38 from under his arm, sticking it in my own waistband.

"Now back up," I said, "hands high."

"Look who dropped in," intoned a deep, firm voice.

Meyer Lansky sat casually on a couch, legs crossed, in the sitting area of the big one-room suite; Harold Christie sat across from him in a comfortable armchair. Lansky, in light blue sport shirt and dark blue slacks, wearing sandals and socks, was smiling; he seemed faintly amused by my entrance.

Christie, who wore a rumpled canary-color linen suit with a red bow tie, looked astounded, and dismayed, the money-color eyes wide and blinking. He looked ten years older than when I first met him, at Westbourne, not so long ago; also skinnier, the flesh hanging on him like another rumpled suit.

Between them was a coffee table on which were their drinks and a briefcase that I figured belonged to Christie. A well-stocked bar was at the left, and a double bed was over at right. The two of them—but for the bodyguard and me—were alone.

I ignored Lansky; also Christie, who was saying, "What in the hell are *you* doing here, Heller? What in the hell is he *doing* here?"

"Tell your friend in the hall to come inside," I told the bodyguard. "Tell him Mr. Lansky wants to talk to him."

He nodded.

"Meyer," I said, "tell him no signals. Otherwise I shoot up the place."

"No signals, Eddie."

Eddie nodded.

He poked his head out and said, "Boss wants to see you."

The burly guy in the two-tone suit came in with *Ring* magazine under his arm and his guard down.

"What the fuck . . . ?"

But he didn't argue with the nine-millimeter in my one hand as my other took his .38 out from under his arm. Now I had two of them in my belt, Zapata-style.

"In the toilet," I said, pointing the way with the nine-millimeter. "Immediate seating. . . ."

I locked them in by wedging a chair under the knob.

"Get yourself a drink while you're up, Mr. Heller," Lansky said cordially.

"No thanks."

"Suit yourself. It disappoints me that you think you have to go to such absurd lengths to see me. If you wanted to stop by, all you had to do was call."

I stood between them, Lansky at my left, Christie at my right. Lansky was obviously unarmed and Christie wasn't the type.

"You're understaffed tonight, Meyer," I said. "Two of your best boys are missing."

The sharp, dark eyes tensed; otherwise, his weak-chinned homely face gave an impression of unconcern.

"And what two boys would those be?" he asked blandly.

"The two boys that were with you at the Biltmore, last time we spoke."

"You're mistaken. Those two had the weekend off. They didn't make this trip."

I smiled pleasantly. "Are you sure? Maybe I didn't describe them well enough. There's one with a bad toupee and a cheesy little mustache, although you might not recognize him now because I shot off one of his ears and, well, put three or four rounds in his face."

Lansky's eyes tightened even more, but otherwise his countenance didn't change; Christie's mouth was open, and he was trembling—that old witness-box flop sweat was starting in again.

"The other one has a scar, kind of shaped like a lightning bolt, on his left cheek, I think it's his left cheek, with a kind of round face, oh, and a new touch—there's a hole in his forehead . . . about here."

Lansky nodded once. "I believe I do know who you're referring to."

"You should. You sent them to whack me out tonight."

He shook his head no; gestured gently with an open hand. "You're mistaken. I believe what you're saying—I believe they did what you say they did, and that you did what you say you did. But I didn't send them. Did you, Harold?"

Christie reacted as indignantly as if he'd been slapped. "Certainly not!"

I looked at them, one at a time, and laughed. "Why the hell don't I believe you, fellas? A couple of stand-up citizens like you."

Lansky sat forward; his manner was reasonable. He didn't seem frightened, unlike Christie, who looked on the verge of wetting his pants. "Mr. Heller, why in the world would I want to have you killed? Before tonight, at least, you've done nothing to offend me."

"He's insane," Christie said. "He insists on trying to put the blame for Harry's death on me!"

"Well, *I* certainly had no part in Sir Harry's death," Lansky said flatly.

"I think you did," I said. "I think Harold here asked you to send two of your strong-arm boys . . . specifically, my uninvited, now-deceased guests this evening . . . to help convince Harry to change his mind about blocking your mutual efforts to bring casinos into the Bahamas. But Oakes was a tough old bird, and he put up a fight and got himself killed—after which your two boys improvised that voodoo routine, to confuse the issue."

"Mr. Heller," Lansky said, shaking his head, smiling like a disappointed parent, "you're the one who's confused."

"Oh really?"

"Really. If I wanted to put gambling into the Bahamas, Harry Oakes couldn't have stood in my way."

I was holding the nine-millimeter on him, but his calm, hard eyes were equally on me, and similarly deadly. And what he was saying echoed things Freddie de Marigny had told me in his jail cell. . . .

"Gambling already is legal here," Lansky said. "Merely suspended for the duration of the war. The law does forbid Bahamian residents from gambling, which is fine." He might have been delivering a lecture on traffic safety at a junior high school. "The point is to get tourist trade. But with the war on, Mr. Heller, there are no tourists to speak of."

"Which means," Christie said edgily, bitterly, "there is no rush whatsoever to put casinos into the Bahamas!"

"Harold's right," Lansky said. "This doesn't become a pressing issue until after war's end . . . and even then, Sir Harry couldn't have stood in my way. He would've had to be on the Executive Council to consider gaming license applications—and he wasn't. He was a powerful man, yes—but he didn't wield any power with Bay Street. He was an outsider, and he liked it that way."

"Heller," Christie said earnestly, "Harry didn't give a damn about gambling in the Bahamas—he didn't care about the *Bahamas* anymore! He was gearing up to move to Mexico City—surely, you knew that. . . ."

"No matter what either of you say," I said, gun tight in my hand, "the two assassins who killed Sir Harry Oakes were *your* men, Lansky! The same two men that the dead Lyford Cay caretaker saw that night, the same two men I shot the shit out of about a fucking hour ago!"

Lansky may have been worried now; he could see that I was wound a little taut.

"Mr. Heller—if those two were responsible for Sir Harry's death, it wasn't at my say-so. It was some . . . free-lance assignment they picked up."

Christie seemed to settle back in his chair, trying to disappear into it.

I turned the gun on him. "Then *you* hired them . . . you knew them, through your friend, here—"

"Heller," Christie said desperately, "I had nothing to do with Harry's death! I loved the man!"

"Mr. Heller," Lansky said, and he risked leaning out and putting his hand on my wrist—not the wrist of the hand with the gun in it, but my wrist. "I'm a Jew."

I looked at him like he was nuts.

"*You're* a Jew, aren't you, Heller?"

"Well . . . yeah. I suppose."

"You suppose! It's not something you have to think about, man! You think that evil bastard Hitler would take time to think about it?"

The homely little man actually seemed upset. Finally.

"What the hell are you babbling about, Lansky?"

When he spoke, he bit off each word, like a telegram he was

dictating. "Do you really think I'd knowingly get in bed with a bunch of goddamn fucking Nazis, just to make a *buck?*"

It was like cold water had been thrown on me. "Nazis?"

Christie was glaring at Lansky.

I looked from one to the other. "What the hell do you mean—*Nazis?*"

Lansky let go of my wrist. "I've already said too much. You got balls, Mr. Heller, and brains, but right now you need the latter more than the former."

A sick feeling was growing in the pit of my stomach.

Lansky stood. He put his hand on my shoulder and whispered, "Go. Go now, and this is just an honest misunderstanding. Stay, and . . . well, you're either going to have to kill everyone here, or wind up with me mad at you. And we don't either one of us want either one of those things, do we?"

Christie was sitting there like a toad in a suit, sweat and desperation all over his face. I might have to talk to him again—but I didn't want Lansky around. Suddenly I knew that Lansky was damn near an innocent bystander in all this.

Suddenly I knew how big a mistake I'd made.

We were frozen there for what seemed like forever and was probably thirty seconds. Lansky stood looking patient, Christie sat looking distressed and me, I probably had the same green pallor as when I'd climbed down the building bathed in that pale green light.

"You gentlemen must have business to do," I said, backing up, gun in hand, but lowered. "If you'll excuse me."

"This time I will," Lansky said. "Why don't you just use the door this time?"

I did.

Twenty-seven

It was approaching two o'clock a.m. when I returned to Hog Island. I'd gone to Dirty Dick's to think and drink; I held myself to two rum punches, but didn't hold back on the thinking. Despite the several hours I'd been gone, Daniel was waiting for me at Prince George Wharf, with the little motor launch. He had seemed nervous bringing me over, muttering about the bad storm, even though by the time we made the trip, the storm was a memory. Heading back to Hog Island, in the wee hours, under a black starless moonless sky, even the sea had settled down. Calm again.

So were my nerves. The rum had done it. And the thinking.

The cottage was dark. I flicked on the light: no sign of Fleming, whose "tidying up" had been limited to removing the two dead bodies. Otherwise, the scattered glass from the broken doors and window, slivers and shards and jagged chunks, the shot-up sheets and blankets and mattress, scattered shell casings, the holes the .45s had punched in the walls, even the glistening pools of blood here and there, not dry yet thanks to the humidity, were testimony to what had happened here, a few short hours ago.

The mansion was not dark—several lights were on, and I hadn't left them that way. Perhaps Fleming had, when he made his phone call for corpse-disposal assistance. He'd left the keys on the bed, and I walked over to the house down the palm-lined path and went in the kitchen way.

I found her—stumbled onto her, is more like it—in the round living room where two nights ago we'd been celebrating de Marigny's victory amid the Inca artifacts.

She was pacing, almost prowling, before the blandly benign portrait of Wenner-Gren, her slim, full-breasted figure wrapped in a pink silk peignoir; she was smoking and on the coffee table between the facing curved couches was a bucket of ice with an open bottle of champagne.

"I thought you were going to Mexico City," I said.

She turned quickly, startled. For an instant her face was frozen with incredulity, then it melted into a smile. Even at two in the morning, those bruised lips were rouged red.

"Nate! God, I'm glad to see you! I was so desperately *worried!*"

She rushed to me; under the sheer robe was a sheer pink nightie and where the pinkness of it ended and the pinkness of her began was a mystery she would no doubt allow me to solve. She hugged me, and made sobbing sounds, though she wasn't sobbing.

"You're alive!" she said into my chest.

"And well." I smiled at her, holding her gently away from me. "What about Mexico City?"

She shook her head as if she had to clear it to answer my mundane question.

"Oh . . . all the flights were canceled, due to that bloody storm. Wasn't another Mexico City connection for two days, and that would've been too late for the meeting Axel needed me for. I chartered a little boat back from Miami."

"I see."

"Let me get you something to drink." She moved to the liquor cart. "Do you want rum? Or some of this bottle of Dom Pérignon left from the other night?"

"The champagne. Please."

She went to the coffee table, poured me a bubbling glass and said, "What in hell happened?"

"What do you mean?"

"At the cottage! I got back about an hour ago—Daniel was gone, and the cottage was a shambles! It doesn't take an expert to know that somebody shot up the place. Nathan, there's *blood* on the floor—and all that broken glass."

"Yeah. I saw."

She narrowed her eyes, studying me over the rim of the glass she was handing me. "You . . . you weren't there when what happened happened, were you?"

I took the champagne. "Oh, I was there."

She frowned. "Well, goddamnit, man! Talk to me! Did someone try to kill you?"

I walked over to the couch and sat; she sat across from me on the opposite couch, sitting on the edge, knees together primly like a schoolgirl, and with a schoolgirl's wide, round, innocent eyes.

"Two men with guns came in and mistook some sheets and blankets for me. Fortunately I was sleeping on the couch at the time."

"What did you do?"

"I shot one in the face three times. Or four. The other one has a bullet in the head."

That knocked her back, just a bit. She blinked the lush lashes, swallowed, and said, "Where are the bodies?"

I shrugged. "I don't know. They were still there when I left to go over to Nassau, to confront Harold Christie."

Her eyes got even wider. "You confronted Christie? What the hell did he say?"

I shrugged again. "He denied sending 'em."

"What did you do to him . . . ? You didn't . . ."

"Kill him? No. I didn't do a thing to the slimy little bastard. Say . . . tell me—when you saw the cottage in a shot-up shambles, did you call the police? Is anyone on the way?"

She made a meaningless gesture with the hand with the cigarette in it. "The phones seem to be out. I was frightened, Nate. Thank God you're here."

I nodded sympathetically. "You should get some rest. We should sort this out with Colonel Pemberton and his men after sunup sometime, don't you think?"

She shuddered. "Oh, I simply *couldn't* sleep."

I looked at her for a long time.

Then I said, "You know what would relax you?"

She shook her head no; she sucked on the cigarette, holding in the smoke a long time.

"A bedtime story."

As she blew the smoke out, her smile turned one-sided and

wicked. "A bedtime story?" She shook her head again, her expression wry. "Heller, you *are* bad."

"No," I said. I pointed at her. "You're bad."

She froze again, momentarily, then laughed it off, blond hair shimmering. She raised an eyebrow and her glass. "What happened to my bedtime story?"

I put my hands on my knees. "Once upon a time there was a grizzled old prospector who spent years and years looking for a fortune in gold. Finally, one day, he found some gold. Quite a lot of it, and it made him enormously wealthy, and so he married his sweetheart and had a wonderful family and moved to a tropical isle. But one day a war broke out in the outside world, and though he and his family were safe on their island, the prospector worried that this war might threaten his fortune. Then a former king and two very wealthy men—one who owned land and another with a great big boat—invited the prospector to start a bank with them, in a foreign land. To storehouse their money until the war was over."

Di was frowning; the bruised lips were pulled tight and thin, and her blue eyes were cold, peeking out of slits. "I don't think I much care for this story."

"Okay," I said. "Let's talk about real life, then. Sir Harry was all for ducking wartime currency restrictions; what's a little money-laundering between friends? But greedy as he was, hypocritical old goat that he was, Harry saw himself as a patriot. How would the man who personally funded five Spitfires for the RAF react if, say, he discovered that Banco Continental's primary customers were Nazis . . . hoarding money they looted from Europe, building themselves enormous nest eggs they could look forward to, no matter how the war came out?"

She sipped champagne. "You're talking nonsense, Nathan."

"I don't think so. I think Harry was just patriotic enough—and wealthy enough—to tell Wenner-Gren and Harold Christie and the Duke of Windsor to kiss his big fat rich behind. He'd been making plans to move to Mexico City, and had made several trips there in recent months, and on those trips he got a better picture of what was going on at Banco Continental. And he didn't like what he saw." I sat forward. "Sir Harry was going to blow the whistle, wasn't he? On the whole sordid scheme!"

She threw her head back and shook her hair and laughed her

brittle British laugh. "There is no such scheme, you silly man. Banco Continental is a legitimate financial institution, and while the Duke and others may be moving some money around in a questionable, even *unpatriotic* manner, as you might put it, there's nothing truly sinister going on."

I had a sip of champagne myself. Smiled at her. "Remember that dark unidentified fluid in Harry's stomach that the prosecution never managed to identify?"

"Yes. So?"

"You know what I think?"

"What do you think?"

"I think when Christie had dinner at Westbourne that night, he drugged Sir Harry's drink, or maybe his food."

She smirked. "Now why would he do that?"

"Not to kill Harry—his dear old friend. Just to subdue him; make him easier, safer, for you to handle."

"For *me* to handle?"

"You." I laughed, once, harshly. "You know, every single one of the red herrings you threw my way—Harry chasing women, the stolen gold coins, Lansky's casinos—had a grain of truth. The gold coins probably *were* stolen the murder night—by you. After all, you're the one who saw to it that that native had a gold coin to sell us."

"Me? Are you insane?"

"Don't knock it—it got me out of the service. And the Lansky/Christie connection obviously is very real, even if the casinos they eventually hope to open together weren't anything Harry gave a damn about. And I think maybe Harry did have an eye for a pretty face and well-turned ankle, which, added to his grogginess from being drugged, is what made it safe for you to invade his room that night, even if he did have a gun at his bedside."

She gestured to herself with cigarette-in-hand. "And why would I do that?"

I pointed to the oil painting over the fireplace. "Your boss, Axel Wenner-Gren, may have ordered it . . . or it may have been your own play, looking after your employer's interests. I'll never know the answer to that—unless you care to tell me."

"I'd rather you continue telling me—sharing these strange, imaginative fantasies of yours. For example, tell me, would you,

Nate, how a delicate creature like myself might accomplish such a brutal act as the murder of Sir Harry Oakes?"

I threw my hand out and clutched the air; she flinched.

"By reaching out," I said, "to the Banco Continental's own Harold Christie. You had him get you a couple of mob thugs to lean on Harry. To scare him. You had them rough him up, threaten to give him more and worse if he didn't keep his trap shut; but Harry only spit blood in your eye—swearing he'd go public, taking Wenner-Gren, Christie and all the King's men down with him."

"Nonsense."

"He was on the floor, on his face or on his knees, damn near beaten to death. Your thugs had gone too far—so you finished him off: shot him behind the ear, four times, close-range, with small enough caliber a gun that the bullets didn't even pass through his head. Maybe you even used his own bedside gun—it's missing, after all, and a .38 fits the profile."

Bingo! The Bahama blues flared just a bit when I mentioned Harry's gun; she *had* used it.

"Then you made a makeshift blowtorch out of the flit gun, using denatured alcohol from the toolshed, setting the bed on fire. After which, you and your mob help flipped the corpse onto the burning bed, and played voodoo. A scorched corpse, a few feathers, and presto—an obeah kill."

She laughed, shook her head, lighted up a new cigarette. "Really, Heller. You should be writing for radio. *Inner Sanctum*, perhaps."

"You may have really intended to set a fire and burn Westbourne down, but I doubt it. I think you just mutilated the corpse to muddy the waters. Maybe you stole the gold coins to back up the voodoo angle, or could be you're like Harry: you just plain like gold."

She sucked smoke; looked at the ceiling, playing bored and disgusted.

"Anyway, after you'd taken your time doing a thorough, sick job of it, you and Lansky's boys left. Christie had left long before, after paving the way for you and your thugs by drugging Harry; he'd also picked up your two assistants when they docked at Lyford Cay, getting spotted by the unfortunate Arthur. Then Christie dropped off his unpleasant passengers at Westbourne and went to spend the night with his mistress. But either in the middle of the night, courtesy of a phone call from you, or when he returned in the morning, he found how tragically wrong the attempt to coerce Sir Harry had gone. Christie quickly changed his story, pretending to have been asleep next door all the time. He was too much the gentleman to involve his lady friend, who he prompted to say nothing."

Now she was shaking her head, smiling patronizingly. "I do so hate to disappoint you, but this is all the most ludicrous pipe dream. Nancy de Marigny is my dearest friend—even if I had done this *dastardly* deed, her husband is the last person I'd have ever framed for it."

"I never said you framed Freddie. Your half-ass voodoo cover-up was meant to suggest some nameless black boogie man. The *frame* was courtesy of Barker and Melchen with a nudge from the Duke—whose role in this, I believe, was limited to taking Christie's advice to call in those two very special Miami cops."

"Oh, that was *Harold's* idea?"

"Probably. Could have been yours. At any rate, somebody told the Duke to bring in these two corrupt, mob-connected coppers. Somebody told him that by doing that he could contain the crime. And he did as he was told. After all, he's involved in Banco Continental up to his royal white Nazi-loving ass."

Di's head was back; she was smiling coolly, eyes glittering, apparently amused. "So, then—what is it exactly you imagine I am? Some Nazi dragon lady?"

"No. I think you're just June Sims from the East End—poor white British trash who fucked and schemed and cheated her greedy little way to the top. How *did* your husband die, anyway?"

Her face went blank. The moral void behind her pretty mask was frighteningly apparent, for an instant; then she managed a part-seductive, part-sarcastic smile.

"Well—I take it that question, which I don't intend to dignify with a response, is the conclusion of your 'bedtime story'?"

"Almost, although I'm not sure everybody lives happily ever after. I'm also not sure whether you had poor Arthur killed or not—Christie could just as easily have had that done. So we're up to the part where you call that two-man goon squad back in to finish the job. That is, finish me."

"Oh, *I* tried to have you killed? Why, that simply slipped my mind—now, why did I do that, again?"

"I started making noises about keeping the case alive beyond the de Marigny trial—that made me a loose end that needed tying off." I grinned. "You want to know something funny?"

She shrugged; her breasts stirred beneath the pink silk. "Sure. I like to laugh."

"I know you do. You're a fun girl. What's funny is I didn't completely tip to this till your 'boy' Daniel started making like Willie Best."

"Willie Best?"

"Willie Best. Mantan Moreland. Stepin Fetchit. All those funny colored boys in the movies who get so scared, so 'spooked'—feets do yo' stuff."

Now her expression was frankly irritated. "What the bloody hell are you talking about?"

"I think you'll appreciate this, bigoted bitch that you are. Daniel just about jumped out of his black skin when he saw me show up to use the launch, after I survived the attack by your two would-be assassins. That pair didn't dock a boat here at Shangri La, did they? They arrived in Nassau by clipper—and Daniel brought them over to Hog Island in the launch! At your behest, like when he told me the phony story about the gold coin."

Her eyes tightened, just barely, but I knew I'd hit pay dirt again.

"You must have instructed Daniel to keep to the dock, no matter what sounds he heard from the grounds, and mind his own business and not worry about it when Mr. Heller disappeared. Or maybe he was going to help dispose of the body in one of the boats. Only there I was, an hour later, standing on Daniel's dock, a white ghost looking for a ride. Hell, he was still having kittens when he brought me back here! I'll bet he's halfway to one of the out islands by now." I laughed. "The only native you ever lowered yourself to hiring gives you away. That is rich."

"Rich," she said. Then she said the word again, savoring it, leaning forward: "*Rich*. Like you could be. Like we could be. . . ."

"Oh, please. It took Meyer Lansky, of all people, to make me see the truth. I'm a Jew, lady. Your people think I'd make a swell lampshade."

She frowned. "I'm no Nazi."

"No—you're worse, you and your boss Axel Wenner-Gren. The

Nazis are sick fucks, but they believe in *something*. You? You're just in it for the money."

The truth of that stopped her for a moment. Then she smiled and it seemed sad; whether genuine or not, I couldn't begin to say.

"I've been good to you, Heller. We've had good times together." She slipped the flimsy dressing gown off her shoulders; she thrust back her shoulders and displayed her two deadly not-so-secret weapons, straining at the sheer silk nightie.

"You've been very good to me," I admitted.

She leaned forward, hovering over the coffee table; it was if she were about to climb over. Her breasts swayed hypnotically, tiny points hard under the sheer silk.

"I *own* you, remember?" Her pink tongue licked her red upper lip, like a child removing a milk mustache.

"That was more a rental deal."

"Come on, Heller . . . I think maybe you even loved me a little. . . ."

"I think sometimes ambergris turns out to be rancid butter."

She sneered. "What the bloody hell is *that* supposed to mean?"

All that gold Sir Harry searched so long and hard for turned out to be just so much rancid butter, too, hadn't it?

"It means no sale, lady."

She slipped her hand in the champagne bucket and rustled in the ice and I thought she was going to pour herself another drink; instead she filled her hand with a little silver revolver and I dove off the couch, but the shot rang in the room as she caught me in the midsection. It was like being punched, followed by a burning. . . .

I had the nine-millimeter out before she got her second shot off; I was on the floor, on my side, and my bullet went up through the glass of the coffee table, spiderwebbing it, and catching her about the same place hers had me, but mine was the bigger gun and it doubled her over in pain as her hand clutched the blossoming red, the silver revolver tumbling from her fingers, scooting across the hardwood floor.

Her pretty face contorted. "Oh . . . oh. It hurts. . . ."

She fell to her knees, holding on to herself, red welling through her fingers.

"I know it does, baby." I was hurting, too—a sharp wet hot pain and blackness was closing in.

"I'm . . . scared . . ."

"I know. But don't worry. . . ."

She looked at me desperately, the blue eyes wide and seeking the hope I held out.

"In half an hour," I said, "you'll be dead. . . ."

Twenty-eight

I was back in Guadalcanal, back in my shell hole, but it wasn't the same. It wasn't raining and it wasn't wet and tropical flowers—red and blue and yellow and violet and gold—were everywhere. All the boys were there—Barney, that big Indian Monawk, D'Angelo too, with both his legs—nobody was shot-up or bleeding at all, they were in spiffy dress uniforms one minute and then loud tropical shirts and slacks and sandals the next, and we would sit on the edge of the shell hole and sip champagne from glasses served to us off silver trays by gorgeous native girls in grass skirts and no tops. Sun streamed through swaying palms and Bing Crosby interrupted his rendition of "Moonlight Becomes You" to introduce me to Dorothy Lamour, who asked me if I minded if she slipped out of her sarong because it was so tight, while Bob Hope was going around telling dirty jokes to the guys. I asked where the Japs were and everybody laughed and said, They're all dead!, and the Krauts are, too, and we all laughed and laughed, but the only thing wrong was, it was too hot, really way too hot. Dorothy Lamour looked at me with sympathy in her big beautiful eyes and said, *Let me soothe you*, and she wiped my brow with a cool cloth. . . .

"Dreaming," I said.

"You're not dreamin' now," she said.

"Marjorie?"

"Shhhh." Her beautiful milk-chocolate face was smiling over me; her eyes were big and brown and as beautiful as Dorothy Lamour's. . . .

"You still got a fever. You just rest."

"Marjorie," I said.

I smiled.

She wiped my brow with the cool cloth and I drifted away.

Sunlight woke me. I blinked awake, tried to sit up but the pain in my midsection wouldn't let me.

"Nathan! I'm sorry! I'll shut the curtains. . . ."

I heard the rustle of curtains closing. I was in her cottage, in a nightshirt in her little bed that folded out from a cabinet. I could smell the flowers in the bowl on her table; I had smelled them in my dreams.

Then she was at my side, pulling up a chair to sit; she was in the white short-sleeve blouse and tropical-print skirt she'd worn that first night she invited me in for tea.

Her smile was radiant. "Your fever, it broke, finally. You remember talkin' to me at all?"

"Just once. I thought I was dreaming. You were wiping my face with a cloth."

"We talked a lot of times, but you were burnin' up. Now you're cool. Now you know where you are."

"Help me sit up?"

She nodded and moved forward and put the pillow behind me. I found a position that didn't hurt.

"How did I get here?"

"That British fella, he brought you here."

"Fleming?"

"He never said his name. He looks cruel but is really very sweet, you know."

"When?"

"Three days ago. He stops in every day. You'll see him later. You must be hungry."

The pain in my stomach wasn't just the bullet wound.

"I think I am hungry. Have I eaten anything?"

"You been takin' some broth. You want some more? I got some conch chowder."

"Conch chowder."

"Banana fritters too?"

"Oh yes . . ."

She brought the food to me on a little tray, but insisted on feeding it to me like a baby, a spoonful at a time; I was too weak to resist.

"Marjorie . . . you're so pretty . . . you're so goddamn pretty. . . ."

"You better sleep some more. The doctor says you need rest."

The doctor, as it turned out, was de Marigny's friend Ricky Oberwarth, who had lost his part-time position with the Nassau Jail because his medical examination of Freddie hadn't backed up Barker and Melchen's singed-hair story. Oberwarth—a thin, dark man in his forties whose glasses had heavy dark frames—stopped by later that morning and checked my wound and changed the dressing.

"You're doing well," he said. He had a slight Teutonic accent, reminding me that he was a refugee from Germany, one of the rare Jews welcomed to Nassau, thanks to his medical expertise.

"It's sore as a boil. Don't spare the morphine."

"You only had morphine the first day. And starting today you're on oral painkillers. Mr. Heller, you know, you're a lucky man."

"Why do doctors always tell unlucky bastards like me how lucky they are?"

"The bullet passed through you and didn't cause any damage that time and scar tissue won't take care of. Still, I wanted you in hospital, but your guardian angel from British Naval Intelligence forbade it. He wanted you kept in some out-of-the-way place, and since you hadn't lost enough blood to need a transfusion, I relented."

"How did he know to bring me here?"

He had finished changing the dressing, and pulled down my nightshirt and covered me back up, like a loving parent. "I don't know. Your friend Fleming isn't much on volunteering information."

When the doctor had gone, I asked Marjorie if Lady Oakes objected to my presence.

Her smile was mischievous. "Lady Eunice, she doesn't know about your presence. She's in Bar Harbor."

"What about Nancy?"

"She doesn't know, either."

"I killed a woman."

She blinked. "What?"

"Oh God, I killed a woman. Jesus. . . ."

She climbed onto the bed gingerly and held me in her arms like a big baby, which is exactly what I was crying like. I don't know why—later, in retrospect, killing Lady Diane Medcalf seemed not only logical but necessary and even admirable. She was at least as evil as any mobster I ever knew.

But right now I was crying. I think I was crying for the death of the funny, bitchy society dame I had thought she was—not the slum girl who clawed her way into royal circles, though maybe she deserved some tears, too.

Marjorie never asked me what I meant; she never asked me about the woman I said I killed. She had to have wondered, but she knew what I needed was comfort, not questions, let alone recriminations.

She was a special girl, Marjorie—one of a kind, and when I look back, I wonder why I didn't drag her off to some out island and raise crops and kids, black or white or speckled—who gave a shit, with a woman like this at your side?

Which is why I cried so long. At some point the sorrow or guilt or whatever the hell it was I was feeling for Di merged with the overwhelming bittersweet ache I felt knowing that this sweet woman who was holding me, comforting me, nursing me back to health, was as lost to me as the dead one.

My tears weren't just for Di. They were for both the lovely women I'd lost in the Caribbean.

Fleming appeared in the doorway that evening like a pastel illusion—light blue sportcoat, pale yellow sport shirt, white trousers. He looked like a tourist with exceptional taste.

"Back in the land of the living, I see," he said, smiling faintly. Marjorie had only one small lamp on, and the near darkness threw shadows on his angular face.

Marjorie stepped to the door, glanced our way shyly. "I'll just walk outside in the moonlight while you gentlemen are talkin'."

Fleming turned his smile on her, melting the girl. "Thank you, my dear."

Beaming, Marjorie slipped outside.

Fleming's smile settled in one cheek. "Lovely child. You're fortunate to have a nurse with such exceptional qualities."

"She thinks you're sweet, too."

He withdrew a smoke from his battered gold case. "Most women do. Would you like one?"

He meant cigarettes, not women.

"No thanks. The mood's passed."

"How *is* your mood?"

"All right, considering. Hurts a little."

"Your side or your psyche?"

"Choose your poison. Why did you bring me here, Fleming? How did you know to bring me to Marjorie?"

"You really don't remember?"

"Remember what?"

His smile crinkled. "Asking me to bring you here. You were barely conscious, but you clearly said, 'Marjorie Bristol,' and when I asked where to find her, you said, 'Westbourne guest cottage.' Then you put a period on the sentence by spitting up some blood."

"What about Diane? She is dead, isn't she?"

He nodded. "There are services tomorrow. Nancy is quite crushed, poor girl. You see, Diane died in a boating accident— went down with the craft that bore her name. Body wasn't re- covered—lost at sea."

I laughed without humor. "You secret agents really are good at 'tidying up,' aren't you?"

"We have to be, with the likes of Nathan Heller making messes. Besides, you're *lucky* we're so fastidious. If I hadn't come back to Shangri La to tidy up further, after disposing of that carrion, you'd be lost at sea, as well."

"So that's how you stumbled onto me."

"Yes. Now—tell me how it happened."

"How I killed her, you mean?"

He nodded again, blowing smoke through his nose like a dragon. "And what led up to it, if you don't mind."

I did, including dropping in on Lansky and Christie, and my theory about the Banco Continental being a Nazi repository.

"Very insightful, Heller. Banco Continental is indeed where much of the Nazi spoils of Europe are cached. Of course, the Banco is much more than that."

"Isn't that enough?"

He shrugged. "Among Banco Continental's other significant in- vestments and holdings is its funding of a syndicate supplying Japan with oil, as well as platinum and other rare metals. That same syndicate has cornered the market in hemp, copper and mercury as well—crucial war materials for the U.S."

"And you agree with me that Harry got royally pissed off when he got wind of all that?"

"Not only do *I* agree," the British agent said, "your FBI does as well. I've checked with them. Sir Harry had made some preliminary contacts."

"Jesus. I ought to go into the detective business."

"Or the spy game. That was an impressive showing, the other night—quite a savage beast lurks beneath that relatively civilized exterior of yours."

"Gee thanks. Tell me—do you think the Duke knows his precious Banco is an Axis operation?"

"I would imagine not. At least, I would hope not. My thinking is that Wenner-Gren kept certain of the members of his consortium in the dark about various aspects of Banco Continental's activities. Trust me when I say the Duke will soon be briefed in detail, and cautioned to curtail these activities in future."

"Where does that leave me?"

"As pertains to what?"

"As pertains to the Oakes case. Nancy de Marigny hired me to stay with it, you know!"

"I'm afraid that's out of the question. Neither your government nor mine needs the sorry scandal of the Duke's activities publicly aired. Perhaps when the war is over."

"What do I tell Nancy?"

"What did you promise her, exactly?"

I told him about seeing Hallinan and Pemberton; about the letter they'd requested from me.

"Write the letter," he said. "If I were you, however, I would not be specific about the new evidence . . . hold that back for another day."

"Because on this particular day, the Duke will quash any investigation?"

"Certainly. But by writing that letter, your pledge to Mrs. de Marigny will be fulfilled. I think with the imminent deportation of her husband, and the tragic death of her best friend coming upon the heels of the loss of her father, Nancy Oakes de Marigny will be ready to get on with her life."

He was probably right.

"This still isn't over, you know," I said.

"I should say from your standpoint it is."

"Not hardly. There's still that son of a bitch Axel Wenner-Gren to deal with. If I have to paddle a canoe up the Amazon, I'll find that fucker and put a bullet in his brain."

"And why would you do that?"

"Because he masterminded the whole goddamn affair!"

"Perhaps he did. Or perhaps Diane Medcalf took it upon herself to do these things. The answer to that question is at the bottom of the sea."

"I don't care. I don't care. Either way, it's still the fault of that evil cocksucker. As Meyer Lansky was kind enough to remind me, I'm a Jew. I'm not going to sit back and let these Nazi bastards get away with murder."

He was lighting up a fresh cigarette; he seemed vaguely amused, and that pissed me off.

"What the hell is so funny, Fleming?"

He waved out his match, twitched a smile, said, "Sorry. It's just that Wenner-Gren is no more a Nazi than the late Lady Medcalf."

"Well, what the fuck is he, then?"

"Among other things, he's the architect of Swedish neutrality, Goering's financial advisor, Krupp's front man . . . and so much more. He's just not a Nazi, per se. But he *is* one of a consortium of some of the richest, most powerful men in the world—men who exist on a level above and beyond politics."

"You mean Christie and the Duke and Wenner-Gren weren't alone in their Mexican banking scheme."

"To phrase it in the American argot: not by a long shot. Included, among various wealthy, respected Europeans, are some of the most prominent and influential American businessmen."

"Backing Nazis?"

"Making money. Your General Motors poured one hundred million dollars into Hitler's Germany, and they are hardly an isolated example. Heller, I would be content, were I you, with having dispatched the villains you've managed to dispatch. Aspiring to the shit list, as you might well put it, of that particular powerful consortium would find you rather on the deceased side, in very short order."

I sat up sharply; it made my midsection hurt but I didn't give a damn. "So Christie walks. And Axel Wenner-Gren . . . shit, I never even met the son of a bitch. . . ."

"You should leave it that way." He shrugged, drew in smoke. "The great villains of the world seldom get what they deserve."

"Hitler will—Mussolini just did."

He exhaled a blue cloud. "Possibly—but they are, after all, only petty politicians. And who's to say Adolf himself won't wind up in South America with all that bounty Wenner-Gren helped storehouse?"

"Do you believe that?"

Fleming's smile was sadly ironic. "I'm afraid, Heller, the masterminds of evil only meet their due justice in the realm of fantasy. Best leave it to Sax Rohmer and Sapper."

"Who are they?"

He laughed. "Nobody, really. Just writers."

It had been a week and a half and I was, for the most part, healed. Certain wounds never heal, but I was getting used to that. I walked on the ivory beach under a poker-chip moon with my arm around Marjorie Bristol's waist; she wore a white scoop-neck blouse with coral jewelry and the full blue-and-white-checked skirt with petticoats that swished.

"You saved my life," I said.

"That British man, he saved your life."

"He saved my body. You saved my life."

"Not your soul, Nathan?"

"A little late for that."

"Not your body?"

"That's yours anytime you like."

We walked some more; Westbourne was silhouetted against the clear night sky. The sand under our feet was warm, the breeze cool.

"Not mine anytime, anymore," she said.

We turned back and walked until we were near the cottage. She removed the skirt, stepped out of the petticoats; she was naked beneath, the dark triangle drawing me. I put my hand there while she pulled the blouse over her head.

She stood, naked but for the coral necklace, washed with moonlight, unbuttoning my shirt, unzipping my trousers, pulling them around my ankles. I stepped out, barefoot; took off my shorts. I was wearing only the fresh bandage she'd applied about an hour ago.

We waded in, not so deep that I got my bandage wet. We stood with the water brushing our legs and embraced and kissed, kissed deeply, in every sense of the word. She lay in the sand half in the water and I eased on top of her and kissed her mouth and her eyes and her face and her neck and her breasts and her stomach and my lips brushed downward across the harsh curls stopping at wet warmth where I kissed her some more.

Her lovely face, ivory in the moonlight, lost in passion, was a vision I would never forget; I knew, as I was impressing that image forever in my mind, even as I pressed myself within her, that we would never do this again.

We lay together, nuzzling, kissing, saying nothing at all; then we sat and watched the shimmer of the ocean and the moon reflected there, breaking and reforming, breaking and reforming.

"Just a summer romance, Marjorie?"

"Not 'just' a summer romance, Nathan . . . but a summer romance."

"Summer's over."

"I know," she said.

Hand in hand, we walked back inside.

Twenty-nine

I wrote my letter, although I mailed it directly to the Duke of Windsor with carbon copies to Attorney General Hallinan and Major Pemberton. In it I spoke of recognizing the Duke's "deep concern for the welfare of the citizens of the Bahamas," as I addressed him on a matter of "great importance."

"During the incarceration and trial of Alfred de Marigny," I wrote, "no adequate investigation was possible. Statements and evidence which failed to point toward the defendant were ignored."

I closed by saying that "I, and my associate, Leonard Keeler, would welcome an opportunity to work on the Oakes murder case. We would willingly offer our services without compensation."

I received a curt letter from Leslie Heape saying, thank you, no; and I heard nothing from Hallinan or Pemberton. Eliot later told me that at around the same time, President Franklin D. Roosevelt had written the estimable Governor of the Bahamas to offer the services of the FBI in the case. FDR's offer was declined, too.

I wrote Nancy, stepping aside from the case and enclosing copies of both my letter and the one from the Duke's flunky, and my bill with itemized expenses. She wrote a brief note of thanks and enclosed full payment.

Fleming had been right about her: Nancy had other, more pressing problems. Within a week of the end of the murder trial, de Marigny and his pal the Marquis de Visdelou were convicted and fined one hundred pounds each for illegal possession of gasoline. Within three weeks, Freddie—appealing neither the gasoline conviction nor the deportation order—hired a small fishing boat and a crew and, with Nancy at his side, sailed to Cuba.

She didn't stay at his side long, however—after only a few months she moved to Maine for dance lessons and sinus surgery. De Marigny had been denied a visa to the United States, and within a year his marriage to Nancy was over.

Nancy returned to the Oakes family fold, although she remained just as convinced of her ex-husband's innocence as her mother was of his guilt. In fact, Lady Oakes was from time to time the victim of extortion schemes in which she traded money for evidence of Freddie's guilt.

The entire Oakes family had a rough go of it. Two of Nancy's brothers died young—Sydney (who I never met but over whose affections Sir Harry and Freddie had clashed), killed in an automobile accident; and William, of acute alcoholism before he reached thirty.

Only Nancy's younger sister, Shirley, seemed to have a charmed life: a law degree at Yale; classmate and bridesmaid of Jacqueline Bouvier Kennedy; marriage to a banker who shared her liberal philosophies and worked in support of black businessmen and politicians in Nassau. But after her husband went into business with Robert Vesco, their fortune was lost, their marriage over, and Shirley herself was crippled in a car crash.

There were family squabbles, too, among the Oakes clan—over money and possessions. Sir Harry left a considerable estate, but nothing like the two hundred million he'd been said to be worth.

Apparently the other investors of Banco Continental enjoyed a windfall when Sir Harry was silenced, as much of his fortune had seemingly already been moved south. Now it had simply gone south, and the Oakes trustees couldn't find it, and the family just had to make do on the odd ten million or so.

The former Mrs. de Marigny remained unlucky in love—she was all set to marry a dashing Danish Royal Air Force officer, but the prospective groom was killed in a plane crash in 1946. A long love affair with an English matinee idol ended when he decided marriage might upset his female fans. In 1950 she married Baron Ernest von Hoynigen-Huene, whose title turned out to be more impressive than his financial status, but the union lasted long enough for Nancy to give birth to two children, a boy and girl, who were to fill her life with joy and frustration. Nothing unusual about that.

Her society-page romances between marriages included the heir of a famous French wine family; Queen Elizabeth's male secretary; and a central figure in the Christine Keeler–John Profumo scandal. Nancy did get around. She married again in 1962, and divorced a decade or so later. Perhaps the oddest footnote in her story is that, last time I heard, she was living in Mexico, in Cuernavaca—the country of her father's downfall, the city of her father's sinister associate Axel Wenner-Gren's wartime exile.

Nancy—despite countless operations and continued ill health— remains to this day a handsome woman; I haven't seen her in years, but photographs attest to her enduring beauty. Apparently she's remained relatively cordial with Freddie, who has in the intervening years led the sort of checkered yet storybook existence you might expect.

De Marigny became a man without a country, shunned by not only the United States and Great Britain, but his homeland Mauritius. In Cuba, palling around with Ernest Hemingway, Freddie was the target of an apparent murder attempt, shots ringing through his bedroom window; he decided to leave the tropics. He went from being a seaman with the Canadian merchant marine to a private with the Canadian army, but his application to become a citizen of that country was denied, anyway. He bounced around the Caribbean—steering clear of the British possessions he was barred from—and spent some time in the Dominican Republic. Finally in 1947 he was granted a U.S. visa, only to discover that funds being held for him in New York were lost in the estate of a dead broker.

He walked dogs for rich old ladies, sold shoes and peddled his own blood on his road to a Salvation Army soup kitchen. But his luck was better than Nancy's: in 1952, having worked his way up from selling aluminum storm doors to operating a Los Angeles marriage agency, he wed Mary Taylor, an American girl, a union which has sustained to this day, I understand. They had three sons and have lived in Florida, Cuba and Mexico but mostly in Texas, where I'm told they still reside. Supposedly Freddie has been moderately successful in several businesses, including lithographing. He still sails.

The friendship between the Marquis Georges de Visdelou and Count Alfred de Marigny apparently did not survive the Oakes trial. De Visdelou is said to have asked young Betty Roberts to marry him, only to be rejected; forlorn, he went to England and joined the British army. Apparently the French Foreign Legion didn't have any openings.

Betty Roberts, on the other hand, was said to have gone to New York, where the newspaper columns announced her impending marriage to a Russian count.

Immediately after the war, five months short of a governor's usual term, the Duke of Windsor and his Duchess left the Bahamas. Never again did Great Britain entrust its former King with a position of even the remotest responsibility, despite constant applications from His Royal Highness; he and Wallis spent their remaining years golfing, gardening and attending fancy dress balls, making the New York–to–Palm Beach, Paris–to–the–Riviera circuit. Windsor died of cancer in 1972, and Wallis lived to the age of ninety. At her burial in 1986, she was granted the concession of being buried next to her husband in a royal plot.

I didn't keep track of everybody. Occasionally I bumped into somebody who shared a piece of information; sometimes an obituary caught my eye. My friends—like Sally Rand and Eliot Ness —I stayed in contact with over the years. I did keep in touch with Godfrey Higgs, who kept me up to date, before he passed away.

Of the attorneys, only Ernest Callender, retired and respected in Nassau, remains alive at this writing; but they all had remarkable careers. Hallinan was knighted and was appointed Chief Justice of Cyprus, dying in 1988. Adderley flourished in both his law practice and in politics, but died of a heart attack on an airplane after representing the Bahamas at the coronation of Queen Elizabeth II.

The Nassau police officers have retired, Colonel Lindop to suburban Wimbledon, Captain Sears and Major Pemberton in Nassau, with Pemberton working as secretary of the Bahamian Chamber of Commerce, last I heard. Whether any of them are still alive at this point, I don't know; but they were all decent enough men.

The same, of course, can't be said about Captains Barker and Melchen. Barker was brought before the International Association of Identification, which condemned his work on the Oakes case; under a cloud of accusations of mob links, Barker was allowed to leave the force on permanent sick leave. In the wake of the Oakes debacle, Barker—who had upon his return sustained an injury in a motorcycle crack-up—turned to illegal drugs for relief from pains real and psychological. As he spiraled into complete addiction, he abandoned his wife and grown son, also a Miami police officer.

Meanwhile, his partner Melchen was suffering under similar clouds of censure and suspicion, and quietly retired from the force, dying of a heart attack in 1948.

Barker promised his wife and son he would reform and begged to be allowed back in the home, which he was. But one night in 1952, Barker's son found his father brutally beating his mother, and the son interceded, leaving his father a bloody unconscious heap on the floor. In the wee hours of the morning, Barker came to, and went after his son with a .38. There was a struggle and the Duke of Windsor's fingerprint expert was dead.

After the war, many British citizens fled their new socialist government and confiscatory taxation for the nearly tax-free Bahamas, and in so doing, sent property values soaring and made Harold Christie an even richer man. Lyford Cay was developed into a haven for the very wealthy; high fences, sophisticated security measures and their own police station protect the rich and the famous, whose life-styles include a marina littered with motor cruisers and yachts, where once a native caretaker named Arthur, his murder not only unsolved but long forgotten, stood watch.

Harold Christie not only lived to see his tropical dream come true—his Bahamas were now both home to the rich and tourist magnet second to none—he saw himself rewarded with knighthood "for services to the Crown." Sir Harold Christie finally married— a Palm Beach divorcée—but, for all his position and prosperity, lived out his remaining days in the shadow of suspicion.

I suppose I didn't make Christie's life any easier when, in postwar years, I boasted in newspaper and magazine articles, as well as on radio and TV broadcasts, that I could still, even at this late date, solve the Oakes case. Evidence had been suppressed, I would say, and a prominent Nassau citizen was being protected. . . .

After all, over the years there had been odd, unexplained occurrences seemingly related to the case: shortly after the war, various out-island natives turn in over twenty-five thousand dollars' worth of gold coins to the government, which term them "pirate treasure" despite the oldest dated coin being 1853 and other coins dating as recent as 1907; in 1950, a female reporter from Washington, asking around about the Oakes murder, winds up stripped, raped and dead at the bottom of a well; that same year, a stevedore drunk in a bar in California boasts of knowing who killed Sir Harry Oakes, is questioned by the FBI and held for questioning by the Nassau chief of police, who flies in and tells the press that the stevedore has correctly identified the killer, yet neither the FBI, Scotland Yard nor the Nassau police reopen the investigation; later, Harold Christie's own secretary is mysteriously murdered.

Finally, in 1959, with the political power of the Bay Street Pirates foundering, a prominent figure in the Bahamian government, Cyril St. John Stevenson, introduced a resolution to reopen the Oakes investigation.

"I could point my finger at the man responsible," Stevenson said.

Seated not ten feet away, in the House of Assembly, was a glowering Harold Christie, who nonetheless lamely tried to save face by voting along with the resolution.

When the resolution passed, the Governor of the Bahamas, Sir Raynor Arthur, referred the matter to Scotland Yard, which declined to get involved.

Nonetheless, Christie felt haunted by the case. "It gets tiresome," he told the press bitterly, "being pointed out on the street, wherever you go—'There he is, that's the man who did it!' "

Today, in Nassau, his legacy is just that: ask about Harold Christie and you're more likely to hear him described as a murderer than as the man who brought prosperity to those tropical shores.

He died in 1973 of a heart attack.

Erle Stanley Gardner continued writing his best-selling mysteries, of course, although he later got some competition from Ian Fleming. After the war, Fleming left Naval Intelligence and turned to a career in journalism; he wrote his first spy novel on a lark, vacationing in Jamaica, which is where he'd been stationed when I knew him. Fleming's thrillers invariably focused on mastermind villains who met well-deserved fates, often in their tropical-island strongholds. When asked by friends and journalists if he'd ever killed a man during his own spy days, Fleming always said he had—once.

As for Gardner, his observations of the many injustices that surrounded the Oakes case led to the eventual formation of the Court of Last Resort, an organization designed to "improve the administration of justice." Specifically, a board of experts was gathered to look into cases where gross miscarriages of justice may have been done. Leonard Keeler was the member in charge of polygraph, and Gardner invited me to head up detection. Many "underdogs" were aided in this effort, and someday, in another forum, I may discuss some of those cases.

Casinos finally did come to the Bahamas, but not until Castro's coming to power in Cuba made it necessary for Meyer Lansky and his business associates to seek new venues. In 1963, after generous "consultant's fees" were paid to various prominent Bahamian politicians, a casino opened on Lucayan Beach on Grand Bahama island. The FBI tracked the deliveries of the large amounts of cash from this first Bahamian casino to a man in Florida. That man was Meyer Lansky.

But the American press got hold of mob involvement in Bahamian casinos, and the scandal that followed finally ended white-minority, Bay Street Pirate rule in Nassau; the black-dominated Progressive Liberal Party came into power in 1967 and has been there ever since.

Of course, gambling has been there, too. A casino was even built on the former site of Westbourne, and Hog Island—sold by Axel Wenner-Gren to Huntington Hartford in 1961 in a twenty-million-dollar deal arranged by Harold Christie—became Paradise Island, home to high-rise hotels and glittering casinos.

Eventually Meyer Lansky became, as had Alfred de Marigny for too long a time, a man without a country: faced with federal indictments, he left the U.S.A. for Israel, which despite generous cash contributions eventually turned him away; after stops in Switzerland and South America, Lansky returned to the States, but was acquitted. He died in Miami Beach, just another retired business executive, in 1983.

One of the things that amazed me over the years, as I followed from a distance the fortunes and foibles of those involved in the Oakes case, was how seldom Axel Wenner-Gren's name turned up anywhere. His public stance was that of philanthropist; however, one of his research foundations was (and is) devoted to the study of eugenics.

In 1960, a stewardess I was seeing invited me to fly with her to Nassau on some free tickets for a long weekend of (this is how she put it) "funning and sunning on the beach, and fucking and sucking wherever." It was a sincere invitation, and I accepted. If this sounds like a low-life response to a vulgar suggestion, keep in mind I was fifty-five and she was twenty-seven, and how many more offers like that could I hope to get?

Out of either nostalgia or habit, I got reservations at the B.C. It hadn't changed much, and in fact was looking a little long in the tooth; but then, so was I. One evening, after my stewardess friend (whose name was Kelly and who had green eyes and blond hair in a Jackie Kennedy cut) had kept her promises, we dined at the Jungle Club, which hadn't seemed to change a bit from when Higgs brought me here, over a decade and a half ago.

We dined in the shade of indoor palms under a thatched umbrella at a green table, enjoying conch chowder and a meal that included grouper and a pepper pot, and one of the sweet young saronged things came over and said, "Are you Mr. Heller?"

"Yes?"

"A gentleman would like to speak to you."

The waitress pointed to a table across the way.

"Oh. Okay."

I didn't recognize him at first—and why should I? I'd never met him, really.

He stood, as I approached, and smiled in a disarmingly boyish manner for a big, older man: fleshy, pink-faced, his hair stark white, eyebrows wispy and all but invisible, a soft oval face with a nose enlarged with age and small wet eyes peering from flesh pouches. He was casually dressed, in a pink-and-white short-sleeve sport shirt and white slacks. He looked sturdy for a man pushing eighty, but he also looked like a man pushing eighty.

"Ah, Mr. Heller!" he said in a melodious voice touched with what I took for a Scandinavian accent. "At long last."

Who the hell was this guy? I studied him, knowing I'd seen him somewhere before.

Seated at his table was a dark-haired handsome young man in a cream-color suit with a dark tie. He looked vaguely familiar, too, but not as familiar as my old friend who was extending his hand, which I shook. It was a firm handshake, despite his age.

Then I remembered.

I remembered the benignly, blandly smiling portrait above the fireplace, among the Inca masks, in the round living room.

"Axel Wenner-Gren," I said numbly.

"This is my friend Huntington Hartford," he said, gesturing to the handsome younger man, who smiled tightly at me, and we shook hands. "Please sit with us."

I did.

"How did you know who I was?" I asked. "We never met."

"I've seen your picture in the newspapers, many times. So many interesting, important cases you've been involved with! You should write a book."

"Maybe after I retire."

"Ah, you're much too young to even think of retiring. Me, I'm beginning to divest myself of material concerns. My friend, Hunt, here, is trying to talk me into selling him Shangri La."

"You still live there?"

Wenner-Gren smiled and shrugged; his manner was avuncular. "Winters, only."

His dinner guest—the A&P heir who was worth fifty to seventy million, roughly—excused himself and rose. I wondered if that was prearranged.

Still smiling, Wenner-Gren leaned in and he patted my hand; his hand was cold. Like a goddamn ice pack.

"I have kept track of you, over the years. From time to time, you speak of the Oakes case, don't you? To the press."

"Yeah, I do."

"It will never be reopened, you know. Some foolish people tried, last year, unsuccessfully. Even now, that whole matter is an embarrassment to the Bahamas and to England, as well."

"I know."

"Then why continue discussing the case? I'm just curious."

"It's good publicity. I mention the Lindbergh case, too, sometimes. That's why I have branch offices all over the country, now. Back in Chicago, we call it capitalism."

He smiled, more to himself; no teeth, just bloodshot apple cheeks. "You're an amusing man. You have a reputation for a rough wit."

"I also have a reputation for leaving well enough alone."

He nodded. "Very wise. How very wise. You know . . ." And he patted my hand again. Cold! "I've wanted to thank you, for so many years."

"Thank me?"

Now his face was somber as he nodded again. "For . . . eliminating that problem."

"What problem?"

He licked his lips. "Lady Medcalf."

I didn't say anything. I was shaking a little. This smiling eighty-year-old philanthropist had me shaking.

"I know what you did," he said, "and I'm grateful. And it gives me great pleasure to finally let you know, personally, that she was acting on her own devices."

I nodded.

Then he smiled broadly. "Well, here comes Hunt again. Mr. Heller, I'll let you get back to that charming young lady. Your daughter?"

"No."

He beamed. "Isn't that nice! Good evening, Mr. Heller."

I said something or other, nodded at both of them, and walked numbly back to the table.

"Who was that?" Kelly asked.

"The devil," I said.

"Oh, Heller—you're so bad!"

"What did you say?"

She looked at me curiously. "I don't know. What *did* I say?"

"Nothing. Nothing."

She wanted to stay to watch the limbo contest, but I wanted out of there. That was the last weekend I spent with that particular stewardess; seemed I hadn't been much fun, on our little getaway, after a certain point.

Axel Wenner-Gren died of cancer a year later. His fortune was estimated at over one billion dollars.

It wasn't till 1972 that I got back to the Bahamas, this time with a woman closer to my own age, who I happened to be married to. In fact, it was our honeymoon and my wife—second wife, actually—had always wanted to see the Bahamas.

Specifically, she wanted to see Government House, because she'd been so taken as a girl with the bittersweet love story of the Duke and Duchess of Windsor.

Nassau hadn't changed much, although the ways it had changed weren't for the better: American fast-food joints on the fringes and, on Bay Street, interminable T-shirt shops and an offer of drugs from a ganja-reeking black guy every few paces.

But there was (and is) a time machine known as Graycliff, a large old rambling Georgian Colonial home near Government House that first opened its doors as a small hotel back in 1844.

The honeymoon suite, by the poolside, is a small separate building amidst an exotic tropical garden. The hotel restaurant—you dine here and there on the main floor, but we preferred the porch—is five-star.

The first evening we were there, after a meal that included goose-liver pâté with truffles and a Hollandaise-smothered steak as thick as a phone book and as tender as a mother's touch, we were served steaming hot soufflés in custard cups.

"I've never had coconut soufflé before," my wife said.

"I have. And as good as this place is, they'll never beat it."

She was having a taste. "Hmmm. You better try some and see if you still feel the same way. . . ."

I broke the light brown skin and spooned the orangeish white custard and tasted its sweetness, the shredded coconut, the hints of banana and orange and rum. . . .

"What's wrong?" She leaned forward. "Too hot, dear?"

"Yellow Bird," I said.

"What?"

"Nothing. Waiter!"

He came over, a young handsome black. "Yes, sir?"

"Could I speak to the chef?"

"Sir, the chef is . . ."

"I have to compliment him on the dessert. It's important." I pressed a ten-spot into his hand.

My wife was looking at me like I was crazy; it wasn't the first time, and it was hardly the last.

"Actually, sir, the chef doesn't prepare the desserts and the pastries. His missus does."

"Take me to her."

My wife was confused, and half-standing.

"Please, dear," I said, patting the air with one hand. "Just wait here. . . ."

I went back by the kitchen and waited and in a few seconds that were an eternity, she came out, wearing a white apron over a blue dress not unlike the maid's uniform she wore so long ago.

She didn't recognize me at first.

"Marjorie," I said.

Her face—her lovely face, touched by age but gently—looked at first incredulous, then warmed, and she said, "Nathan? Nathan Heller?"

I took her in my arms; didn't kiss her. Just held her.

"I'm here on my honeymoon," I said.

I let go of her and we stood apart, but rather close. Her hair was lightly sprinkled with white, but her figure was about the same. Maybe a little thicker around the hips. We won't discuss my gut.

She smiled widely. "Only just now you get married?"

"Well, this is the second time. I think this one's going to last, or at least outlast me. And you're married to the chef?"

"For twenty-five years. We got three little ones—well, not so little anymore. Got a boy in college."

My eyes were getting wet. "That's so wonderful."

Her brow wrinkled. "How did you . . . ?"

"That soufflé. One taste, and I knew you were responsible."

"So you ordered that! It's still good, isn't it?"

"Still good."

She hugged me again. "I have to get back to work. Where are you stayin'?"

"Right here. We have the honeymoon suite."

"Well, I simply must meet your wife . . . if she won't mind sharin' you, just a little. You have to excuse me, now—"

"You know where to find us."

She started to go back in, then turned and looked at me, and her expression was half happy, half sad.

"Tell me, Nathan—do you ever think of your Marjorie?"

"Not often."

"Not often?"

I shrugged. "Only when I see the moon."

We visited a little, during the week my wife and I were there. Not much—it *was* our honeymoon, after all.

But Marjorie told me something, in one of the few moments we had alone, that sent me whirling back in time just as surely as had that coconut soufflé, only not so sweetly.

It seemed she had run into Samuel, once—the missing night watchman from Westbourne—about ten years after the murder. . . .

He had told her that on that awful night he had seen things and people at Westbourne that had scared him; and that Harold Christie had come around later to pay him and the other boy, Jim, to "disappear" for a while.

Everything Samuel had told Marjorie, and which Marjorie was now sharing with me, confirmed the story I had told Lady Diane Medcalf, so very long ago, in the aftermath of a tropical storm on Hog Island, during carnal hours, right before she shot me and I shot her.

I Owe Them One

Despite its extensive basis in history, this is a work of fiction, and a few liberties have been taken with the facts, though as few as possible—and any blame for historical inaccuracies is my own, reflecting, I hope, the limitations of conflicting source material.

The major liberty I have taken is in the telescoping of time; while the murder of Sir Harry Oakes did take place in July 1943, the trial of Alfred de Marigny did not end until November. I am purposely vague in *Carnal Hours*, implying these events took place within several months. Both the preliminary hearing and the trial itself have been compressed to spare the reader the countless delays and redundancies of the real proceedings; nonetheless, I have attempted to accurately portray what occurred.

Most of the characters in this novel are real and appear with their true names. Any readers intimately familiar with the case will realize that I have omitted a few players, chiefly Frank Christie, who was his brother Harold Christie's business manager and who some theorists place in the thick of the murder and cover-up; in fact, Frank was among the first people Harold Christie called from Westbourne after the discovery of Sir Harry's body. However, from my point of view Frank Christie served merely as an extension of his brother's will, so certain things sometimes attributed to Frank (paying the native watchmen to disappear, for example) have been laid at Harold's feet.

Another major missing player is Raymond Schindler, the legendary private detective whose role in this version of the Oakes case is given to Nathan Heller. Schindler did many of the things attributed here to Heller, including playing practical jokes on the cops and talking the Marquis de Visdelou into testifying for his friend Freddie. He also worked closely with Erle Stanley Gardner, whose role in this novel is largely factual.

So is that of Leonard Keeler, although some of the theories and discoveries Keeler makes are actually new additions to Oakes lore. With the help of indefatigable researcher Lynn Myers, who spoke to numerous fire marshals and forensics experts, two new theories were developed: the probable use of the bug sprayer as the makeshift blowtorch; and the use of a smaller-caliber revolver at close range, to produce the four wounds that were, absurdly, considered the work of a bludgeon by "expert" witnesses. Lynn's expert witnesses included Sergeant Jake Baker and Detective Bob Warner of Carlisle Borough Police Department, and Fred Klages of the Pennsylvania State Fire Marshal's office.

Ian Fleming's involvement in the case is fanciful; however, British Naval Intelligence did indeed track the Duke of Windsor's activities during the period Fleming was stationed in the Caribbean.

Diane Medcalf is a fictional character. In real life, Axel Wenner-Gren's wartime affairs in Nassau were looked after by a baron and baroness—George and Marie Trolle; Baroness Trolle was Nancy de Marigny's confidante during the ordeal of the trial. Private eye Schindler and his friend Leonard Keeler did in fact stay with the Trolles, even burning up some valuable furniture in their experimenting. However, Lady Medcalf's fictional treachery is not meant to cast any suspicion on these real-life figures.

On the other hand, the theory that a minion (or minions) of Axel Wenner-Gren committed the crime has valid historical underpinnings.

Marjorie Bristol is a fictional character, although she has a historical counterpart in a housekeeper who worked at Westbourne.

My longtime research associate George Hagenauer, whose many contributions include slogging through volume upon volume of Nazi spy research, spent hours in libraries gathering book and newspaper references, and on the phone discussing with me the ins and outs of this convoluted case. George is a valued collaborator on the Heller "memoirs" and I continue to appreciate his contribution and friendship.

Lynn Myers, the nicest glutton for punishment I know, again dug in and did research rivaling George's; he located the rarest of books and magazine articles and deserves much more than these simple thanks.

Going to great lengths, both Lynn and George found fragmented versions of the lengthy Hearst-syndicated coverage of the case by Erle Stanley Gardner, which together added up to one complete set of what became perhaps my single most valuable research tool. Gardner's on-site observations of both Nassau and the trial's participants give the lie to the general notion that Perry Mason's creator was a limited stylist and poor observer; he was, instead, keen-eyed and insightful and capable of many a well-turned phrase. Also, a Gardner article, "My Most Baffling Murder Case" (*Mercury Book-Magazine*, January 1958), was a useful summary of his views on the Oakes affair. Tina Maresco of Spahr Library, Dickinson College, helped assemble the Gardner material.

Another person was instrumental in the writing of this book: my talented wife, writer Barbara Collins, who accompanied me on a research trip to the Bahamas in January 1990. While I would not bother denying even to the IRS that we had a pleasant time, Barb was her usual intelligent, diligent self in seeing to it that our primary pursuit was the ghost of Sir Harry Oakes. Like Heller, we stayed at the British Colonial, which at this writing is still owned by the Oakes family; the assistant manager of the B.C., Nigel Bethel, took time out of a busy schedule to help us in our efforts.

Unquestionably the most valuable research aid we discovered in the Bahamas was a remarkable individual named Romeo Farrington of Romeo's Executive Limousine Service, who took us on a lengthy tour of New Providence, away from usual tourist haunts, to give us a sense of the real place, and the history surrounding it.

Of the handful of books published about the case, the most comprehensive is *The Murder of Sir Harry Oakes* (1959), published by the Nassau *Daily Tribune*, a collection of the contemporary coverage from that paper. Other books on the case were extremely helpful: James Leasor's 1983 *Who Killed Harry Oakes?*, which begins as nonfiction and takes a lengthy excursion into speculation, and is the source of the now widely accepted (and in my opinion erroneous) theory that Lansky was responsible; *King's X*

322 _Max Allan Collins_

(1972) by Marshall Houts—a veteran of Gardner's Court of Last Resort—which focuses on the trial, with later editions including a new chapter detailing Harold Christie's successful efforts to have the book banned in the Bahamas; and _The Life and Death of Sir Harry Oakes_ (1959) by Geoffrey Bocca, the only biography of the victim, with an excellent account of the case marred only by a naive endorsement of Harold Christie as an admirable, blameless individual.

Alfred de Marigny has written two autobiographies: _More Devil Than Saint_ (1946), a picaresque account of his colorful life leading up to a rather sparse account of the murder and trial; and _A Conspiracy of Crowns_ (1990), written with Mickey Herskowitz, which deals in detail with the case and with de Marigny's subsequent life. Together they form one complete, fascinating portrait. Oddly, in his recent book, de Marigny does not mention having written _Devil_ (and does not list it in the "selected bibliography"), and even tells of giving up his plans to write such a book, back in the forties, after murder attempts!

One footnote about de Marigny: after his acquittal and into the 1950s, de Marigny would say he owed his life to private eye Raymond Schindler; but in his more recent book, de Marigny dismisses Schindler's contribution as minimal and complains at length that the detective charged an exorbitant fee. Other research tends to confirm his earlier opinion.

Also, de Marigny goes out of his way to praise and exonerate Christie in his 1946 book, but lays the crime at Christie's feet in his recent one.

Countless books have been written about the Duke and Duchess of Windsor; I used primarily the following: _King of Fools_ (1989), John Parker; _The Woman He Loved_ (1974), Ralph G. Martin; _The Duchess of Windsor: The Secret Life_ (1988), Charles Higham; and _The Woman Who Would Be Queen_ (1954), Geoffrey Bocca. Two books on the Duke's time in the Bahamas were particularly helpful: _The Duke of Windsor's War_ (1982), Michael Bloch; and _The King Over the Water_ (1981), Michael Pye. Incidentally, Sally Rand's Red Cross Benefit performance, which embarrassed the Duke, is chronicled in several of these volumes.

Biographies that helped me shape the portraits of characters include _The Life of Ian Fleming_ (1966), John Pearson; _Sally Rand: From Film to Fans_ (1988), Holly Knox; _The Case of the Real Perry Mason_ (1978), Dorothy B. Hughes; _The Case of Erle Stanley Gard-_

ner (1946), Alva Johnston; *Vesco* (1987), Arthur Herzog; *Meyer Lansky: Mogul of the Mob* (1979), Dennis Eisenberg, Uri Dan and Eli Landau; *Lansky* (1971), Hank Messick; and *Little Man: Meyer Lansky and the Gangster Life* (1991), Robert Lacey. Two autobiographical works proved useful: *A Unicorn in the Bahamas* (1940), Rosita Forbes; and *My Political Memoirs* (undated, but post-1983), Sir Henry Taylor.

The elusive Axel Wenner-Gren's stultifyingly vague philosophical/political tract, *Call to Reason* (1938), provided an epigram and, between the lines, glimpses of an idealized world state—"reason," in Axel Wenner-Gren's view, was a synonym for "science." A more coherent portrait of Wenner-Gren was found in "The Sphinx of Sweden," a chapter in *American Swastika* (1985), Charles Higham.

Various magazine articles on Raymond Schindler were perused, but more helpful were *The Complete Detective* (1950), a biography/casebook of Schindler written by Rupert Hughes with an Erle Stanley Gardner introduction; and *Great Detectives* (1966), Robert Liston, which has an excellent Schindler chapter.

"The Reluctant Heiress," a chapter in *How to Marry the Super Rich* (1974) by Sheilah Graham, influenced the characterization of Nancy Oakes de Marigny.

Good discussions of the Oakes case were found in *The Encyclopedia of Unsolved Crimes* (1988), Daniel Cohen; *Great Unsolved Mysteries* (1978), James Purvis; *Unsolved: Great Mysteries of the 20th Century* (1990), Kirk Wilson; and *Unsolved! Classic True Murder Cases* (1987), edited by Richard Glyn Jones. "The Myths About the Oakes Murder," a 1959 *Saturday Evening Post* article by John Kobler, provided information unavailable elsewhere. Perhaps the best single account of the case, however, including the book-length ones, is "Who Killed the Baron of Nassau?" by Alan Hynd, collected in *Violence in the Night* (1955).

The wartime Nassau depicted in this novel may exist only in the author's imagination—and, with luck, the reader's; but the following books gave my imagining a grounding in reality: *The Bahamas Handbook* (1927), Mary Moseley; *Bahamas: Isles of June* (1934), Major H. MacLachlan Bell; *Circling the Caribbean* (1937), Tom Marvel; *Paradise Island Story* (1984), Paul Albury; *The Caribbean Islands* (1968), Mary Slater; *Historic Nassau* (1979), Gail Saunders and Donald Cartwright; *A History of the Bahamas* (1986), Michael Craton; *The Caribbean* (1968), Selden Rodman; *Bahama Islands* (1949), J. Linton Rigg; *Islands in the Wind* (1954),

William T. Redgrave; *The Caribbean Cruise* (1935), Harry L. Foster; *The Pocket Guide to the West Indies* (1935), Sir Algernon Aspinall; and *Ports of the Sun* (1937), Eleanor Early. Also a 1939 *National Geographic* article, "Bahama Holiday" by Frederick Simpich.

Finally, I would like to thank my editor, Michaela Hamilton, and her associate Joe Pittman, for their enthusiastic response to this novel, and for suggestions to improve it; and my agent, Dominick Abel, for his continued support, both professionally and personally.

MAX ALLAN COLLINS is a two-time winner of the Private Eye Writers of America "Shamus" award for best novel for *True Detective* (1983) and *Stolen Away* (1991). The other entries in the acclaimed cycle of "Nate Heller" historical thrillers—*True Crime* (1984), *The Million-Dollar Wound* (1986), and *Neon Mirage* (1988)—have been Shamus-nominated their respective years, as was the title novella of the Heller collection, *Dying in the Post-War World* (1991).

In addition, Collins has written three contemporary suspense series—Nolan, Quarry and Mallory (a thief, hitman and mystery writer respectively); and several historical thrillers about real-life "Untouchable" Eliot Ness. He has been nominated for Mystery Writers of America "Edgar" awards for both fiction and non-fiction.

He scripted the internationally syndicated comic strip "Dick Tracy" from 1977 through 1993. With artist Terry Beatty, he is creator of the comic-book feature "Ms. Tree" (nominated for a 1991 "Will Eisner" Comics Industry Award), and has scripted the "Batman" comic book and newspaper strip. He has coauthored critical studies on Mickey Spillane (with James Traylor) and TV detectives (with John Javna); a book collection of his film reviews for *Mystery Scene* magazine is forthcoming. A rock musician since the mid 1960s, he is still performing and recording.

Collins lives in Muscatine, Iowa, with his wife, Barbara, and their son, Nathan.